Adult PB

Wak

G000140060

Hunger Town

Born in Adelaide, Wendy Scarfe graduated from Melbourne University and later trained as a secondary school teacher. For over four decades she has written poetry and novels in her own right and non-fiction works with her husband, Allan Scarfe. Her novels show her interest in history, political conflicts and social injustice. Writing in *Australian Literary Studies*, Dr Katherine Bode commented that Wendy is 'an important and innovative contemporary author' whose books offer a 'difference'.

Wendy Scarfe lives in Warrnambool with her husband. They have three daughters, a son and four grandchildren.

By the same author

Poetry
Shadow and Flowers
Shadow and Flowers (enlarged edition)
Dragonflies and Edges (with Jeff Keith)

Novels
The Lotus Throne
Neither Here Nor There
Laura My Alter Ego
The Day They Shot Edward
Miranda
Fishing for Strawberries
Jerusha Braddon Painter
An Original Talent

Non-fiction (with Allan Scarfe)
A Mouthful of Petals: The story of an Indian village
Tiger on a Rein: Report on the Bihar famine
JP His Biography
JP His Biography (revised edition)
Remembering Jayaprakash
Labor's Titan: The story of Percy Brookfield, 1878–1921 (eds)
All That Grief: Migrant recollections of Greek resistance to fascism,
1941–1949
No Taste for Carnage: Alex Sheppard, a portrait, 1913–1997

Educational Books (with Allan Scarfe)
People of India
The Black Australians
Victims or Bludgers? Case studies in poverty in Australia
Victims or Bludgers? A poverty inquiry for schools

HUNGER TOWN

A novel

Wendy Scarfe

WILLOUGHBY
B. H.
9 FEB 2015
WILLOUGHBY
CITY LIBRARY
CANCELLED
WILLOUGHBY
CITY LIBRARY

**Wakefield
Press**

Wakefield Press
16 Rose Street
Mile End
South Australia 5031
www.wakefieldpress.com.au

First published 2014

Copyright © Wendy Scarfe, 2014

All rights reserved. This book is copyright. Apart from any fair dealing for the
purposes of private study, research, criticism or review, as permitted under
the Copyright Act, no part may be reproduced without written permission.
Enquiries should be addressed to the publisher.

This is a work of fiction embedded in some major political events in Australian
history. The people in it and their relationships with any organisation or
occupation are the product of my imagination and do not represent any real
person living or dead. The cartoons are also works of my imagination.

Cover designed by Stacey Zass, Page 12
Edited by Julia Beaven, Wakefield Press
Typeset by Wakefield Press
Printed in Australia by Griffin Digital, Adelaide

National Library of Australia Cataloguing-in-Publication entry

Creator: Scarfe, Wendy, 1933–   , author.
Title: Hunger town: a novel / Wendy Scarfe.
ISBN   978 1 74305 336 2 (paperback).
Subjects: Australian fiction.
Dewey Number: A823.3

Government
of South Australia
Arts SA

fox creek
wines

Australian Government

Australia Council
for the Arts

Publication of this book was assisted by
the Commonwealth Government through the
Australia Council, its arts funding and advisory body.

For my husband Allan with love.

My legions ne'er were listed, they had no need to be:
My army ne'er was trained to arms – 'twas trained to misery!
It took long years to mould it, but war could never drown
The shuffling of my army's feet at drill in Hunger Town.

'My Army, O My Army!'
Henry Lawson

Contents

Part 1

Judith and Harry

THOSE FURTIVE SHADOWY FIGURES, gliding along the wharf or scurrying like rats seeking a hole to hide themselves, haunted my childhood. Unbidden, they hovered always at the edge of my dreams. Even as an adult. Awake, I told myself that they were only poor destitute sailors who had jumped ship and now searched fruitlessly for a new berth. Often they were Indian or Chinese, unable to speak English, adrift in that no-man's land where all is foreign, inexplicable and threatening. Without money, they scrounged to survive.

Early one morning when night shadows on the sea had barely lifted I saw one swimming near our hulk. With one hand and clumsily treading water he grabbed at scraps of food waste my mother had thrown overboard with the slops. At first I thought the sleek hair smooth on the round head was a seal but then a sliver of sun transfixed him and he swam in a circle of light. I saw his face and his eyes moist and black. He stared at me expressionless, snatched a piece of soggy crust, stuffed it in his mouth, swam back to the wharf and clambered up the ladder. His clothes stuck to his thin angular body and where the sun burnished the folds of wet cloth they glistened like fish scales.

I raised my hand to wave, to acknowledge his cleverness – a piece of soggy bread did not seem distasteful to me. His trick, so like a seal, delighted me but he did not look back from the wharf and I lowered my arm feeling foolish. I had intruded and there was something I had failed to understand.

I didn't tell anyone about the swimmer but for several weeks afterwards I observed what my mother put in the slops bucket and when she wasn't looking I added one or two slices of bread. On other quiet mornings, when the sea clicked and ticked and sniffled rhythmically against the side of our ship and the sun made spangled streaks across a calm surface, I waited at the railings for the man to swim out and claim the bread. But he never came again.

Others came at night, always skulking along the wharf, deeper patches of feline black with murky edges. Faceless, they glided out of the gloom, passed our hulk and were drowned in the sea of darkness.

I was eight and in those days we lived on a hulk in the Port Adelaide River. My father's job was to supply coal to the large ships in the Outer Harbor that could not enter the river, and to work the winches. When our hulk was not engaged in coaling it was moored to the wharf and it was at these times that I saw the shadowy men.

My father kept a gun and I often watched him oil and clean it. His wariness of the 'wharf rats', as he called them, sat oddly beside the stories he told me of his agility and courage on the masts and riggings of windjammers. He had no fear of the sea but an uneasy almost superstitious dread of those wraith-like creatures. His fear was catching, but I separated those ghostly apparitions from the swimmer with the piece of bread. He had been no more frightening than the occasional stray dog scavenging for food.

One dark night I saw two men fighting on the wharf. One was tall and heavy, the other shorter and thinner. The tall man struck the other so fiercely that his feet lifted off the ground like an acrobat and he fell with a thud even I could hear. The tall man then kicked him while the other scrabbled to escape his boot, scrambled to his feet and ran. As the tall man turned towards me I saw from my porthole that it was my father. He came quietly up the gangplank, stole across the deck and entered his and my mother's cabin. I heard them whispering. Then there was silence. I never told him what I had seen, but some days later, as he oiled his gun, I asked him if he were afraid of the wharf rats. For some moments he was silent and I thought that he had not liked my question. Then he said, 'When I was a boy I had an uncle in Denmark and from there we would skate across the straits to Norway. In winter the sea froze and the ice was a white road. I was only a boy but all my companions were big men. I can't abide puny, weak men.'

'But weren't you scared of falling into the sea?'

'No.'

'Could you swim?'

'We all could swim. Not that that would have done us much good. To fall through ice is the end.'

'Did someone teach you?'

He laughed. 'No one taught us anything. We learned ourselves, the hard way. That's what men do.'

I recalled the swimmer with the bread stuffed in his mouth. He, too, must have taught himself, as men did.

'Are all the wharf rats puny?'

'Yes, the waste from ports. Anywhere in the world. No good on land, no good on ships.'

'I can't swim,' I said.

'No.'

'Should I teach myself?'

He tweaked my hair, a casual dismissive gesture. 'Of course not. You'll drown.'

But now when I stood at the railings and looked at the sea I thought about the swimmer and imagined my father skating on a fragile ice-bridge above seething depths and my world became divided between people who could swim and those like myself who couldn't. There was no ice here but what if some day I, too, had to skate across the sea and falling through it found it was the end?

The sea was my constant companion. Sometimes in the early morning a mauve mist shrouded it and on a moon surface our ship lay suspended between sky and sea. Then the fog would lift, not all at once but as if the sun took fistfuls and shook it apart. The sea had a voice. It moaned and sighed, sobbed, gulped and hiccuped, and on still nights its muffled rolling rumble reminded me that it crashed on distant beaches. There were constant smells: the sour stench of wet ropes, damp wood hot and sweetened from the sun, the dense gluggy smell of oil, and the hot acrid metal smell of the winches. There was the comforting smell of coffee and bacon and hot toast from my mother's galley and the thick juicy onion smell of stew. And all these smells belonged to our hulk and the sea and were different from the smell of land houses. These smelled of polishing wax, soap and confined spaces.

The sea seemed no longer benign. To fall into it was the end. Where once I had gazed no deeper than the surface, now I peered into the depths, searching for those imagined dead sailors my father sometimes recalled.

'Lost souls,' my mother had sighed.

'Lost bodies,' my father had guffawed. 'Don't be sentimental. Anyone can get another soul, but once a body's fish food – pouf! No more – soul or body.'

Were those bodies there? I searched the limpid surface. Below it deepened to cloudy green and finally became an impassable dark wall. They wouldn't be held down by stones, as in a grave-yard. They might pop up at any minute and stare at me with moist black eyes. What if the puny wharf rat had died during another swim and any time I might catch a glimpse of him?

When I was very small and on deck I had had a heaving line attached to me to save me from falling overboard, but now I had grown out of it. My father made me a swing, a bosun's chair suspended from the yardarm and I delighted in flying upwards and outwards over the railings and the sea that glinted beneath me. It was this activity that brought to a head the problem of whether I should learn to swim. My mother was always ahead of my father in foreseeing consequences. He mocked her caution. They argued about my swing. 'It's dangerous,' she said in her no-nonsense voice.

'Rubbish!'

'And if she falls?'

'If, if, if,' he mocked. 'It's always if with a woman. If she takes no risks she'll never grow.'

She pursed her lips. 'I'm her mother and I say it's dangerous. She can't even swim.'

He muttered rebelliously but she was adamant: either the swing was cut down or I learned to swim or both. He conceded grudgingly, 'Then I'll teach her to swim.'

My mother looked doubtful and shook her head.

Impatient, he roared, 'Isn't that what you want?'

She was tight-lipped. 'Don't shout at me. And if you teach her to swim, don't shout at her.'

Suddenly he laughed and folded her in a bear hug. 'Two women to order me about.'

'Oh, you,' she protested, struggling free and rearranging her clothes, but she was smiling.

My father's teaching methods were rough. He was not a patient man. He tied a rope about my waist and shakily I climbed down the Jacob's ladder, trembling with excitement and terror. At first he held the rope firmly. I flailed with my arms and legs, while he yelled instructions, to use my arms as paddles, to kick harder. The water was very cold. I had no swimming costume and my skimpy clothing clung about my limbs. I tired quickly but after a few moments my father had convinced himself that I had the hang of it. He relaxed the rope. Instantly the water closed over my head. I worked my arms and legs frantically, struggled to the surface, sucked a breath, screamed, filled my mouth with water and again submerged.

The sea became my battleground. Now it was harder to reach the surface, to breathe. I fought but again my mouth and eyes filled with water and blindly I choked and panicked. Then the rope tautened and I found myself gaspingly on the surface. I screamed again, a piercing terrified wail, 'like a lost seabird' my mother later told me. It was my mother's terrified face I first saw as together they dragged me on to the deck. I continued to wail.

'Stop that noise!' my father shouted at me. 'You're not going to die.'

I tried to stop my teeth chattering but now great shivers attacked me and I couldn't stop shaking and sobbing. Between wrapping me in a blanket and trying to soothe me my mother raged at my father. 'You fool, you thick-headed fool!' she stormed. 'Never one moment's careful thought. You idiot! You thick-headed, impatient idiot!'

She helped me up and continued to mutter, 'Fool, idiot, brainless. I had to marry the stupidest man alive,' and as she led me away I glanced back to see my father looking ashen-faced and guilty.

She brought me warm clothes, a hot drink and tucked me into bed with a hot water bottle. All that day she refused to look at my father and I caught him throwing anxious, beseeching glances at her. I felt sorry for him. Their troubles seemed to be my fault. I had failed to swim. I had caused all this misery.

'I'll try harder next time,' I promised my father, in a whispered attempt to ease the anger between them.

'There won't be a next time,' he snarled, turning his temper on me.

And I never forgot this small injustice.

The bosun's chair also seemed to be at fault. Now the thought of flying over the sea filled me with horror and I shuddered. But my father refused to cut it down. My mother was not to be drawn. To my father's 'Do you want me to take it down?' she was surly. 'Do as you please.'

I didn't use it again but it occupied my thoughts as a kind of private dare, a challenge to my courage. What if, one day, I again flew over the sea? Half of me wanted to show the other half that I was not afraid.

My father was a six foot three blond Norwegian. He had no formal education and could only read haltingly. But as a boy he had led a tough life with the Icelanders and could speak their language as well as Norwegian and English. He married my mother, a woman also tall and strongly built, and living on a hulk was his compromise between life on the land and on a windjammer.

Our hulk was 'a de-luxe class ship converted' I heard my mother tell a friend. My parents had a large bedroom, two cabins joined together. I had no idea what 'de-luxe' meant but the beauty of my parents' bedroom entranced me. The walls of various inlaid wood glowed in different shades and had a satin touch. There were no portholes, only windows looking over the upper deck, some with patterns of birds and flowers in coloured intricate designs. Light through these windows fell in strands on the polished woodwork turning it to emerald and crimson and sapphire. Then, when I ran my hand across the silky smoothness, colour stained my fingers. I had a small cabin with a bunk bed on the wharf side of the ship. From my porthole I watched the shadowy wharf rats and they seemed little different from the hungry, nervous cats and dogs that also searched warily.

My schooling was irregular. Sometimes when my father had to work the winches and unload the coal it was impossible to row me ashore and walk me to school. My mother often did this but not in rough weather. We had very few books on the hulk.

'The best education a man can get is from life. Schooling,' my father told my protesting mother, 'is a waste of time.'

'And for a woman?' My mother was sarcastic.

He looked nonplussed. 'A woman? She'll marry I suppose.'

'And be as ignorant as you?' she snorted.

Instead he took me to the Working Men's Club. She told him it was unsuitable for a child but he over-rode her concerns about its rowdiness. 'It's the best education,' he asserted. 'She can see how most people have to live and educate themselves. I'm not going to have her growing up a lazy privileged snob.'

'Much chance of that,' my mother flared. 'She doesn't even know how to wear girl's clothing.'

And it was true, although it didn't concern me. I lived in boys' clothes because they were more adaptable on the deck of a ship.

'She only mixes with men,' my mother continued. 'She's growing up. It's unsuitable.'

It was his turn to snort. 'She's still a child.'

'Then you should take her places suitable for a child and not a men's club.'

But he won the day. She brought out her full arsenal of surly unbreakable silences but he ignored her and went about his tasks whistling.

'My father says working people have to educate themselves,' I quoted piously.

'And that's why you need to go to school, if only to get the rudiments of learning. And I had to marry an uneducated man.'

It was a variation on her complaint that she had married the stupidest man in the world. As I grew older I wondered why she had married my father. One day I heard them shouting at each other and saw her throw a plate of stew at him.

I froze, horrified at such violence and fearing his reaction, but he only glanced down at himself, picked off a few bits of meat, gave a great guffaw of laughter, enfolded her in his arms, and kissed her loudly with smacking lips. She responded and soon they were both roaring with laughter.

Years later a family friend said to me, 'Your mother and father had a tempestuous marriage when they were young.' I was puzzled. It had seemed a normal marriage to me. Then my viewpoint shifted and I saw my parents from a distance, the detached observer. 'Yes,' I said, 'I guess you are right. That explains a lot.' But even then I was not certain what I meant by 'a lot'.

My father and I walked to the Working Men's Club. He always took my hand when we crossed the rail lines, weaving along the bitumen apron that fronted the docks. The rail lines weren't bumpy and I didn't trip but the huge warehouses that loomed over us threw impenetrable shadows far darker than the night. These made me nervous. I was comforted to have the strength of his hand.

The Working Men's Club was a noisy place. I had imagined that a place of education would be hushed and serious. Many of the workers or the unemployed who came there had been soldiers in the Great War. Although demobbed some years ago they were still rowdy and ribald and, although years older than I was, had a youthful iconoclastic zest for life. I wondered later if having been deprived of their youth they constantly sought to relive it and reclaim it. There was a bar with plenty of beer and a smoking room rarely used. The whole building had a blue misty cigarette haze and smelled of warm sweaty clothes, tobacco and yeasty staleness.

I was the centre of attention. They called me 'a pint-sized socialist' and roared with laughter. I was pleased but embarrassed when they spoke about me over my head. They vied with each other to teach me ribald songs and urged me to join in while they sang 'Mademoiselle from Armentieres'. They were kind to me in small ways: they competed with each other to find me a chair and sat me upon it as if it were a throne. Then they would buy me lemonade and watch me drink.

Sometimes one of them would wink at me, 'You won't be drinking lemonade for much longer.'

'Yes,' I asserted, 'I will. My mother does.'

They treated this remark as a huge joke, roared with laughter again, and slapped their thighs.

It seemed someone was always winking at me and laughing at some secret amusement.

'Why do they always wink at me?' I asked my father.

'It's their way.'

And as I continued to look puzzled, 'They're a good bunch. It's tough being a working man and a returned soldier.'

Not all the men at the Club joked and winked at me. One man sat apart in a corner of the room. He was skeletal thin and the bones of his skull formed hard ridges on which a little hair sprouted. He sat with downcast eyes and his lips mumbled unintelligible words as he wrung his hands.

Sometimes someone took him a glass of beer, put it in his hand, folded his fingers about the glass and, before he could slackly drop it, helped him lift it to his mouth. Once he looked at his helper and large tears started from his eyes, ran down his cheeks and he sobbed. On another occasion someone kindly touched his shoulder but he leapt up and screamed, 'Quick, boys, it's coming! Gas!' and he fumbled frantically at his body. Finding nothing there he screamed again.

Several men gently took his arms and spoke softly to him. They tried to ease him out of the room but at the door he fought them off. 'I won't go back,' he sobbed. 'I won't.'

My father's friend Frank saw me watching and came to my side. He was a bluff Irishman. 'Don't be upset, darlin',' he said, 'or afraid. He's only someone's poor bastard of a son wrecked by the war. You can't send a man to hell and expect him to come home sane. The war's done for him. He's harmless. Just always scared.'

His explanation didn't make things any clearer to me. The war had no reality for me but I was ashamed to have been seen watching. It was as if a skin had been peeled back from this weeping man revealing something too painful for my eyes.

My father didn't know what I had seen and I never told him or my mother. When I returned to the hulk I drew a picture of the man and placed it with other drawings in a special box. When I drew things that upset me I didn't feel so sad.

I didn't mind the lectures that took place in a big room of the Working Men's Club. Words fascinated me and the words I heard there were different from the words spoken at home. It struck me that maybe words belonged in families and lived in particular places: Marxism, Lenin, socialism, revolution, capitalism, unions, were words that belonged in the Club. Nobody there complained about them but when I mentioned them to my mother she closed her mouth firmly and said, 'You're too young to understand that sort of thing. I don't want you to use those words.'

'Why not?' My father was belligerent.

'They'll get her into trouble.'

'What trouble? Shouldn't she learn?'

'I'm not interested in your theories, your big man's dreams. I know plenty of women who'd like to put more food on the table now, not in some pie-in-the-sky future. I don't want her head stuffed full of unreal fantasies.'

But I continued to enjoy the songs beefed out at the meetings and without understanding the passion caught something of the fervour and was excited by the song about the red flag died with the blood of workers. The nobility of its sentiment of sacrifice engulfed me.

My mother must have convinced my father that it was all beyond my comprehension for, as a sop to her, he allowed me to take some pencils and paper so that I might occupy myself while he argued with his friends. Surrounded by faces, I amused myself drawing them and I later added my sketches to the collection I kept in my drawer. On those occasions I first experienced the joy of privacy. Although I was encircled by people they demanded nothing of me. To be apart but happily occupied is not loneliness. Many of the men were poorly dressed. My mother was forever washing and ironing and even my father's work clothes were clean and mended. But many of these men wore old shirts with ragged stained collars and button-less threadbare coats. Once I heard a rustle of paper and saw one surreptitiously pick up a newspaper left on a chair and quickly stuff it down inside his shirt. I couldn't imagine why he wanted to steal a newspaper. As I looked he caught my eye but he didn't wink, in fact he reminded me of the swimmer with the piece of bread. Instead he turned a deep red, hurriedly got up and shuffled away.

'Don't some people have enough money to buy newspapers?' I asked my father.

'It's difficult for them.'

'I think I saw a man steal one at the Club.'

'Steal? Why? Don't be silly.'

'He hid it inside his shirt.'

'He wasn't stealing. He needed it.'

'Can you take things if you need them?'

'Sometimes.'

This was a new thought about stealing. I was ready to pursue it with more questions but he quelled me. 'It's tough being a working man. You'll understand one day.'

But that night I overheard him talking to my mother. She said, 'Our women's group will find something for him to wear. Too many unemployed men are keeping warm with newspaper. There's a shirt of yours, Niels.'

'Yes,' he said, 'but I don't have enough shirts for them all.'

She was bitter. 'Years at war, their youth stolen, and now unemployed. What is this country coming to? The nation's gratitude is a mockery.'

After the lectures some of the men played billiards. My father didn't play. He told me he needed to talk union business with others. One evening I had used all my drawing paper and, bored, I wandered about looking at the several closed doors. Rather, I thought, like *Alice in Wonderland*, my favourite book. Which door, I wondered, should have *try me* written on it. The one near the corner of the room seemed to be rarely opened, or if it were people came and went through it one at a time. Clearly business was not talked there. I watched it for a while but it remained shut and tonight no one entered or left.

On tiptoe, and feeling guilty, I crept to the door, gingerly turned the handle and opened it enough to peep in. Inside was dim but light enough to make out a wall of bookshelves. It was a library. Nobody was there. I pushed the door wider and stole in.

The rows of books astounded me. I had a few books given to me as Christmas or birthday presents but except for *Alice in Wonderland* most were annuals. I had read and reread these until the covers fell off. I was amazed that the world held so many books and wondered if they were all at the Working Men's Club.

I shut the door behind me and a soft silence engulfed me. I breathed quietly and tiptoed to the shelves. The room was poorly lit so I stood up close to read the titles. I noticed that they were all in alphabetical order. The first two 'A's were Aristotle and Aristophanes: strange foreign names. I took down the Aristotle and read inside that it was translated from the Greek. I didn't know what translated meant but once we had had a Greek sailor visiting on our hulk. Short and muscular, with dark hair and eyes, he spoke a mixture of English and Greek. My father had called him 'an original Ulysses', a son born by, in and on the sea. So I supposed that this was the Greek the book talked about.

I turned the pages, discovered after all that they were in English and that Aristotle had been born over 2000 years ago. Shocked to be holding a 2000-year-old book I held it gingerly. Its covers were still intact. Perhaps nobody had ever read it and I was the first to open it. If it had lasted all this time I mustn't damage it, and with the utmost care I replaced it on the shelf.

I wasn't aware of the elderly white-haired man who stood at my shoulder until he spoke softly and I smelled his tobacco breath. 'That's a very very old story.'

I jumped nervously. 'Yes, I know. It says two thousand years. I haven't harmed it. I was just looking.'

His laugh was a wheeze. He caught his breath and coughed. 'No, no, girlie, that book isn't two thousand years old. It's what's in it that's ancient. It was written by a Greek in Greek and has now been translated into English.'

He took it off the shelf. 'See, this is just a re-print.' To my horror he thumbed the pages carelessly. I didn't confess that I was still confused about translation. 'See,' he continued, 'reprinted in 1910. Quite recent, really.'

He handed it to me. 'You like reading?'

'Yes,' I replied and then was silent, for in the presence of all these books I felt ashamed to confess how few I had read. It seemed my fault. That no one had given me the opportunity to read books didn't assuage my sense of inadequacy.

'Then, maybe you can find something here that suits you.'

He assessed me with squinting blue eyes and a smile that wrinkled the corners of his mouth. 'Perhaps not Aristotle. How old are you?'

'Eleven. Nearly twelve.' It was not quite the truth because my eleventh birthday had been but a week ago, but somehow I felt I must defend myself, make myself as old as possible.

'Then, Nearly-Twelve,' and the creases around his mouth and at the corners of his eyes wrinkled again, 'have you read any of Jack London's stories?'

I shook my head.

He led me along the shelves until we came to the Ls, took down two books and handed them to me. I read the titles: *White Fang* and *Call of the Wild*. I turned the pages. There were no pictures, just printed words, hundreds of pages. Daunted, I appealed to him, 'I won't have enough time tonight to read them here.'

He smiled at me, and although his eyes were kind I wondered why he looked a little sad.

'You can take them home, you know.'

'To keep?'

'No, to borrow, girlie. All you need to do is sign that book on the table by the door, write down the title of the book and your name. You can keep the books for two weeks and then if you need you can borrow them again. Who did you come with?'

'My father.'

'Then, he can return them if you can't.'

'Yes,' I said, clutching the precious volumes, 'and when I have read these I can borrow others?'

His eyes strayed from me to the shelves, lingered there and he sighed. 'It may be difficult for you, girlie.'

Difficult! That's what adults said when they really meant impossible.

'I'm not allowed to borrow any more – only these?'

My spirits fell. A door had opened and shut. Like Alice I was too big to enter the magic garden and too small to reach the key on the table.

'I'm nearly twelve,' I protested, and knew there were tears in my eyes.

'No, no, girlie.' He looked unhappy. 'You may borrow any books you like. But they are adult books and you won't find them much fun.'

Reprieved from my sick disappointment, I beamed at him. 'Adult books don't worry me. Next time I shall begin at the As – Aristotle and Aristophanes.' I stumbled and he corrected my pronunciation. 'Every fortnight I shall borrow a new book and one day I will have read all the books in here.'

He rubbed his chin and smiled at me. 'Nearly-Twelve, you astound me. Artistophanes,' he chuckled, 'that'll be an interesting read. It's always good for the old and cynical but maybe the young and hopeful can also enjoy it. I look forward to meeting you again in a fortnight.'

Sometimes our hulk anchored alongside a foreign ship and seamen from the Far East visited us. The Indian boys, who worked for a pittance at the most menial jobs on British ships, loved my mother and called her Mummy-ji. When they visited us they wore their own clothes, the same in summer and winter: baggy cotton trousers and a long over-shirt to their knees. In winter they clutched their arms around their chests in an effort to keep warm. My mother scrounged in second-hand clothing shops for old jumpers and jackets and decked out they were a motley group. Her favourite was Ganesh, with his large doe-like eyes and mouth full of bright white teeth, but she enveloped them all in kindness. She stood aside in her precious galley while they prepared us curries so hot that they exploded in our heads like tiny volcanoes and a lava of sweat poured down our faces and necks. They brought us small gifts of food that my mother accepted reluctantly but when they tried to spoil me with tiny brass pots inlaid with bright metals or sweet-smelling sandalwood boxes she told me not to accept them.

'They are too poor. These little things represent a lot of money to them.' But in the face of their puzzled hurt she relented and I kept my row of tiny brass jars well polished so that if they ever visited my cabin they would not be disappointed in me.

My father was scathing about their poverty and working conditions. 'Bloody British,' he stormed. 'Think they own the bloody world. Built their empire on the backs of these poor bastards.' And for once my mother didn't disagree.

On hot days they were like children having fun. They jumped or dived from the deck of our hulk, clambered up and down the Jacob's ladder. Ganesh made a mock of his British masters by holding his nose and strutting stiff-legged to the side before he jumped over. They discovered the delights of swinging in the bosun's chair across the water and then catapulting themselves from it with a great splash.

I watched enviously.

'Come,' they called. 'Come.'

'I can't swim.'

'Come. We'll teach.'

'Can I?'

My mother was anxious. My father disappeared, supposedly to find some jobs. I heard my mother mutter that he always avoided decisions.

Eventually, as they trod water circling the ladder, a ring of happy inviting faces, she let me climb down.

'Don't let go,' she called.

But Ganesh drew me away from the ladder, protectively supporting me, and gradually I felt the water hold me up. They encouraged me to dog paddle from him to the ladder and cheered my efforts.

So I learned to swim.

When they climbed from the water to dry themselves their thin cotton garments clung about them and with surreptitious curiosity I peeped at the shape of their bodies. In the library under H I had found a history of art and looking at the illustrations of the sculptures I realised for the first time what a man's body looked like. I secretly noted how the thin clothes clung to a little knob between the boys' legs. Guiltily, I hid my curiosity from my mother but maybe she detected it for she complained to my father that their clothes were too revealing.

'But to spoil their fun ... They can't be much older than she is. What do you think, Niels?'

He mumbled something.

'Yes,' she said, but sounded doubtful.

The boys continued to visit and they continued to throw themselves off the ship into the water. I continued to swim with them and observe their shape. And, of course, I had now read Aristophanes and knew about Lysistrata. I knew that it was a rude play but understood little. Now, with the help of the Greek statues and the wet clothes on the boys, I began to put two and two together.

When I was fifteen my father found me work in a local cafe at the Port where the wharf labourers went for lunch. I had protested angrily, 'I don't want to spend my life slinging hash in some down-and-out dump.'

My father had responded with equal anger. 'You're not going to be a lazy spoiled woman.'

'I want to stay at school,' I said.

My mother looked troubled. 'We can't keep you at school. You have to earn your keep.'

'Yes,' he was short, 'things are getting bloody tough. There are a lot of poor unemployed bastards now and we're going to have more strikes on the wharves. Do you realise what will happen to my work if the ships are idle?'

I was silent. I had seen poor men at the Working Men's Club.

My work at the Chew It began at eight o'clock and I walked there from our hulk. The timber wharves were short and square and stuck out into the river like a row of ground-down molars. I crossed the wide bitumen thoroughfare webbed with rail lines and lipped by huge warehouses that flanked the shore side. Often a pall of black smoke from the copper smelter and ship smoke stacks hung in the still morning air, immovable until the sea breeze dispersed it.

I wound my way into Lipson Street, which was always busy. Horse drays and motor vehicles jostled and manoeuvred for space on either side of the railway line that ran down the centre of the road. Little dockside engines, collecting wagons of cargo, trundled all day to and from the port. The clanging of their warning bells was incessant. Sometimes it was a relief to turn out of the crowds into Jane Street, the little lane where I worked at the Chew It.

The dump served thick soup, hunks of bread and stew. Smelling of onions, boiled cabbage and rancid fat, it was ridiculed as the

Chew It and Spew It. Most of the labourers knew my father and except for an occasional leer kept their distance and their hands to themselves. Usually I was called Duck or Love or Girlie, never Judith. If they wanted my attention they shouted across the room. But usually they were patient, indifferent to the style of serving, or even the taste of the food, so long as it was hot and heaped generously on their plates.

The tables were of rough wood covered with newspaper. It was easier to replace the food-stained sheets than scrub down the tables. However once a week it was my job to do this and, armed with a scrub brush, a bucket of soapy water and a gutful of resentment, I lathered and sweated and my arms, my back and my neck ached and I hated my father, who continued to extol the virtues of manual work.

The years had not made me more feminine. My mother reproved me for my unrefined language and manner but there was little reality in her admonitions for apart from her I had few practical examples. I had grown up in a world of men and the women I read about in books were fantasies from another world.

I had worked my way through the library to S and was now reading Shakespeare's plays. It had been a strange process, as if the books I read were the measurement of my growth. I wasn't certain whether I understood more in them because I had acquired more years or whether a pool of accumulated knowledge gave me an illusion of maturity beyond my years.

I was not a pretty girl, although my mother defended my appearance by saying I had a strong face. When I complained of my appearance one day my father surprisingly said, 'Yes, a strong face. That's why we called you Judith. Many years ago I saw a painting of Judith slaughtering General Holofernes and I thought, with luck I'll have a daughter like that. Strong.'

My mother laughed. 'She won't go slaughtering anyone. You think action can solve anything.'

In my mirror a square heavy-jawed face stared back at me. My nose was straight and so was my mouth, more sullen than serious, and un-smiling. My hazel eyes weren't too bad, I supposed. I wore my heavy long blonde hair dragged off my face and in a plait down my back. Like 'a brawny Norwegian peasant girl' my father said, 'a toiler in the vineyards not a lily of the field'.

My father's biblical knowledge surprised me.

'His father was a pastor,' my mother smirked.

'My grandfather?'

'Yes, your grandfather.'

'And as mean an old bastard as ever was,' my father snorted. 'Religion's just another sort of tyranny. And when did it ever help the working man? I ask you that, Eve. Religion is the opium of the masses.'

He confronted my mother as if she were the defender of God, the Church and all religious belief, but she only patted him on his hand and said, 'How cruel to send you to sea when you were a mere child.'

In one of his about-turns he said, 'It was the making of me.'

Years later I realised he was not defending the mean old bastard of his father but his own successes. He couldn't bear to think that neglect had in its own way defeated him. This was my father's vulnerability.

As for myself I was growing bored with his constant references to 'the working man' and 'the working class'. I was beginning to wonder if it was a belief almost as tyrannical as religion.

Usually labourers were the only customers at the cafe. So the shabbily dressed but clean young man who came regularly for a cup of tea and a bun puzzled me. I glanced at him as I hurried to and fro from the kitchen, but he ignored me. He always had a book on the table and never lifted his head from his reading. When he absently ordered the same tea and bun I amused myself with a private bet: threepence if he mumbled his thanks, sixpence if he looked up, a shilling if he did both.

The more he ignored me the more challenges I set myself. My gambling debts mounted. I would take myself to the pictures if he looked at me. The new picture house at the Port was very glamorous. Maybe I would buy myself a new dress if he spoke to me. Maybe his eyes were grey or blue or brown. If none of this happened I promised myself I would help my mother do the washing and not complain.

I continued to lose my money, didn't go to the pictures, didn't buy a new dress and did lots of additional housework.

Why I bothered to pay myself my self-imposed debts I don't know. It was silly, but it all allowed me to think about him. I was far too curious about him. But to intrude on his privacy risked a humiliating set-down, far worse than years ago trying to wave to the swimmer.

Nonetheless, one day in a moment of courage and defiance I asked him what he was reading. He glanced up at me and I realised that his myopic eyes hidden behind thick glasses saw me through a haze.

'Marx,' he mumbled, '*Das Kapital*.'

I had come across Marx in the library and battled with *Capital*.

'In German or in translation?' I now knew what translation meant and I expected he should appreciate my learning but before he could respond someone yelled, 'Hey, Duckie, you serving or what?'

I flounced around and shouted back, 'What do you mean "or what?" Wait your turn.'

I turned back to the reader but his head was again bent to his book. Neither my comment nor my shouting had drawn his attention. A memory from a childhood fairytale made me smile. He was a male version of *The Princess Who Couldn't Laugh*, only his fault was he couldn't converse. I'd take no further notice of him. And why should he notice me? I was a nobody, an unbeautiful, uneducated waitress in a slop shop. Depression engulfed me. This shabbily dressed reader of books who ignored me had no idea how I boiled with a passion to escape my drudgery.

He continued to come for his tea and bun. I continued to plonk it in front of him with a terse, 'Will that be all?' and I stopped making bets with myself. If he didn't care to look at me then it was his business and I tried to shrug off my disappointment.

As most of the lunchtime diners were regulars a new visitor rather better dressed than most and with a disdainful air took my notice. We had only a fixed menu and as I put his soup in front of him he picked up a corner of the newspaper-tablecloth on his table and said, 'What's this?'

I didn't like his tone. 'A newspaper?' I was tart.

'Yes, I can see that it's a newspaper, girlie, but what's it doing here? Don't you throw newspapers in the bin?'

The patronising 'girlie' angered me. 'Yes, after you've made a mess on it.'

He looked at me coldly with his thin eyes set too close to his nose.

'Take it off,' he said.

'No.'

'Take it off! I won't eat my meal on newspaper. I don't make a …' he hesitated, as if spitting out an unappetising word, 'mess.'

'Then there is no need to take it off.'

I dumped his soup in front of him. Some spilled over the edges of the plate onto the paper.

'Oops,' I said, 'so sorry,' clearly not meaning it. He froze an instant and then before I realised his intent he threw the bowl of soup at me. It was hot. My thick woollen skirt saved me from being burned but I felt the heat of it on my thighs. The blood drained from my face and then rushed back so that my face as well as my legs felt on fire.

'You bastard!' I shouted. 'You bloody bastard!'

A moment of abrupt silence fell on the room. Then, as one, every man in the room, except for the *Das Kapital* reader, was on his feet. Chairs scraped back or crashed over as they surged towards me. The soup thrower was hauled to his feet and in a circle of angry threatening labourers shrank miserably. His disdain had gone and his face had the quality of a hunted rabbit.

'I've seen him about,' someone growled. ' He's a boss's man.'

'Organising scab labour, are you? A dirty scab yourself?' And they pushed him around the circle.

He pleaded piteously. 'No, fellows, no, just eating lunch.'

'Then you're a spy?'

'No,' he bleated.

'Listening to our talk were you?'

'No.'

'Insulting our Judith?' For the first time I heard them speak the dignity of my name.

'Didn't mean anything.'

'Not mean anything when you threw your soup at her?'

He was silent and wary. The shifty feral silence of a hunted animal. He cringed.

'Apologise and call her "lady".'

'Apologies, ma'am,' he whined.

'Louder! And she's not the Queen.' Someone prodded him.

'Apologies, lady,' he screeched.

'Oh, let him go.' The *Das Kapital* reader had, unbeknown to me, approached the melee. 'Let him go,' he repeated, 'we have other things to worry about beside a single bloody blackleg.'

They hesitated and I was surprised they accepted his authority.

The soup thrower was hustled out the door and given a hearty shove that sent him tumbling. As he scuttled away they shouted with laughter and slapped each other on the back as if triumphant.

Meanwhile the reader had returned to his book.

I stood hesitating in the middle of the room but finally

approached him. 'Thank you,' I said. 'If there had been a fight I might have lost my job.'

'Yes,' he said and looked up. 'Better change that skirt. So you understood bits and pieces of *Das Kapital*?'

Surprised, I stared at him. He had actually heard me earlier and remembered what I had said. At my obvious astonishment a slight smile lifted the corners of his mouth.

'Amazing,' he said. 'She understands some Marx. Quite amazing.' He returned to his reading.

And now I knew his eyes were grey. Jubilantly I remembered my challenge to myself. I would take myself to the pictures and see a new Mary Pickford film and maybe buy a new dress.

On Sundays I put on my best dress, hat and gloves and went to the Botanic Gardens to stroll with my closest friend Winifred, secretly nicknamed 'Weepy Winnie' because in bursts of sentimentality she would dissolve into tears. Just about anything set her off: a lost kitten mewing under a bush; a ragged child begging for a penny. Her feelings were utterly indiscriminate so she was mocked, but gently so. I was certain that if Winnie had not been pretty her outbursts would have appeared incongruous and feeble-minded.

She had no doubt about her attractions. Sometimes I thought unkindly that she cultivated me because by comparison she shone more brilliantly. Her pansy-brown eyes were large and soulful. Her mouth was what romantic novelists called a rosebud, her skin a glorious pink and white, her face a delicious heart-shape. She had the knack of filling her eyes with tears when she wanted to seem affected and the tears would drown the pansies, overflow and run down her cheeks but never did her eyes or nose redden and she never sniffed.

Her art amazed me. She only had to glance at a boy or a man for them to liquefy. They blushed, gushed, stammered, took her hand, then, overcome with embarrassment at their private infatuation, released it and blushed, gushed and stammered again. Even older women pronounced that she was a sweet girl and in many ways she was. There was no malice in her.

I thought her feather-brained but liked her and enjoyed her bright company. She tried to take me in hand and improve my dress sense but I was plain and didn't see the point of dressing myself up. My clothes were clean, neat but unimaginative. They didn't attract anyone's eyes and for that I was grateful. I always felt that I would look rather silly flirting and consequently was more awkward and self-conscious than I needed to be.

Weepy Winnie flirted outrageously.

We had wandered along North Terrace and passing through the elegant cast-iron portals entered a green oasis bright with spring flowers. It was a mild day, pleasant before the summer heat and there was a mixture of the stylishly dressed and those shabby in ragged coats and shoes with broken soles that flapped as they walked. Those dressed well walked with confidence and chatted and laughed with ease and ignored the ill clad who, unable to compete and aware of their difference, often hurried by with bent heads as if shamed by their misfortune. I had the impression that rather like the shadowy wharf rats in my dreams they were there and yet not there.

We strolled along the paths, passed the statues of two white dogs that children had polished from constant patting, and loitered before the goddess Amazon astride her rearing steed and defending herself against a tiger. I wondered briefly about this mythical world that meant so little to me. We peeked in the windows of the Palm House with its mellow creamy stone work and grand glass dome. Still chatting we meandered across the finely trimmed grass and as we emerged from behind some trees I saw a man with a starved expression bend swiftly and surreptitiously to snatch at a cigarette butt. He had first glanced about him, like some hunted animal that sees a tid-bit but can't gather enough courage to steal it, then, having cautiously assured itself of its safety, makes a quick grab. A sweet statue of Diana gazed down on this moment of humiliation with marble indifference.

I halted, shocked by his misery. Winnie tugged at my arm. 'Don't look,' she whispered. 'Come away.'

I shook her off. 'Why not?'

The ubiquitous tears filled her eyes. 'He's embarrassed. Poor man. He's ashamed. He doesn't want us to see.'

She was right but her tears irritated me. 'Stop crying, Winnie. It's ridiculous.'

This time she actually sniffed. 'Seeing things like this spoils my afternoon.'

It had certainly spoiled mine.

It was this Sunday afternoon, even more than slavery at the Chew It and Spew It, which gave me a sharp sense of class division.

Winnie, in her pretty clothes and her parents who owned a men's clothing store in the city, clearly belonged in the upper strata of society. My father was a labourer and I slung hash in a cheap eating place to other labourers. So I supposed that I was working class. Several rungs below Winnie.

Something in society divided us and without offering us a choice placed us where we were. But I wasn't knowledgeable enough to understand how this had come about. I fretted over this.

When we tired of strolling, and when Winnie grew bored with commenting on the clothes people were wearing, we made our way to 'The Stump'. This part of the gardens was the domain of spruikers, religious ratbags, political theorists, tin-pot messiahs. It always promised to be entertaining.

Each speaker had his box, usually an old soap box or vegetable crate, and mounted thereon shouted his message to a crowd that drifted from speaker to speaker. The audience contributed to the fun with witty interventions or ribald mimicry. There were no women speakers and it often seemed we were the only two women in the audience.

Winnie looked about with bright eyes. 'It's such fun.'

The first time we had come here I had asked, 'Are all these people just allowed to get up and shout whatever they like?'

She had giggled. 'Usually. But my father says the City Council has had just about enough of free speech and they are thinking of introducing permits. He doesn't mind the religious nuts but he thinks that there are too many political speakers and they may be causing unrest. Anyway, I prefer the religious ones. The political ones are so earnest.'

This Sunday she dragged me over to a small group standing in front of a red-faced bellicose man with sparse hair and a large wart on the end of his nose. His box still bore the label SOUTH AUSTRALIAN TOMATOES.

Winnie whispered to me, 'Give him a minute, he'll see us and begin to talk about Jezebel. I think he hates women. I suppose plenty have rejected him. It'll be that wart.'

True to her prediction he brayed about the evils of Jezebel, then went on to trumpet the evil of dissenters and non-conformists. In a stentorian voice he condemned our adulterous generation, the evils of false worship, paganism, Marxism, rationalism. In hushed tones he breathed the beauty of redemption, salvation and the flight of the anointed who winged unerringly into a new heaven.

'What do you think happened to the *old* heaven?' Winnie giggled, and as he turned his wrathful eyes upon her she poked out her tongue at him and, openly laughing, pulled me away.

I went with her, irritated by his puerility. 'Do they all spout such drivel? Are they of sound mind?'

'Probably not. But if they weren't so mad we couldn't laugh at him.'

I chewed this one over. The mad, like the poor, are to be pitied my mother had told me but I didn't feel pity for the man with the wart on his nose and he didn't amuse me. He had held the crowd in the palm of his hand. Whether devotees or mockers they were all mesmerised, listening and responding in their own ways. His sort of madness disturbed me. He was a bully and I hated bullies.

I followed Winnie reluctantly. There were several other orators, all perched on their boxes, like birds come to rest. Some had megaphones and they drowned out their neighbours. Away on his own and addressing a small group was a thin man of medium height. He had an English cap on his head and wore a well-used tweed jacket. I recognised him as the reader in my cafe. Winnie was looking elsewhere for entertainment but I gripped her arm. 'I know him,' I whispered.

Immediately arrested, she peered at him. 'It's a bit hard to recognise him under that cap. Are you sure?'

'Yes.'

'Where did you meet him?'

'At the Chew It and Spew It. He's the reader.'

'Ooooh.' Winnie's attention was now fully focussed. 'Glasses and all?'

'Yes. Glasses and all.'

'Let's go closer. Maybe he'll recognise you. You look much nicer in your Sunday clothes.'

'I don't want him to do that.'

'Why?'

'Don't know. Just don't.'

'You are a silly old thing.'

I didn't tell her that I was ashamed to work in that cafe; ashamed that I was not better educated; and mortified that he had seen the soup thrown at me. However I was curious and stood at the back of the group with Winnie. Perhaps, I thought, he's so short-sighted he won't recognise me.

He was speaking: 'All history is the story of class struggle. The economic exploitation and political domination of class by class has always existed. The poor man gets less than his due. The rich man lives by exploiting the poor.

'The state is an executive committee for managing the affairs of the governing class. The poor are excluded from any active part in the state or the law. We have one law for the rich and quite another for the poor.

'But, comrades, we are in the last stage of humanity's march towards a classless society. The proletariat will overcome capitalism and bring in a new classless society. You are all part of this historical evolution ...'

'Oh gawd,' Winnie rolled her eyes. 'And my father thinks he's dangerous.'

She was kind. His audience pilloried him.

'Get a real job, Professor.'

'Swallowed a book, have you?'

'Yeah, the book of the Comical Party. Came in the post from Russia, did it?'

Certainly he had no skills as an orator. He was actually pleading with his audience to listen to him. I didn't want him to be bullying like the warty religious fanatic but his lack of fire annoyed me. 'Come on, Winnie,' I said, turning aside, 'let's go.' Others were also drifting away.

'What a dry old stick,' Winnie said.

I glanced back. Suddenly he jumped down from his box, hurried towards us and snatched my hand. 'Here,' he shouted, 'here is a daughter of the working class. Not your idle rich dressed in silks and satins. She has to work every day. Tell them what you think of capitalism,' he insisted, still gripping my hand. 'Tell them what it's like to be a poor woman in grinding employment.'

The audience had stopped its flight and scarlet with embarrassment I was the centre of all eyes. Furious with him and with sniggering Winnie, the smirks of a watching policeman and the cries of 'Go on, girlie, get it off your chest,' I allowed myself to be dragged back to the box. There was little I could do since he had such a clutch on my hand.

In desperation to get the whole thing over, I shouted, 'Capitalism stinks and you should all know it.'

I jumped down and ran to escape the cheers. I scrambled through the growing crowd, 'Doubtless here to see a woman make a fool of herself,' I fumed.

A burly fellow in a coat without buttons patted me on the back. 'Good on yer, girlie. I'll tell my missus. We need more like you.'

I ignored him.

Winnie trotted beside me, bleating that I walked too fast.

'Wear sensible shoes,' I snarled.

I wasn't aware that my tormentor had followed us until I felt the light touch on my shoulder and his voice. 'Please, Miss Larsen, wait a minute.'

I swung around, glaring at him and he stepped back, perhaps expecting that I would strike him. 'How dare you?' I flared. 'Make an idiot of me in front of, in front of ...' I stuttered and gestured wildly to include the whole gardens and everyone in it.

He flushed. 'I didn't m-m-mean ...' he stammered. 'You were so ...' he hesitated, 'thrilling.'

'Thrilling?' That stopped me. 'Thrilling?' I choked. Winnie giggled. I pinched her arm and she yelped.

'What do you mean, *thrilling*?' My indignant voice was an embarrassed squeak.

He was much thinner than I had noticed in the Chew It and Spew It – not aristocratic thin, more starved thin and his sensitive mouth worked nervously.

'I think she was thrilling, too,' Winnie said coyly and batted her eyelashes at him.

Could she never let another girl have her moment of attention?

But to my delight and her chagrin he ignored her.

'It was thrilling because it was brave,' he said. 'I always knew you would be brave,' and as I remained silent he added desperately, 'and full of spirit.'

He blushed again.

Heavens, I thought, he's shy. Instantly I was sorry for him. Shyness I understood. Still resentful, I didn't feel like making the effort to put him at his ease but I could not be so rude as to ignore him. 'Do you come here often?' I asked stiffly.

'When I can.'

'You find it worthwhile when so few listen?'

He looked downcast. 'We must try. The proletariat need to be educated about the class struggle.'

I laughed. 'And you think this will convince them?'

My mockery peeved him. He flushed again. It was an irritating habit, particularly in a man.

'We don't look for immediate results.'

'No,' I said. 'That is obvious.'

Winnie and I had begun walking towards the main gardens. He fell into step beside us without being invited. In the Chew It and Spew It he had aroused my curiosity, even earned my gratitude for intervening in the fray over the soup thrower, but now his insistence on dogging us annoyed me. There had been some romantic mystery about him in the cafe; now he was just an ordinary and tactless young man. I chatted to Winnnie and ignored him. She looked embarrassed and kept glancing first at me and then at him. It seemed that he didn't know how to extricate himself and leave. He continued to trot beside us.

Finally, in her pretty engaging way, Winnie asked, 'We don't know your name.'

'Nathan,' he said hastily. 'Nathan Ramsay.'

'Then, Mr Ramsay, how do you do?' and she held out her hand.

He shook it seriously but in no way showed that he was smitten.

'We must return home now, Mr Ramsay. Perhaps we will see you here another time.' And she smiled her dismissal.

He hesitated, looked anxiously at me, and, as I didn't respond, mumbled, 'I'm sorry if I embarrassed you. Very sorry. I thought they'd listen to you. I'm not very good at making people listen.'

'No,' I said, 'you're not. Good day.'

He hovered a minute, perhaps waiting for me to add something but I turned away.

Winnie reproached me, 'That poor young man. You crucified him. He tried to apologise.'

I was tart. Her reproach hit home but I wasn't going to admit it.

'If you can't succeed in something by your own efforts then you shouldn't drag someone else in to help you. He's hopeless and had better stick to reading his books.'

I recalled him lifting his head from his reading to peer at me. How well did he see I wondered with those frightful thick lenses? Maybe he was almost blind. Had I been cruel?

'I wonder what happened to his box while he was following us. Someone must help him carry it. He wouldn't be strong enough to lift that crate on his own. Why are there so many hungry-looking people about, Winnie?'

She was surprised. 'Are there? I hadn't noticed.'

'You hadn't noticed?' I stopped abruptly in the middle of the path so that a woman ran a stroller into the back of my legs. She apologised profusely while I said it was my fault. We both laughed and she passed on with her baby.

'How do you mean you hadn't noticed, Winnie? You saw the man snatch up the cigarette butt. There have been dozens of people looking as if they haven't a penny to their name. Even Nathan, Mr Ramsay, looks as if he needs a decent meal.'

Winnie had a soft heart. 'I think he's what they call a Bolshevik,' she said kindly. 'They're all down at heel. I suppose that's why they're always talking about helping the poor. You would need to be poor to understand what it's like. It's hard for someone like me, although I can see what you mean. He definitely looks hungry. He has a sort of hopeful, expectant look, like my brothers have when they come home from boarding school and they expect to be fed. I don't know whether he's hopeful in that way at all.'

Winnie's observations made some sense but I didn't think it was necessary to be poor to understand. Some of the things I had read in books suggested to me that one could learn about what it was like to be poor. It wasn't necessary to experience it. But I wasn't certain that Winnie would understand my reflections so I squeezed her arm and told her she was doubtless right and that from what I knew about Bolsheviks they did want to help the poor.

She looked at me anxiously. 'In the right way? I'd like to think well of him. He did look hungry.'

'How should I know, Winnie? I wouldn't know if it were a right way or a wrong way but listening to Mr Ramsay I would say that there might be a useful way or a useless one.'

She giggled. 'I suppose, poor man, that he hoped to be inspiring.'

We reached the garden entrance but were arrested by a bellowing shout. 'Weepy. Wait!'

Winnie looked back, startled, and then a wide grin transfigured her face. Dropping my arm she sped across the grass to greet the tall young man bounding towards her. She threw herself into his arms and he lifted her, swung her round, and put her down.

'How are you, Weepy? It's ages since I saw you.'

She straightened her clothes and beamed at him. 'You, Harry, what are you doing here?' She glanced about. 'No girl?'

He put on a mournful face. 'They don't love me any more. Not like you do, Weepy.'

'Oh, Harry! You! Don't call me that. You know I hate it. You only do it to tease. This is my friend ...' She had forgotten me and now looked about, relieved to find that I had followed her and stood nearby. I wondered who Harry was.

'This is my friend, Judith.' She pulled me forward. 'And this is my cousin Harry, my favourite cousin. He's a scamp, the family scamp.'

Harry grinned at me. 'Pleased to meet you, Miss Judith.'

I smiled back. From his shock of wild copper hair, freckled snub nose and humorous upturned mouth, to the jaunty carriage of his head and loose eager stance, he was joyousness. I was certain it would be impossible for him to ever stand still.

'Where are you off to?' he asked, including me in his bright glance.

'Judith and I are going to have afternoon tea. Want to come?'

'I'll shout you both,' he said, and walking between us tucked an arm through mine and Winnie's. 'Where to?'

'Rundle's, and you can't pay for us, you never have any money. No job, no money.'

'You sound just like your father, Winnie.' He deepened his voice, stuck out his chest and pontificated, 'Young man, you'll never get on in life if you don't work. No work, no money, my young man, no work, no money.'

'I'm never sure why I'm "my young man" as I don't really belong to him.'

Winnie said severely, 'Your father's dead and your mother's a widow. She needs help and you just fritter your life away being funny. After all, my father's money does help you.'

He looked chastened, but merrily so. 'Well, you can now rest, Judge Winnie. I have a job.'

'Oh, yes?' Winnie sounded sceptical. 'And who'd give you a job?'

'Oh, yes,' he mimicked her, 'you'd be surprised. And it's a man's job.'

She looked at him suspiciously. 'What do you mean a man's job? What prank are you up to now, Harry?'

'No prank. Am I always to be misunderstood?' He faked

an injured look. 'Your father has found me an apprenticeship.'

'Where? What in?'

'I'll be a turner and fitter in a foundry.'

'A foundry?'

'Yes, a foundry. Why do you have to be told things twice, Winnie?'

'Won't that be a lot of hard work?'

'Probably.'

'Will you enjoy it?'

'I always enjoy what I do.'

'Is it suitable, Harry?'

He looked at her quizzically. 'Darling, Winnie, it's very suitable for a poor widow's lad,' and this time his laugh had a sharp edge to it. 'And what do you think of my good fortune, Miss Judith?'

I hesitated. I had once peeped in the doors of a local foundry. It had been hot and noisy, the floor was of dirt and it was full of huge machines driven by great belts that surged up to revolving wheels in the roof. It all looked very dangerous. While I watched a young lad grabbed one of the belts and hung on while it took him a ride to the roof. He yahooed triumphantly but I held my breath in terror for him. Just before the belt rolled over the wheel he let go and plummeted to the ground.

A foreman shouted, rushed across the shed, and swiped him a backhander. 'You fucken stupid cretin. Do you want to kill yerself? We've had one death already this week. You wanna be a second?'

Then he saw me. 'And whatdya want?'

'Just looking,' I said.

'Well, Just Lookin', look somewhere else. We can do without visitors lookin'. You may think this is a three-ring circus with fucken trapeze artists but it's only a foundry with Tom Fool boys I try to keep alive.'

I told my father.

'Bloody machines,' he said, 'no guards. A boy in that foundry had his head crushed in that machinery. They carried him out on a stretcher and flung a couple of hessian bags over him. Then they sent for his mother to identify him. Bloody disgrace and the government tells us we don't need unions.'

All this I remembered as Harry waited for my reply.

'They're dangerous,' I replied. 'You must be careful.'

'Careful,' Winnie mocked, 'careful. You're asking Harry to be careful? Not likely.'

She hadn't seen or heard what I had. Her ignorance annoyed me. He preened himself, living up to his reputation of being wild, I thought.

'Boys get killed in foundries,' I said soberly.

'Not me, Miss Judith,' he boasted. 'I'm immortal.'

It was useless to do other than play along with his mood. Already I had sounded like some middle-aged know-all.

'We've been to The Stump,' Winnie laughed, changing the subject. 'Judith knows one of the Bolshies there.'

'No I don't, Winnie.'

'Yes, you do,' she carolled, 'you do, do, do. She does, Harry. And he's so earnest. He made her speak from his box and the box had South Australian tomatoes written on it. I nearly died laughing.' She was embellishing the story. The tomato box had belonged to the religious fanatic. I felt hurt. She was enticing Harry into joking at my expense. But surprisingly he didn't laugh.

'Shut up, Weepie, you're embarrassing your friend and the Bolshies are not all stupid. Sometimes I listen to them, too, and they talk some sense. I think one day I might become a Bolshie, too.' The moment of seriousness abandoned, he was laughing again.

His mercurial changes were tiring. It would be hard to know when he was sincere.

'And join a union?' Winnie was aghast. 'What would my father say?'

'I can hear him now,' he said. 'I give that young ne'er-do-well a chance in life and what does he do? He throws it away to become a Bolshie.'

He gave me an I'm-a-naughty-boy-but-you-love-me look. It worked and I smiled at him, but my thoughts about him and the foundry were not happy ones.

Winnie and I paid for the tea and cakes, sharing the cost of Harry's, as he said with mock apology that he wasn't in the money just yet. He parted with a cheerful kiss on the cheek for Winnie and a friendly handshake for me.

'I'm sure,' he said, with a twinkle, 'that you'll be very good for me, Miss Judith.' He strode off whistling 'If you knew Susie like I know Susie Oh. Oh, Oh what a girl'. I didn't know whether to be flattered or annoyed but had experienced that first telltale rush of affection that Harry would always be able to inspire.

Winnie walked with me to the railway station so I could catch a train to the Port. She lived on the other side of the city. Even suburbs divide us, I thought, envisaging her pink stone house set in a thriving garden and comparing it with our hulk and my small cabin.

Winnie squeezed my hand. 'I can't come next week. A family get-together. Are you free the week after?'

'OK, one o'clock at the entrance.'

'Yes, and maybe we'll go to see the Bolshie again.'

'No, Winnie, please.'

She teased, 'Perhaps he'll come to the Chew It and read his books.'

'Maybe.' I was uncertain about whether I wanted to see him.

'These Bolshies are unpredictable,' she pronounced. 'Do you think that Harry means what he said?'

'About his job?'

'No, silly, about being a Bolshie. My father … Heavens, you can't imagine what my father would say.'

'Then you'd better not tell him.'

'As if I would. I never tell him anything about Harry. But, you know, Harry's a real risk-taker.' She shook her head. 'Even as a child he had to climb the highest tree to the highest branch. He used to tell me how he would dare himself to do things and then make himself do them.'

I remembered my terrified longing to have the courage to swing the bosun's chair over the sea and understood Harry. 'Yes,' I said, 'safe can be boring and boring is usually safe.'

She looked anxious. 'Do you think he'll be safe in the foundry? You seemed uncertain. Do you know what they're like? Do they have very big machines?'

'Yes.'

'Dangerous machines?'

'Yes.'

'What sort of machines?'

'I don't really know. My father says they are lathes and slotting machines and presses and there is a boiler and a coal-burning donkey engine and they all need guards around them.'

She looked terrified. 'Presses, lathes, slot-machines – they all sound remorseless. If they need guards, surely they'll have them, Judith, won't they?'

'I don't know. I suppose it depends on the owner.'

'Aren't owners made to do it?'

I shrugged. 'Not according to my father.'

'So Harry might …,' she choked, 'Harry might get caught in one of those dreadful machines and killed? Or his hands might get crushed.' She burst into tears. 'Oh, Judith, he only wants to become a pianist. He can play anything. Just has to hear a tune and he plays it. Has been doing this since he was a little boy.'

I was perplexed. 'Why the foundry? Surely with that skill …'

She blew her nose. 'There's not much money in it. Just an occasional job at the Blood House, playing for dances. He doesn't mind the fights there. He can look after himself. He's good at boxing. Sometimes he plays in the dance halls at the Semaphore but it's not regular work.'

'And he has a piano?' I asked.

'No, of course not. How could his mother afford a piano?'

'Then how has he learned to play?'

She began to snivel again. 'By begging anywhere there is a piano. Sometimes at our house when my father's at work, sometimes at the local hotels. They're pleased enough to let him play and entertain but they don't pay him anything. They say it's their fee for lending him the piano for a couple of hours. Sometimes music shops give him a go to advertise their wares. People come in to listen when they hear him playing.

'And he dances, too, Judith. Quite divinely. I've heard some of the girls call him "Twinkle Toes". He's just got rhythm in his bones. His father wasn't much of a provider and my mother says that Harry's a lot like him. But it's no job no money and I'm sure he'll be killed in the foundry.'

She started to cry again. Passers-by paused to stare, their looks hesitant and doubtful. Quelled by my frown, they moved on. As they glanced back with concern I begged her to stop. 'Crying will do no good, Winnie. He'll just have to be careful at the foundry – and sensible.'

'Careful?' she wailed. 'Sensible? You don't know him.'

It seemed that Harry was good at everything except earning a living. His choices seemed no more unpleasant than the Chew It and Spew It was for me. I thought sourly that maybe a foundry would be good for him.

I sat in the non-smoking compartment with the women and children. Through the door window I could see a couple of working men lounging in the open vestibule, smoking and occasionally hawking tobacco spittle out the carriage doorway. Unkempt and unwashed they folded their arms about themselves to keep warm as the fresh breeze zipped through the vestibule. It seemed that wherever I saw ill-clad people they were folding themselves in to keep out the cold. I thought about Harry and impossibilities. He could play anything on the piano and he could dance and box but now had to earn his living in a hot dirty foundry.

I recalled the workers in their heavy leather aprons feeding the huge coal-fire furnace. Its stomach of molten fire vented heat and showers of brilliant sparks rained about them. I had flinched as if personally attacked but regardless of the danger they continued to open the iron doors and shovel in more coal. With each fuel load the volcanic centre roared into powerful life and momentarily the workers were black figures silhouetted in the mouth of Hell. That their faces, eyes and hair were not seared was a miracle.

I had made some drawings of the workers in their leather aprons and sketched the boy suspended from the huge belt. Barely able to hold on, he was a figure dancing in space, carefree but precarious, his grip on the belt as tenuous as his grip on life.

Earlier when my father expressed his anger at the unprotected dangers of the foundry I had taken out my drawings and rather shyly shown them to him and to my mother. My mother, busy preparing the evening meal, glanced at them cursorily. 'Yes, dear, very nice,' she said. My father grunted dismissively, 'Those leather aprons are bloody heavy to wear all day.' And at the sketch of the belt-swinger, 'Bloody idiot. I'd take a belt to him, no mistake. And it wouldn't be the one he's riding like some crazy cowboy.'

Although not certain what it was I had expected or even wanted from them I had hoped for more. Disappointed and deflated I returned my sketches to the drawer. Over the years I had accumulated quite a pile of them.

Reflections about Harry's fate had brought my own life into focus. Lack of education doomed him to the foundry; lack of education doomed me to the Chew It and Spew It. My life stretched before me a desolate dreary wasteland of drudgery. I read of other women with different lives. They weren't always happy but it seemed that their strivings had some dignity. Even the tragic endings were beautified and uplifted by passion. In the pages of a book, women's lives unfolded meaningfully and their fantasy lives made my own seem worthless by comparison. Sunday excursions to the gardens with Winnie seemed minor diversions, sweet but pointless interludes. In fact, I was set to have a real fit of the blues.

My mother watched me gloomily pick at my food and suggested that I accompany my father to the Club to change my books. As our financial situation worsened, she fell back on my love of reading as some consolation she could offer me. I knew she felt guilty that I was unhappy and knowing her financial struggles I felt miserable for inflicting my gloom on her.

This emotional tangle passed my father by. Hard physical work from childhood had been his lot. He lacked the imagination to perceive that for me it might not be enough. So my mother watched and worried and suffered for me silently. I was coming to dislike my father and didn't think that a trip to the Club would help me but in the face of her worry I agreed to go.

'Got over your grumps?' my father said. Sulking, I refused to give a yes or no answer.

'Still feeling sorry for yourself?' he needled me and in a hectoring voice told me how lucky I was to have a job, three meals a day and some pleasures in life. He had never been able to stroll in the gardens with friends or go to the cinema, all he had had to do was work and damned hard work it had been. I should be grateful that my life was so much better.

Close to tears, I resented his attack. My mother intervened: 'Stop it, Niels. Stop harassing her. You've said enough. More than enough. Button your lip and take your daughter to borrow some books. You should be grateful that you can offer your daughter something more than you had. She needs other things for her life. We all need other things.'

He grumbled and I would have liked to refuse to go but after her intervention it was impossible. In a fit of defiance, to assert something that was individually mine, I took out several of my drawings, placed them in a folder, collected my over-due books and went with him. Maybe, I thought, Joe will be there tonight and we can talk.

I kissed my mother goodbye. She had turned on the wireless and taken out her darning. The wireless was her consolation and tonight she listened to George Wright singing 'Drink to me only with thine eyes'. Afterwards he might sing 'Comin' through the rye' and she would hum along happily. She loved the soft senti-mentality of these songs. Once I saw her with tears in her eyes listen to Nellie Melba sing 'Home Sweet Home' and it had been sweet, excruciatingly sweet, a nostalgia at once painful and beau-tiful. My father scoffed, calling it fairy floss, a lament for a world that in reality never existed, but she ignored him. She needed a small world that was hers alone.

I looked forward to meeting Joe Pulham, the old librarian I had met five years earlier. He had become my friend. He still did odd jobs at the Club but his cough had grown worse. Now he needed to sit down when he talked to me and the words often struggled out between gasps of breathlessness. He was quite direct with me about his illness. 'Leaded,' he said, 'we're all leaded in the printing industry. The lead slugs, you know. Gives us all dickey hearts. Industry is a grand killer, Nearly-Twelve.'

He always called me Nearly-Twelve. When I reminded him my name was Judith he chuckled. 'I know,' he said, 'Judith Emma Larsen, but if you don't mind I'll keep on calling you Nearly-Twelve and then I won't forget the little girl who planned to read Aristotle and Aristophanes.' He always laughed, then coughed, when he said Aristophanes as if he had some secret joke.

Maybe Joe would take some real notice of my drawings. Over the years he had talked to me about the books I had borrowed. I think he had read most of them. 'Reading's the only education most of us could get,' he said. He didn't say who 'us' was but as I grew older I knew that 'us' meant the class of people we lived amongst. It didn't mean family. Joe never mentioned his family. It meant those who were poor. Now that the hopeful days of the early twenties were passing the number of 'us' had grown. My father spoke angrily of 'us' when he meant waterside workers and unionists; my mother spoke of 'us' when she meant women struggling to put food on the table or keep the family clothed with constant washing, darning and mending. 'Us' certainly meant a large group opposed to 'them' who did not have to struggle.

In our discussions Joe had introduced me to Aristotle's very important question: What is the purpose of living? I recalled Joe's amusement as he reflected, 'A huge question, that, Nearly-Twelve. Now if I had the answer to that ...' He didn't give me an answer to Aristotle's question but waited patiently for me to ask, his eyes intent over the top of his glasses. That is how Joe and I talked. He would introduce an idea from a book and then wait for me to ask an appropriate question.

'Well, Joe, did Aristotle have an answer?'

He was gleeful. 'He did, Nearly-Twelve, he did, but whether it solves anything I don't know.'

'And what is the purpose of living, according to Aristotle, Joe?'

He looked at me triumphantly. 'To be happy, Nearly-Twelve.'

I gaped. 'Is that all? Anyone could have come up with that idea. And how are we all to be happy? My father says people will be happy in a socialist state. My mother says people who believe in fantasies will always be unhappy. I'm not sure which one I should believe in, my father or my mother.'

'No, Nearly-Twelve, Aristotle didn't have such a down to earth answer as your father or mother. He said people could be happy if they behaved in the right way and behaving in the right way was being moderate. For instance, someone might have a lot of courage and think that courage made them happy but if they had too much of it they could be foolish.'

It was an interesting idea but quite frankly, at that time, I didn't think that Aristotle had a great deal to offer and wondered why he had been around for two thousand years.

It wasn't until I saw the boy at the foundry, tenuously clutching the belt as it surged dangerously to a revolving wheel that could crush him in an instant, that I recalled Aristotle and his view on foolishness and moderation. Aristotle would have called him a downright idiot. It had been comforting to have my thoughts confirmed by someone wiser. It gave them substance and authority. That, I decided, was at least one of the purposes of books.

When years earlier I had asked Joe to explain to me what Aristophanes was saying, he had given his secret chuckle, 'The thing is, Nearly-Twelve, Aristophanes made people laugh at silliness and when you make people laugh you can get away with a lot of criticism. I suppose there were as many silly people in Greece two thousand years ago as we have to put up with now.' He sighed, coughed and asked me at that time, 'How old are you now, Nearly-Twelve?'

'Only thirteen,' I had said, crestfallen.

'Then, Only-Thirteen, perhaps you need to grow a bit to understand Aristophanes. He'll wait, you know. He's been around a long long time.' He stopped, wheezed and gasped for breath.

'Are you not well, Joe?' I had asked.

'No, Nearly-Twelve, you could say that and you wouldn't be exaggerating.'

Joe understood many things and he seemed to have lots of time. When I had finished reading Jack London's *White Fang* and *Call of the Wild*, I told him how my father had also lived in a very cold place with the Icelanders. He had looked amazed.

'Well now, I never knew that.'

'And can speak their language.' I was determined to impress through my father.

My father's hard life had been a source of pride then and I wanted to boast of it.

'Are you educated, Joe, if you can speak another language?'

'It helps,' he said. 'It helps.'

'Jack London was an adventurer,' I said, 'like my father. There's a piece at the start of the book about him. But he never had the happy life Aristotle talks about. I suppose he wasn't moderate.'

Joe managed to laugh again without coughing. 'You kill me, Nearly-Twelve. You kill me. Jack London moderate? Not by a long chalk. A happy life? Probably not. But an interesting one. Lots of experiences.'

'He killed himself the book said.'

Now Joe was sober. 'Yes, I believe so.'

'Why would someone do that, Joe?'

I had puzzled over this because I had seen the smallest most unimportant creatures dash away from danger to live: a bird with a broken wing fluttering in protest; a fish gasping and flapping on the deck in an effort to regain the sea. If they struggled to live why would a man give up?

Joe agreed, 'Very strange, Nearly-Twelve, very strange, indeed.'

'And he didn't even have industry to kill him.'

'There are other things, Nearly-Twelve.'

In reflecting on death with me Joe prompted my thoughts about life.

That night when we arrived at the Club my father was grabbed at the entrance by his two friends Jock and Bernie. Jock was a small thickset belligerent Scotsman. Bernie-Benito, was a lank Italian with large soulful eyes and a soft mouth like a baby. They were an odd pair, but inseparable.

Jock had emigrated from the shipyards of Glasgow. Bernie had fled an Italy that was becoming increasingly fascist under Mussolini. My father said Bernie was a fanatical and fiery communist who had seen the writing on the wall. When he smiled at me with his soft liquid eyes, a smile that seemed to loosen his features so that only kindness showed, I couldn't imagine him being fanatical about any idea. Jock, always at his side, often slapped his back and called him 'my fascist friend' and roared with laughter.

Catching on to a few of my father's ideas, I asked why he called him a fascist if he was a communist. My father laughed. 'It's the name. He shares a name with Benito Mussolini, the Italian prime minister. They're both Benito. It's not an insult, it's affection.'

Jock and Bernie nodded to me but their absorption was in their latest political grievances. 'Our bastard of a prime minister, Bruce, plans to reduce wages. Says we have to compete on foreign markets. Us poor working men can be caned but those Queensland landholders, those robber baron bastards, they don't have to reduce their incomes. I tell you, Niels, we fought for very little when we fought for the English.'

Jock's rich Scottish accent burred his words but they were forceful enough. Bernie nodded. Jock usually acted as spokesman for them both. They moved away enclosing my father in their resentment. Ignored, I went to find Joe.

He was at his desk, reading. The room was silent, dimly lit, and still held the musty smell of old books.

'Why, Nearly-Twelve,' he still called me this. 'I haven't seen you for some time. Your books are overdue.' He pretended to look stern and I grinned at him.

'I'm a working girl now, Joe, and don't have much time to read.'

'That's a pity, Nearly-Twelve.'

I sighed, dispiritedly. 'I know.' And in a mood of desperation I appealed to him, 'What is to become of me, Joe?'

'In what sense, Nearly-Twelve?'

'I don't know.'

His expression became compassionate. 'Are you unhappy?'

'Yes,' I burst out, 'of course. I have a terrible job and no hope of anything better. I don't have any education and I don't think I have any talents. My mother has a hard life as a domestic drudge and her satisfaction now is to escape into sentimental songs. They don't appeal to me. I can't abide too much sweetness and I don't want to listen to music that looks back so sadly. I want a future.'

He was quiet and put his hand over his mouth to suppress his cough. 'Yes,' he said, 'of course you want a future. You're young and it's your right. If that isn't your right, then why did we get into the goddamn awful war? What a waste.'

I had never heard Joe swear before, and looked at him, startled.

'Yes, Nearly-Twelve,' he repeated, 'a goddamn awful war, an unnecessary one, and an unproductive one. The only people who win in a war are the rich ones.'

This time his spasm of coughing racked his whole body. Over the years he had grown thinner, his skin had now a grey hue and his hair, once thick and white, fell in cotton-wool wisps about his ears.

'You're not well, Joe.' I was ashamed of my concentration on myself. He repeated his words from years earlier, 'You could say that, Nearly-Twelve. You could say that. But what is that folder you have on your lap? Have you brought me something interesting?'

I blushed. 'It's nothing, Joe.' He was clearly very ill and I shouldn't be bothering him.

'Well,' he said, 'I'd like to see what nothing is.'

Shyly I took out my drawings and put them in front of him. He studied them thoughtfully, one by one, occasionally pushing his glasses up on his nose. Then when he had looked at them all he started again. Sometimes he turned one so that the poor light fell more strongly on it and he held it closer to his face peering at it. I noticed large brown spots on the back of his hands. Finally he looked up at me.

'Well,' he said, 'well, well, well. Who would have thought? How long have you been doing this, Nearly-Twelve?'

'Since I first came to the Club.'

His intensity puzzled me, as he kept returning to examine the drawings.

'Well,' he said again, 'well, well, well. You know, Nearly-Twelve, when I worked as a compositor on the *Argus* we printed sketches and cartoons of everyday life, but few were as good as these. Now I could readily find a caption for this fool boy swinging on the belt, but equally important is your background sketch of the foundry. Our Australia is entering the urban and industrial phase of its life and artists will begin to reflect this world. There were artists in the last century who had to find their Australian-ness in the land-scape. Recently some fools told us that our Australian-ness has been born of going to war and that's nonsense. Now in peacetime many of us are becoming city people. Artists will reflect that.'

Overwhelmed by his burst of knowledge, I protested, 'But, Joe, I'm not an artist.'

He grinned. 'Maybe you're not but maybe you are. These are very good. Could you leave the belt-swinger with me? And this one of fuelling the furnace? I have a mate on the *Workers' Weekly*. He may be able to do something with them.'

'Do what, Joe?'

'Leave it with me, Nearly-Twelve. Leave it with me. And you must keep on doing these. They're very good.'

He took down a book from the shelves and handed it to me. 'Have a look at these. They are drawings by Goya, a Spanish painter.'

'I saw them before, Joe. They're ugly and queer.' I shuddered.

'Yes, very ugly at times. Quite horrible. But they say some-thing. Have another look. You may find them stimulating. We don't learn just from pleasant things. Have a think about the way he draws.'

Joe opened a door for me, a small crack that let in just a smidgeon of light. A week later it was extinguished, because Joe died suddenly.

I continued to waitress at the Chew It and Spew It, but now the regulars called me Judith and occasionally enquired about my health. It was as if they expected the soup-throwing incident to have permanently scarred me and they drew me comfortingly into their own circle of victimisation. They were warm in a rough way. I responded with a smile or a laugh and their company made my work easier and more pleasant. But Nathan, the reader, didn't come for his bun and tea any more.

In the occasional spare moment when I wasn't serving or cleaning I sat down with my sketchpad and, remembering Joe's encouragement, drew from memory the faces I had seen that day.

I had wanted to attend Joe's funeral but both my parents were against it. 'Only men will be there,' they said. 'It's no place for a girl.'

A month after Joe's death Winnie and Harry came to afternoon tea. My mother was delighted that Winnie and I were friends. Winnie's pretty ways comforted her with a dream that I might learn to be more feminine. In her realistic moments she doubted this possibility, even blaming herself for this not happening. I jokingly teased her, 'What sort of imbecile would you want me to be? A weepy?' I grinned and put my arm about her and she laughed with me.

As Winnie teetered up the gangplank my father looked askance. She looked gorgeous in a tangerine dress and a wide-brimmed cream hat. Harry offered his hand to help her balance and she giggled, first at him and then appraisingly at my father. He was still a handsome Nordic man with eyes the sapphire blue of ice caves and as she fluttered her absurdly long eyelashes at him his skin flushed a dark mahogany.

Later he subjected us to his outrage. 'She tried to flirt with me, at my age. Her no older than Judith. The little minx. I don't know what young people are coming to these days. Absolutely no respect.'

His strictures amused my mother. 'You want her to regard you as an old man, Niels?'

'No, no, of course not.' And again he blushed like a boy. 'Just some respect,' he mumbled, discomforted by her amusement.

But she was having fun. 'I'm sure next time she'll find lots of respect for you, Niels, when she notices all those grey hairs.' She put out her hand and ruffled searchingly in his mane of blond hair. 'Here's one,' she laughed, plucking it out.

He shrugged her off. 'I haven't any grey hairs. My hair's always been blond. It's the sun here. It bleaches everything. I get tired of the endless bloody sun. I could do with a northern winter and the cleanness of cold snow.'

'The coldness of cold snow you mean,' she sighed. 'People go crazy in places where the sun shines feebly for only half a year. What are you talking about? – all that nostalgia nonsense.' Then she sighed again as she always did when my father dug up memories of his youth.

However, when Winnie had stepped on to the deck he had been full of gallantry and courtesy like a king receiving some foreign empress to his court, I thought, with a mixture of jealousy and resentment.

'Just in case,' he said, 'you stumble over a rope. Ships are unpredictable places, but then they are adventurers on the high seas and they ride the wild winds.'

She opened her eyes wide at this burst of poetic language that amazed me.

She thanked him sweetly and clung to the support of his arm a fraction too long. My mother appeared, broke the spell, and took charge.

He was less gallant and more wary with Harry. I could see he was struggling to categorise him. Harry did not look the typical foundry worker. His body carried little heavy muscle, yet he was not puny. An athlete, I thought. Harry is a runner, he has the lithe fluid movements of a greyhound or a dancer. Brawn wouldn't get Harry out of trouble but speed and flexibility might.

Harry held out his hand to my father with a frank engaging smile. 'How do you do, sir?'

My mother slipped her hand over her mouth to hide a smile and my father, startled, had a moment of suspicion, but Harry's openness convinced him that no mockery was intended. Relieved, he shook Harry's hand, and soon they were deep in conversation about the foundry.

Mostly occupied by Winnie's chatter, but deeply curious, I garnered only slivers of their conversation. My father mentioned the machines and Harry nodded. In fact, he nodded a lot, as my father did most of the talking.

'Poorly paid … no compensation.' Harry looked sober.

'Came to the foundry begging for help?'

They were speaking about the mother of the boy who had been killed. Harry's voice was quiet: 'Four other children.'

'Bloody disgrace.' My father's voice was loud and strident, as it always was when he was angry. 'Bosses for you. Did she get anything?'

Harry shook his head. 'The boss reminded her she was only entitled to the award.'

My father snarled. 'The award. A starvation award. You watch yourself in that place, Harry.' He placed a protective hand on Harry's shoulder. 'You watch yourself, my boy.'

In the space of a few moments Harry had wheedled himself into my father's affection. Yet I had seen other instances of my father's kindness to young workers.

'We took up a collection for her,' Harry said, 'me and the other boys. It's too late to bury him but it might help.'

My father snorted: 'And those Holier-Than-Thous doubtless prayed over him and swindled his mother that there would be joy for him in the After Life. Religion,' he snorted again and spat into the sea, as if relieving himself of a nasty taste. 'A big lie to stop the working man from complaining.

'Complaining!' he was caustic. 'That's their word for what we want. We don't complain, we fight the bastards. Has anyone told you about the waterside strike in Perth in 1919? A wake-up call to us all. The ship-owners tried to bring in scab labour to work the *Dimboola*. The lumpers showed them. They threw the scabs into the Swan River. Mounted police charged the protesting women with bayonets. Let them try their tricks here. Our river is as good as the Swan. We'll show them.'

My mother interrupted them to call them to afternoon tea but my father continued to dominate the conversation until she put a hand on his arm. 'Give the boy a break, Niels. I'm sure he'll come again and there'll be time to tell him more of your stories.'

'Yes, yes, of course. I didn't mean to bore you, Harry. But you youngsters need to know what is what. Get the right ideas now and you won't go wrong in the future.' He laughed a little self-consciously and in a rare moment I saw him not as a virile young man enduring the hardships of Iceland and windjammers but as a man approaching middle age. He had married late and was now in his late forties. Physical work had taken its toll and his arms had begun to develop an aged skinniness.The backs of his hands, once fair-skinned, had sunspots. He wanted to impress and I was grateful to Harry for his patience.

Harry assured him that he wouldn't go wrong in the future. Then, turning to me, said, 'By the way, Judith, your friend Nathan often comes around at the foundry.'

'He's not my friend, Harry.'

Winnie poked me in the ribs, rolled her eyes at my mother, and shook her head, denying my denial.

'Stop it, Winnie,' I said, 'my mother will think …'

'And what should I think?' My mother was quick.

'Resigned,' I said. 'I met him at the Chew It and Spew It. I told you about the soup incident.'

'Oh, that.' She dismissed any suspicion she might have had and I threw a warning look at Winnie, who grinned naughtily at me and said, 'Her hero, Mrs Larsen.'

I was growing tired of Winnie aligning herself with others to embarrass me but I was curious and asked Harry, 'Why does Nathan come around the foundry?'

'He talks to us when he can and gives us leaflets on workers' rights and about the Free Speech meetings. The boss always shouts that he'll have him for trespass but can't because he joins us when we have a smoke-o and that's usually off the premises.'

My father looked thoughtful. 'This Nathan's a smallish chap with a quiet manner and spectacles? A communist, I think. They're not a bad lot. Just too fixed in their ideas.'

'And that coming from you, Niels?' My mother laughed.

'Well,' he said, caught off-guard, 'well, there are lots of groups in the labour movement.'

'All with fixed ideas.' She was caustic. 'All disagreeing with each other.'

She got up and cleared the table. 'Now, for heaven's sake, let's have a rest from politics.

'We have a piano, Harry. Perhaps you'd like to give us a tune.'

We had been sitting in the galley but now my mother led the way into a larger cabin converted to a sort of sitting room. Harry approached the piano as if it were some religious icon. His face glowed. He ran his fingers lightly and lovingly over the woodwork. 'May I?' he asked, but before anyone could reply he lifted the lid and struck a few notes. 'It's well tuned,' he said, and, comfortably confident, pulled out the piano stool and sat down.

My mother hovered beside him. 'Do you need some music?'

'Can't read it,' he laughed. 'Never learned. But here is,' and he launched into 'If you knew Susie like I know Susie, Oh, oh, oh what a girl'.

Winnie had said that he had rhythm in his bones and she was right. In the zest and joy of his playing I felt the real Harry was revealed and wondered if he was the same man who had listened so earnestly to my father. Now he was playing 'When my Sugar walks down the street' and this morphed into 'Nothing could be finer than to be in Carolina'. Finally he finished with a soulful rendition of 'We'll build a dear little, cute little love nest'.

'Oh, Harry, that was beautiful,' my mother breathed. 'You and the piano talk to each other.'

'Yes,' my father grunted, 'very nice, most enjoyable.'

But now Harry had eyes only for my mother and they smiled at each other like two pieces of chocolate that melt together. My father was forgotten. I pitied him. With Harry my father's strident tones had quietened. He had been gentle, almost tender. I had watched this transformation puzzled and a little suspicious. Even at seventeen I sensed an emotional simplicity about my father that left him vulnerable to the more sophisticated.

Harry was a natural sophisticate. A charmer. Maybe a manipulator. Did he genuinely respect my father or was it only a game, played by someone who thrived on being liked?

Work continued at the Chew It and Spew It from eight in the morning until six at night. When I wasn't waitressing I cut up vegetables, washed dishes, mopped floors, washed cleaning cloths and tea towels. I complained to my father that I hadn't been hired for this extra work and ought to be paid for it.

He said, 'Thank your lucky stars you've got a job. A bit of extra work won't hurt you. It's only a bit of domestic labour.'

My mother stiffened and looked daggers at him. 'Only domestic labour,' she said in her tone that meant 'don't say anything more'. He mumbled.

When he had gone she said to me quietly, 'You don't want to lose your job, Judith. You'll just have to grin and bear it. Maybe,' she added as a sop to my anger, 'we could find some way to help you get training at night school, perhaps in shorthand and typing at the Adelaide School of Mines. Office work is nice for a girl. We wouldn't want you to end up in a factory, working on a conveyor belt.'

Harry fell into the habit of visiting us on Sunday afternoons. At first he had come with Winnie but then he began to drop in on his own to chat with my father, charm my mother and beg an invitation to play our piano. He confided to me childhood memories of Winnie and often mentioned Nathan, who still lectured the foundry workers. I got the impression that Winnie had convinced him Nathan and I were friends and that my denials were some sort of maidenly reticence.

I was irritated and disabused him sharply. He looked so hurt that I hastily reassured him that, although I didn't care for Nathan personally, I was interested in his ideas. This pleased Harry and he began to talk enthusiastically about communism. Occasionally I caught my mother glance from his eager face to mine and she would smile indulgently as if she had some secret knowledge.

Some weeks later Harry came on board for his usual Sunday afternoon tea,. He was still full of his usual enthusiasm and mad keen for me to accompany him to a Communist Party meeting.

'I don't know, Harry,' my mother demurred.

Challenged by her doubtfulness over a political matter, my father instantly asserted that I should go, that it would be educational for me.

My mother continued to object. It wasn't that she was directly influenced by the anti-Bolshevik sentiment around us but indirectly it made her suspicious and careful. Besides, she hated being pushed by my father.

Harry wheedled, 'I'll look after her, Mrs L. You know that with me she's in the greatest care. I'll be like a father to her.'

This preposterous statement and Harry's mock solemnity made her laugh and once she laughed at Harry she was defeated. My father, aware that Harry's persuasive tricks were better than his, kept quiet.

The meeting hall we entered was cold and characterless. It was a space and nothing more. It had been a mild day but the evening closed in with a sharp wind off the sea and the dank smell of impending rain. Our footsteps on the bare wooden floor echoed eerily and chairs pulled back screeched a protest. We were the first there and found ourselves tiptoeing to seats in the middle of the room. 'Let's go up front,' Harry said, but I shook my head. I could see Nathan seated at a table at the front of the hall and after the incident in the gardens I had determined to keep my distance. He shuffled through a heap of papers, diligently taking notes, only occasionally looking up to comment to a man who leaned over his shoulder. The other man was Jock from Glasgow. There was no mistaking his squat pugilistic stance. There was no sign of Bernie-Benito.

'How many come?' I whispered to Harry. It seemed irreverent to speak out loud.

'I don't know. This is the first time I've been. Nathan invited me. He asked me to bring you along. He said he knew you, that you'd met at The Chew It and Spew It.'

'Yes,' I said, non-committal.

'Then you do know him?'

'Sort of.'

I wouldn't be dragged into any relationship with Nathan. He was more unpredictable than Harry, and that was saying a lot.

'He admires you. He says you're a true proletarian.' Harry was not to be put off. 'Come on, Jude, tell me what's between you two.'

'Mind your own business, Harry. There's nothing between us.' I was annoyed.

'Wow,' he said, putting up his hands in mock self-protection. 'Sorry. Didn't know you felt like that. Tell Uncle Harry all about it.'

'Shut up, Harry. Don't try to wheedle me as you do my mother. I'm up to your tricks.'

He put a careless arm about me and gave me a squeeze. 'OK, Miss Larsen, I'll be good.'

More people had drifted in, about three dozen in all. They looked ordinary, cleanly but poorly dressed, tired and subdued. Winnie would have called them earnest but I felt they were there to fulfil a duty. Bernie-Benito was amongst them. With his loose frame and ungainly gait he looked like a benign rag doll. He drooped into a chair in the front row and, like one who speaks English as a foreign language and feels the need to shout, yelled, 'Good evening, comrades.'

Jock replied cheerfully, 'Shut up, you little fascist bastard. Can't you see we're working?'

Bernie-Benito doffed his cap, grinned and lolled back in his chair, rocking it precariously on two back legs. '*Avanti popolo*,' he hummed under his breath.

I felt that Bernie-Benito would carry a knife and smile charmingly while he used it.

There were no women present, except myself, so when two other women entered I took particular notice of them. Harry with over-done gallantry jumped up to welcome them. His greeting interrupted their conversation and their glance of dismissal was a hurtful rebuff. He returned flushed and embarrassed. 'I suppose it's our first night here and I shouldn't have intruded.' I looked at him with pity and he blushed again.

'You should recognise when people are downright rude to you,

Harry.' I was going to add, not everyone will like you, and thought better of it. After all, I knew what it was to be mortified.

I studied the two women. They were dressed in sombre clothes: black skirts and coats, with matching cloche hats. One wore a fake fur tippet about her neck. Thin sandy hair escaped in wisps from under their hats and their complexions were colourless, unaided by rouge or lipstick. They looked like a pair of unpleasantly self-sacrificing acolytes.

'I'd say, Harry, they lacked moderation and probably lead a thoroughly unhappy life. I hope all the comrades are not like that.'

Harry did not appreciate my reference to Aristotle and now, recovered from his moment of embarrassment, was looking about him with bright expectant eyes. My eyes followed the two women as they walked to the table. Nathan jumped up and kissed each on the cheek.

'They must be family,' I commented to Harry. 'Is he married?'

'No. Sisters, I think. He said they were coming to support him.'

I giggled. 'Revolution's a family affair, then?'

'Shush, Judith.'

'Shush yourself, Harry.' He grinned at me. 'Stuck up bitches,' I said.

He sucked his breath on a laugh and squeezed my hand.

We had expected to be part of the evening but now felt like aliens. Harry was clearly disappointed. I supposed Nathan's interest in him made him believe he was special and would be included. I was peeved because, although I did not want to be claimed by Nathan, neither did I want to be ignored. So, naturally, I was prepared to be antagonistic to whatever followed.

I can't say I was pleasantly surprised by Nathan's speech but I found myself becoming interested in what he had to say. After his botched address at the gardens I had expected the worst but here there was no need for him to be an inspirational orator.

He began quietly and with conviction. Much of what he said

confused me. My knowledge of history and political theory was limited. I felt I had acquired some education in untidy snatches. I was rather like a cloth on which a number of patches of different colours and shapes had been sewn to fill in holes. But no patch matched or related to another. There was no overall design. I recognised that Nathan had a pattern of thinking; a set of ideas that fitted together and this was orderly and pleasing.

He began with references to the Russian Revolution, which happened when I was eight, and although interesting they were beyond my comprehension. I vaguely recalled excited conversations in our galley but at that time I was more interested in the swimmer searching for a crust of soggy bread. I didn't know that Russian soldiers on the battlefront had deserted, nor that Russian peasants burned manor houses and took over the great landed estates. The only farmers I knew were the people who lived at fly-blown Piggery Park and tried to make a living rearing and selling pigs. My mother and I had gone there once to take some clothes for the children of a chronically ill man. The mother, an exhausted, harassed woman, had offered us tea, scooping a handful of flies off the milk before she poured it into our cups. My mother had said hastily that she only drank black tea and I only drank water.

Nathan said that the Russian Revolution had made capitalist society afraid of Bolshevism. He spoke of Kerensky, Lenin, Mensheviks, Petrograd and Trotsky. I didn't know who they were. He asserted that Russian bosses would have preferred the German invasion to a workers' revolution in Russia and that speculators had been allowed to commandeer food so that workers were starved into submission. The Russian Revolution was the end of capitalism that for too long had rolled like a juggernaut over working people destroying them, their wives and their children. History was the history of class war. The economic structure of society determined all else. Until people controlled the means of production they would never be free. The working class and the employing class had nothing in common.

That's right, I thought resentfully. I've got nothing in common with my boss. When he owes me money for overtime he wriggles out of paying it and although I'm employed as a waitress I'm also a skivvy. But, on the other hand, I reflected, the rest of the working class doesn't help me, nor does my unionist father.

My thoughts returned to Nathan. He peered at his notes, holding them close to his face. I remembered the moment he looked at me in the Chew It cafe, his eyes magnified and swimming myopically behind those dreadful glasses. Perhaps that was why he never looked at his audience. He couldn't see us. Poor Nathan.

He found his place. World revolution was coming, he said. It was inevitable. The capitalists' war, created through their greed for colonies to enslave poor workers in poor countries, had sown the seeds of their own destruction. It had torn apart the fabric of society and allowed people to see for themselves the evils of capitalism. There had been people's revolts in other countries besides Russia. In Germany itself the Communist Party was growing and no wonder. The Treaty of Versailles had subjected the German worker to penury and starvation.

He spoke for over an hour. Occasionally he reached for one of the reference books heaped on the table and searched laboriously for a quotation. He was learned. But, heavens! How tediously ponderous. Most of his audience had worked a long day and I heard an occasional snore broken by a hiccup as the sleeper jerked awake. His sisters seemed oblivious of the time and the hard seats. They sat upright and nodded frequently. But as the evening drew on his speech seemed interminable. My concentration started to fail me and his words merged into a haze. I shifted restlessly. Harry, always more impatient than I was, crossed and uncrossed his legs, clasped and unclasped his hands, rubbed his thighs, played a tune on his knee with his fingers, hummed a little under his breath, and tapped in time with his toe. I poked him and he stopped. He was bored and finally so was I. Clearly Nathan didn't know when to stop.

My thoughts wandered to Joe. I had once asked him if he believed in revolution. I had picked up a few points from Marx's *Capital*. He had looked startled. 'Do I believe in revolution, Nearly-Twelve? Wherever do you get these huge questions from?'

'Books, Joe.'

'Of course, where else do we get our ideas from? How silly of me to ask. Do I believe in revolution? I don't really know. Change, certainly. But revolution? I'm too old for violence, Nearly-Twelve. After the war there doesn't seem to be much point in it and then there's history. I suppose at my age I take the long view. Instant results are a dream.'

'So you don't believe in revolution, Joe? And you think Marx ought to have taken the long view?'

'I didn't say that, Nearly-Twelve. Marx had some very sound ideas, better than a lot around now, but it's best to pick and choose from what someone says or writes, not swallow it whole. I wish I knew. It's hard to accept in old age how little one really knows and just as I think I may have got a grip on things something unexpected comes along. There's a new book out, Nearly-Twelve. *Mein Kampf*. It's in German so I can't read it but some have and apparently it's a thoroughly nasty book, written by a thoroughly nasty bloke – Adolf Hitler I think his name is. The world will be in a pretty pickle if he gets power.'

He coughed. 'I'm reminded of Matthew Arnold's poem that we're on a darkling plain with ignorant armies that clash by night. Sometimes writers are prophetic. It would be bad to come out of one goddamn awful war and be dragged into the next because Europeans can't get along with each other. Them and their goddamn rivalries. Most of us came here to escape their mistakes and just brought them with us, leaving us still on a darkling plain and with plenty of ignorant armies.'

Joe always talked to me as if I was another adult and although my comprehension was limited I still felt my mind stretch and reach out to his ideas. They were wider, more expansive than my father's and far less limited than my practical mother's.

Finally Nathan's speech was over. The audience gave three relieved cheers and Jock from Glasgow took over. By contrast he was belligerent and fiery. He wasn't interested in history. As he spoke the audience, aware of his passion, came alive. It was a clarion call. Those who had lolled in their chairs listening to Nathan straightened up. There was an atmosphere of preparation and readiness. Jock raised his fist and shook it. 'Comrades,' his Scottish burr lengthened the word so that it rolled off his tongue and rumbled around the hall, 'comrades, the workers of Australia are under siege and we must ready ourselves to fight. To fight, comrades.' He punched the air. Voices from the audience cried, 'Yes, hear, hear.'

This is what they've waited for, I thought, not Nathan but a man to lead them.

'Direct action to fight the capitalist bosses is what we need, comrades, direct action to defeat the Crimes Act, direct action to fight for the right to free speech. We will fight the tyrannies of the master class, and you, comrades, will be in the vanguard of the action.'

While the loud chorus of 'hear, hear' strengthened I saw Bernie-Benito flick his fingers across his throat in a gesture of slitting it. I hoped it was merely bravado. Now Jock lowered his voice, as if in reverence, and his audience leaned forward, silent, listening.

'The twelve IWWs, the twelve Industrial Workers of the World, your persecuted brothers, comrades, railroaded into jail on lies and corruption. They have a right to speak. They should be heard, not silenced by that viper, Prime Minister Bruce. Donald Grant, my fellow Scotsman, knows what poverty is. You, comrades, know what poverty is. Donald Grant, because he's an IWW is prevented from telling you, the working man, what comes to the poor in any capitalist country. In the British Isles, he says, "If Christ came back to earth he would weep to see how women and children lived." I've been there, comrades, and know it's true. Lived? Comrades, lived isn't the word. Barely existed would be closer. Barely existed. Shall we, too, barely exist? Our babes starve while the likes of Bruce drag down our wages and prevent us from trumpeting our protests?'

He paused. 'Bloody Bruce!' someone in the audience snarled. Around him sounded rumbles of agreement.

'That's right, comrades,' Jock applauded. 'The Crimes Bill strikes at the heart of democracy and strikes at your right to shout out against injustice. Oppose it, comrades. They tell us it is against atheistic communism but, comrades, it's against anyone who protests, anyone who believes they have some rights to the sort of life the bosses lead. They'll fine us and jail us, comrades, that's their Christianity. Now is the time to rise up and throw off your oppression.' He raised both hands in the air and shook them as if casting off the weight of shackles.

The audience cheered and leaped to their feet. He sat down, smiling grimly. The audience, a little deflated after their surge of defiance, also shuffled back into their seats. It had been truly rousing stuff but I had years of defences built up against my father's haranguing and instead of being swept away by the public emotion I felt oddly aloof. Nathan called the meeting to order and asked for those who volunteered to help organise Free Speech rallies to meet him afterwards.

To end the meeting we all rose and the sisters led everyone in singing a song I had heard before at the Working Men's Club. It began with *Arise ye workers from your slumbers, arise ye prisoners of want*, and a chorus: *Then comrades come rally and the last fight let us face, the Internationale unites the human race*. Beside me Harry grimaced and fidgeted. 'They're singing flat,' he whispered in my ear. 'They need somebody to set the note.' He endured it to the end, sighing heavily.

Nathan had seen me and clearly intended to speak to me before we left but I was swift in dragging Harry to the door. A quick look back and I saw Nathan surrounded by admirers. Harry had forgotten his boredom at Nathan's speech. 'Isn't he marvellous?' he said. 'They call him "The Professor". He knows everything about history. He's a back-room boy.'

'What on earth does that mean, Harry?'

'He educates people but doesn't do any of the action stuff like Jock.'

'That must be comfortable.' I was cynical. 'Maybe he's no good at the action stuff.' And I remembered his botched speech in the gardens. Jock was certainly superior as a crowd rouser.

But Harry wasn't listening to me. With dreamy eyes he recalled that Nathan had told him that in the Soviet Union he could be a musician or a dancer and the state would pay for him to have tap-dancing lessons and support him while he was learning. 'Nathan,' he said, 'maintains that in the Soviet Union society is run from each according to his ability, to each according to their needs. Isn't that a grand idea, Judith?'

Caught up by his enthusiasm, I said, 'I could be paid to draw and not have to work at the Chew It and Spew It.'

He was a little hesitant at that. 'To draw? I don't know about that.'

'Yes, Harry, to draw.'

'Well, if that's your ability, I suppose it would be all right.'

Remembering Joe's advice to me, I retorted, 'Yes, that's my ability. You haven't seen any of my drawings and they're not there for some pie-in-the-sky state to make judgement.'

He was contrite. 'I didn't mean that, Judith. Truly I didn't mean that.'

'No,' I was surly, not quite forgiving. 'I haven't shown them to many people, only Joe at the Club.' I wanted to say that Joe had remarked they were very good but I was suddenly shy. 'Dear Joe,' I said sadly. 'He was my friend for many years. Will you come to the cemetery with me, Harry? I'd like to put flowers on his grave.'

He looked solemn, nodded and took my arm.

We were alone in the cemetery. Warm spring days had brought out the wild freesias. Their sweet scent followed us as we searched for Joe's grave and eventually found it. There was no headstone, only a small wooden cross, painted white, with 'RIP Joe Pulham' in black. I laid a small bunch of flowers on the raised earth of the grave.

'Didn't he have any family?' I asked Harry.

'I don't know, Judith. I never knew him. Was he English by birth?'

'I don't know.' Suddenly it seemed a fault in me that I had never known anything about Joe's private life. 'He was a compositor on the *Argus* and later worked on some socialist paper, I think. He was leaded, Harry.'

'Poor bloke. Lead's a terrible poison.'

'Yes, he told me that industry is a grand killer. Whenever I read the newspaper I think of him. I don't know why it is that when we benefit from something new in society it always seems to have been bought with someone else's sufferings. Look at your job now, Harry.'

He was subdued. 'You know, Judith, I'd like to learn to tap dance.' He laughed self-consciously. 'I don't suppose there's any money in that, unless, of course, I become some great Hollywood movie star.'

He did a few dance steps on the path. I felt sad but laughed with him. Joe would not have minded his dancing.

Some weeks later a parcel arrived for me, and a letter bearing the name of a legal firm. Inside the parcel were three books: an anthology of poems and two novels by Charles Dickens –*Great Expectations* and *The Old Curiosity Shop*. They were inscribed 'To my dear friend Nearly-Twelve with whom I had wonderful discussions about books and life. May your future be bright and your talents recognised. Best regards, Joe Pulham'. In the envelope was a brief letter from the lawyer saying Joe had left the contents of his flat to be sold and the proceeds given to me. They were forwarding the money and would I please send a return letter of acknowledgement.

Shocked and overwhelmed with sadness for a lonely man who had only me to whom to leave his meagre bequest, I sat down, clutched the books against my body as if they had some human warmth and wept. Memories of Joe merged with my visit to the cemetery and the lonely white cross and for some reason I also recalled Harry, his hair bright in the sunlight, his body young and flexible, dancing on the path, and what had made me laugh briefly now made me weep bitterly for futile dreams.

My mother found me sobbing and put her arms about me. I showed her the cheque. 'You and father should have it,' I hiccuped. 'You never have much.'

'Rubbish,' she said briskly. 'It's yours. You keep it for the future. Maybe that night class at the School of Mines or perhaps some proper drawing paper and good pencils.' I was surprised. 'I thought about your drawings,' she said, 'afterwards. You should do more of them. Maybe it's your talent.'

I hugged her.

That summer was a scorcher. We took our mattresses onto the deck and slept under canvas awnings set up by my father. When we were docked he pulled up the gangplank; when we were anchored in the Outer Harbor he considered us safe. Winnie now visited with Harry on most Sundays. We drooped in deck chairs, hoping for a cool breeze off the sea. Towards evening it usually came but there was never much strength in it.

Harry looked longingly at the water. 'A dip would be nice.'

'There's been a shark seen in the area,' my father warned.

Winnie squealed. 'A shark! Good heavens! Are we safe?'

Harry was impatient. 'Don't be an idiot, Winnie.'

She pouted. 'Oh, you, Harry.'

Winnie's life was so comfortable that she needed to assert her sensitivities. I thought, if Winnie ever has a personal problem she'll make it her life's work.

Curiously the mention of the shark pricked Harry's interest. He got up, wandered over to the railings, and looked into the water. 'What are all those bottles doing floating about?'

'Empty beer bottles,' my father said. 'They're a damn nuisance.'

My mother was half asleep. 'Anyone who collects them will make a bit of pocket money.'

'Ah,' Harry said, and I recognised the birth of one of his adventurous ideas.

'No, Harry,' I said automatically.

He grinned at me. Winnie looked from one to the other of us. 'What does she mean, no, Harry? What have you got in mind now?'

'We could take the little boat out and collect them.' He was eager. 'I could do with a little extra cash. My dancing pumps have holes in them.'

'Our banana boat,' I laughed.

'Why do you call it that?' Winnie asked.

'We don't really know,' my mother said sleepily.

'Yes, we do,' my father asserted. 'I've been to the West Indies and it reminds me of the boats that carry bananas there.'

'Well,' Harry said, 'now it could carry empty beer bottles.'

'Dead marines,' I corrected.

'Dead marines?' He was puzzled.

'Yes,' I grinned, 'our banana boat and dead marines and I'll bet my father doesn't know why they're called that.'

He grunted.

'What about it, Mr Larsen?' Harry pleaded.

'No, Harry,' my mother said, 'don't be tiresome. You can't manage to row and collect bottles on your own.'

'Judith could come with me, or Winnie.' He threw her a wicked look.

On cue she squealed again. 'No, Harry, there's a shark out there.'

'Oh, for heaven's sake,' now I was impatient, 'a shark won't hurt us in a boat. Besides, it's days since it was seen and it's probably gone out to sea.'

'You're very tiresome, Judith, and you, too, Harry,' my mother repeated. 'Both of you always so restless.'

'Oh, let them try it,' my father said. 'Judith is often in the boat anyway and it will fill in their afternoon.'

I changed into more suitable clothes, leaving Winnie bleating that we were leaving her out and it would serve us right if a shark ate us. Harry said, 'Shut up, Winnie.' We scrambled down the Jacob's ladder and untied the small rowing boat.

'Let me row,' I advised. 'I've been doing it for years.'

'No, Harry asserted. 'I'm just as good at it.' I sighed. He was always so over-confident. He rowed towards a flotilla of bobbing bottles. 'You lean over, Judith, and collect them while I ship the oars and keep things steady.'

I leaned out as far as I could but the bottles remained out of my reach. 'You'll have to row a little closer, Harry.' He tried but the bottles kept bobbing away from our pursuit.

'The rowing creates a wash that pushes them away,' I complained.

'No it doesn't. You just don't reach out far enough.'

'Any further and I'll fall in.'

'Girls,' he snorted, 'always making excuses.'

I rounded on him. 'Girls! Don't lump me together with girls, as if we are all incompetent idiots. You just row the boat so I'm close enough to reach the bloody bottles. It was you, remember, who wanted to collect them, not me.'

'OK,' he said, 'sorry, I forgot you're so touchy.'

'Touchy?' I muttered. 'Touchy?' And in exasperation I half rose so that I might lean further over the side and reach the bottles.

'Careful!' he called as the boat rocked viciously.

It happened in an instant. One minute I clutched a bottle in my hand, the next I catapulted into the sea. My first thought was that it was delightfully cold. My next thought was the shark. Panic seized me.

'Harry!' I screeched. 'The shark!'

He leaped to his feet. 'Where, oh my God, Judith, where?' He flung himself on his knees and reached out to clutch my hand. The boat rocked perilously. He tried to drag me over the side. The boat tipped.

'Where's the shark?' he panted. 'Did you see it? Oh, my God, it's all my fault. Hang on, Judith.' He was frantic in his terror.

I clung to the gunwale of the boat, trying to help him lift me in. The boat leaned sideways. 'You'll have to put your weight on the other side,' I said, 'and I'll try myself. I can't swim back to the hulk, Harry. I'm too afraid,' I moaned.

He scanned the sea for a telltale fin. 'Where did you see it, Judith?'

'No,' I said, a bit calmer, but treading water gingerly, 'I just thought about it, that it might be around.'

He stopped trying to help me. 'You just *thought* about it? It wasn't actually here?'

'No.' I looked shamefaced.

He roared with laughter. 'Oh, Judith,' he said, 'you're an absolute card.'

Balancing the boat as best he could he helped me scramble over the gunwale. I felt his arms warm about me and smelled the sweet sweat on his neck. As my face touched his cheek I trembled and it wasn't because the water had been cold. I sat down, shivering a little and we laughed at each other.

Before the summer reduced us to melting exhaustion there had been a huge free speech rally at The Stump. Charles Reeve and Donald Grant, two of the Industrial Workers of the World previously jailed under the War Precautions Act for opposing the war, addressed a crowd of some six thousand people.

I recalled being moved by Grant's comment that if Christ came back to earth he would weep for the abysmal poverty of working people and it prompted me to draw Joe Pulham's grave. On a gravestone I inscribed 'RIP JOE PULHAM, KILLED BY INDUSTRY, OCTOBER 1926' and above the gravestone I sketched a weeping angel offering a laurel wreath.

It was my first attempt at drawing a cartoon. Previously I had sketched in a haphazard manner anything that took my interest. But for some months now I had found myself searching out and studying the cartoons in newspapers. Their power to convey an insight in a few sharp lines fascinated me and I knew that, if I could create work like this, it might give purpose and meaning to my drawing. So, feeling brave but presumptuous, I sent my cartoon to the *Sun News Pictorial*. They regularly published cartoons. Maybe they would take it.

Despite the Board of Governors of the Botanic Gardens swearing that no IWW would ever speak there, the demonstration had gone ahead. Harry had been jubilant. 'It was a triumph,' he said. He had heard all about it when he had gone to see Nathan and Jock about volunteering to help with propaganda for the Free Speech campaign.

Nathan and Jock were elated by the size of the crowd. Even though Donald Grant had called the communists 'tin-pot Lenins of the Comical Party', Nathan was forbearing. After all, they had staged an enormously successful event. 'However,' Harry chuckled, 'Jock was livid. He fumed that "Donald Grant was a base double-crossing stab-in-the-back bastard". Hadn't he stuck his neck out to support a bloody IWW and now Grant rewarded him with treacherous comments behind his back. The IWWs were always determined to undermine the Communist Party. You couldn't trust any of them.'

Nathan, Harry told me, had responded quietly. 'Not quite behind your back, Jock. Six thousand people heard it. We must ignore these pettifogging differences and work together. We all have a common goal.'

'Do we?' Jock snarled.

Harry smirked. 'I don't think Jock liked being dismissed as pettifogging but he seldom argues with Nathan. Nathan was very forgiving, Judith. After all, it was quite a public slur. A bit mean.'

'Forgiving?' I snorted. 'Pious, you mean.'

My father had been both amused and exasperated by Harry's story. 'Fat chance we have of those two lots working together. You should see them in the union.'

The temperature continued to rise. Fires exploded in the Dandenong Ranges behind Melbourne. People fled for their lives. A call went out for all able-bodied men to volunteer for fire-fighting. Harry went.

A thick pall of smoke hung over Adelaide from fires in the Adelaide Hills. We breathed its grey heaviness; the sky a vermilion haze through which a fierce sun struggled. The smoky sunlight did strange things to the light and the day looked as if it were lit by an opalescent moon rather than a bright sun.

My father couldn't go fire-fighting. Trading ships couldn't

hang around the harbour for days waiting for fuel. In the midst of the heat wave we chugged to the Outer Harbor to fuel a coastal trader. Our hulk had an iron hull and this increased the heat on board.

Coaling was an exhausting job. A team of men worked with my father and were dependent for their lives on his skill at the winch. The coal lumpers brought their own tools – shovels, baskets, boots, ropes and their own physical strength. The gear on the collier – winch, rope and baskets – had to be rigged so the coal could be shifted from down below up to the deck before moving it into the ship that was being coaled. The baskets were attached to the rope that ran through a pulley and a winch on the deck above the hold. The shovellers worked in the hold filling the baskets with coal, but if the winchman brought the basket up too quickly the heavy load could fall on the men below.

Fear of killing the men in the hold made my father's life at the winch enormously stressful. At times he had to stand at the winch for up to forty hours and not make a mistake. My mother told me that often he woke in the night, sweating with terror from a nightmare in which he had killed a shoveller. As a child I simply accepted the gangs of men moving about our hulk but now, with Joe's death, I observed their terrible work. This, too, was a grand killer of men.

The Chew It and Spew It was so hot that one day I fainted and had to be driven home by a friend of my boss. My mother pursed her lips when she saw my white sweating face. 'That's enough,' she told my father. 'She's not going back.'

But through 1928 unemployment was worsening. He had a permanently worried look and constantly urged my mother to save what she could. She scrimped on everything.

I lay on the deck on a mattress with cool cloths over my head. He was distressed. 'I don't know what to do, Eve. On a union count we guess one in five of our men is out of work and this bloody government is talking of bringing in immigrant labour to undercut our wages.' He was grim. 'I'd like to see those immigrant scabs employed as coal lumpers. That'd be a joke. The government would need to import an army of giants to take on that job.'

It was the first cry of despair I had ever heard from my father and it wrung my heart.

Later I said to my mother, 'There is the hundred pounds from Joe.'

'No!' she was fierce. 'We're not going to take everything from you.'

I returned to the Chew It and Spew It.

Harry had agreed to help advertise the next street meeting by putting up posters around the area. This was part of a continuous campaign to defeat the ban on street meetings. Before an illegal meeting was held volunteers went out at night and secretly stuck up posters on walls, trees, lamp-posts, shop windows, giving the date and place of the next meeting. Sometimes posters were distributed during the day at shopping areas but there volunteers had to be fleet of foot to escape watching police.

The three of us, Winnie, Harry and I, were to say that we were going to the Saturday night pictures and afterwards I was to spend the night at Winnie's home. I felt guilty lying to my mother and uncomfortable seeing the easy charm with which Harry beguiled her. Sometimes Harry's duplicity bothered me.

In my mother's eyes nothing could be more innocent or more desirable. That I was included in Winnie's family life delighted her. She constantly worried about my isolation on the hulk and I realised she feared I might suffer the same loneliness that she experienced. It was not that she didn't go out or have women friends but because of the difficulties in visiting us she couldn't have that easy drop-in lifestyle.

When friends visited it was usually as a result of a formal

invitation. They expressed amazement at our different way of life and mother preened herself on their admiration for the strangeness of it all. She showed them over the hulk. But their visits were intermittent and rare and often relationships died for lack of proximity.

'It's out of sight out of mind,' my mother sometimes remarked bitterly, 'and it's always me who has to make the visits. They won't bother to come this far although it's only a tram ride from the Semaphore and a bit of a walk along the wharf.'

But I knew that it was also the problem of the times when we were docked. Finding us at home was unpredictable and friends grew tired of trying to visit when times convenient to them were not possible for us.

I also felt guilty at involving Winnie.

'She'll love it,' Harry was casual, 'and we need her. You have to stay somewhere and I need you.'

'But her parents won't love it.'

'Come on, Judith, put your outsize conscience in your pocket. You're always worrying about something.'

'Yes.' But I was doubtful.

Harry came for me with his usual assurance to my mother that I would be quite safe with him. We took the train from the Port into the city and then a tram to Winnie's suburb. From the tram stop we walked along the footpath. The houses here hid behind high walls, overshadowed by leafy trees. Winnie's home, built from the lovely Adelaide pink stone, was double fronted with a central door and windows on each side opening onto a wide veranda.

Inside, a passage ran centrally to a kitchen at the back. Bedrooms and living rooms opened off the passage. They were high ceilinged with decorative cornices and plaster rosettes circling central light hangings. The large lounge room had a glittering chandelier. Winnie's bedroom had two single beds and a long window, which overlooked the garden. My cabin would have fitted into a third of the room and even the beauty of my mother and father's cabin could never match the elegance of this house. This house said 'money'.

'Winnie,' I said, suddenly anxious, 'perhaps you shouldn't come with Harry and me tonight.'

Awed by my surroundings I had a terrified feeling that Harry and I held something exquisite and fragile in our hands and by a moment's carelessness we could smash it into small pieces. I don't know why at that moment I thought it a crime to endanger Winnie's beautiful lifestyle. Perhaps it was akin to the feeling I had had many years earlier when I dropped a delicately carved wooden box Ganesh had given me, breaking it into several pieces.

This house was luxurious beyond my wildest dreams, elegant and peaceful. I envied Winnie, but I wanted no part in destroying it. Winnie's eyes filled with the ubiquitous tears. 'You and Harry always leave me out of things these days. Harry used to be my special friend.

'Oh, Winnie,' I cried, 'I'm so sorry. It's not like that at all. Harry loves you. You're his favourite cousin. Of course you must come with us.' She brightened and dried her eyes.

Winnie's parents were away for the night and had happily agreed to allow her to stay home so long as I was there also. 'They think that you're a solid, hard-working, admirable girl,' Winnie said, rolling her eyes, 'and, of course, there is also our dog to take care of both of us.'

She patted a large lolloping good-hearted Labrador that would have loved to death any intruder but because he was a dog he was considered a protector. He did have a deep bark but it was more joyous and welcoming than threatening. 'It's hard to know with dogs,' she said wisely. 'Now if I were threatened, who knows?'

I regarded the grinning snuffling beast that had laid his head trustingly on my lap and could not imagine him attacking anyone, even to defend Winnie. But then even the gentlest can fight for the ones they love, I thought. Maybe, we're a lot like dogs.

'I would have liked a dog,' I said, 'but it was impossible on the hulk. We had a cat called Emerald because of her green eyes but she found her way into the hold and died under a fall of coal.'

I had never been allowed to cuddle Emerald. My mother feared her fleas. Some years earlier, before I was born, there had been a scare in the Port of an outbreak of bubonic plague from foreign ships. So we kept a cat to control the rats and then my mother worried that the cat might be a carrier. So I had grown up with an uncomfortable, sometimes embarrassing fear of animals.

Winnie said it was their cook's night off but she'd left some cold meat and salad for us, and some cake. We sat around the table which the cook had set for Winnie before she left. We munched in conspiratorial 'brotherhood' Harry said. I said 'sisterhood'. This seemed to delight the other two so much that they laughed uproariously.

Harry had brought three old paint tins with clag in them and three brushes. The tins had handles so were easy to carry. He also had a pocketful of gypsum pieces, which he had stolen from the gypsum works at the Port.

'What's that for?' Winnie and I asked together.

He grinned. 'For writing on the road.'

Winnie took a piece and turned it over in her hand. 'That would have been great for drawing hopscotch when we were kids. I never had enough chalk.'

Harry reclaimed his piece and pocketed it. 'I'll do the writing on the road.'

'And why is that?' she bridled. 'I've drawn on the pavement many times.'

'When you were a kid.'

'I haven't forgotten how. It's not difficult.'

'You take orders from me tonight, Winnie, or you don't come.'

She pouted. 'Oh, you, Harry.'

To fill in time after tea we played several games of Animal Grab. We were tense, nervous and excited and shrieked hysterically at our own antics. We waited until it was that time of night when, if people were going out, they would have left, and if staying at home they were settled in to listening to the radio, reading or entertaining friends.

I had brought a small case with me and changed into some serviceable and darker clothes.

'Should we black our faces?' Winnie was eagerly dramatic.

Harry guffawed. 'You are an idiot, Winnie.'

'Well?' she was defensive.

'Well,' he mimicked, 'if a cop catches us what will he make of a pretty little girl with a blackened face?' She blushed.

'It's quite a good idea, Winnie,' I said to mollify her, 'but Harry's right. We need to look normal.'

She was still put out and said regretfully, 'I suppose so.'

At about ten o'clock we collected our gear and set out. The streets were quiet and heavily shadowed. A sliver of moon threw only a pallid fitful light. We were apprehensive and jittery. We jumped when a possum coughed a throaty sepulchral sound and Winnie shrieked.

'Shut up, Winnie,' Harry hissed. 'But you don't have to go on tiptoe, you idiot.'

I took her arm. 'Let's try that lamp-post,' I whispered. 'It looks like it's got a nice smooth surface.'

'Let me try,' she whispered back, 'please.'

'OK.' I stood beside her as if more experienced, which, of course, I wasn't. Harry, a little further along the street, was slapping posters on a house wall.

Winnie selected a poster and held it by the corner in one hand. With her other hand she tried to slap clag on its back. It puckered and crinkled and flapped against her arm. She put the brush back in the can and took out a cloth she had brought to clean her fingers but the poster had now stuck to them.

'Bother,' she said. Then, 'Oh, dear.' She giggled. 'I've made a hash of it, Judith. What do I do now?' She started to peel the poster away from her fingers and the now gluggy paper tore in half. In exasperation she crumpled it into a ball. 'Damn,' she said. 'What a mess.'

Benefitting from watching her disaster, I said, 'Let's do it this way. We'll put the poster face down on the lamp-post, slop on the glue, peel it off and replace it right way up.'

'Is that what Harry's doing?' She peered along the darkened street.

'Probably.' I held another poster for her against the lamp-post and she happily slapped on the clag. We peeled it off and re-stuck it right way up. It worked.

'Hurrah!' Winnie was triumphant. 'You are clever, Judith.' She surveyed our work. 'It's not quite straight,' she said and tried to swivel it around so that it sat squarely, but it had stuck. She compromised by using her cloth to carefully wipe the edges clean of any clag.

While we had messed about Harry had stuck up several more posters. He returned to find us. 'What on earth are you girls doing? We have dozens of these things and not much time.'

Winnie wiped her poster once more and with her fingers carefully firmed its edges against the lamp-post. 'If a job's worth doing, Harry,' she said sententiously, 'it's worth doing well.'

'For goodness sake, Winnie, it doesn't need to look pretty. Come on.'

The streets continued to be very quiet. Once or twice a passer-by looked at us oddly but in the main we met no one and never a policeman. I supposed that at this end of Adelaide police didn't think Saturday night patrolling necessary. Everyone would be too well behaved. At the Port drunks would be rolling out of the various pubs and there would be fights and police to arrest them.

Before the movies were due to finish and people poured out of the picture houses we scuttled back to Winnie's. Harry went home. We did our best to wash the clag off our hands, faces and hair. Eventually we got into bed.

'That was such fun, Judith,' Winnie giggled. 'Can we do it again?'

'Perhaps.' I was sleepy.

'Judith?'

'Yes.'

'Do you love, Harry?'

'Of course, everyone loves Harry.'

'Yes, I know that, but do you love him?'

I pretended to be asleep so I didn't need to answer her.

Harry had breezed through the incident with his usual easy confidence. Winnie was too innocent to recognise the danger. But I had been afraid and in a constant state of apprehension at breaking the law. After all, we had all been brought up to respect authority.

Naturally we had to follow up our evening's work of putting out the posters by attending the meeting. Harry had been to several and knew the ropes.

'They're actually pretty tame,' he said. 'The meeting is advertised, as we did. When the time comes the speaker, with a couple of helpers, brings along a box. Of course the police have also learned about the meeting and are hovering about. The speaker mounts his box and begins. After a few minutes the police move in and demand he stops. If he continues they seize his box, often tipping him off, then they arrest him. The crowd is ordered to disperse and any lingerers may also be arrested. And that's all there is to it: pretty flat really; a sort of continuing game between protesters and police. Nobody gets hurt, except, I suppose the speaker, who may get a bump on his backside. Most get dismissed from the police station with a warning. The police seem rather bored by it all.'

'Who are the usual speakers?' I asked. 'Nathan? Jock? Anyone else?'

'Yes, both of those and Frank and Izzie. Frank appeals to the Irish Catholics there. He recalls the anti-conscription days and Cardinal Mannix. And many in the crowd love it and applaud. You can hear their Irish voices reclaiming their heroic past and spruiking for another Mannix to take on the government. The Irish do a lot of living in the past and never seem to forget any injury done to them.

'Then there's Izzie. He's a Jewish chap and he's very very interesting, Judith. He speaks about a book *Mein Kampf* and the German threat.'

'Yes,' I said. 'Adolf Hitler.'

Harry was surprised. 'You've heard of him?'

'Yes. Joe Pulham. He said it's a nasty book written by a thoroughly nasty bloke and that if he ever gets any power the world will be in a proper pickle.'

Harry looked sober. 'Everyone in the Communist Party is talking about it and worrying. But you know, Judith,' all at once he was merrily confiding, 'sometimes I think the communists revel in thinking themselves victims. I guess it's just another book.'

The meeting was held at a corner of the crossroads near Victoria Square. Quite a crowd had gathered. Jock was billed to speak and Nathan stood unobtrusively behind him. I noticed that Bernie-Benito was in the front row. Wherever Jock went, Bernie followed. My father had accompanied us. 'It's no good, Harry,' he said, 'unemployment has seriously worsened this year and the bloody mayor has no right to stop people venting their anger. Why shouldn't they say they are destitute? Their kids starving?

I know this meeting will be joined by a lot of unemployed men. Then we'll see who can or can't speak out. And let the police try to stop them.'

Dusk was darkening into night and more people began to gather as we arrived. Suddenly there was a sound of marching feet. I looked around and saw a large contingent of at least four hundred men bearing down on the meeting. Those at the front of the march held a large banner FREE SPEECH FOR ALL – WORK FOR THE WORKERS. They swelled the crowd, surrounding and merging, while their leaders stood to the side holding up the banner. They were a motley group, some hefty, some weedy, all in shabby clothes and down-at-heel boots, their faces rock-like with determination. Harry's eyes flew around the crowd, taking it all in. 'This is more like it, Judith.'

I, too, caught the excitement. It rumbled through the crowd as if it had a single continuous heartbeat. But having arrived in such triumph, the marchers were now a warm if robust group. 'Evening, comrades,' they shouted, waving to friends or colleagues they knew, and they pushed their way through the crowd shaking hands and slapping backs. A sense of common grievance and common purpose united everyone.

Jock mounted his box. The police stirred, suddenly watchful, alert, waiting, rather, I thought, like a dog which scents unwelcome visitors. Quietly they moved to encircle the crowd and quietly they drew nearer to the box.

Jock began with his usual gesture of raising his hands and shaking them as if to throw off shackles. The crowd cheered. 'Fellow slaves,' he trumpeted, 'slaves of the capitalist system, throw off ...'

The police rushed the box, seized it and knocked him backwards. We heard the thump as he hit the road. The box was only a plywood vegetable crate and a couple of cracks with batons broke its top. Two police manhandled Jock and began to hustle him through the crowd. 'Move on!' they shouted. 'Meeting's over! Move on!'

Strengthened by an army of four hundred unemployed the crowd, instead of dispersing, closed around them.

'Move on!' the officer in charge bellowed, 'and clear the way!'

The crowd remained a wall of defiance. From the unemployed a burly workman grabbed what remained of the box and lifted it above his head. 'Here is your platform, comrades, your free speech platform. Smashed. Like our wages, our families, our future. Are we going to endure this suppression?'

'No!' roared the crowd. 'No!'

Beside me Harry was bobbing up and down, trying to see over all the heads what was going on. I cringed beside him. The press of bodies around me was claustrophobic and frightening. Somehow I had become separated from my father and I looked for him anxiously and fruitlessly. Harry still held my hand and I clung to him.

'Tame?' I laughed uncertainly. 'Not exactly tame, Harry.'

But there was too much noise for him to hear me.

The police and Jock were corralled together in our midst and no one seemed to know what to do except shout and there was plenty of that. Suddenly a cry went up, 'Horses, cops on horses, mounted.'

Like a swarm of fish dismembered by a shark, the crowd splintered. Released from the suffocating enclosure I saw before me a row of remorselessly advancing horses and mounted police with batons in their hands and as people ran they caught them in flight and clobbered them about the shoulders, backs, heads and faces. Some fell to the ground and were trampled beneath the hooves.

It was dark now but there were enough streetlights to see it all.

'Harry,' I screamed, 'they're killing people. Dad,' I shouted, 'Dad, where are you?'

Frantically I searched the shapes of the fleeing people but he wasn't there. Harry tightened his grip on my hand. 'Run, Judith,' he said, 'quick. We can dodge along the side. Quick.'

We ran.

'Into the square,' Harry panted. 'It's railed. We can hide in there.'

There seemed to be police everywhere, on foot, on horses. We heard more shouting and screams and groans. The square was within reach. The railed area seemed a haven. We entered it at full speed but others had had the same idea. A melee of police and protesters fought each other. They surged around us enclosing us and now there was no escape.

A couple of police grabbed Harry and shoved me aside. They pinned him against the railing and I saw their batons flail him. He struggled and tried to protect his head and face. They increased their attack. They would kill him.

I leaped at one of them, hurling my weight against his shoulder, trying to push him away to deflect the horrendous blows, but he threw me aside. 'Out of the way, girlie,' he snarled.

Then, instinctively, I did what women throughout centuries have done to divert attention. I screamed at the top of my voice, over and over, 'Rape! Rape! Rape!' And to be convincing, 'Help! Police! Help! Rape!'

I threw myself into the garden behind me, and continued to scream.

The police thumping Harry heard me and swung around. I saw their faces white masks in the darkness and shouted again, 'Help! Help me! Rape! He's getting away!'

From the ground I couldn't see Harry but I saw Bernie-Benito loom out of the darkness, a tall panther-like figure in dark clothes that merged with the night. I saw the flash of his knife but he did not strike for the two policemen had turned their attention to me.

'Rape,' I moaned, and from shock burst into hysterical tears. It was no pretence as I sobbed and sobbed.

The police stood irresolutely, looking down at me. I had rubbed dirt into my legs and along my jaw bone. I must have looked a desperate sight. They spoke in low voices to each other. 'Take her to hospital?'

'What if she accuses us?'

'She looks pretty bad.'

'Rape's a hanging offence.'

'Hard to prove our innocence.'

'She's with the protesters. Probably a lying little bitch.'

'But it looks genuine.'

'Yes, and we don't want to get the blame. No way I'm going to try to defend myself in a rape trial.'

They melted into the darkness.

I lay there for a long time it seemed. At first the noise of the affray went on around me. I heard grunts and shouts and muffled thuds and groans and curses. Occasionally I heard the sound of running or stumbling feet, then it quietened and I heard people urgently calling names and sometimes more stumbling steps. It was odd that no one had fallen over me. Now I remembered where I had thrown myself. Grass, twigs and clumps of dirt stuck into my back. Probably I was in a garden bed.

Eventually there was complete silence and only the darkness breathed around me. I relaxed. Perhaps I would go to sleep here. That would be nice. My mind and my body were strangers to each other and I had no intention of trying to stand up. Stray thoughts flitted through my mind but I felt nothing. I hadn't been able to find my father. I hoped that he was not dead like Harry. With curious detachment I thought of my poor mother.

The darkness was soft and kind and protective. They hadn't found me before; they wouldn't find me now. I could hide here forever. My mind drifted. I was in a dark picture house and suddenly out of the blackness a brilliant image of Harry spread-eagled against the railings, his face a mask of blood, flashed on the screen. I put my hand across my eyes to shield myself from its horror but it was still there inside my head, not on a screen.

The flash of brilliant light was something else. It bobbed around and a voice accompanied it. 'Judith,' it called, 'Judith, are you here?'

I shrank. I wasn't here. I wouldn't answer. There were murderers in the darkness.

The light bobbed nearer. I peered at it between my fingers.

'Judith,' the voice was questing, insistent.

Still I remained silent.

'It's Nathan,' the voice said. 'Are you here?'

Nathan, not a murderer.

I tried to speak, to call out, and failed twice before I managed to croak, 'I'm here.'

'Where?'

'I don't know.'

He floundered around.

'In the garden, I think.' My teeth clattered like castanets.

He found me, dropped to his knees and played his torch along the length of my body. He drew in his breath on a hiss. 'Judith.' His tone was the same as my mother's when she questioned me determined to get at the truth. She had been severe and always said, 'Now I won't brook any lies, my girl.'

'Judith,' he repeated, 'have you,' he gulped, 'have you been … interfered with?'

I stared at him, bemused.

'People in the square. They're running everywhere. Someone yelled at me that the bloody police had raped a girl. Your clothes, Judith. You look …' He choked.

Now I understood his fear but it was unimportant.

'No,' I answered wearily. 'Of course not. I screamed rape to try to save Harry. He's dead, isn't he? And my father? I couldn't find him. He must be dead, too, or he would have come searching for me.' Tears of abandonment sprang into my eyes and ran down my cheeks. 'Just leave me, Nathan. I don't want to go home and tell my mother my father's dead – and Harry. She'll be so sad. It's all my fault. I lied to her, you know about going out to stick up those posters. If we hadn't done that we'd never have gone to the meeting.' Now I was sobbing.

'Please, Judith,' he begged, 'please.' He shook my arm gently. 'Neither your father nor Harry are dead. Your father has been arrested, that's all, and Harry was spirited away by Bernie-Benito. He's taken him to the hulk. We can protect him there.'

'Not dead. Neither of them.' Relief surged through me. My father was alive and Harry was safe with my mother.

'Taken him to the hulk. But what have they told my mother? She'll be frantic about me.' I was shouting at him, although it came out a poor croak. 'Has anyone been stupid enough to tell her I've been raped?'

'No, of course not.'

'Well, I haven't and she ought to be told.'

'Yes,' he said, 'but I must get you home. Please help me. You must ...' he hesitated, 'you must dress yourself.'

'I am dressed. Don't be silly.'

'No.' And I detected the embarrassment in his voice.

I ran my hands down my body.

While I had screamed rape I had thrashed around on the ground to keep the police attention away from Harry. My calf-length skirt was scrunched up around my thighs. Just for an instant an irrelevant and amusing thought took the place of the night's carnage. This is the third time that my meeting with Nathan has been a humiliating experience for me. Then I was annoyed. Why should he be embarrassed? If he's so timid as to quail at the sight of a half-dressed woman then there's not much hope for his courage in a revolution.

I wriggled and wrenched my clothes into place. 'I'm ready,' I said.

He took my arm and helped me to sit up. The world spun.

'Don't rush it, Judith.'

'That's not likely.'

I sat for a few minutes, my head in my hands. Then again he took my arm and helped me to my feet. My legs trembled as if bones in them had dissolved.

'Try a few steps.'

I tottered. It was a very strange sensation. He put his arm around me, supporting me. 'Thank you, Nathan. But how are we to get home?' I giggled a little. 'I can't walk all that way.'

'A friend of Frank's has a car. He has been helping people home or to the hospital.' He stopped.

'The hospital?'

'Yes.'

'What a terrible night,' I groaned. 'Why, Nathan, why? It was only a meeting.'

He didn't answer. He helped me out of the square to where Frank's friend Pat had parked his car. Pat saw my faltering steps and Nathan supporting me and sprang out of the car to help.

'Oh, me darlin', me poor brave darlin',' he crooned, 'have they hurt you? You're all right, then?'

What silly questions people asked in their anxiety. 'Yes,' I said tiredly, 'I'm all right.'

'She's all right,' Nathan repeated.

Vaguely annoyed, I looked at him. All right? What a stupid assertion. I didn't think I'd ever be all right again.

The drive to the hulk was quiet. It was hard to believe that there had been such a desperate affray so short a time ago and in this peaceful city. It wasn't so late that everyone was in bed and there were lighted windows with shadows of people moving within. How safe the houses looked. My terrible memories had the unreality of a nightmare. I dozed a little in the car. Nathan and Pat talked in low voices in the front. I wasn't interested in what they said. Harry was not dead and my father, though arrested, would come home. It was enough that they were alive.

They helped me limp along the wharf. Now I was aware of pieces of me I had hurt. The sour salt-water smell and the oily reek of moored boats were comfortingly familiar. The sea slurped against the pylons, its rhythm an eternal and tranquil refrain that would chorus long after our deaths.

At the hulk they helped me balance on the gangplank. I moved slowly across the deck. My mother was in the saloon. Harry lay stretched on the couch. Dr Banks, our family doctor, leaned over him. He was a bald-headed rotund man with a brisk manner when arriving and leaving but he never hurried his visits. He had attended all my childhood ills – measles, chicken pox, sore throats – always with concerned advice. He was short but he still blocked my view of Harry, so it was a particularly homely and reassuring scene.

Frank and Bernie sat on the other side of the saloon. They looked an odd pair: Bernie garbed in funereal black, Frank, a wizened whipcord of a man, a 'meagre man' he once told me 'with a body that doesn't require much feeding. Such a body was handy to have in Ireland'.

They saw me first and glanced quickly from me to my mother. They half rose, then sank back again, their relief enclosing me in the conspiracy. Bernie put a light finger to his smiling lips as if to wipe something away. It was a secret gesture, warning me that he knew who had screamed rape but would never tell. He nodded as if in casual greeting. Bernie, I thought, had had a lifetime of keeping secrets.

'Mum,' I said.

She looked up, startled. Shock at my sudden appearance, then relief, then joy transfigured her face. I noticed how exhausted she looked. 'Judith,' she screeched. The bowl she held clattered to the floor, spilling a stream of reddened water. She dropped the cloth she had been holding and rushed at me. 'Judith.' Her arms enfolded me and crushed me against her. 'Judith,' she repeated, 'Judith.'

She pushed me away, grabbed my shoulders and shook me vigorously. 'Where have you been? I've been beside myself with worry. And your father?' She looked past me to the darkened deck. 'Where's your father?'

'They've arrested him.'

'Arrested him?' She stared at me blankly. 'What for?'

'I don't know.'

She fixed her eyes on Nathan, who was standing hesitantly behind me. Pat had retreated into the deck shadows where he couldn't be seen.

'And this is all your fault?' she rounded on Nathan. 'My daughter looking as if she has been dragged through a garden hedge, Harry half-dead, my husband arrested. This is all your fault.' Her voice crescendoed until she was shouting. 'Look what you have done. You with your stupid Bolshie ideas.'

'No, Mum,' I protested, 'no, it wasn't Nathan's fault. It was the police. Please don't shout. There's been so much shouting tonight.' My voice shook. 'I don't want to listen to any more shouting.'

She took a deep gasping breath.

'And Harry?' I pleaded. 'How is Harry?'

Now angry at me for defending Nathan, she swept back to Harry's side dragging me with her. 'See for yourself, my girl.'

Harry looked terrible. Both his eyes were shut and the swelling round them was red and angry. Purple and black bruises had erupted under the skin of his cheeks, neck and arms. His lips were broken and bleeding. His hair was matted with streaks of dried blood my mother had failed to wash away. He didn't move.

'Harry,' I whispered, cradling his hand. My shock was too great, even for tears. I turned to Dr Banks, mute with fear. He patted my shoulder. 'He'll live. It looks worse than it is. No structural damage. He's lucky. Young people are tough.'

No, I thought resentfully, no they aren't. The cemetery is full of the graves of children not tough enough to withstand diphtheria, measles, whooping cough, even typhoid. Whole families of children gone in one month. Doctors weren't always right.

'They bashed him,' I said angrily. 'They didn't need to.'

His mouth tightened. 'No, but I daresay I'll also find a few young policemen waiting for my attentions in the hospital.'

'We weren't armed with batons,' I said wearily. 'They had the advantage.'

Then I recalled seeing the flash of Bernie-Benito's knife. What if he had used it? The thought of what might have eventuated filled me with terror. There was nothing in my life that had prepared me for such visceral conflict.

Dr Banks insisted on having a look at me. Regardless of my protests he felt the back of my head, pursing his mouth when I winced. 'You've got a good-sized abrasion there. Your mother will clean it.'

He shone a bright light in my eyes, twisted my neck this way and that, ran his fingers down my spine, tapped my knee, examined the scratches on my leg and asked what I had been doing with myself. Had I, too, been part of the affray?

I lied that I had run and fallen, skidded on a small stone, and that's when I had lost Harry. From the corner of my eye I saw Frank and Bernie lower their eyes to examine their hands. They had rested them on their knees and did not move or look up.

Dr Banks grunted disbelievingly. He left some prescriptions for Harry, some pain killers and a sedative to help him sleep. He said he would look in again tomorrow, put his medical equipment back in his bag and snapped it shut.

My mother accompanied him out of the saloon. Nathan moved out of the doorway to let them pass. I had forgotten that for all this time he had hovered irresolutely in the doorway. As in the gardens when he trotted after Winnie and me, he seemed unable to decide when it was time to leave. As Dr Banks passed Nathan I heard him say to my mother, 'I don't care much for the company she keeps.'

I got up, gently replaced Harry's hand on the couch and turned to Nathan. 'I'm sorry,' I said. 'Everyone has been very rude to you and Pat. Please excuse us. I think it's the result of shock. My mother is so angry that she has to blame someone.'

I put out a tentative hand and touched his sleeve. 'Thank you for finding me and thank Pat. Later, perhaps, we'll be more like ourselves again.'

He nodded, his eyes luminous behind his thick spectacles. I remembered how, when he had flashed his torch on me, I had seen pinpoints of light dancing in his glasses. How odd I had thought then that he has survived all this and managed to keep them on. He was also uninjured, but I didn't ask him about that. It was strange that a man so decisive about ideas was lost in a social situation. He didn't know the appropriate time to end a speech. He didn't know when or how he should leave. His vulnerability touched me. As well as finding me tonight he had defended me at the Chew It and Spew It.

He said that he and Pat would go now Harry was in good hands. Perhaps tomorrow or later he could come again to see him. Would he be welcome? He was tentative.

'Of course,' I said, 'but later.'

He and Pat passed my mother. She managed a brief but reluctant thanks.

'Dr Banks had no right to speak to him in that way,' I said. 'He wasn't there. Nathan and Pat helped me tonight. It wasn't Harry's fault. It wasn't mine and it wasn't Nathan's and Pat's.'

Frank and Bernie-Benito had also risen ready to leave. 'We'll go, too, mum,' Frank said. 'Harry's in good hands. Should we do anything else?'

'Yes,' I said. 'Could you tell his mother?' I found a piece of paper and wrote down her address. 'Don't frighten her but she must be told. Ask her to please wait until tomorrow to visit.'

Frank took the paper. Bernie-Benito took my hand and held it lovingly. 'Judith,' he crooned, 'Judith.' And his eyes large and soulful reminded me of Winnie's Labrador resting his head on my lap. He had spirited Harry away, probably carried him. His rag-doll appearance was deceptive. There were balls of muscle in his sinewy arms. I reached up, kissed his cheek and whispered, 'Thank you, Bernie, thank you for everything.'

The next morning my mother put on her hat and gloves to go to the union office. To dress respectably was her defence against the chaos our world had become. We had taken it in turns to watch over Harry during the night and anxiety and weariness had aged her. I made her a cup of tea and some oatmeal porridge, but although she drank several cups of the tea she only poked the porridge around and eventually left it.

'I can't eat,' she said. 'I must go to the union office. They'll know what has happened to your father. It's better I see them than front up at the police station. I don't see any of us being welcome there.' She looked spent and bitter. 'I'm sorry, Judith, it's very hard on you. You need rest yourself. Are you all right?'

That question again. 'Yes,' I repeated for the umpteenth time. How many people now had I reassured? 'I'm all right.'

'You don't look it.' She was doubtful.

I managed a smile. 'Looks are deceptive.'

In another situation she would have been suspicious and pursued my assertion. Now at the limit of her endurance, she gratefully accepted it. 'You're a good girl, Judith, a good girl.'

She left. I drank a cup of tea and forced down a few mouthfuls of the porridge. I hoped the food might warm me for I felt chilled. Harry still slept. Overcome with lassitude, I wrapped myself in my blanket and sat again in the uncomfortable chair by his side. In the morning light his injuries looked harsher, more cruel, the bruises uglier, the inflamed puffy swelling about his eyes discoloured and raw, his lips cracked. But he was still alive. I dozed. My head jerked forward. I slept.

Dr Banks' arrival awakened me. He hurried in, brisk and urgent. He had not shaved and his eyes were bloodshot with fatigue. He examined Harry. 'Wake up, lad,' he yelled at him.

Harry stirred, tried to move and groaned.

'He'll live.' He patted his shoulder. 'There's many a lot worse.'

But his confident medical comparisons failed to reassure me.

'Give him a few days.' His tone gentled. 'And now the truth, young woman. Where were you two last night in this mess?'

I had done enough lying. 'The Square,' I said. 'Victoria Square. The railed area.'

He grunted. 'A good thing you were. I've a patient in hospital with the print of a horseshoe embedded in his back. His vertebra may be crushed. Stupid fools the lot of you. Mounted police,' he snorted, 'on the streets of Adelaide. I don't know what our society is coming to.'

I remembered the arrival of the four hundred unemployed men at the Free Speech meeting. 'Starvation,' I said. 'Unemployment. Desperation.'

He looked at me keenly and shook his head. 'Well, I have enough to do without this sort of thing.' And he stumped out.

Harry managed to whisper, 'He's gone?'

'Yes. He's our family doctor. Don't try to talk.'

'No,' he sighed, and relapsed into sleep.

Three hours later my mother returned. She walked heavily as if bowed beneath a burden too heavy to carry and sank dispiritedly into a chair. As was her habit, she removed the long hat pin, took off her hat and laid it carefully on the table. Then she pulled off her gloves and laid them neatly beside her hat. Her next step was usually to find her apron and put it on, but today she just sat, too overwrought to move.

'There were a dozen other women at the union office, all of us, poor working-class wives, all with the same worry. We waited ...'

'For three hours, Mum?'

'They weren't unkind to us, just distracted.'

'But to make you wait for three hours?'

'They had no time. People rushed about everywhere. There was constant commotion, constant coming and going from Matty Gibbs's office; agitated people shouting at each other; fuming about intimidation of the union, retaliation, retribution, throwing down the gauntlet to the government, tumult, anger and wild talk. Every face was grim and hostile. There were a couple of newspapermen but they got brushed aside and eventually left.

'When Matty came to speak with us he apologised. He said the morning had been almost beyond his management skills. Everyone, so-to-speak, was armed and seething. He told me that last night's attack by the mounted police had swelled the mutterings for forming a Workers' Defence Army. Like they had in Broken Hill a few years back.'

I knew the Union organiser, Matty Gibbs. He was a courteous man who always managed to negotiate conflicts with fairness and reasonableness but latterly, as the economic situation worsened, he had become more strained, more uncertain of his abilities. Unemployment and the Crimes Act now divided most of his workforce from the rest of the community. He was beginning to feel they were all under siege.

'He was sympathetic to us,' she said. 'Some of the women there have children and are desperate for their husbands to return to whatever work they have. One woman said that only the soup kitchen run by the Salvos stands between them and starvation. He looked distressed, Judith. The burden of social ills falls heavily on those with a conscience.'

I dismissed her sympathy for Matty Gibbs. 'It's his job to help.'

'No,' she denied, 'that's the problem. The meeting was organ-ised by the Communist Party, not the Union. Strictly speaking the Union has no involvement.'

'No involvement? But my father's a Union man.' I could see that explaining it all to me tired her further, but I had to know. I could feel the indignation swelling in me. 'Are we to receive no help? Not even from the Waterside Workers' Union?'

'They will help as far as they can, Judith. Matty promised that Union lawyers would represent your father and others and if necessary they will put up money for bail or bonds. However if the choice is between either jail or a fine they can't guarantee to pay the fines. It could amount to quite a lot and the Union is strapped for cash. Their priorities are the families of unemployed Union members and they can give them little enough.'

Tears ran down her face. 'What are we to do, Judith? If there's a fine we must pay it. Your father mustn't go to jail. He can't lose his job. He's a winchman. The ship owners won't put up with delays.'

She wept with her head against my shoulder and I clutched her as if I were the parent and she the child.

'We have so little money saved.'

'I have some.'

'Oh, no, Judith. That was to be yours, your future.'

'Well, I won't have any future if we don't have a now. Whatever it is I shall pay. I am quite determined.'

I knew she was relieved but now tasted the bitterness of acceptance.

In the afternoon Winnie and Frank and Harry's mother visited. Harry's mother was a timid, defeated creature who looked at her injured son as if he were the ultimate disaster in her life.

One glance and Winnie burst into tears, wailing, 'Oh, Harry, you look absolutely awful.'

'Thanks, Weepy,' he whispered. 'That's good to know.'

His mother took a handkerchief and wiped her eyes.

We're going to have a crying competition now, I thought.

'Your job, Harry. At the foundry?' his mother questioned, faintly and hopelessly.

'No need to worry, Mum,' Frank intervened. 'We're sending a couple of blokes around to speak with his boss. I'm sure they'll make him understand.'

'How kind of them,' she murmured. 'I've not met his employer but please thank him for me. I'm sure Harry will be grateful.'

'Did you hear that, Harry? So kind.'

Harry had heard. He looked at me from the one eye he had managed to open and it held a flicker of his old sense of humour. Harry's mother was clearly incapable of reading the meaning behind Frank's words. She was a simple woman and defenceless because of it. I wondered how Harry had inherited or learned so much sophistication – possibly from his long-dead father. The tree people sprang from often grew strange shoots.

My mother, always kind to the vulnerable, made tea and served scones to console Harry's mother. The three left eventually and I hoped we'd have no more visitors. Harry was clearly exhausted.

My father returned home that evening. He had been bonded to appear in the magistrate's court at some future date. Unshaven, heavy-eyed and crumpled, he looked dog tired. My mother put her arms about him. Over her shoulder he saw me.

'You're all right, Judith?'

'Yes.'

'I've been worried. And Harry?'

'The police beat him up,' I said. 'He's in the saloon. But Dr Banks says he'll recover.'

'That's good.' He reached for a chair and sat down. Careful, measured, slow movements, so unlike his usual vigour.

'I'm whacked, Eve. It's hard to believe that a night in the cells could so exhaust me.' He tried to smile. 'After all, I've done a stint of forty hours on the winches, but jail, there was something villainous about it, something brutalising and hellish in being shut away. Too much of it and I'd be defeated. It's the inaction, the helplessness. One could so easily get to feel worthless. I kept remembering the windjammers and freedom.'

My father was not given to self-reflection. This tired old man with a confused expression was shockingly new to me and I was devoured by a rage so venomous that its poison consumed me. My father was demoralised, Harry beaten near to death, my mother distraught and afraid, some man I didn't know had the imprint of a horseshoe on his spine. It wasn't justice I cried out for, it was revenge, primitive, pestilential revenge. If authority had degenerated to such shamelessness then where were we, its help- less victims? Our feebleness had not been because we were bad characters or transgressors, our weakness lay in being unarmed. We had been lured into a situation where the violence had been apportioned unequally. That was the root of the problem. We could remedy that. Our first defeat need never be our last. The communists were right. We couldn't beat the police unless we had guns.

These were wild thoughts, bitter imaginings but later, when I had quietened and thrust out the idea of guns, the core of my conviction remained.

Three days later Nathan visited and brought along his sisters. I was surprised. After all, they didn't know Harry – had indeed ignored and insulted him at the meeting hall – but now they assumed a graciousness that was as irritating as their previous rudeness had been.

They walked into the saloon confidently and without being asked. Certainly a hulk is odd, in that there doesn't seem to be a formal front door, but some sort of hesitation on the deck would have been courteous. My mother, her antennae alert to any superior patronising, took in their appearance and manner and stiffened. Nathan's introduction was clumsy. 'My sisters, Miss Abigail and Miss Adelaide,' he mumbled, eyeing my mother warily. 'We hoped to visit Harry. That is, if it's convenient. That is, if he's well enough. Judith said ...' he stammered and looked at me appealingly; his eyes large and defenceless like some bush creature, behind huge spectacles.

How could a man so dominant in his opinions be such a weakling in dealing with people? 'This is Nathan,' I felt compelled to remind my mother. 'You remember, he brought me home.'

'I remember.' Her iciness did not melt.

'I'll take them in to see Harry,' I hastened. 'He has been moved into my cabin for his privacy.' I suspected that Harry would not enjoy their visit, although he might be pleased that Nathan showed his concern. Personal touches meant a lot to Harry. They showed affection and he craved love.

'There isn't much room,' I said as I showed them in and retreated to the saloon.

'Has there been a funeral in their house?' my mother was sarcastic.

'Not as far as I know. They just seem to like black.'

'Dreadful colour, so draining for an ageing woman. Makes you look like a death's head, particularly if you're scrawny.'

'Shush,' I laughed, 'they'll hear.'

'Let them. Waltzing in here as if they owned the place – and uninvited, too.'

'I invited Nathan.'

She sniffed. 'Not his sisters?'

'No, not his sisters.'

They reappeared a short time later and hesitated in the saloon.

My mother didn't ask them to sit. Miss Abigail said, 'Nathan would like to spend a little more time with the young man.'

'Harry,' I said, 'his name's Harry. You met him at the Communist Party meeting.'

She looked disbelieving. 'Is he then some follower of Nathan's?'

'No,' I said, 'he's not a follower of anyone. We came to the meeting only out of interest.'

I knew that this was not quite true about Harry. He had followed Nathan, too much like an acolyte I had thought at the time, but I had no intention of giving his sisters the satisfaction of knowing this.

'We are forming a Women's Defence Army and looking for recruits,' Miss Adelaide began abruptly. 'Would you care to join us?' She looked expectantly from me to my mother.

'Defence Army? Women?' I was puzzled.

'Defence Army?' My mother was coldly antagonistic. 'And what will that do?'

'We will march with our men, but in front of them. At future protests we can't leave them unprotected to be picked off by the police.'

'And how will a group of women stop that?' My mother was incredulous.

'The police won't attack women. Our vigilance will save our menfolk.' Miss Abigail was the Greek chorus.

My mother snorted scornfully. 'And you will swallow that fantasy? You have the gall to expect my daughter to risk another baton charge from mounted police in order to protect your brother? Hasn't he caused enough trouble? You might just as well ask the police not to bash anyone who is wearing spectacles.' She laughed derisively.

Miss Adelaide drew herself up, offended, rather, I thought, like the Queen in *Alice in Wonderland*. Any minute now she would shout the order, *Off with their heads*. I would have thought they'd had enough but she persisted, 'We understood that given your experiences you'd like to help.'

'Our experiences?' my mother choked. 'I'll help,' she said, 'but at a Salvation Army soup kitchen. That's real help.'

Now their scorn matched hers. 'Bolstering up the system? Handouts?' Miss Adelaide scoffed. 'Amelioration rather than revolution? Helping people survive so they won't fight? Promising them rewards in heaven for their miseries?'

'You've never had children, have you?' my mother threw at them. 'No children to watch starve?'

They were silent, affronted.

'I thought not.' She stormed to the saloon door and pointedly held it open. There was nothing they could do except leave. She huffed and puffed back to the galley and clattered saucepans around to relieve her angry feelings.

I didn't know what Nathan was talking to Harry about and didn't much care but I gave the argument between my mother and Nathan's sisters careful thought. My mother had been outraged at the thought of our involvement in a Women's Defence Army. Certainly Nathan's sisters had assumed too much. It seemed that they had confidently considered that martyrdom had made us good pickings for their cause. However, unlike my mother, I did not reject the idea of matching physical violence with confrontation but it would have been easier for me to accept their proposal if I had disliked them less.

Half an hour later Nathan also left. I think he would have liked to talk with me but my mother's mutterings from the galley daunted him.

I went to join Harry.

'Have they gone?' he whispered.

'Yes.'

'They're still singing flat.'

I laughed, recalling Nathan's meeting and the botched rendering of *The Internationale*. 'And quite out of tune. For all their fine political principles they were visibly offended when my mother lumped them with her as working class women.'

He frowned, puckering his brow in his effort to remember. 'We ran into the square, Judith?'

'Yes.'

'The railed area?'

'Yes.'

'There were lots of people and fighting?'

'Yes.'

'Two cops grabbed me and started to hammer the daylights out of me.'

'Yes.'

He paused, thoughtful. 'A woman screamed? She kept on screaming "Rape!" The cops stopped bashing me. I think they went to look. I couldn't help her.'

'You didn't need to.'

'No.'

He considered me. 'It was you, Judith?'

'Yes.'

He looked worried. 'You weren't?'

'No, of course not.'

'It was to save me?'

'To try.'

He chuckled feebly. ' Thanks, Judith. You are a card. Such a card.' He reached me his hand. The effort of talking had again exhausted him and he lapsed into a light doze.

Very gently I leaned over him and touched his lips with mine.

On the brink of deeper sleep, he smiled. 'Butterflies,' he sighed.

After a week Harry had recovered enough to go home. Frank, Pat and Nathan all came to help him along the wharf and into Pat's car. My mother cried a little to see him go and hugged the part of him that did not hurt to be touched. He did his best to grin at me. 'Do I remember some butterflies?' he said.

I blushed.

'What a card you are, Judith,' he chuckled. 'Won't be long before I'm dancing again and I'll shout you a threepenny hop at the Bloodhouse.'

I returned to my work at the Chew It and Spew It. My boss scowled, 'There was no need for those two union heavies to come around here threatening me. I wouldn't have sacked you. It's too hard as it is to find good workers.' And that was as much recognition of my labours as I was likely to get.

However I was surprised and a little embarrassed. What could I say about the union heavies? I knew they had gone to the foundry on Harry's behalf but had never imagined they would think of me. Perhaps I owed my boss a sort of indirect apology. Irresolutely I looked at him.

'Well, haven't you any work to do?' he grumbled some more.

With all the terrible events of the previous days I had forgotten that I had sent my drawing of Joe Pulham's grave to the *Sun News Pictorial* so it was with surprise that I opened a letter from their editor. He had returned my drawing but accompanied his refusal with a courteous letter. 'The drawing is good,' he wrote. 'It shows considerable promise.' He assumed that such a feeling cartoon must have sprung from some painful personal experience, but for a newspaper a cartoon had to be topical. It must encapsulate a particular event and display a clear viewpoint. The best cartoons were satiric or ironic or funny. He suggested that I study the work of Will Dyson. He wished me well and hoped that I would continue to draw. If I produced others his paper would be happy to consider them.

Apart from Joe's opinions this was my first experience of a

judgement of my work from an outsider. That my drawing had been treated with serious consideration lifted my spirits. I felt that a part of me, previously ignored, was now acknowledged. Maybe there was some place for me in a world that I had never before dreamed of entering. Again, like Alice, I had come to believe that I would never fit through the door into the magic garden. How pertinent *Alice in Wonderland* was to our deepest fears and hopes, how relevant its images that time could never consume.

While Harry lay prone on my bunk bed and I watched over him I had been unable to forget that last horrifying image of him before I flung myself to the ground and screamed, 'Rape!' Strung against the iron railings that reared above his head like the obscene arms of a crucifix, he was helpless to resist the vicious flagellation. Each time that image imprinted itself on my retina I felt so ill that the need to vomit nearly overwhelmed me. Part of me needed to draw that image to free me from its pain but another part cringed and retreated from re-living it.

Now, with the editor's letter, my thoughts returned to Joe Pulham. He had taken a book of Goya's etchings from the shelf, handed it to me and told me to look and learn from them. That, too, I had forgotten until now. In fact, I remembered guiltily, I had also forgotten to return the book to the library. I searched, found it, and sat down to turn the pages thoughtfully. Some of the drawings were incomprehensible; I supposed they were dependent on an understanding of Spanish history and culture. But the series *The Disasters of War* arrested me.

Before the riot and the police bashing they would have meant little, a brutality that took place in another country at another time and alien to me in its ferocity. But now experience had changed my viewpoint and I saw in their savagery the agony, pity and suffering of people at war, the nobility of defiance that ended in useless defeat, the clarion call for liberty. These were not just Spanish works, they were universal in their message and power and they were about ordinary people, like Harry and me and Nathan and my mother and father and Jock and Frank and Pat and darling innocent Winnie, who might have been in that square and seen what I had seen and lost her sweetness and trust for ever.

If Goya could face such vile events and record them then I could draw Harry as a crucified Christ. I wasn't religious. My father had cured me of that and my mother's church-going was wishy-washy at best, but I could see there were universal symbols that we all recognised and responded to no matter what our political beliefs. Donald Grant, an IWW, had spoken of Christ returning to earth and weeping for the poor and this image resonated with people and stirred their sense of right and wrong. Some symbols were perhaps particular to local cultures. I suspected that perhaps some of the animal images in Goya's works were more local to Spain but the image of the tortured Christ was universal.

So I began my drawing of Harry and the two policemen, one striking him, the other with baton raised and I wrote the caption beneath: *Defenders of free speech*. I was aware as I drew that somehow I was not fully catching the sense of Harry's body beneath the clothes but I did my best and when it was finished I set it between two sheets of cardboard and sent it to the *Barrier Daily Truth* in Broken Hill. This I knew to be a radical miners' paper that might appreciate my viewpoint.

Following the *Sun News Pictorial* editor's advice I went to the Institute at the Port and requested any interstate newspapers that might have featured some of Will Dyson's cartoons. I found several and a book of his works published in 1919. They were full of images of capitalists with huge bellyfuls of lard spurning abject women and children or thrusting heroic workers back into the pit of poverty. But, like Goya's, his cartoons – of Australian soldiers at war – were realistic and tragic. Their nobility lay in their suffering, not in some fake set of heroics, and what struck me more than anything else was the complexity of the drawings.

Some were bitter angry political statements, like *Peace and Cannon Fodder* published in 1919, depicting three of the leaders of Europe and Woodrow Wilson after the signing of the Treaty of Versailles. There is a child weeping behind a pillar but they fail to see him.

Joe had said to me that we would rue the Versailles agreement, that it was a pitiless exercise in revenge. Nathan had also spoken of the starvation of German working people and Adolf Hitler had written his terrible book. Did Dyson's cartoon foretell that the terms of peace would again let loose the dogs of war? A shiver ran down my spine.

In both Goya's works and Will Dyson's there was a strong honest mind behind the works, a passionate integrity. I returned home thoughtful. My mother had hoped that I might spend some of my hundred pounds on training for office work but shorthand and typing seemed an empty future. Instead I decided I would spend some of my money in enrolling at the Adelaide School of Art. There I could learn to draw. That is what I wanted to do with my life.

I had needed to spend some of my hundred pounds on my father's fine but we had been relieved that he didn't receive a jail sentence. Jock, knocked off his box and kicked around, had received a month's jail as had several of the other unemployed marchers, accused of causing the affray. Now I hesitated about enrolling at the School of Art. In the circumstances it seemed self-indulgent, a training that didn't ensure a job at a time when money was becoming more and more the measure of all things. I dithered between longing and guilt. I didn't like to discuss the matter with my mother. It was a decision on my behalf I hesitated to impose on her.

My doubts about this dream grew as I accompanied her on weekends to the Salvation Army soup kitchen. She and three friends, Ailsa Thornhill, Mavis Jones and Brenda Danley, volunteered to assist the overstretched Army workers seven days a week. There was a kitchen at the back of the Army hall and an old wood-burning stove. Brenda Danley's son was conscripted to collect firewood and whatever else might burn. Ben was fourteen and had left school but there was no work for him. School fees were beyond his parents, so he hung around the Port with a gang of other lads and his mother worried about what mischief they might get up to. Some of the wood he brought in was palings from someone's fence that had disappeared during the night. 'Fences I don't mind,' she said, 'although if the police catch him ...'

I knew that stealing was now a way of life for many. 'You're a good girl, Judith,' she added. 'Such a strength to your mother. Boys are different.'

My mother begged free milk from the dairyman. She had to water it to make it go round all the children and I went from door to door at the stores and fruiterers collecting anything that once they would have thrown away: cauliflowers browned, cabbages a bit slimy, carrots growing whiskers, potatoes with long white tentacles of shoots, mouldy onions that we peeled down until the skin showed white. The butchers were cajoled and upbraided. The day my mother unwrapped two shanks that already smelt high and found them crawling with maggots was a day I never forgot. For her, it was the final outrage, that she should be given for the destitute something so disgustingly inedible. She stormed back to the butcher dragging me in her wake and flung them on the counter. 'Look at these,' she shouted. 'Look at them. Lousy with maggots.'

The butcher eyed them without expression. He had, I think, become inured to angry women aggressive in their need. 'Well, Mum,' he said, 'them's surely maggots. I won't deny. But what do you expect for nothing? Glow-worms?'

My mother stopped in mid-shout, her mouth gaped. I laughed. It was untactful but there was little enough to laugh at these days.

'Glow-worms,' my mother stuttered at last.

The butcher looked from my mother to my laughing face and grinned. 'You know,' I said, 'it's for the Salvos, their soup kitchen. The Lord won't forget any kindness you do.'

He looked abashed and muttered, 'Didn't know you were Salvos.' Still mumbling he went into a back room, brought out a stack of soup bones, slapped them on some newspaper and handed them to me. My mother, dumbfounded, thanked him and we went out. 'That was well done, Judith,' she said. 'A timely lie, although perhaps not a real lie, just an implication.' And I thought, in her way, my mother is as puritanical as any Salvo.

I badgered my boss at the Chew It and Spew It to help. He had always seemed a mean and disagreeable man but now he showed a side that surprised me. 'If a bloke is unemployed, Judith, just give him his stew and don't ask questions. You'll know because he'll ask for tick. If someone comes in for a bun and a cuppa and says they'll pay tomorrow, ignore it. Better that they're here and not at the pub. Better for their missus and the kids. They'll talk here and that's OK too. I hope, Judith, that you can continue to work here. I'll not give even a crust to some dirty scab to take your place. Not,' he added with crude cynicism, 'that it'd be a mite of bloody use employing some out-of-towner that can't even speak the language. The Port is family.'

Then he asked me if I'd accept less pay because times were so tough. My wages were skimpy enough as it was. There had been no yearly increments as I grew older. I wasn't certain whether all this preliminary self-righteousness was to soften me up. It was hard to tell from his bland plump face whether the workings of his mind were honest or not, and yet if he wasn't completely noble then he wasn't entirely mean either. I accepted his offer, knowing that my employment might in the long run be as uncertain as everyone else's.

At the end of each day he filled a bag with leftover vegetables but I learned to open it and smell what was inside. If the smell was the sour odour of rotting vegetables I tipped them out on the kitchen bench and re-sorted them. I would look at him reproachfully and repeat what now had become a mantra: 'And these are good enough for the Salvos?' And he would find some excuse. He had done it in a hurry. He hadn't noticed the rotten potatoes. We understood each other.

From my childhood I had noticed poor individuals: the swimmer after a crust of bread; the man in the gardens sneaking a cigarette butt; the man at the Club stealing newspaper to put under his coat; the unemployed returned soldier weeping; the poor hawkers who came regularly and tentatively up our gangplank offering mothballs and bits of this and that for sale. My mother purchased mothballs and afterwards laughed sadly as she told me moths and silverfish did not inhabit a hulk.

But these had been individuals, shocking because they stood out isolated and alone amongst those better off. Now everyone looked poor. At the soup kitchen gaunt and desperate women, their children clinging to their knees, lined up with men shuffling and defeated or angry, surly and defiant, and the children were spindly, the bones of their faces prominent, their skin pallid and blotched with sores.

The Depression, like a quagmire, swallowed the Port. Family after family was sucked into the bog of unemployment, even the most humble of their expectations gutted. Many, barely making do on the edge of existence, now looked starvation in the face. Day after day women struggled to feed and clothe their families, endlessly sewing and mending so that the few clothes they had left did not completely fall apart. They made small articles that their husbands could hawk around the Port, cadging a few pennies from neighbours as desperate as themselves. Men endlessly applied for jobs that only a few could get, hundreds of them queuing day after day at the Labour Exchange, all in their one good suit and hat. Most were turned away humiliated and bitter with disappointment and despair. They all wanted jobs, not charity, but it was the soup kitchens that kept them alive and staved off famine.

I watched this endless queue of pathetic people with their billies and saucepans and found myself bereft of understanding. Years later I was to learn that when The Great Depression fell on us Adelaide was hit first and hit hardest.

Harry quoted Nathan that it was all predictably the nature of capitalism and until the working class understood that they would always be victims of booms and busts. But this abstract analysis left me unsatisfied. To understand it was not to cure it. It wasn't like a bilious attack for which a particular remedy could be prescribed, it was a number of illnesses all attacking the body at the same time and tearing it apart. But my mother wasn't interested in the big picture; not then, anyway. As far as she was concerned feeding hungry people was the first thing to be done.

Mrs Grenville, Harry's mother, asked me, my mother and, of course, Winnie to afternoon tea on Sunday. Harry handed me the invitation written on elegant parchment and in a matching envelope. The formal words were in a careful copperplate script.

The afternoon tea was to thank us for our kindness to Harry when he was ill. 'You don't have to come,' he said as I opened the invitation. He sounded apologetic as if the invitation was some sort of burden. His diffidence puzzled me, and to be reassuring I accepted enthusiastically. However this seemed to only increase his embarrassment and, scarlet in the face, he hurried away.

'My goodness,' my mother said. 'We'd better wear our best clobber for this do. To look at Harry you'd never believe that he came from such upper class folk.'

So all dressed up for the occasion in hat and gloves, we were quite unprepared for the pitiful genteel poverty of Harry's home and his mother's sad little pretensions. It was a small brick house with a narrow untidy front garden, the grass still a scruffy brown from the Adelaide heat. It occurred to me that it would be a good thing if Harry spent some time tidying it. I'd point this out to him next time we were alone.

Inside the house was shadowy because most of the blinds were either partly or fully drawn. It smelled of old furniture, its fabric embedded in years of accumulated dust. The couch and chairs in the parlour were sprinkled with crocheted antimacassars. One had slipped from its marshalled position on the back of the couch to reveal a tear in the cloth underneath. The carpet was threadbare although a hand-made rag rug concealed what I assumed was the charred area in front of the fireplace.

Mrs Grenville greeted us as timidly as she had on the hulk. Harry tried to cover for her nervousness by briskly taking my mother's coat and hat and talking quickly and rather too loudly.

Winnie had arrived before us, pretty as ever in a light green skirt and matching blouse. She jumped up and gave me a hug. 'Doesn't Harry look well? I was so terrified when I saw him at the hulk. You looked awful, Harry.'

'So you told me, Winnie.'

'You remember?'

'Of course.'

'I thought …' she stopped.

'That my brain had been affected?'

'Well, you did look awful. And I read in the paper that some poor woman was raped. In the Victoria Square, Harry.'

Harry opened his eyes wide in amazement. He didn't look at me. 'I never heard about that.'

'Really, Winnie,' Mrs Grenville reproached faintly, 'not nice.'

Winnie ignored her. 'You were too sick to know, Harry. But it was in all the papers.' She spoke with the confidence of someone who believes in the veracity of the press. 'You couldn't be expected to know. But everybody was talking about it.'

I concentrated on the intricate design of a crocheted doiley on a small side table and looked up at Mrs Grenville. 'Have you made all these lovely antimacassars?' I interrupted Winnie.

She smiled tremulously. 'In our school days we were all taught needlecraft and the art of fine writing.' She looked at me expectantly.

'Yes, of course, your lovely invitation.'

On queue I had tiptoed through my praise, aware that Harry would see through me. My mother was silent but I knew she was taking in the dreary room, assessing it and adjusting her expectations of upper class living.

Harry's mother had little conversation and I felt tongue-tied so we were grateful that Winnie chattered aimlessly, a pleasant prattle: her dog had adopted the next door kitten and now they both slept together; she had purchased a lipstick in the latest colour but it was too red, you know that crimson red that makes a sort of slash across your face, too harsh, she hated harsh colours; she had been to see the latest Pearl White film. Pearl White always gave her a thrill.

Mrs Grenville responded feebly. To the dog anecdote she said 'How strange'; to the lipstick story 'How disappointing'; to the film a nondescript murmur which might have been either approval or disapproval.

Winnie's bright glances enclosed us all but mostly centred on her aunt. At one point she caught my eye and the tiniest flicker of awareness made me wonder if this babble of inanities had been a deliberate performance to help manage what was becoming a very awkward afternoon.

Eventually afternoon tea was served from a trolley, also set with crocheted doilies. Harry wheeled it in and then went back to the kitchen for the large teapot, which he placed on a stand on top of the trolley. Beside the teapot was a small jug of milk, a sugar bowl and a single plate of thin slices of bread and butter.

On the lower shelf of the trolley was a collection of cups and saucers, all of delicate English bone china but none of the cups matched either the saucers or the accompanying plates. I looked at this wretched collection of exquisite china and imagined Mrs Grenville scouring the second-hand shops of Adelaide for beautiful things that she could lovingly look at and hold. And, indeed, as she poured us tepid cups of weak tea and handed around the sadly parsimonious slices of bread it seemed to me that she caressed the china as fondly as anyone would touch the hair of a loved child. It was a doll's house party, a melancholy pretence and an assertion of gentility in the face of grinding poverty.

Harry fidgeted with painful embarrassment and looking at him I recognised beneath his usual bright gaiety the restless resentment that made him seek out Nathan and cling to his beliefs. Clearly he was painfully mortified that his mother could not share with us the sort of honest abundance my mother served from her galley. Mrs Grenville appeared unaware that his glances at her revealed both his pity for her plight and resentment at his.

Thankfully the afternoon tea was at last over and Harry jumped up to wheel out the trolley. His mother now seemed less anxious as if serving the afternoon tea had been the hurdle she most dreaded. She prattled on about Harry's job at the foundry; at the kindness of the men who had spoken to his boss; how it was just a matter of time before he was promoted to the office, even perhaps made a partner in the firm. She ignored Harry's mumbled protest, 'No, Mum, it won't happen. Please.'

At his interruption she hesitated a second, then smiled. 'Of course it will, Dear.' And to me it seemed that her smile held the same fondness she had shown her teacups. Her fantasy about Harry's future now seemed to give her the confidence to ask my mother what she did because it must be very interesting to live on a ship, even if it was a little dangerous.

My mother responded sturdily. I was certain she was fed up with the pretences. 'For the last few weeks I've been giving my time to the soup kitchen at the Salvation Army hall. There are many families in the Port where the breadwinner is out of work and many single women struggling to make do. Judith helps by cadging food from various shops and we manage to provide a tidy meal for all the people who come. The butcher gives us offcuts of meat and this boiled up with plenty of vegetables and thickened with barley makes a wholesome meal. Two or three-day-old bread is good and can be broken into the soup. People come with their billycans and saucepans and mostly it's a happy community occasion.'

As Mrs Grenville listened to her she flushed painfully and my mother stopped abruptly. Winnie rushed in, 'The poor souls. How lucky we are to live better.'

Harry sat slumped in his chair. I caught his eye and smiled. The look he gave me was one of total dejection. The afternoon had been enough agony for him. I searched desperately for something to say. 'It's the children, you know. How fortunate, Mrs Grenville, that Harry is a grown man. You can be so proud of him and he plays the piano so beautifully.'

She replied in a die-away voice, 'The piano. Oh, yes. But a partnership in the foundry is what he needs.'

I looked desperately at my mother. Rescue us, my eyes pleaded.

She responded determinedly. 'Well, my husband will be expecting his tea.' She got up, thanked Mrs Grenville and smiled at Harry. 'Where have you hidden my coat and hat, Harry?'

He brought her coat and gallantly helped her put it on.

'Thank you,' she said and patted his hand. 'He's a good boy, Mrs Grenville, a good boy. We're glad he's well again.'

She bustled out and I trailed behind her with Winnie. Harry took my arm. 'See you soon, Judith?' he asked anxiously.

'Of course,' I said.

When we reached home my mother said, 'I could have bitten out my tongue, Judith. I never thought until I saw her face. She thought I was suggesting that she should come to the soup kitchen for a meal. Mind you, she looks as if she needs it. But some can't bear to think they've come down in the world. What a poor soul she is to plague herself with pretensions and expectations so unreal. To be so afraid. I don't know how much support that Harry gives her.'

'I think he gives her all his earnings from the foundry,' I said, but he may keep some of the few bob he earns at the dance halls.'

She shook her head. 'That house, Judith. Isn't it wonderful to have the clean sea air of the hulk?'

My boss was in a bad temper. He was in a fix. He grumbled, 'It's all these free loaders, Judith. I expected a few, the odd free meal until they got on their feet again, but more come every day. It's a bloody deluge. Chew It is packed and they all demand what others had yesterday and the day before and the day before that. Do they think I own the Bank of England? Neimeyer in disguise or something? Jesus Christ, Judith, I'm going broke. You'll have to tell them. Nothing on tick. Payment first, food after.'

I looked at him disbelievingly. 'I can't do that.'

'You'll have to.'

'You expect me to tell them that while you hide in the kitchen?'

'Don't be impertinent with me, Judith. You'll judge differently when we close down and your job as well as mine is up the spout.'

He wheedled, 'You're a good girl, Judith. They'll take it from you. I don't want any violence.' He looked shamefaced. 'I thought I was being generous.' His round babyish face looked so miserable that I felt sorry for him.

'You were, but a lot of your customers are single blokes and there's no government help for them.'

'And there'll be none for me,' he said flatly.

I hadn't realised that he was unmarried. All these years the Chew It and Spew It must have been his family, his link with our community. I was trapped, caught between my own fear of losing my job, his despair at losing the Chew It and Spew It, and my horror at turning away hungry men. I felt all my earlier disgruntled surliness return. Once again circumstances beyond my control were forcing me to do something I hated, and depriving me of choice. In a voice tight with anger and frustration I said, 'Very well.'

'You're a good girl,' he pleaded.

'No,' I snarled, 'don't say anything more. You know and I know that I have little choice.'

'You needn't be so rude about it,' he grumped. 'It's not my fault.'

'And it's not my fault that you're making me bell the cat.'

Usually so hail-fellow-well-met, he was silent and his fat body looked crumpled and shaken.

But of course it wasn't his fault that the Chew It might close, and it wasn't my fault. Whose fault was it then? I asked myself angrily.

I dreaded the lunchtime rush of customers. As I diced vegetables in the kitchen I debated with myself how to say the dreadful words. Should I be cheery and casual and try to carry it off with a bright confident we'll-have-no-nonsense smile, or should I be humble and apologetic but firm in the face of their distress? Would it be better to be cold and distant or warm and sympathetic with their plight? The anticipation was agony.

At twelve o'clock a large group of customers arrived. I stationed myself near the entrance to the cafe, stiff with anxiety, prepared to tell them one at a time, but they brushed past me with a quick nod or brief g'day and rushed to find seats, jostling each other for a perch. Confused I didn't know what to do. Silent and miserable I just stood as if rooted to the spot by the door.

The drone of noise escalated. Then someone called, 'Hey, Judith, what about a meal?' Cheerfully they chorused, 'We're waiting, Judith, just waiting for you.'

I cleared my throat but no sounds came out. Their cheer defeated me. They were mostly gaunt men but in their shabby suits and ubiquitous felt hats they asserted what dignity was left to them. My voice was stuck. I swallowed as if trying to get rid of a fish bone. It was all too much. I couldn't tell them. I burst into tears and stood sobbing, a helpless and hapless figure in the doorway.

An abrupt silence fell on the room. Someone I didn't know jumped up and came to me. 'Why, girlie, what is it? What has so distressed you?'

A murmur of sympathy ran round the room and I saw them look puzzled and questioning at each other.

'Was it our chiacking, girlie?' my helper asked. 'We meant nothing by it.'

I shook my head. Between sobs I got some of it out. 'It's the cafe.'

'Closing,' someone said, in a flat dispirited voice and they all sighed.

There was a faint intangible movement in the room as if everyone having dispensed with hope now resettled themselves resignedly in their seats.

'Yes and no,' I struggled to find the right words. There weren't any. They waited.

'Spit it out, Judith,' one said at last.

'We can take it,' another added.

'Don't be scared.' This was perceptive.

Brutality took the place of tact. 'The meals are no longer free.' At last I had said the fearful words. They had come out very quietly as if subconsciously I hoped that they would have faded to disappearance and nobody would hear.

The young worker who stood at my side handed me a large white handkerchief. It was thin with a couple of holes but spotlessly clean. Some woman had made a Herculean effort to see that her son or husband went out to find work with a cleanly laundered and ironed white handkerchief. Pity for the little efforts people made to keep their pride overwhelmed me and with a mumbled apology to the whole room I stumbled from the cafe into the kitchen.

'You tell them,' I stormed at my boss. 'You tell them. I'm going home. I don't care if your whole bloody cafe collapses about your ears. It's your cafe. You face them.'

He ran after me as I reached the back door. 'Please, Judith.'

Still crying, I shook my head.

He said, helplessly, 'Tomorrow. Come to work a little later tomorrow. That'll be OK. I can manage on my own.'

I took no notice of the self-pity in his voice.

I slept late next morning and by the time I rose my mother had left for the soup kitchen. Preparations for the midday meal distribution began before eight o'clock.

Our hulk had not been bunkered beside any steamer in the Outer Harbor for several weeks. Winchmen were not needed so every morning my father went to the Waterside Workers' pick-up point at the junction of Lipson and Nile streets, to see if he could fluke a day's loading work on the wharf. The pick-up was an insecure haphazard arrangement for hiring wharf labourers but at best it might give him a full day's work.

Now rumours flew around the Port that instead of the single morning pick-up there might be a change of regulation to allow for two pick-ups, one in the morning, one at midday. I regularly heard angry talk between my father and his friends that this was the thin end of the wedge, a ploy by ship owners to reduce wages even further. How could men who lived at a distance from the Port attend two pick-ups? Unless they had bicycles they couldn't go home between them, perhaps to do a bit of gardening, and waiting around brought in only a small amount of appearance money.

The pick-up point was now dubbed 'Poverty Corner' and in the smouldering discontent around me I heard the rumblings of rebellion.

Fear of changes that worsened their working conditions left everyone on edge and my father, wretched and helpless in the face of what was happening to him, frequently snarled at my mother. She urged me to be patient because it wasn't his fault and he needed to let off steam. But I resented his constant spleen. Too often he made her the butt of his anxiety.

When, in a petty taunt, he yelled at her to buy herself some new clothes because she was getting to look like an old hag, I exploded. 'Then bring some money home yourself, you old bastard,' I stormed at him. 'My mother's doing her best. New clothes! How the hell can she afford new clothes? Have you noticed that now she has to put cardboard in her shoes because the soles are so thin? And that she comes home exhausted to prepare you a meal because she has to walk home from the soup kitchen? Soon only the soup kitchen will keep us alive.'

His face had crumpled and for the first time in my life I saw my father weep.

'Enough, Judith,' my mother said sharply, 'enough.' And she put her arms about my father and led him into their cabin.

Overcome with guilt and shame I stood helplessly on my own, aware suddenly that in their marriage my parents were an entity and that between them was a bond I would never understand. In this situation I was merely a beloved outsider. As I took a chair and sat on deck in the morning sun I reflected on this.

My boss at the Chew It could wait for me. My days there were already numbered. We both knew this but in the time left he was now dependent on me. For the small petty ways he had cheated me over my wages I could now have my revenge. He could wait. Wait and wonder whether I might turn up to work at all.

I settled myself more comfortably in my chair. To both fore

and aft of the hulk a row of tugboats and steamers nose-to-stern groaned and sighed against their moorings. In the gentle swell they sidled against their ropes and rubbed against each other, creaking. An occasional gasp of black smoke from a steamer funnel ballooned into the air and dispersed with a filmy greyness. Early sunlight glittered on the warehouse walls but sent long shadows across the wharf.

On our banana boat – I smiled as I remembered Harry and the dead marines – three cormorants sat upright, immobile as pieces of charred wood. Two silver gulls swooped and squarked in a dog fight above me. They settled themselves on the deck, but apparently too close for comfort one lowered himself aggressively, jutted his beak and darted wrathfully at the other. His unwanted companion took off with a rebellious squawk, circled low over the hulk and then returned to a safer perch further along the deck. The first aggressor resumed a jaunty pose, strutted and muttered his winner's satisfaction and then fell into a quiet dream, resting on one leg. What it had all been about, goodness knows.

I returned to my cabin, collected my drawing pad and pencils and sat again to happily occupy myself drawing the scenes around me. The next hour I spent working and my worries fell away. What a joy my life would be if I could do this every day, even perhaps make some money out of it to justify enjoying myself.

At last I put on my work clothes and wandered along the wharf peering at some of the unfamiliar names of the trading ships. The *Milora* was being loaded with wheat but the usually busy wharf was ominously quiet. I crossed the Port Road into Lipson Street and passed 'Poverty Corner', but there was no one there. I went on by a couple of the hotels.

Men standing outside talked loudly in groups. They gesticulated angrily. I caught the word 'Beeby' and someone spat disgustedly. Someone added, 'Justice Beeby' to a ribald round of contemptuous comments. 'Justice? What a fuckin' joke that is.

And he's a Labor man, mates. So he tells us. On the side of the workers. My fat arse.'

They did not see me as I strolled, taking the long way round to my job. Their anger lay like a scar on my previous enjoyment of the bright morning. At the Labour Exchange I saw more men, hundreds of them, patiently queuing.

My boss greeted me with effusive pleasure. The experiences of my walk had chastened me. We were all in this together. I made no excuses for my lateness but immediately got to work to help him with preparations for lunch. He fussed anxiously over how much we should prepare. He didn't suppose that he'd have a lot of customers. He didn't want to waste food but on the other hand he didn't want to run out. I did what he instructed me to do and didn't give him any lip.

Lunchtime was very quiet. There wouldn't have been a dozen customers, far quieter than my boss had expected.

'Perhaps tomorrow,' he said, 'tomorrow things will have settled down. They're angry today. Tomorrow they'll be calmer.'

I didn't have the heart to tell him that it was not a matter of calmness but of money. Besides, when he stopped deceiving himself, he would know this.

Nathan's arrival startled me. I hadn't seen him for weeks. He had never come for free meals. He looked neat, his shabby clothes clean and pressed, his hair cut, his chin shaved. His shoes had been shined but I had no way of knowing whether he, too, put cardboard in their thinning soles. Clearly Miss Abigail and Miss Adelaide were devoted to his appearance.

When I had asked Harry about his whereabouts he said that Nathan and Jock were busy organising a local branch of the Communist Party. Soon it would be a real political party with membership books and membership fees. He expected that he would join.

'Will there be many others?' I had asked.

'About thirty, I think.' Harry's casual response failed to conceal his excited anticipation.

I was sceptical. 'I suppose it will grow.'

'Certainly. Look about you, Judith. It's bound to grow.'

But I knew the waterside workers my father worked alongside. They scoffed at the Bolshies. A lot of hot air was the usual derisive and dismissive comment. All talk. Intellectuals they call themselves. Like to see them down here lumping a hundred and eighty pound bag of wheat or coal. And they want to tell us what our lives are all about.

Now I said cheerfully, 'Hello, Nathan. Should I get you a bun and a cup of tea?' I grinned at him, recalling his earlier visits to the Chew It.

He had arrived in a hurry, hotfoot with impatience, but now, as he met me, he hesitated, awkward and diffident. Something was afoot and I waited expectantly. From experience I knew that nothing stirred Nathan except some political event so shortly, when he relaxed, I would hear the momentous news. Behind his thick spectacles his eyes shone and he clutched a newspaper in nervous hands. Had some disaster occurred?

Frightened, I looked from the newspaper to his face and back again to the newspaper. Whatever I didn't want to read about was there in it. I took a deep breath. 'You'd better tell me, Nathan.' I tried a little joke. 'The Bank of England's gone bust? Australia's bankrupt? The army has taken over the government? Tell me if there's anything worse than that.'

He flushed. 'No, of course not. Not bad news at all. In fact ...' he thrust the paper at me, 'see for yourself.'

I took it gingerly. Sometimes news can bite; sometimes I didn't want to read it. I looked down at the open page and through a miasma of anxiety saw my cartoon of Harry in Victoria Square looking back at me.

It was a copy of the *Barrier Daily Truth* Nathan had brought me. They had published my cartoon on the second page along-side an article headed POLICE BASH UNEMPLOYED. Stunned I reached for a chair and sat down. I seemed unable to shift my eyes from it. It was mine but publicly displayed. I felt it was the work of a stranger.

'It's good, Judith.' Nathan had at last relaxed onto a chair beside me. 'I didn't know you could do this sort of thing. On the way here I passed Harry at the Labour Exchange and showed it to him. He said you had always done drawings and had a lot of them.'

'Yes,' I said. 'What's Harry doing at the Labour Exchange?'

'The foundry has reduced his hours. He only gets work now for one week in two. It's only a matter of time.'

'Did he say anything about my cartoon?'

Nathan hesitated and looked embarrassed. I knew that Harry had said nothing. Now I was irritated that Nathan had shown my work to Harry pre-empting my triumph. I was also hurt that Nathan, not Harry, had told me about his job worries. Recently I had felt that the sad afternoon tea had erected a barrier between us. He didn't want our pity. He felt humiliated by it. The bright face he showed us was at times a mask to hide his misery and discontent. Now presumably he couldn't bear having to tell me that he might be jobless.

I sighed to myself. We'd all be jobless soon. We couldn't afford the niceties of hurt pride that Harry had learned from his mother. Maybe he needed the Communist Party to give him an outlet.

Nathan interrupted my thoughts. He was saying earnestly, 'I work on the *Despatch* you know, Judith. I'm their chief compositor. They should take some of your work.'

'The *Despatch*? Not likely, Nathan. With your political views I don't know how you can work for them; why they employ you.'

The *Despatch* was an imposing Gothic blue-stone building in Lipson Street and I was always cynically amused to read the Latin insignia over the entrance. Inscribed in a semi-circle from which radiated fake sunrays was the masthead inscription *Tantum eruditi sunt liberi*. I knew that this meant 'only the educated are free'. Joe Pulham had told me it came from the Greek philosopher Epictetus. I regularly jibed at Nathan that it peddled propaganda, not education.

'Why do you put up with its hypocrisy?' I asked.

He shrugged. 'Why do they employ me? Best man for the job. They put up with my politics and I put up with theirs. I guess that's how a good society should be run.' He tapped my cartoon. 'Not like this, with police bashing people for their opinions. When you do some more cartoons let me have them and I'll use my influence. Generally newspapers like controversial cartoons. They help sales. Look at Will Dyson. Even *Punch* took his cartoons.'

I thanked him. I couldn't make him out. While talking about his work he was assertive and confident. A few minutes earlier he had looked as if his body, and there wasn't much of it, was some sort of heavy encumbrance he didn't know where to put down.

When he had gone I still sat marvelling at my cartoon, now actually printed in a newspaper. Eventually I returned to the kitchen. No matter how jubilant I felt, the dishes would have to be washed and dried.

'That your Bolshie friend?' my boss asked.

'Yes, I suppose.'

'He was in here some years back.'

'Yes.'

'Been seeing a lot of him?'

'Some.'

'He's got tickets on you, has he?'

'No, of course not.' His interrogation irritated me.

He sniggered. 'No, of course not,' he mimicked me. 'I'd know that panting eager look anywhere.'

'It's not like that.' I was annoyed. 'He brought me this.' And on an impulse I showed him my cartoon.

125

'Jesus,' he said, 'you have got hidden talents. Who'd have thought? You could knock me down with a feather. A second Will Dyson.'

I showed my surprise. His knowledge was unexpected.

'Think I'm an ignorant bastard, just because I run the Chew It? And I know you all call it the Chew It and Spew It. Doesn't worry me. Not stupid, Judith. Just uneducated. But I know a thing or two you mightn't for all that. Don't know how much longer we'll be able to stay open. Got any other prospects?'

I shook my head and clutched the newspaper.

He grimaced. 'You hang on to it. You may have a future there.'

Part 2

Waterside Warfare

IN THE END it wasn't a difficult decision to make. Shortly I would be unemployed. There were no work prospects for me. Clearly I had some talent and it was sensible to develop it.

I had not apologised to my father for my harsh abuse and he hadn't indicated in any way that he blamed me for it. But he was more affectionate and considerate with my mother and she was tenderer with him. He gave me his blessing and a rare kiss.

I dressed in my one good dress, a chemise that came below my knees. It was factory made. Waistless, it looked like a nightie but it was the fashion. Amongst other women I might look unattractive but not odd.

I took the train into the city and made my way along North Terrace to the imposing three-storey Exhibition Building with its ivy-clad walls and square turreted tower. It was the School of Design and Painting. I searched nervously for the entrance. My appointment with the principal was at two o'clock and in my anxiety I had arrived half an hour early. I found the office, was shown a hard-backed wooden chair, and instructed to wait.

The entrance hall was high ceilinged, painted an off-white colour, cavernous and smelt cold. I was used to the luminosity of light on the hulk. There were paintings on the walls but they looked rather old and faded.

At two o'clock a door to my right opened and a middle-aged woman, in a dress to her ankles, bustled out. She wore spectacles on the end of her nose and peered over them at me. 'Miss Larsen?' she questioned in a deep musical voice.

I nodded and got up.

'Then come in, my dear. So sorry to have kept you waiting. Have you eaten?'

I nodded again.

'Of course you haven't. You've come from the Port, haven't you? My assent didn't seem necessary.

'Ella,' she called over her shoulder to the young woman typing in the office, 'Ella, please make us a cup of tea and some biscuits would be nice.'

She urged me ahead of her into her room. Unlike the corridor it was bright from light flowing through the window that over-looked North Terrace. It was an untidy attractive room. Papers lay higgledy-piggledy on a large desk; on the walls were pinned dozens of unframed drawings and small bright jewels of paint-ings. She drew forward a chair so that I sat opposite her at the desk. Carelessly she shoved the papers to one side. A few fell on the floor. Instinctively I bent to retrieve them for her.

'Leave them,' she said. 'Not important. I'll pick them up later. We are all at sixes and sevens at the minute because Miss Armitage has retired.'

I looked blank.

'Miss Letitia Armitage. She has been our painting mistress for twenty-six years, an inspiration to us all, particularly the students. We have just held a farewell function for her and must now get down to the very difficult task of running the place without her.' She looked quizzically at me over her glasses. Her eyes were large, a little protuberant but exceptionally kind.

'They say no one is indispensable, but as we try to sort out who will follow her, and that's a daunting task, I wonder.'

The tea arrived and a plate of biscuits. She poured me a cup and handed me the biscuits. 'Things are bad at the Port?'

'Yes,' I said. 'Very bad.'

'Have you work?'

'No. I had work but the cafe is closing.'

'So much closed,' she said, shaking her head. 'So much. Some of our students arrive looking so pale and washed out that we have to ask if they have eaten. Please help yourself to the biscuits.'

I wondered if I, too, looked pale and washed out.

'So you want to enrol here, Miss Larsen?'

I nodded and she looked amused.

'You can speak to me, Miss Larsen.'

I blushed and she laughed. 'This is not an interrogation. I have here some of your work.'

'Yes. You requested it with my application.'

'It shows a lot of promise, Miss Larsen, but it is of a particular style. What is it you want to achieve here?'

'I want to be a political cartoonist.'

She raised her eyebrows.

'Like Goya and Will Dyson,' I said.

'Goya,' she said sharply, 'was a lot more than a political cartoonist and Dyson, our home grown genius he may be, and champion of the down-trodden, but he has always had to struggle with his draughtsmanship, the outcome I would think of having no formal art training.

'Some critics have accused him of not being a natural draughtsman.' She grimaced. 'Who is? These things have to be learned. It's only sloppy to assume that natural will do. It rarely does. The great artists base their work on solid learned principles and that is what we teach here.'

I was humbled by the certainty with which she spoke of my two heroes. 'Then, can you teach me?'

'No.' She smiled kindly at me. 'I can't. My forte is china painting and I'm quite certain that won't interest you.'

I said nothing, for to agree with her would sound rude and to falsely praise china painting would appear to be currying favour. I think she understood my silence.

'Most of our classes are combination lessons in drawing and painting and you'll benefit from broadening your skills.

'You'll notice that most of our teachers are women. We're very proud of that. And,' she added, assessing my plain factory-made clothes, 'we don't just cater for rich bored young ladies who like to dabble. You'll find most of our students are as dedicated and hard working as our teachers.'

Once again she thumbed through my work, then looked at me thoughtfully. 'I think Miss Taylor will suit you. Her name is Stella Mary Taylor but she likes to be called Marie and if you manage to give it a French intonation she'll be tickled pink. She spent several years in Paris before the war and has exhibited at the Salon de la Societe des Artistes Francais. In her life classes she insists on nude models. You won't mind that will you?'

I shook my head.

'She's a very skilled and dedicated artist. She has kept herself alive for years working in a flower shop. She has imbibed a revolutionary bent, presumably from her French experiences. I think you'll do well together. Her father is a wealthy grazier but she likes her independence. I fear that her work in the florist's may finish soon. People can't afford flowers in a depression. However,' she sighed a little sadly and then smiled at me, 'flowers will still grow despite what we humans do to each other and whether we are able to sell or buy them doesn't matter to them. They will always be there to delight us and that's a great comfort, Miss Larsen.'

My classes were only on a Tuesday and Thursday so when I was not there I helped my mother in the soup kitchen. I grew used to the queues of women and children and some men waiting quietly both in and outside the Salvation Army hall.

Mrs Danley and I would fill the boilers with hot soup from iron cauldrons bubbling on the antique wood-burning stove in the Salvos' kitchen. We would carry them panting into the hall. Then we would struggle to lift them onto the tables. We had found that if we put them on the floor the constant bending to fill the ladles and then the receptacles hurt our backs. So did the lifting, so we were between Scylla and Charybdis. The boilers had handles but the heat and weight made our task arduous. Because I was young and Mrs Danley was a massive muscular woman the task was allotted to us. Until Herbie arrived.

Herbie had started to come every day for his meagre midday meal of soup and bread. He was a beanpole of a man with thin greying hair that hung over his frayed collar and baggy pants held up by a length of string. His age was indeterminate but I had noticed that with many of the unemployed men it was difficult to judge how old they might be. It was as if poverty had interrupted the normal timeline of their lives. He might have been thirty or he might have been fifty.

He watched Mrs Danley and I struggle with the boiler. 'Too heavy for you, missus,' he said, 'and for you, girlie.

'Hey, Perce,' he yelled down the queue, 'give us a hand here. Need some help for the ladies.'

Perce lumbered out. He was a good-natured but slow-witted hunk of a man with arms like legs of mutton. Herbie and Perce took over the job of lifting the boilers. As they heaved them onto the tables three cheers often went up from the waiting queue and there was the occasional 'Good on yer, mates'. Perce flushed with pleasure at this praise and Herbie looked satisfied.

When it was their turn to have their billies filled we always gave them an extra helping. No one complained at this special treatment, at least I never heard any resentful comments. It was more often 'Poor old Herbie' – a generous and grateful sympathy.

Once I asked around where Herbie lived. There were shrugs. 'In the camp by the Torrens River' was the general opinion 'with the other unemployed blokes.' I had seen the camp. It was a collection of makeshift lean-tos, made of bits of wood, cardboard, old sacks, tin and canvas. There was a small bricked-in area for a fire and a few buckets for carrying water from the river. I had made drawings of it and captioned them *The working man's paradise* and sent them to the *Despatch* where Nathan worked. He had offered to try to place my cartoons.

One Monday a woman came in to the hall with two small children, a frightened boy of about six and a silent pale little girl of about four. Their mother, anxious and nervous, carried only a small saucepan, hardly enough for one meal, let alone sufficient for a family. One side of her face was stained by a purpling-greenish bruise. The hand that held the saucepan shook.

Immediately Herbie went to her side. 'Been beating you up again, missus?'

She nodded. Tears ran down her face and she clutched her daughter's hand. The little boy stood silent and stiff. Herbie took her pathetic saucepan. 'We can do better than that,' he said loudly. 'We can do better than this, can't we, Mrs Larsen?' he shouted across the hall and waved the saucepan above his head. The woman cringed, embarrassed, but Herbie saw no shame in it. He marshalled her and the children to the front of the queue. Everyone shuffled back and made room for them.

My mother found a good-sized saucepan with a lid and Herbie ladled the soup into it up to its brim. Then he squashed on the lid. Liquid squelched down its sides forming a messy glutenous patch on the table. Mrs Danley, supervising the distribution, sighed but said nothing. She went out into the kitchen and returned with a bowl of water and a cloth to mop up the mess. No one would think of reproaching Herbie. My mother and her friends had a secret pact to tolerate him whatever minor inconveniences he caused.

In triumph Herbie handed the dripping saucepan to the woman. 'There you are, Mrs Blighty.'

His eyes were caught by the pale still children. 'Milk,' he said, 'they need milk. We need milk for the children,' he ordered me loudly. 'They need to take some milk home.' He patted them on their heads. 'Miss Judith will see to that.'

I hurried to the kitchen, amused to be running at his bidding, searched for and found an empty bottle. I washed it and rinsed it in hot water always boiling in an iron kettle on the stove. That day I was in charge of milk distribution for the children. 'Our battle against rickets' my mother had forcefully persuaded the local dairy farmers. It was skim milk, not wanted after the cream was removed, and usually sold to pig farmers for a pittance. My mother cadged it for the children, shaming the dairy farmers into forfeiting the few pence they received if they sold it.

Herbie led the family out the door. 'I'll be back later,' he called over his shoulder. 'Perce, you get some other bloke to help lift the boilers. I have to see Mrs Blighty home and have a talk to her husband.'

Having organised his foot soldiers, he went out. A couple in the queue laughed and although not a hearty laugh it was good to hear. Perce was chiacked. 'Got yer orders, Perce? Jump to it.' Perce flushed again but looked proud. Someone said, 'That's Herbie all right'. Another, 'He'll straighten that Blighty bastard out.' And a third, 'Far too quick with his fists.'

That same day Harry bounced in to the hall. I hadn't seen him for several weeks and, as I had been so busy coping with my own affairs, had not met with Winnie to hear news of him.

As if we had met only yesterday he bounded up to me and gave me a bear-like hug. 'How do, Comrade Judith?' His cheer was genuine, unforced and unapologetic. I wanted to be annoyed at his neglect and appear remote and hurt but my mother's warm welcome undermined my intentions.

'Where have you been, Harry? We've missed you.'

'The foundry closed, Mrs L. Jobless now, isn't it great? Hated that place. The smell of quicklime made me gag.' Despite his bravado he was shocked.

'The Chew It closed, too,' I said. He wasn't entitled to have the shock of joblessness on his own.

'Well, you'll be as overjoyed as me. You hated that place.'

'It was a job,' I said tightly, 'and money. How are you managing? And your mother?'

'In a minute,' he said cheerfully, 'I'm going to find a place in the queue and take her home a bowl of your delicious soup. See, I've brought my billy.'

'Harry!' I was horrified. 'Your mother. How will she— ?'

'Judith,' he interrupted me, the humour fallen away, 'Judith, we're all in this together, and the sooner we realise that we are working-class people, all with the same working-class problems, the better it will be.'

'Better for whom?' I asked tartly. 'You've been talking to Nathan.'

'And why not?' He was defensive.

Yes, I thought, why not? Nathan's ideas made some sense.

'So, comrade Judith, how about a bit of soup for a poor working-class boy?'

But there was a certain bitter twist to his mouth, an ironic gleam in his eye, which made me wonder if he had managed to grow into the new clothes he had put on. 'Don't call me comrade,' I was peevish. 'It sounds false. You don't have to prove your Bolshie leanings to me.' He grinned.

'Did you see my cartoon in the Broken Hill paper?'

'Of course. Nathan showed me. He was very impressed.'

'And you, Harry?'

He shifted uncomfortably. 'It was me, wasn't it?'

'Yes.'

'I hate to remember, just hate it, Judith. But Nathan said I should be proud and that you're a genius and would be a great help to the Communist Party.'

'So?' I questioned. I waited expectantly.

'I thought it was quite good.'

'Thank you, Harry,' I mocked. 'I'm glad that you and Nathan approved of it.'

He grinned at me again and the few weeks in which he hadn't contacted me were forgotten.

'How are you living, Harry?'

He was serious. 'I play the piano at a couple of dance halls at The Semaphore. They pay me six shillings a night until midnight. After that the dancers have to take up a collection for me to go on playing. Usually that brings in another couple of bob. I tried the Labour Exchange but there's no foundry work and as you know they ballot the few jobs that are around.

'It's pretty humiliating, hanging about to see if your name gets drawn out of a hat. The blokes hate it. Some of them pretend they don't care. They strut around blowing out their chests, telling everyone that today their luck is in, and then they switch their mood and become cynical. How fortunate they'll be to get one day's work and be able to return for another good luck ballot. It's all bravado and when they don't get picked they look crumpled and defeated. Some of them just leave, give up, they can't stand it any more.

'At least I earn something piano playing. Most of the other poor bastards can't do anything except a bit of manual work. Nathan's right, Judith. The way our society runs just stinks. And you, what are you doing? Working here all the time? Has your dad any work?'

'A little,' I said. 'Winchmen are more in demand than lumpers. There are fewer of them. But it's hard because not many ships are coming in and he's needed less.'

'Then you're here every day?'

'No, I've enrolled at the School of Design and Art. I'm studying drawing.'

His eyes widened. 'You have?'

'Yes, I have, Harry.'

'Oh, Judith, lucky you. Do they teach tap dancing at this art place?'

I laughed, but was uncomfortable. There was envy in his voice and I didn't know how to respond to it. 'I don't think so,' I said. 'It's not a school of dance.'

He recovered himself and his normal generosity. 'Good luck to you, Judith. I guess I'll have to wait until we have a communist state and they pay me to learn to dance.'

His longing was so real that I couldn't laugh at him and I felt both guilty and resentful at his response to what was for me such a minor opportunity that might never lead anywhere.

When he left I went into the kitchen to help wash the boilers, cauldrons, saucepans and ladles we had used. I thought of Herbie and his uncomplicated generosity. There were days when he was a little overpowering and we had to grit our teeth. Sometimes he would patrol up and down the line pushing people into a more orderly row, or he collected a child who had strayed, admonishing them to return to their parents and not get lost, although there was little likelihood of that in the enclosed hall. Sometimes he took it upon himself to greet or welcome people. For the elderly or pregnant he fussed around and found a stool or old wooden chair. If anyone, particularly a woman, looked exhausted he pottered into the kitchen and made a pot of tea in an old tin teapot. Then he carried the cup out to her. For all these small services and his stalwart help, Herbie was loved.

My mother dug out an old flannelette shirt of my father's and carefully re-washed and pressed it. She also found an old cardigan and woollen socks. When she gave them to Herbie with a careless, 'You might find some use for these' he took them gingerly, turned them over, and examined the cloth carefully as if he were buying from the best store in town. At last he looked up at my mother.

'Thanks, missus,' he said, 'they'll come in handy,' but she swore that not long afterwards she recognised the shirt on a frail young man new to the soup kitchen. He coughed and looked consumptive. She never mentioned the matter to Herbie but she wondered to me where the cardigan and socks might have gone. Certainly Herbie never wore them.

'Gone to a good home,' I said.

She laughed. 'It will certainly be a needy one.'

I thought about Herbie and my thoughts about his kindness were like an oasis for me because day after day there was little but anger and bitterness at the Port.

In a few days Justice Beeby's ruling about the new award for the waterside workers was to be brought down in the Arbitration Court. The papers were full of it. The *Despatch* and the *Register* trumpeted the claims of the ship owners for lower wages. Profits had fallen. Fewer ships entered the harbour. To save the country, workers now had to do 'a fair day's work for a fair day's pay'.

On my walk to and from the soup kitchen I passed knots of men arguing, gesticulating, shouting, thumping rolled-up copies of the newspapers on their hands, boiling with indignation that they were accused of not doing a fair day's work and blamed for the rotten state of the country.

But beneath the defiance was fear. I felt it at the soup kitchen where desperate women muttered the word 'strike' to each other and shuddered as if it were a death knell. The few days' work their husbands now got was better than nothing. Anxiety swept like a contagion through the community. Everybody waited and the waiting was agony. My father went about grim faced.

'If Beeby sides with the ship owners for a two pick-up will you strike?' I asked him.

'It's a last resort,' he said heavily. 'Strikes are pretty hopeless in bad times. The union is short of funds. We can't support people.

None of us want it but there's a point beyond which men can't be squeezed. Beeby is a labour man. We can only hope he sees our plight.'

But I knew that his hope did not match his expectation. Whatever Beeby's labour background my father did not trust him. And he was right not to do so, although being proved right wasn't much consolation.

Justice Beeby agreed with the ship owners that two pick-ups for wharf labour, one in the morning and one in the afternoon, would help the economy. Personally I couldn't see the connection but it sounded grand in the headlines, as if by a single stroke of the pen Beeby had saved the country. Now fleets of ships would steam into our ports, more wheat and coal would be loaded, profits would skyrocket.

'My fat arse,' my father said and spat his disgust and disillusionment into the river.

My mother knew it meant a strike and, thinking not only of us but the women coming to the soup kitchen, she prepared and served the tea with a listless hopelessness. My father tried to console her. 'It may not come to a strike, Eve. Our disputes committee will meet with the bosses. Perhaps ...'

'Perhaps, Niels,' she said tiredly.

He jumped up and hugged her. 'Not my brave girl,' he said. 'This is not like you, Eve.'

'Just a bit tired,' she said, an admission that we had never heard before.

It was the sense of betrayal that wounded so deeply. Although there had been little expectation that Beeby would consider the unionists, there had also been a lingering deeply seated faith that a labour man was always a labour man. People felt bereft. There seemed to be no one they could trust.

Shock was the first reaction, followed by disbelief, dismay, disgust and finally fury. Justice Beeby and his rulings could go to hell. When did the Arbitration Court ever help working people? Someone sang, 'We'll hang Judge Beeby from the nearest bloody tree,' and soon everyone was singing it, defiant and belligerent. The police could hardly arrest people for singing but they watched suspiciously. Copies of the *Despatch* and the *Register* were seen shredded and floating in the sea where men had pitched them.

The two pick-up system meant a reduction in wages. Anyone lucky enough to get a day's work on the wharves now only got half a day. Any man who lived a distance from the Port and failed to get work for the first pick-up had to hang around for three hours to try his luck for the second. If that, too, failed he went home with only the pitiful amount of appearance money. This was the final stab in the back for the Port already buffeted by long-term unemployment.

My father was working at the Outer Harbor loading three-bushel bags of wheat on the *Minnipa* when Beeby's decision became law. He arrived home late in the afternoon having trudged the eight miles. 'When we heard,' he said wearily, 'we called a stop work. We were all mad as hell and voted not to return to work. We left the bags of wheat on the wharf and just walked off. I hope the rats get into the whole bloody lot of them. The cockies are no help to us.'

'They're doing it tough, too,' my mother said. 'Wheat prices are down. Some are walking off their farms.'

My father drank his cup of tea, exhausted and dejected. 'So we fight each other and that's how it's likely to be and we'll probably put more energy into that than fighting the bosses. We don't mean to kill the poor bloody cockies while we struggle for ourselves but what else can we do? There'll have to be a strike. They'll have us on starvation wages soon.

'And you know, Eve, they're pushing the situation so they can bring in scabs to take our jobs. It's always been their intention. It's as clear now as the nose on your face. We'll have to compete with starved ignorant Italians and down-and-out Europeans who can't find work in their own country and come here expecting a workers' bloody paradise.'

He laughed bitterly. 'Let's all sing a new hit tune for September 1928: "We'll hang Justice Beeby from the nearest bloody tree".' He slumped off to change his work clothes. He looked haggard and my mother care-worn.

It seemed that now we were all dragging along, one minute gritting our teeth with a determination to survive, the next given to spurts of anger and protest and this emotional roller coaster repeated itself day after day. Just when we felt nothing more awful could happen, it did.

I was in this dispirited mood when, on my way to the soup kitchen, I ran into Nathan outside the Labour Exchange. He greeted me enthusiastically. 'Your cartoon in the *Barrier Daily Truth* is going everywhere, Judith. Everyone is talking about it.'

'Everyone in the Communist Party you mean, Nathan? All thirty of them?'

He looked put out and I felt mean, but I was in no mood for Nathan's fantasies. He had the *Despatch* tucked under his arm.

'Helping capitalists distribute their lousy propaganda are you, Nathan? How can you bear to print their lies?'

He looked at me as if I were some ignorant child who couldn't see past her nose.

'It helps the cause.'

'What cause?'

'Our cause.'

'And how's that?'

'It makes people see exactly what capitalism is and does.'

'No it doesn't. It persuades them that it's OK.'

He pursed his mouth. 'You don't understand, Judith. Through their suffering working people will eventually become enlightened and then we'll be able to lead them to a new order. It happened in Russia. It can happen here.'

'How simple you make it all sound, Nathan. I sent a cartoon to the *Despatch*. Did you see it?'

'No,' he said, 'when?'

'About ten days ago.'

'I'll look for it. We're not indifferent to the plight of the poor.'

We? I thought. Just where did Nathan stand in all of this? In one breath we were the Communist Party, in the next breath we were the *Despatch*.

Excusing myself I left. I was needed at the kitchen. I didn't mention Harry. I didn't feel comfortable talking about Harry to Nathan. I didn't want him to feel that we shared Harry.

At first I had been nervous about attending art classes. It was many years since I had experienced the disciplines of learning. I feared that what I wanted to do would be scoffed at by those better off, better educated and more talented. My humble cartoon in the Broken Hill paper now seemed a nothing, only praised by those who loved me or were like-minded. It could not possibly achieve merit in a wider world. I was a fool to leap from years at the Chew It and Spew It into this new world, unknown and possibly unknowable.

I made it down the passage as wobbly in the legs as a sick person who has lain in bed too long. Perhaps that's what I am, I thought gloomily. I nearly turned tail and ran. My familiar even if confining world suddenly seemed comfortable and safe. I could manage to do my cartoons on my own. I didn't need to subject myself to this. We at the Port were battlers. I could battle alone.

I had turned to flee when the door to the art room opened and a diminutive woman with shingled hair, sparkling eyes, and a mouth too generous for her tiny face, looked at me with startled surprise. One glance and she read my nervous hesitancy.

'Miss Larson? It must be. Miss Judith Larson. I was just coming to look for you. I said to the other girls, we have someone new today and the pauvre enfant, she will be terrified. So here you are and I don't need to search.'

She took my arm and patted my hand. 'I'm not French, you know. Just good down-to-earth Aussie from the bush. But I had many happy years in Paris before the terrible war. You would have been only a petite enfant then.' She shuddered. 'But I like to remember the good times. So you'll forgive my little lapses into French.' With comforting chatter she gently guided me into the art room. After the dimly lit passage it was surprisingly bright. It was also joyfully untidy. There were easels and tables cluttered with objects: a pumpkin, some onions, a blue vase with a chipped fluted top, a couple of old saucepans and a milk can. The smell was a mixture of paint, turpentine and oils. Eight young women in smocks sat in front of easels. They looked up and smiled at me.

'This morning, Miss Larson, I think you should just get to know us and observe, otherwise it is too overwhelming, *n'est-ce pas?*'

At her French a couple of the girls grinned.

'See,' she said, 'they have a little giggle at me.' She dropped her hand on one of the girls' shoulders. 'Ruby thinks I'm a great joke, *n'est-ce pas?*'

Ruby cocked an eye at her and responded in French, *'Pas du tout, M'selle.'*

The class descended into giggles.

'Ruby,' she said, 'is always a little bit cheeky, but in this scruffy head,' and she touched her hair lightly, 'is the mind of an artiste. Ruby can see her whole painting in her head before she even picks up a pencil or paint brush. Do you do this also, Miss Judith? Do your first visualise it in your mind's eye?'

'Why, yes,' I said, surprised at her perception. 'I do. Always.'

She nodded and looked satisfied as if I had confirmed something important.

Miss Taylor, or Miss Marie as she wanted to be called, let me sit peacefully and listen to her advising her students but after an hour or so she took my folio, which lay on the desk at the end of the room with a higgledy-piggledy collection of other work, and came to sit beside me. There was no formality of sitting across the desk from her. She just drew up a chair and sat down. I felt not a student but an equal.

'These are very good,' she said, turning over my drawings.

I had done some additional cartoons, sharpening their meanings with ironic biblical quotations. I had learned from studying Goya's work that there was a depth in the symbols we all recognised.

I had drawn two cartoons of the soup kitchen: one of Mrs Danley ladling soup into the billycan of a single man while a long queue of others waited and disappeared behind him. I had given it the caption *Give us this day our daily bread*.

A second had been prompted by the women's constant fears that one day they'd have no food to give out because the little shops which usually supported the poor had given so much on tick that now they, too, were going broke. Soon the little extra they found to help the soup kitchen would cease.

In this cartoon I drew two women speaking to each other while they held a plate with five loaves and two fishes on it. The people in the queue were turning aside in despair and trudging away. The caption read: *But this is all we have today*.

Miss Marie looked from the cartoons to me and her face was sad. 'It is very hard at the Port?'

I nodded, embarrassingly close to tears. The sympathy of a stranger and the anxiety of the morning choked me. She saw it and was brisk.

'Very good, Miss Judith, and very original. But here and here,' she pointed to parts of my drawing, 'your line, tone, proportion, perspective ... Your natural talent needs refining. We must be able to see the bodies through the clothes. The impact will be greater. You'll benefit from our life classes.'

She asked me about my pencils and paper and gave me advice on what to buy. I looked dismayed. She patted my hand. 'Never mind. These we can supply. We have a fund. A small one to help.'

I flushed. This was charity. We all struggled against it.

She was matter-of-fact. 'These days there are many poor, Miss Judith. You should not feel insulted. It is not your fault. There are other girls here we help. Should art cease because stupid men wreck the country?'

My art classes became a joy, a respite and an escape from the slow boiling anger that consumed those I loved. All those who had refused to comply with the Beeby Award and had walked off the *Mannipa* had been sacked, including my father.

At a loose end Harry had taken to hanging around the soup kitchen. With his youthful ebullience he soon charmed the women, and began to assume, with a certain lordly air, special rights to help. Of course he stood on Herbie's toes, and unable to compete with Harry's glamour, Herbie retired sulky and hurt.

He tried to organise the queue but Harry disorganised it by fiddling jigs on the old second-hand violin he had bought and taught himself to play. The children were delighted and in a circle about him bobbed up and down happily to his tunes. He was like the Pied Piper of Hamlin.

Herbie hovered helplessly, his sense of orderliness threatened. When he tried to lead the children back to their parents he was hurt by their reproach to leave them because they were having fun.

I watched poor desolate Herbie standing confused and unwanted and remonstrated with Harry. He was immediately contrite. 'What a fool I am, Judith. What an insensitive clot.' And he thumped himself on the chest. Immediately he rushed up to Herbie and shook his hand. 'What a great bloke you are, Herbie, and what a wonderful job you do here. I didn't mean to interfere, you know. Now you tell me what I can do to help. You're the boss.'

Mollified and forgiving, Herbie explained to him the routine of the kitchen and the distribution. It wasn't complicated and Harry already knew it but he listened intently to his instructions, murmuring agreement and assurances that he would do exactly as Herbie wanted. Herbie patted him on the back and called him a good boy. Harry gave me his irrepressible wink.

In the afternoon Harry walked back to the hulk with us. We didn't talk about my father's sacking. What was the point of endlessly dredging up our anger so that when we had eventually shovelled a great heap of dirt we could stand around helplessly wondering what to do with it? Nor did we talk about the increasing numbers of people at the soup kitchen and our diminishing sources of food supplies.

The Salvation Army called for help from other churches, in wealthier areas of Adelaide, but now there were many more soup kitchens all struggling for a pitiful supply of leftovers.

It was a sunny afternoon and I took off my hat, pulled up my sleeves and let the warmth seep into my face and arms. Beside me Harry wheeled his bicycle. His shirt sleeves were also rolled up and the fine gold hairs glinted along his arms, a soft fuzz that stirred as the muscles flexed and relaxed. He had fine wrists and long fingered hands with spatulate fingers, what my mother sentimentally called 'pianist's hands'. A few gulls squatting in a row on a rooftop suddenly took off with piercing shrieks, zoomed wildly to and fro, then settled again on the same rooftop. Perhaps they knew what it was all about. Their frenzy seemed meaningless to me. Sparrows jostled for space in a dust hole on the footpath. They fluffed cheerily, companionable and content.

Some new manure from a passing horse and cart steamed thickly on the road. In a minute someone would rush out and shovel it into a bucket, either to dry for fuel or put on their small vegetable patches. The horses could hardly keep up with the demand for manure. Where possible people helped themselves. No one grew flowers now, only vegetables, in any available space. Along the wharf, rows of unemployed men sat with hopeful fishing lines. Boys rode their bicycles to the outskirts of Adelaide and in bush areas trapped or hunted down rabbits. Jock and Bernie occasionally brought us a rabbit and I imagined Bernie's slick silver knife skinning and gutting it.

My thoughts had drifted to the days since my father's sacking. When we reached the hulk my mother made a pot of tea and we sat quietly around the table. She was too tired to talk. The tea was weak. It was the third infusion. She no longer threw out the tea leaves after the first brew but poured them through a sieve, carefully dried them and used them again and again. After the third infusion they were too insipid to re-use and regretfully she threw them away. These small parsimonies wore her out.

She hated collecting our food rations and more often now I went in her place. I was ashamed to bring the inferior food home. She tried not to turn it over and examine it in disgust but the meat was frequently too strong for her liking and the vegetables were rarely fresh. The flour often had the telltale spider webs of weevils and every morning we ate large bowls of oatmeal porridge with treacle. 'Good sustaining food,' my mother said stoutly as she served it and we ate it stolidly and determinedly. There was no point in longing for something tastier.

When my father caught a fish we feasted. Jock and Bernie-Benito dropped in regularly. When they brought a rabbit my mother stewed it with onion and we shared it with them, pleased if only in a small way, to be able to eat with friends. Jock was worried about Bernie-Benito and told my father about it. Bernie was not an Australian citizen.

'The bastards might deport him,' Jock snarled. 'They're hunting down radicals. Say they're an undesirable influence. Let them try to send him back to that murderous thug of a Mussolini.'

He thumped Bernie on the back. 'We'll hide you, won't we, mate?'

Bernie grinned and his fingers strayed towards the knife in his belt.

'Should you carry a knife, Bernie?' I asked suddenly. 'You don't want to give the police excuses.'

He understood the word knife and looked at Jock. Jock raised his eyebrows at me, disbelievingly. He translated. Bernie beamed at me and spoke in Italian. Jock shook his head and chuckled. 'He says not to worry, Miss Judith, it's only for rabbits.' But Bernie and his future added another dimension to our fears.

On this occasion, as we sat round the table, Harry had been unable to find a topic for cheery conversation. He left early and I walked with him to the gangplank. He frowned. 'Does your father pull this up every night?'

'Sometimes.'

'He should do it always. Do you see men skulking along the wharf in the night?'

'Occasionally.'

'They may mean no good, Judith.'

'I know. But, oddly, Harry, they've always been there. Ever since my childhood. Once I saw one of them swim out to the boat for bread my mother threw overboard with the slops. It's a long time ago but I remember because it was the first time I saw someone desperate for food. Now we're all like that.'

He took my hand. 'What time do you finish at art school on Tuesdays and Thursdays?'

'About four.'

'Then I'll meet you there. Maybe we can get some time together that we don't have to share with someone else.'

'I'd like that,' I said. It was true. Our friendship always seemed to be a community one, shared either with Winnie, my mother or father, the people at the soup kitchen, even Nathan.

The following Tuesday Harry waited for me outside the Arts School. I found him leaning against the wall, his bicycle propped beside him. He was humming his favourite tune, 'What'll I do when you are far away and I am blue, what'll I do?'

He came eagerly to meet me. I was leaving with Ruby and several other girls. They recognised the tune, giggled and cast simpering sidelong glances at Harry. He smiled at them, a dazzling animated smile that sweetened his face and lit his eyes. They blushed, entranced, and hesitated, longing for an introduction.

After I had introduced them and they had left with many backward looks and a lot of hand waving, I reproached him for embarrassing me. He laughed. 'You're not ashamed of me, Judith, are you?'

'Only of your conceit, Harry.'

'Ooops,' he said.

'Oh, Harry, you,' I retaliated, mimicking Winnie.

He grinned, pulled my work bag over his shoulder, took my arm and with his free hand wheeled his bike. 'Instead of going straight down North Terrace to the railway station let's go a long way around,' he said. 'I might get to talk to you.'

The streets through which we strolled were new to us and pleasantly strange. Isolated from a throng of people we had never met before and were likely to never meet again, we felt happily marooned. At first our conversation was desultory.

'Are you enjoying art school?' Harry asked.

'Yes, I love it.'

'Have you done any more cartoons?'

'Yes. I hope to sell a couple. We need the money.'

'Who doesn't?' he grunted, but there was no edge to his grumble. Money and troubles were remote from us.

'So you've joined the Communist Party, Harry?'

'Yes.'

'Do you believe in all that?'

He looked at me seriously. 'I think I do, Judith. It makes sense to me. I've read the books Nathan gave me and thought about his ideas. It's a kind of a relief to find some explanation for what is happening. I've been very confused and now a lot of things are clearer and strangely I'm happier, not because I'm better off, but because I understand.'

'Yes,' I said, 'I can see that makes sense. When I was a little girl I asked Joe Pulham about Aristotle.'

'Aristotle?' He was perplexed.

'A Greek philosopher, before Christ.'

'Oh,' he said. 'That's a long time ago. Did they have philosophers then?'

'I think so, at least they had Aristotle. He said that the best way to live was to be moderate.'

Harry looked puzzled. 'I don't know how that would solve anything.'

'No, perhaps not. Maybe he was just giving advice on how to go about things.'

He furrowed his brow, then laughed. 'Perhaps we can share Aristotle with the ship owners who sacked your dad. You should come to a Communist Party meeting again, Judith. You'd enjoy it and maybe find a subject for a cartoon.'

'Like Nathan's sisters? A pair of Medusas.'

He shouted with laughter and several people turned to look at us.

'Shush, Harry.'

'Shush yourself, Judith. When you make me laugh, I'll laugh. I wish Nathan would laugh properly, right from his belly. It's usually a rather constipated snicker or snigger. It makes me uncomfortable.'

'It's probably living with those two sisters. They'd constipate anyone.'

He threatened to chortle again and I squeezed his arm.

'Really, Judith, you're such a card. I suppose you know that Nathan carries a torch for you.'

'I know no such thing, Harry.'

'No such thing,' he imitated me in a prunes and prisms voice.

I recalled my previous boss's comment that Nathan had tickets on me. 'I don't think his sisters like me,' I said.

'Probably not,' he agreed. 'It's hard to know if it's because Nathan idolises you or because his adoration isn't reciprocated.' He looked at me solemnly. 'Either way he can't have you. You're my girl.'

'Really, Harry,' I protested, 'don't be ridiculous. I don't belong to anyone.'

He sang softly, 'You're like a plaintive melody that never sets me free.'

I laughed then. 'Nobody could be less like a plaintive melody than I am, Harry. And now we're nearly at the railway station.'

I took my bag and boarded the train.

'See you on Thursday,' he called after me.

My father had responded with amazing calm and restraint to the news he had been sacked. I think that momentarily he had got beyond anger to a state of cynical detachment where there was comfort in expecting the worst in people and even some humour in being proved right. He shrugged and said it was inevitable but that he worried about my mother. 'She's tired, Judith. I wish she'd ease up on the soup kitchen. There are other women who can help. Even some blokes. It'd keep them out of the pub.' I recalled Herbie and Harry hauling the cauldrons of hot soup and felt comforted by their kindness.

But every morning my mother trudged along Commercial Road to Dale Street and the Salvation Army hall. It was a long trek and she found the return journey after hours of work exhausting. But she wouldn't give it up. 'It's the least I can do,' she persisted doggedly. She found Commercial Road particularly wearing and commented wearily on the unexpected sensation of finding the road congested with busy people seemingly leading a normal life when there was a depression and she was about to meet a large number of people utterly destitute. It was a peculiar shifting from one world into another, as if traipsing out of bright sunshine into darkness. But then she would add, 'Maybe all those busy people on the street have problems we don't know about.' She complained about the difficulties of crossing Black Diamond Corner between Commercial Road and St Vincent Street. There was no help for pedestrians in the congestion and confusion of cars, buses, horses and carts and the wretched dock engines on the rail lines. Their bells were useless. Only that morning she had seen a horse and cart collide with a car. The poor horse, although uninjured, trembled with fright.

'I'm sorry, Eve, that I've lost my job.' He was humble.

She was philosophic. 'Nobody I know has a husband in a job. We're all in the same boat. We've been lucky up to now, but what will happen to our home here on the hulk, Niels?'

I knew that we paid rent to the shipowners but that my father also acted as caretaker of the expensive equipment.

'I don't know,' he said. 'Maybe they'll be glad to let us stay. Everybody remembers the *City of Singapore*.'

The fire on the *City of Singapore* had happened when I was a child but it was burned into my memory, an event both terrible and wildly exciting. Mr and Mrs Danley had been dining with us when the first thunderous explosion rocked our hulk. Momentarily it seemed to jump out of the water and then lurch sideways straining against the mooring ropes. My father leaped to his feet, his chair crashing to the floor and rushed on deck. 'Hell!' he shouted. 'Bloody hell!'

From further along the wharf great balls of fire erupted upwards and outwards to burst asunder in a succession of thunderous explosions. Volcanic heat incinerated the ship. The noise deafened us and we retreated before a searing wind. Firemen with bright metal helmets emerged and receded in the billowing smoke like dancing ghosts. People ran hither and thither panting, shouting, screaming in panic that the fire could spread to other ships.

We watched one fireman caught in an explosion sail like an acrobat into the air and somersault on his head. My mother gasped, 'He'll be killed.' But we heard later that he had survived. His helmet had saved him.

The fire burned for weeks, creeping about the ship, consuming more and more combustibles. Mesmerised I had watched the leaping darting flames that ran like flaming fingers into every little hidey-hole, setting them alight so that, as well as the great fire, there were many smaller feeder fires.

At last the explosions ceased, the fire quietened but still glowed with ugly fervour. When we at last saw the blackened remains a crowd gathered to look and comment, amazed and relieved that the fire had been contained and, of course, conjecturing how it had started, everyone wiser in his opinion than his neighbour. No one had been on board at the time and that was strange. So, of course, there was a suspicion that the shipowners had plotted the fire for insurance. Then someone started a rumour that it had been an anarchist plot and this was taken up in all seriousness.

As we walked back to the hulk my father snorted, 'Poor bloody anarchists. Get the blame for everything. First they're accused of trying to burn down Sydney and now they've come after the *City of Singapore*. God knows why. It's a ridiculous accusation. It's a great cover up for an insurance fraud.'

Now as my mother recalled this event she looked thoughtful. 'They may believe it was arson and in this climate the *City of Singapore* might be a lesson to them, a reminder, a warning that they need a caretaker. Perhaps you could point this out to them, Niels.'

'You mean blame the poor bloody anarchists, throw them to the wolves again?'

My mother looked shamefaced but she laughed. 'It need only be a hint, Niels, an implication, a suggestion.'

It worked. We were permitted to stay on the hulk rent free so long as my father cared for the winching equipment. The letter from the shipowners confirming that he could continue his tenancy was both a relief and an irritation. A final paragraph instructed him, in dictatorial tones, that under no condition was the hulk to be used as a meeting place for any 'nefarious activities'. He chucked the letter on the table. 'Pompous, self-righteous, greedy bastards,' he snarled, his dormant anger fresh again. 'Treat us as little boys, would they, to jump at their bidding. We all know what they're up to. Bringing in cheap labour to work the ships, scabs to work the waterfront. They hold my home over my head as a threat. I'll give them nefarious activities.' And he moved to rip the letter and pitch it in the river.

My mother snatched it. 'It's our security, Niels. At least some sort of insurance.' And she placed it under her recipe books in a drawer.

Up until now I had been shyly tentative about sending my cartoons to newspapers. From childhood I had grown accustomed to my drawing being an escape from anything that disturbed or distressed me: a private world like Alice's garden that once entered would be magically protected.

But Miss Marie subjected me to an outsider's comments and criticisms. She was always tactful, always encouraging, but now my work was no longer a private world. I think she understood my initial reluctance to let in any intruder but gradually she winkled me out of my reticence, and I found myself in happy discussions with her.

However now it was imperative that I earned the right to be at art school. It was no longer a private matter, it was also a family one, and a community one. On the one hand we desperately needed any money that I could make, on the other, Miss Marie encouraged me to believe that the political comment of my cartoons helped people understand what was happening to us.

'Values, Judith,' she explained to me. 'Artists must assert values and the harder times become the harder we must struggle to do this. There is humanity in your cartoons and above everything else we need that now.'

It was an inspiring thought and for a short time I floated with this glorious vision of myself before I bumped back to the ground. Nevertheless, with her faith and the need of my family for the five shillings I might receive if one of my cartoons was accepted, I set about determinedly drawing copies of them.

The *Despatch* had not responded so I sent my drawing of the unemployed camp by the river to the *Sun News Pictorial*. Maybe they would see it as relevant. Surely there would be camps of the unemployed along the Yarra River in Melbourne.

Mrs Danley asked if she could offer my drawing of her in the soup kitchen, with the caption *Give us this day our daily bread*, to the newsletter of her Anglican church. 'I'm quite chuffed by it, Judith,' she said, 'but I want to assure you that it's not vanity that prompts me. It's the editor of the *Despatch*, a devoutly religious man of our church … I'll say no more, Judith. It would be uncharitable of me to point out another's moral discrepancies.' My cartoon appeared in the newsletter and at her request I supplied her with a copy of the two soup kitchen women holding the platter of five loaves and two fishes.

Shortly afterwards I received a letter from the editor of the *Despatch* returning my cartoon of the workers' paradise but requesting permission to re-publish the two cartoons of the soup kitchen. He felt, he said, that they had 'the right moral impact', and would help all the 'good women' at the soup kitchen. There was no doubt, in his mind, that charity to the less fortunate was a Christian duty.

I took this statement of high-mindedness with a grain of salt. I also took, with thankfulness, the ten shillings he sent me for publishing my cartoons – five shillings each. My mother insisted that I keep a little for my fares and paper and pencils but most of it went into buying extra food.

I hadn't expected to receive such notoriety nor the warmth of praise. On the street, at the soup kitchen, outside the Labour Exchange, and on the docks, strangers would stop me, shake my hand, pat me on the shoulder or back, or simply say, 'Good on yer, girlie.' I became 'Our Judith whose cartoons hit the nail on the head every time'. My mother glowed and trod with a lighter step. My father strutted a little, embarrassed but proud. In our miserable world I had brought a little joy to them and I was elated.

Miss Marie said, 'They'll tear themselves apart politically at the Port but they'll all agree with your cartoons and their unity will give them confidence.'

'I think,' I said, retreating from such a grandiose view of me, 'I think, Miss Marie, that that is a little far-fetched. I'm not ready yet to lead them to the Paris barricades.'

She laughed, but her eyes were intense. 'When you do I'll be at your side.'

'No,' I said sharply, 'not again. I was at a brutal demonstration once. The police nearly killed Harry. I saw it all.'

'Ah,' she said, 'your cartoon in the *Barrier Daily Truth*.'

'Yes. And I don't want to do any more such cartoons.'

She looked wise. 'You may have no choice, Judith. Sometimes circumstances drag us in against our wills; compel us.' I shook my head and she did not pursue the discussion.

Of course, our hulk had now become a place for intense political argument. Every decision made by the Waterside Workers' Union Executive, the Disputes Committee, the Trades and Labour Council or Parliament and the shipowners was examined, dissected, disputed and pounded out on our galley table. Jock, Pat and Frank sat around the table shouting at each other while Bernie, lost in the language, watched them with eager eyes. Jock, belligerent and pugilistic as always, declared that now was the time for revolution. The workers were ready, readier than they had ever been to throw over the whole bloody state. The Russians had done it, why not them?

'Och, laddie,' Frank always mimicked his Scottish burr to rile him, 'don't be a daft blithering idiot. A revolution requires guns and all we've got are baling hooks and stones. Have you ever even fired a gun? Besides I don't know whether I like your communist clap-trap.'

Pat, as Irish as Frank, interrupted: 'Even when we had guns in Dublin in 1916 we lost. It's not only guns, it's power and organisation. You've never been in a stoush on the losing side, Jock, have you? You bolshies feed yourselves on theories and dreams. I've had enough of dreams. We lost those in Ireland. I came here for a bit of peace. Poverty I'm used to. I can put up with that, but revolution? You can keep it.'

Jock snarled, 'No guts, the lot of you. If it's not now it'll never be. As unionists we're piss weak. We'll even be forced into a secret ballot over this strike.'

Bernie-Benito, at sea in this altercation, still caught the feeling. At the words 'union' and 'secret' he flicked his finger across his throat. 'Mussolini,' he breathed and began as usual to sing *Avanti popolo.*

'Shut up, Bernie,' Jock said. 'But he's got a point.' He glared at the other three. 'He knows what's in store for us – fascism. It's a creeping death, eh, Benito?'

Bernie again flicked his neck and this time his smile was evil.

'There'll be no secret ballot if I have my way,' my father growled. 'We'll throw the bloody ballot box out the door. Let everyone see who votes for what, who votes to betray his mates. No organisation, union or any other, is going to tell me what to do.'

'Yes,' Frank said. 'On that we all ought to agree. No secrecy. Let the bastards look us in the eye.'

I had gone into the galley to get a glass of water and at the door watched and heard their argument. Jock looked up and saw me. 'There's our Judith,' he said. 'She does bloody good cartoons. Nathan thinks she's a genius. But there's a bit too much charity in them for me. It weakens our cause.'

The strike was inevitable. But despite all the brave talk it was short-lived. There was no cash in the union funds to support members and more and more desperate people turned up at the soup kitchen. Dejected and defeated the unionists straggled back seeking work.

To make sure no further strike action was taken the Bruce Commonwealth Government rushed through the Transport Workers' Bill. Under its provisions my father and others were forced to register to obtain a special licence to work. To make matters worse, these licences could only be obtained from the Volunteer Employment Office set up by the ship owners. It was a ruse, a ploy, for although waterside worker unionists went cap-in-hand to apply for the licences, they were blacklisted. Fuming under the humiliation of what they nicknamed the *Dog Collar Act* the watersiders talked wildly of going on a second strike.

Now no secret was made of the ship owners' intentions to bring in scab labour to work the wharves on lower wages. The government supported the ship owners.

My father and his friends were caught in a vicious pincer because they faced jail under the *Crimes Act* if they went on strike refusing to obey the law.

The arguments at the Port Federation Hall were long and vitriolic. Labor Party supporters bleated that a strike would ruin their chances of being elected. The communists yelled that the Labor Party supporters were bosses' stooges and that capitalism could be overthrown if they only had the courage. The union officials in the Port were afraid of defeat and jail.

Decisions were referred to the Trades and Labour Council in Melbourne. My father snarled that that would be the day when out-of-towners told them what to do. There was no peace in our home as Jock, Pat, Frank, Bernie and my father brawled across the galley table. Occasionally Nathan joined them. He was the quietest of them all but his views only made the rows worse.

I was working on a cartoon when Harry shouted to me from the wharf. I was drawing three figures: a half-starved child, an equally destitute woman, and a man bent double beneath an enormous wheat sack. The woman stood in the doorway of a ramshackle house; the child held an empty bowl. The man bowed under his burden was trudging away from them. On the sack I had inscribed *DEPRESSION*, while the caption read: *Daddy, will they pay you for a fair day's work?* I was arranging and re-arranging the figures, trying to place them in the most telling and dramatic way, endeavouring to convey in a few sparse strokes the destitution of the child and her mother.

Disgust, anger and pity fuelled my drive to create these political cartoons and yet as I worked I felt curiously detached, absorbed entirely in how to make the strongest impact. 'The emotion,' Miss Marie said, 'gives way to artistic discipline, and that creates the emotion, *n'est-ce pas?*' She was consoling me because I had confessed to her that I felt almost self-indulgent for enjoying the process of composition.

So I wasn't thrilled to hear Harry shouting for me and worked on until he bounded up the gangplank and across the deck.

'Judith!' he continued yelling as he burst into the saloon.

I was irritated. 'I'm working, Harry.'

'Have you seen the paper?'

'Yes.'

'Today's *Despatch?*'

'Yes.'

He snatched it off the pile of newspapers on the floor at my feet. They were my material and I searched them for ideas.

'You've seen the advertisement?'

'Yes. I couldn't have missed the advertisement.'

At seven o'clock that morning my father had roared into the galley where my mother was preparing breakfast. He was waving a copy of the *Despatch*, which he flung on the table, his face twisted with outrage and disgust. 'Here, Judith, here's material for your cartoons. We knew this was coming, didn't we? Lying bastards. The word's around the Port – I met a few of the blokes – that a train load of scabs came in last night. They'd lined the tracks and chucked a few rocks. Useless, of course.'

Without waiting for breakfast he had rushed off to the Federation Hall.

I had picked up the paper and my mother and I read it. In large black print the advertisement screamed at us, calling for men to apply for work at Lewis & Reid's Timber Yards. The yard was just north of Robinson's Bridge and No.1 wharf at Port Adelaide. The meaning was clear. Scab labour was to be 'recruited and employed'. As an afterword the *Despatch* made it plain that scab labour ('volunteer free labour') would be introduced the following Friday.

'You're doing a cartoon for it?' Harry looked over my shoulder.

'No, not yet.'

'But it's today's news.'

I sighed. 'They take time, Harry. I have to think. I'm doing one about another issue.'

He looked blank. 'What's more important?'

I sighed again. 'Give me a break, Harry. I can't produce instantaneous cartoons.'

He looked contrite. 'Sorry, Judith. But so much has happened in the last twenty-four hours and you're just sitting here drawing, as calm as can be.'

'Just sitting here drawing,' I mimicked him. 'Believe it or not, I'm trying to keep calm and work. First my father and now you. What else should I be rushing around doing? Go away, Harry.'

He looked nonplussed. 'Well, first, you must know, Judith, they brought the scabs in by train last night.'

'Dad said so.'

'I went to see. There were quite a lot of us. It was like a Wild West show. Armed police at the doorways of the carriages, riding shotgun.'

'Guns?' I was appalled. 'Guns! Here at the Port?'

'Yes, guns. Wouldn't it make a marvellous cartoon, Judith? You could give it an American touch – *I tell you, pard, we'll beat these coyotes yet.*'

I laughed in spite of myself. 'It might work, Harry. I'll think about it. The trouble is that I have an overwhelming number of possibilities to draw. You didn't get involved in any violence? No one was shot at?'

'No. Nathan said we should not get arrested. We have bigger issues to fight for. We must look to the future. We'll know when it is time to make the big sacrifice.'

I looked at him pityingly. 'A sort of deferred martyrdom?' I said sarcastically.

'Really, Judith, I don't know why Nathan still cares for you. You are so nasty about him. After all, he did help you get your cartoons printed in the *Despatch*.'

'He did not, Harry. That was Mrs Danley. Pressure from the Anglican Church, not the communists.'

He was surprised. 'He told me – gave me the impression ...'

'That he had some importance in my life? Some influence?'

'Yes. Well, anyway, I suppose it was a misunderstanding.'

'Sure to have been,' I said.

He grinned. 'You're becoming like your cartoons – too sharp for comfort. Anyway, come on, I've come to get you.'

'Come on where? I'm working, Harry. I told you.'

He took the pencil out of my hand and kissed the top of my head. 'No you're not. You're coming to collect a lot more material. They've got the scabs corralled in the timber yard and the whole town is turning out to have a look.'

'A freak show?'

'If you like. But everyone is mad as hell. A trainload of scabs and that filthy advertisement. Everyone wants to see what those scum look like.'

I was cautious. 'There'll be truckloads of police.'

'We're only going to look.'

'You said that about the free speech rally, Harry. You may be only going to look but others might have different ideas.'

'Oh, come on, Judith. It won't be like Victoria Square. Jock isn't speaking. You'll never have another opportunity like this.' I gave in. 'I'll dink you,' he said.

I followed him to the wharf and, while he held the bicycle, perched myself precariously on its crossbar. 'It won't work, Harry. I'll fall off.'

'Of course you won't. See, my arms will be about you. In a minute, anyway.'

And as I tried to keep my balance by clutching him he leaned towards me and kissed me on the mouth. 'We should get married one day,' he said casually.

'Yes,' I agreed, with equal casualness. 'I'll think about it one day but I have too much to do at present.'

'Thank you, Judith,' he pretended to be rueful. 'It's good to know I'm in the queue.'

'Oh, Harry, you,' I imitated Winnie. We both laughed and I felt comforted that we could always laugh together.

Our journey to the timber yard was perilous and erratic. We lurched across a pothole that nearly tipped us both off. I was laughing hysterically by the time we arrived on the outskirts of the chaotic crowd of men, women and children. Everyone milled around outside the high paling fence, either shoving to see if they could get near enough to jump up and peek over the fence or else eagerly questioning their neighbours as to what they might know or have seen.

Harry pushed through with me and his bicycle and propped it against the fence. 'Climb up, Judith. Have a look.' He supported the bike and a couple of blokes nearby helped me scramble up onto the crossbar. The three of them supported me so I couldn't fall.

'What can you see?' They were avid. 'How many are there? Are they Eyties? Are they scared? Are there police there?'

'A whole crowd of men,' I relayed.

'And?' They were eager.

'They look pretty poor and down and out. And scared.'

'Good. They should be terrified.' My two helpers grunted with satisfaction. 'They'll find there's more to be terrified about tomorrow.'

I was urged to dismount so that others could share my good fortune but Harry demanded his right, as it was his bike. He hung on to the top of the fence. 'There's a few coppers inside,' he reported. 'They're not taking much notice of us.'

'They've been ordered to protect the scabs.' Someone next to us was knowledgeable. 'Full government protection, guaranteed. They've brought in up-country coppers and installed them in the stables down the road, horses on the ground floor, coppers in the loft. Some of them up-country lads have ridden down on their own horses.' He guffawed. 'Country horses will be next to useless in a crowd riot. They'll panic more than the people.'

He spat at his feet. 'That'll be a sight to see. A couple of gunshots and you'll not see them for dust. Police horses! I ask you! As they gallop full tilt down the main street of the Port heading for the hills of home.' He snorted and spat again.

The crowd was growing restless. Inactivity didn't suit them. They needed an outlet for their rage. A couple of blokes wrestled with some palings of the fence trying to tear them loose but they only had their bare hands and it was useless. Bikes were in demand and shared around, but only a few managed to see over the fence. Some of the children started to whine; they were bored and tired and wanted to go home. Women, unable to keep them quiet, began to drift away.

A small knot of men formed in the middle of the mob and a stone and a bottle flew over our heads and into the yard. Immediately things livened up. People searched the ground for missiles and a volley of stones, lumps of wood and glass bottles hurtled over the fence accompanied by a loud chorus of 'Scabs! Scabs! Scabs!'.

The few police, who had hovered at the back of the crowd, grew edgy. Their officer, a local man, tried to calm things. 'Now, boys,' he admonished, 'take it easy. There's no point in chucking stones.'

Their cautions were feeble and futile; there were not enough police to be effective. Most of them were inside the yard. The crowd mocked them and they looked helpless and uncomfortable. Jock and Bernie-Benito arrived just when matters began to look more dangerous.

'Here's real trouble,' I said to Harry. 'Let's go. All we need now is Jock's rabble rousing.' The fence was a terrifying reminder of the railings in Victoria Square. In a riot we could be pinned against it, trapped again.

'No,' he said urgently, holding my arm. 'Wait. I think they've got something else in mind.'

Bernie-Benito edged through the crowd, grinned at Harry, seized his bike and clambered up on it so his head stuck over the fence. Then, in a voice sonorous and resounding, he let fly a harangue in Italian. I didn't understand a word but its passion could not be doubted. I caught the words 'Mussolini' and 'fascism' and 'unions' and '*popolo*'. I had never imagined that Bernie's voice could carry with such resonance. We had grown used to the silence imposed on him by his lack of English.

Jock held the bike and smiled about him with satisfaction and triumph. He had indeed pulled a rabbit out of a hat. Everyone listened to the rich cadences of Bernie's Italian as if by sheer effort we could interpret it. He finished, raised his fist as Jock would have done, and launched full-throated into singing *Avanti popolo*.

The police, who like everyone else had been stunned by the unexpected, now mobilised and tried to push through the crowd to grab him. But the crowd closed ranks. Bernie jumped down from the bike. Briefly I saw his head, then, as he had always managed to do, he melted into the crowd. When the police at last reached the fence where he had been he had disappeared. They knew it was no use questioning anyone. The blank, bland faces all around conveyed quite clearly that no one would tell them anything.

That evening I sketched a cartoon of the morning's events at the timber yard. I headed the cartoon ZOO ENTRY. Over a paling fence I drew a crowd of faces looking in on a gaggle of dishevelled men. On the fence I inscribed FREE LABOURERS. One face in the crowd of onlookers asks another, *What strange animals are these?* I sent it to the *Barrier Daily Truth*.

A week later I was to receive my five shillings and a copy of the issue using my cartoon. I didn't think it was my best work but Nathan and Jock, by this time, had printed copies of it in the *Port Beacon*, a small pamphlet they ran off on a duplicator at Nathan's home. Usually the *Beacon* was full of communist theory and urgings to the proletariat to rise up and throw off the shackles of capitalist oppression. But in this issue they printed my cartoon. Harry sold them around the streets and pinned up a copy of the cartoon in shops and hotels. To the people in the Port mockery became a delightful subversion and laughter a secret unassailable power.

Miss Marie pinned it on the wall of the art class and every time she looked at it she chuckled. 'How you've come along, Judith. From the frightened little girl I collected in the passage to this. So much strength and sharp as a tack.'

The constant hovering police presence at the Port was unnerving. Police seemed to be everywhere and under their eyes I had a perpetual feeling of guilt, although I had done nothing. My insecurity led to an exaggerated anxiety that any harmless action might be construed as illegal. But eventually this uncertainty led to reaction and a feeling of defiance. If nothing I did was safe or harmless then they were the enemy and to hell with them.

The events in Victoria Square had cleaved my trust in the police. I felt sorry for our local men who looked uncomfortable and apologetic in their newly oppressive role, but the extra constables brought in from outside the town looked at us with either grim or impersonal dislike. To them we were neither starving nor desperate. We were simply a bloody nuisance, as I heard one remark.

One afternoon as I had walked home from the soup kitchen one of these new constables, holding a copy of the *Beacon*, accosted me. 'You the girlie who did the ZOO ENTRY cartoon in this paper?'

I froze. 'Yes.' I was icy.

A half-grin spread across his face. 'Clever, aren't you?'

I was silent. What was the purpose of his interrogation? Despite my brave front I felt nervous. Under the Crimes Act I supposed that technically my cartoon 'incited unrest to break the law'. Scabs were now protected by Dog Collar Licences to engage in what was euphemistically named their 'lawful work'. My father's lawful work no longer existed. Nor did the lawful work of eighty per cent of men at the Port. The law had destroyed our right to lawful work.

As these thoughts jostled each other my anger grew, and replaced my nervousness. If he arrested me, so what? Being in court might supply me with plenty more ammunition for another round of cartoons. That'd show the bastards.

He was waiting.

'Yes. It is my cartoon. Do you want to make something of it?'

He looked taken aback. 'No,' he said. 'I just wondered if you'd like to come to the pictures with me on Saturday night. I'm off that night and don't know any girls in the Port.' He was stammering.

I looked at him in disbelief and he stopped, so red-faced with embarrassment that momentarily I took pity on him. 'No,' I said, 'but thank you.'

On the following Friday a small contingent of police arrived at our wharf. We heard the commotion and the noise of lumbering horse-drawn drays and ran out on deck. Men were unloading large wooden barricades. Occasionally, as they heaved and strained and swore, one crashed to the ground. Under police instruction they were sealing off the wharf area.

'Now it's on,' my father grated. 'The *Despatch* said this was to be the day the scabs started. They'll work the *Nardana* shifting wool bales.' He snorted. 'They'll need a few muscles for that. The police expect trouble and trouble they'll get.'

My mother said nothing. She returned to the galley, dished

out our porridge and treacle and made a pot of weak tea. 'Well, they'll have to let me through.' She was determined. 'I'm needed at the kitchen.'

'They'll have to let us both through,' my father was fierce. 'It makes my blood boil. I must be at the meeting at the Federation Hall.'

'And you, Judith,' my mother was anxious, 'you won't do anything stupid?'

'No, of course not. Just some work for school.'

She looked uneasy. 'Harry won't be coming?' She no longer trusted Harry's assurances that I would be safe with him.

'I doubt it,' I said. 'You and Dad can get out but no one will get onto the wharf through those barricades.'

My father looked wolfish. 'For some of us their barricades will only serve as a goad. Wait and see.'

It was far too interesting to stay in the saloon, so I sat on deck and drew what was happening. I watched my mother and father walk along our wharf and speak with the policeman on duty. My mother half-turned and waved back towards our hulk. He must have been satisfied because he showed them a way through. My father had apparently kept his tongue between his teeth, although I'm sure his silence nearly choked him, because there was no sign of any difficulty.

Now the barricades were in place, a few policemen stood around comfortably chatting. They seemed at ease and occasionally patted one of the wooden stanchions as if commenting placidly to each other on their security. Two of them wandered past our hulk. They saw me and hesitated at the foot of the gangplank, clearly debating whether they would come on board. They decided not to.

Further along the wharf were the huge bales of wool waiting to be loaded on the *Nardana* but abandoned because of the strike. They needed expert handling with baling hooks. I wondered how untrained volunteers could cope with their weight and awkwardness. Shipowners, in their ignorance and arrogance, had the hubris to assume that anyone could do a labourer's job. But I knew that years of experience had honed the skills of men like my father and Jock. It had also honed their muscles. It was just as well the scabs were practising on wool bales. A few baling hooks stuck into wheat bags and there'd be grain from one end of the wharf to the other, a good meal for the rats.

The two policemen strolled back. I wondered whether they had made anything of the wool bales. I supposed that it wasn't up to them to measure the difficulty of the job against the incompetence of the scabs. This time they came up the gangplank.

'Girlie,' one of them addressed me.

I smiled engagingly. 'Miss Larsen,' I said. I wanted to say, I don't answer to 'girlie' any more but thought it was better not to antagonise them.

'Miss Larsen, we expect trouble here shortly. We can't answer for your safety.'

'Trouble?' I looked around, pretending confusion. 'Here? Why here?' I slipped a blank page over my drawings.

'What are you doing?' one asked.

'Drawing,' I said.

'Drawing?'

'I'm a student at the art school.'

They were doubtful. 'You're here on your own?'

'Yes. You saw my mother and father leave. He has business in town and my mother works at the Salvation Army soup kitchen.'

They relaxed. Clearly I was a harmless dabbler in the arts and my mother a respectable religious woman. I could see it in their eyes, a benign acceptance for women they classified as sweet and harmless.

'Have you friends in town?' They became fatherly.

'Of course.'

'Then you ought to go there now. It may get rough here. There was an incident last night. We heard that the anarchists planned to blow up one of the tugs.'

'My goodness,' I said, suitably thrilled. 'We heard no explosion. Surely we wouldn't have slept through it.'

'No, of course not. We stopped it. Left two of our blokes on board for the night.'

We had all heard the rumours. The newspapers had suggested dramatically that such a thing *could* happen, and in the present climate *could* became *will*. There were no anarchists at the Port. The police had wasted their time guarding the tug.

'Well done,' I lied. 'Well done.'

They preened themselves a little. 'So you see, you should leave here. We have no men to spare to guard you.'

I looked thoughtful. 'I suppose you are afraid there might be another *City of Singapore*.'

They looked blank. 'I don't think we have any trouble with Chinese,' one said. He looked at his companion with a worried frown. 'Have you heard of any trouble with the Chinks?'

His companion shook his head.

I tried not to laugh. 'Well, that's good,' I said. 'Probably only another rumour.'

They rallied. 'Well, Miss Larsen, if there are Chinese troublemakers as well as anarchists and union thugs, you must leave.'

I felt my jaw tighten. I didn't like their arrogance and had no intention of leaving. However I put on a distressed, helpless look. 'I couldn't today.'

'And why not?'

I pretended embarrassment. 'I'm not very well, today.' I wished that I could blush on cue, however they caught my drift and did the blushing for me. I murmured, 'Sometimes it's difficult being a woman. Every ...'

They didn't let me finish. 'Quite so, Miss Larsen. You'll go inside if there's trouble?'

'Of course. I'll probably feel like it anyway.'

'We'll keep an eye on the hulk, just in case.'

I beamed. 'Thank you. That will be such a comfort.'

They edged away.

'Thank you,' I repeated. 'I do hope there is not too much trouble.' But they had fled down the gangplank and I was speaking to their backs.

They passed a young man lumbering under the weight of a bag of photographic equipment. He struggled up the gangplank, stepped panting onto the deck, put his bag down and shook my hand. 'I'm Jim,' he said, 'press photographer for the *Despatch*. The blokes at the barricade,' he thumbed over his shoulder in their direction, 'let me through, said you'd probably welcome me aboard. I need a good vantage point. Is it OK?' He looked at me speculatively. His eyes strayed around the deck and settled on my drawings laid out on the small table.

'Oh,' he said, in surprise, 'now I get it. You're the Judith who lives on the hulk and draws those marvellous cartoons. Nathan is always singing your praises. He's a friend of yours.'

'Sort of.'

He ignored my doubt. 'Great bloke, Nathan. Wonderful at his job. How he reads the lead slugs upside down and back-to-front I'll never know. He amuses us. One day putting together all this crap about the rights of the foreign shipowners and the next lecturing us about the beauties of life in the Soviet Union. He just about runs the *Despatch* you know.

'Our editor is costive and spends most of his day in the lavatory. He comes out only to check that Nathan hasn't slipped in some Bolshie propaganda.'

He interrupted his prattle to hope that I hadn't been offended. Then he ran on, 'Nathan says you're a down-to-earth girl.' I listened but my attention was riveted on the wharf.

'Find any place you like,' I said absently.

He ambled off and selected a spot on the poop deck. 'Excellent vantage point,' he called. 'I'll set my tripod up here.'

'Good,' I called back.

Shortly afterwards I heard the sounds of scuffling, slip-slopping feet as a disorderly group of ill-clad men straggled along the road and onto the wharf. A couple of barricades were moved to let them through and then replaced. Some hesitated and halted before proceeding. I watched them look back nervously as if they were afraid of pursuit, or maybe they were afraid of being caged between the warehouses and the water. They were a weedy bunch. Only a few showed any brawn. I couldn't imagine how they could lift or even manhandle the bales of wool into the cargo nets.

Accompanied by police they were clearly reluctant and jostled each other in a loose pack, like animals afraid of a predator. If I hadn't been so outraged by their preparedness to steal my father's and friend's jobs I might have felt some pity for their obvious fear. They shuffled past the hulk, looking only ahead of them. They didn't even glance at the police escorting them.

I hung over the rails to see all I could. The police were instructing them but it was the blind leading the blind. Two volunteer labourers tried to manoeuvre a bale of wool but lost control of it. It fell to the edge of the wharf, teetered there and then toppled between the ship and the wharf. Several scabs stopped what they were doing, ran to the edge of the wharf and peered over. There was much gesticulating and shouting. The police, like sheep dogs, herded them back to work. I wondered if the bale were in the river or jammed between the wharf and the ship.

Then I heard a new noise, the harsh, inexorable tread of what must have been an army of men bearing down on the wharf. The police also heard. Those at the barricades sprang to attention and spaced themselves along the wooden barriers. Those who had herded the scabs and now supervised their clumsy efforts to load the cargo nets looked back, clearly in two minds as to where they were most needed.

The ranks of marching men from the Port swung into my view. There were hundreds of them. I recognised Jock and Bernie and Frank and Pat in the lead. I was thankful that my father was not with them at the front. I searched amongst the marchers but could not see him. He would be there somewhere. My stomach churned in trepidation.

Now the police raised their batons in readiness and their superior officer bellowed through his megaphone at the marchers, 'Go back! We don't want any trouble. The volunteers here are legally employed. Stop this march! Go back! Return to your homes!'

But his words might have been confetti wafted and lost on the breeze. With a roar, the marching men swept down upon the barricades, lifted them as if they were match-sticks, heaved them aside and hurled them into the river.

Before this onslaught the police retreated. Those supervising the scabs ran to assist but were thrust aside. They wielded their batons savagely but fruitlessly. There were just not enough of them.

From being a tight phalanx, individuals, armed with iron bars, baling hooks and hunks of wood, broke loose and tore along the wharf. They had the scabs in their sights. Without police protection, some fought to defend themselves. I saw the flash of several knives and blood spurted from the arm of one hefty watersider. With his unharmed arm he lifted the scab and chucked him into the river.

Some scabs tried to pick up the baling hooks they had dropped but as they leaned down they were punched and kicked to the ground. Most fled down the wharf. A couple leapt into the river. Others tried to run up the gangplanks of berthed ships.

'Ran like rabbits,' my father jeered later. 'We couldn't defeat the bastards of shipowners but, by God, we made short work of their minions. They won't come back.'

But I knew it was a false hope.

It was a pathetic debacle and momentarily it looked as if the watersiders could count the day their own. But it wasn't yet over. As they turned to march home, slapping each other on the back, re-living their exploits, shouting triumphantly, a posse of mounted police with foot police behind them blocked their way. Aghast, I saw they were armed with guns and waiting motionless with granite faces. My photographer friend, who had been frantically taking photographs, was also shocked by the threat. 'Bloody hell,' he exclaimed. I felt chilled to the bone with fear.

The Port men saw them but were ebullient, in high spirits at their perceived success, drunk with victory. But then the real battle began. The mounted police advanced quickly with deadly intent and precision. In a silent grim line they simply rode down the unionists. Batons out, they flayed heads, shoulders, arms, faces. They used their horses to knock unionists to the ground and the foot police following beat and kicked the fallen. Several unionists, herded to the edge of the wharf, jumped for their lives. As the water closed over their heads I heard a cheer go up from the scabs, who had regrouped. Lost hats were thrown into the water after the men. Someone yelled, 'Here's yer hats. We hope yer heads are under 'em.'

My father later told us that he had been one of those who had to swim for his life. He climbed the Jacob's ladder of the *Nardana*, discovered a scab hiding on her and was so enraged that he grabbed him, pitched him into the river, and yelled, 'Swim back to Italy you stinking bastard. You and your other fascist mates. I hope you all drown.'

It was warfare. The Port men fought back, punching, kicking, hitting out at the horses so some reared, throwing their riders. They dragged mounted police from their saddles even as batons rained down on them. Horses and men fought and struggled together. The mounted police dragged from their saddles and assailable on the ground were punched and kicked. Horses trod on fallen men. It was a chaos of police, men and horses. The mounted police who kept their seats hit every head without a police helmet. Even from the hulk I could see the blood dark on their batons.

But the struggle was unequal. Some of the beatings were so terrible I feared to look, but felt compelled to see it all. The brutality would haunt me for years to come. I knew this but stood fixed to the railings. Horrified, I thought it would go on until every marcher was dead.

It was Victoria Square all over again but here I was helpless. No wiles of mine would save my father. Frightened, I couldn't spot him in the melee. I hadn't seen him since breakfast time. When he left he had taken a piece of iron pipe with him. My mother saw it but said nothing. There was no point. He would take whatever he wanted and he had a right to try to protect himself. This pipe, more than anything else, had told me what the day might bring. I no longer felt some pity for the scabs. As far as I was concerned they were a squealing rabble, parasites sucking the lifeblood out of other men. They hid behind a police force that served the interests of British shipowners: shipowners, who would not negotiate to end the strike, preferring to find an excuse to employ cheaper and cheaper labour.

It seemed the warfare must go on and on and on. And then a shot rang out, scattering the seagulls that huddled together on the roof of the warehouse. It ricocheted from walls, splintered across the wharf and burst across the river. Its effect was instantaneous. Almost ludicrously everyone stopped, arrested in whatever action they were about to take. Batons remained lifted, legs ready to kick froze.

'Bloody hell,' the photographer working his camera said again. 'Just look at that. They'll kill somebody.'

For a minute nobody seemed to know what to do. Then the police superintendent shattered the silence. 'Present arms,' he shouted. I saw a line of foot police raise their guns. 'Prepare to fire!'

At the same time I saw the marchers hoist their baling hooks. Terrified, I watched them back away, pulling and dragging their injured. Everything was quiet. But ominously so. Someone shouted from the marchers, 'Fire one shot and we'll tear your guts out.' Faced with the line of grim-faced marchers clutching baling hooks at the ready the police superintendent paused. Fearfully I watched this moment of confrontation. One false move on his part and it would be a massacre. I held my breath.

He withheld the order. I sucked in a gasp of air. He called for a spokesperson from the marchers. I saw Jock, Pat and Frank confer, and Frank went forward. He spoke with the superintendent and I saw him point to the guns and raise his baling hook. I couldn't hear what was negotiated but Frank returned to the marchers, spoke with them, and they silently retreated along the wharf. The martial threat evaporated. Dishevelled, bleeding and injured unionists limped away supported by friends. The police straightened their uniforms, collected their wounded and marched away in formation. The clip-clop of horse hooves faded away.

It was over.

A few stragglers from the scabs remained. They had been felled in the battle and now struggled to their feet and lurched towards the entrance to the wharf. Nobody was the least concerned about them. How strange, I thought, they might easily have been men from the Port for one wounded man was indistinguishable from another.

The photographer, Jim, packed up his gear and grinned at me. 'Phew,' he said. 'What a day to write home about. Now I know what it's like to be a war photographer – exciting and terrible.'

The Port labourers struck again, their only hope being that the scabs would prove to be too inefficient to be employed. But I knew that eventually my father and his mates would be defeated. They would finally be forced back to whatever work they could get on whatever wages. I raged at their suffering, their pain and humiliation.

The battle on the wharf had been the moment when my outlook shifted – almost an epiphany. Now I saw my society divided into warring forces and I moved closer to Nathan's views: the inexorable booms and busts of capitalism that he preached made sense. My community was being forced to its knees by forces beyond its control. We, the working people of Australia, were virtually the forgotten people. Poverty made us invisible. All over Australia there were people like us struggling to survive – the timber workers, coal miners, waterside workers in Victoria and Western Australia, all like us, a country divided. The injustice of it weighed on my chest like a huge indigestible meal that produces an unrelenting nausea.

Outrage rather than pity now fuelled my cartoons, and they became savagely political. There was less charity, more biting criticism in them. Without going down Nathan's path to communism and revolution, I attacked those whose power destroyed everything that I loved.

I took on the shipowners. In one cartoon I drew two bloated shipowners toasting each other on the deck of a ship flying a British flag. Beneath them in the water two men are clearly drowning. On their hats, barely visible above the water, I captioned *Unionists*. Looking down on them one shipowner is gloating to the other, *'I can't understand why it took so long.'*

In a second cartoon I drew the room of an impoverished shack. At a table sits another fat shipowner. Opposite him cringe a skeletal woman and starved child with a begging bowl. The caption reads: *You can't expect food when I'm saving the economy for you*. I sent them to the *Sun News Pictorial* but I wondered how they might be received. I was losing my expectation that justice would prevail.

My father had returned from the wharf, dark and silent with rage. I had seen by the wild expression in his eyes that no words could express the depth of his fury. He and his anger were shut away in a place deeper and blacker than the coal hold. My mother did not attempt to speak with him. She bathed the gash in his head and rubbed iodine ointment onto the contusions on his shoulders and back. He thanked her in a tight voice, nodded to me and took himself out on deck to sit alone.

My mother had boiled water for a pot of tea, taken down the tea leaves from yesterday's brew, looked at them with disgust, walked out on deck and savagely pitched them into the river. With a grim face she returned, took a fresh tin of tea from the shelf and made a strong tannin-coloured brew hot and strong. She took a cup to my father and returned. Then she poured one for herself and me. I hadn't dared to intrude.

'I'm sick of this, Judith,' she said.

I wasn't sure whether she meant the weak tea or something else.

She sat opposite me at the galley table and we sipped in silence. Finally she looked up. 'Those sisters of the Medusa who were here when Harry was hurt …'

'Yes,' I said, 'Nathan's sisters.'

She grimaced. 'An unattractive pair.'

'Yes. Very.'

'They talked of a women's army to support the men.'

'Yes.'

'I didn't care for the idea then.'

'No.'

'The time wasn't right, I suppose.'

'None of us could have foreseen this, Mum.'

'They may have. Those sorts of gloomy women are usually right. They expect people to be bastards.'

'They're communists,' I said. 'They believe in the inevitability of class war and violence.'

She smiled at me, a tired, bitter smile. 'What a strange idea,

Judith. Aren't we all humans? But it seems they could be right. I've never been one to hesitate at admitting my mistakes. Life's too short to waste time covering up for pride.'

'I'll talk to Nathan,' I said. 'He'll know what, if any, progress has been made in organising women.'

She nodded. 'That would be a good idea, Judith. This can't go on.'

Later I heard that Frank, Pat and Jock and sundry others had been arrested. They were probably looking at hefty fines or jail sentences. I told Harry that we would like to speak with Nathan's sisters and he promised to pass on my message.

I hadn't seen Winnie for weeks, but now she sent me a note reproaching me for my neglect. It was typical of Winnie to blame me when she had been equally neglectful. She suggested that we meet in town and have lunch together in the gardens. Was I free from class then? I sent a return note through Harry.

Sure enough a week later I found Winnie waiting for me in the corridor outside the office of the Arts School. She looked as pretty and well dressed as always. Since so much had happened at the Port it was an odd sensation to find that Winnie had not changed at all. She had her hair shingled and short little curls bobbed out from behind her ears and across her forehead. She had a charming heart-shaped face and the effect was very fetching. As usual I felt an ugly duckling.

She kissed me and wrinkled her nose. 'Eugh. You smell of oil paint.'

'It's the room,' I said. 'The smell soaks into our skins even when we don't use the paint. I don't notice it any more. I'm so used to it I forget.'

She took my arm. 'I've brought our lunch. So we don't have to find a cafe and have plenty of time to talk.'

'Winnie,' I was suspicious, 'do you think I need to be fed?'

She was never a good liar and blushed. 'Harry mentioned …
the Port … Oh, Judith, he says it's just dreadful.'

'Things are very tough,' I said. 'But I'm a professional woman
now. My cartoons are selling. We are better off than most.'

I didn't tell her that what extra money we had went into the
strike fund. As a family we could scarcely take more than our
needs while others starved. These days everybody I knew seemed
to be surreptitiously trying to feed me. Each morning Miss Marie
arrived with a basket of food. 'The poor models,' she lamented,
'so thin and hungry.' But it was a feeble excuse, for none of them
was thin and hungry, in fact, they mostly looked plump and well-
fed. It was we, her students, she came to feed. Her specialty was
nasturtium-leaf sandwiches. The bread was always fresh, well
buttered and thinly sliced; the sandwiches delicate triangles; the
nasturtium leaves peppery and delicious.

Before the strike and our dependence on government rations
I had never craved nor dreamed of particular foods but now I
constantly longed for an apple or an orange, any fruit or vegetable
freshly picked and served. I think that to Miss Marie nasturtium-
leaf sandwiches were a gourmet delicacy, something she prepared
to delight us. But to me they were a craving satisfied and I was
hard put not to greedily devour more than my share. No one knew
how great an effort it was to refuse the last sandwich on the tray.

To add to our joy she often also brought in a box of chocolates.
Once she caught me trying to wrap mine in a piece of paper to
take home to my mother. She was stern, 'No, Judith, the chocolates are for you. You must not hurt me by stealing them away.'

I was defensive and discomforted. 'Then may I have the empty
box?' I blurted out.

'The box?' She was puzzled.

'Yes, the box. For our soup kitchen.'

'But what use a box?'

'For fuel. We have to scrounge for anything that might burn.

Wood is nearly impossible. People won't give us wood any more. They sell it or keep it for themselves.' I knew my voice had risen. Explaining the situation made it sound so hopeless, so desperate.

Sympathy drenched her face. '*Mon Dieu, ma pauvre.*' Impulsively she hugged me. '*Ma pauvre.* But certainly you shall have all the boxes you need.'

She rushed about the room seeking and eventually finding a large linen bag under a set of folios. She wrenched it out and the folios crashed in a heap on the floor. She ignored them.

'Here.' She held up the bag triumphantly. 'Ruby, Lil, Adie, everyone, here is the bag for chocolate boxes. See, I hang it on the wall for our Judith who needs them for her soup kitchen.'

She turned to me. '*N'est ce pas?*'

'Yes,' I said tearfully. 'Thank you.'

So each Thursday, before I left, she lifted the bag usually filled to the top with boxes and gave it to me. 'A Santa sack,' she beamed and she would look around the class bright-eyed with satisfaction. 'What a lot of beaux you all have. So many admirers to present so many chocolates. But it is sweet to be admired, to be loved. You are the lucky ones, the dear ones.'

As my thoughts had drifted to Miss Marie and the chocolate boxes Winnie had prattled on. We strolled along North Terrace. 'We've all seen your cartoons,' she said. 'Harry is puffed up with pride but my father is not pleased with Harry.'

'Because of my cartoons?'

'No, silly, of course not. I suppose he doesn't much care for them but he's not supporting you. You're not family. But Harry! He's always given Harry's mother an allowance. It isn't much but she manages. He expected that one day Harry would look after his mother himself and now he's lost his job.'

'But, Winnie, it's not his fault. Everyone is losing their jobs.'

She shrugged impatiently. 'I told him that Harry hated his job. He said "So what? Who likes his job? A job is a responsibility and

Harry is sadly lacking in any sense of obligation." He said that Harry probably helped to get himself sacked by being insolent.'

'Winnie!' I was shocked. 'That's not true. How could he say that? Harry! Insolent! What utter nonsense.'

'No, it's not nonsense. Harry has that devil-may-care attitude about everything. My father has to be responsible. He can't go on strike. He has people working for him, people dependent on him.'

'Oh, yes?' I was nasty. 'People he can sack, put on the dole heap?'

She flared, 'A lot you know about it, Judith. Things aren't too good for us either. Daddy has had to cut back his workers. He said one of them cried when he told him. He begged my father to keep him on because he has four children. Daddy was really upset and Harry doesn't help.'

'He can't help, Winnie. You know that. You ought to be ashamed of yourself. Harry is your favourite cousin.'

'He may be, but I know what he's like.'

Now I was really angry. 'No you don't. You don't know what he's like at all. You're just plain selfish.'

She sniffed and her lip trembled.

'And don't play that weepy gag on me, Winnie. It's a put on and you know it.'

She rounded on me, spitting like an angry kitten. 'It's awful for us, too, you know. I have to buy factory-made clothes, lingerie. I always used to have it hand-made. Now I have to wear this dreadful shop stuff because we are poor.'

'Too bad,' I snapped. 'You worry about your underwear while at our soup kitchen we see children so hungry that their bones stick out and sometimes they wear a sack made from wheat bags with holes for their arms and legs.'

I looked her over accusingly. 'You don't look poor to me.'

'It's all your fault,' she wailed.

'My fault? *My fault*?' I was breathless with fury. 'What do you mean, my fault?'

'It's your fault that Harry belongs to a union – the Unemployed Workers' Union. It's not even a proper union but a union of those too hopeless and useless to get jobs. And …' she took a deep breath, 'Daddy thinks he's joined the communists. A Bolshevik in the family. He can't abandon his sister. You've seen how gentle and sensitive she is. He doesn't know which way to turn. He's so angry. He blames you, Judith.'

'Me?' I was outraged. 'Why blame me?'

'It's your influence. You've taken Harry away from his family, stolen him from us, converted him to all these terrible beliefs.'

I gasped. 'You're the limit, Winnie. That's not true.'

I left her and stalked ahead, rapidly and furiously. She ran to catch up with me. Now she was sobbing in earnest. 'I'm sorry, Judith. Please.'

She tried to take my arm but I shook her off. Passers-by stared at us. Why, I thought bitterly, do I have to always be a public spectacle because of Winnie?

'Stop crying,' I snapped. 'You're not a child to be so stupid.'

She ignored me and continued to sob, trotting beside me. 'We shouldn't have gone with Harry to put up those posters.' She gulped. 'Nothing's been the same since.'

I stopped and gaped at her. 'It was over a year ago.'

'Well, that's when it all began.'

'No, Winnie,' I said coldly, 'it didn't begin then. It began when the economy of the country started to collapse – a drought, the copper industry's kaput, we're in the middle of a depression. Haven't you noticed?'

'Don't lecture me. I'm not interested in all that political stuff. Of course I've noticed. Everyone's depressed, including me. I found my mother crying the other day because Daddy had shouted at her. He never shouted. Until now.'

I could hardly believe that she was so ignorant, so lacking in comprehension. Her stupidity riled me. For the first time I noticed that crying made her look plain, not ugly because Winnie could never look ugly, but plain. Her eyes were red and puffy and there were blotches on her cheeks. Suddenly I felt sorry for her and a lot older.

Despite the misery around me I had the comfort of understanding what was happening to us all. I could apportion blame and know that it was the truth. Winnie was drowning in her sea of incomprehension. I recalled Joe's comment about Jack London. When I had asked him why Jack London had killed himself he had said 'there are other reasons for death besides industry'. So there were other reasons for misery. The tentacles of the depression reached into many homes. Everyone, it seemed, suffered according to what or who they were.

Poor Winnie. I took her arm. 'Don't cry,' I said.

She snuffled pathetically. 'And you're not angry with me?'

'Not any more. Let's go and eat your sandwiches.'

We spent the next half hour sitting on the grass of the Botanic Gardens munching placidly. A blackbird scavenged in a mound of dry leaves, raked there by the gardener. Obsessively the bird kicked the leaves aside, scrabbling for worms or other edibles.

'They're such untidy birds,' Winnie said. 'Every morning our gardener sweeps up the path but by next day they've made another mess. Dirt and leaves and twigs everywhere.'

I smiled. 'It's a small inconvenience, Winnie, a very small one.'

She smiled in return. 'I suppose you're right. We'd probably all be happier as blackbirds. They don't seem to worry about other people at all and I suppose they grow older without even noticing it.'

I squeezed her arm. 'It won't go on forever, Winnie.'

'No.' She was dismal. 'Just a few more years. My father says we won't come out of it for a long time. But I won't be young forever, Judith, nor ...' She looked at me as if for the first time realising we were of equal age. 'Nor will you.'

Her sadness was catching. I had never thought about that. To me it seemed that from the time I had claimed to be nearly twelve for Joe Pulham I had rushed on in a hurry to get older. Now Winnie halted me. When my youth had slipped away what would I have?

Sober and more understanding of Winnie, I stood up and brushed the crumbs off my dress. It was certainly an ugly dress. I sighed. Winnie looked up at me critically. 'You should get your hair shingled, Judith. You have lovely hair and it would suit your face.'

I put up my hand and felt my plait. It had been there forever, thick and honey brown, sometimes golden blonde when the sun danced off it. Maybe I could change, look a little younger. Maybe Winnie had a different sort of knowledge. I grinned at her, reached down, took her hand and pulled her to her feet.

'The sandwiches were delicious, Winnie. Thank you. Now I'd better get back to class.'

She came with me to the Gardens gate and we parted. She hugged me and I hugged her back. But that afternoon my thoughts strayed to the idea of a generation of young people lost in time. I had a vision of them all sitting around in a railway waiting room, hoping for a train to take them somewhere, anywhere.

I worked on the concept for a cartoon but despite numerous drawings none of them satisfied me.

Two days later in a small act of defiance I walked into the hairdresser's salon and had my hair cut. Surprisingly, without the weight of my plait, it bounced into waves about my face and a new Judith looked at me from the mirror. As a bonus I was able to sell my hair for wig making and received five shillings for it.

My mother and father were shocked and then resigned when they saw my new hairstyle. 'Oh, Judith,' my mother said reproachfully, but that was all. 'What did you have to do that for?' my father grumbled.

But Harry was angry. 'You should have asked me,' he accused.

Nettled, I snapped, 'And why is it your business?'

'I liked the way your hair was.'

'I didn't. I wanted a change.' I became even more angry, resentful at feeling that I ought to explain myself.

'You might have asked me,' he repeated. 'What did you do with it?'

'Sold it.'

'Sold it!'

'Yes.'

He looked anguished. 'You sold your beautiful hair?'

'Yes. For five shillings.' I was defiant. 'And you needn't be so shirty about it.'

'It's too bad of you, Judith. Too bad. You shouldn't have done it.'

He turned his back on me and stalked off.

I had planned on telling him that I wanted to look young, that time was slipping away from us, and we ought to marry, but now it was all spoiled. Smarting from his anger, distressed and disappointed, I didn't even know if I wanted to marry him. What if he was as bossy over other things – things that to me were more important, like my cartoons and my drawings? I couldn't live with a bossy man.

We were cool to each other for several weeks. Ruby and Lil, who regularly attended Saturday night dances at the Semaphore, invited me to join them at the Palais. Ruby's father had a car and was happy to collect us and take us home.

Ruby was short and plump and her small buttery feet squeezed out around her shoes. Lil, by contrast, was tall and thin with lean muscular arms and long shapely legs.

'She should have auditioned for the chorus,' Ruby giggled, 'instead of wasting her time painting.'

'I like painting,' Lil protested. 'There's no future in chorus lines.'

'Not much in painting either if you're a woman.' Ruby was cheerfully accepting of things. 'Now Judith has the right idea. Political cartoons are the go. There's just so much politics around these days.' She imitated Miss Marie: '"Politics, *mes enfants*, ah, the beautiful politics. It's not love that makes the world go round but the price of potatoes."' She and Lil went off into shrieks of laughter and I joined in.

Ruby looked knowing when she invited me to the dance. 'Your boyfriend plays the piano at the Palais. He has a three-piece band and sometimes the band plays while he comes on the floor and partners us.' She rolled her eyes. 'He is soooo gorgeous. And his slow foxtrot is divine. Before the dance Lil and I draw lots as to who gets to dance with him.' She cocked an eye at me. 'I don't know why we're taking you, Judith. He'll probably only want to dance with you.' And she sighed with exaggerated regret.

The Palais at the Semaphore was a glamorous two-storey building with a dance hall on the second level. Its inlaid wooden floor gleamed after its sawdust polishing and there were still films of dust along the skirting boards after the sawdust strewn on the floor had been swept away. At one end of the hall there was a dais for the piano and band.

Harry looked very handsome in his formal dress suit. It was a little shiny and I suspected that it had been his father's. I recalled my mother once sighing romantically over the actor Ronald Coleman – 'There is nothing so beautiful as a man in evening dress.'

Of course the Palais wasn't as grand as the Ozone Cinema Palace. The Ozone had steel-pressed ceilings and garish green and gilt paint. Harry frequently played the piano there to accompany the silent films and had on several occasions sneaked me in. I relished sitting in the dark listening to Harry mimic on the piano all the tearful, happy, soft, dramatic, fast or slow moods of the films. The music created a breath-taking atmosphere and I hugged to myself my pride in Harry's skill. I imagined that he, through his piano playing, must experience and understand all this range and subtlety of feeling, so it was a little deflating when he laughed at my wide-eyed enthusiasm and dismissed my reverence – 'It's just a script. I play there every night, a bit boring and not really challenging, Judith.'

Despite Ruby and Lil's expectations Harry didn't dance with me. He danced with Ruby and Lil and then Adie and Jess, who joined our party. From their gentle jibes that Harry would monopolise me, Ruby and Lil now became embarrassed. I caught their fleeting glances from me to Harry and back again. They grimaced at each other and shook their heads when they thought I wasn't looking.

I ignored them and when Harry asked one of them to dance I deliberately put up my hand and either gently ruffled my hair or patted it into place. Out of the corner of his eye he watched me and pursed his mouth. I pretended not to care as he introduced me to Karl, a solemn German boy who had no sense of rhythm whatever. As Karl blushed and asked me to do the quickstep, Harry whispered in my ear, 'Serve you right. Now you can go for a walk with *Karl.*'

I survived the night fending off the puzzled and curious glances of my friends. They sympathised, but in an irritating and coy way. 'Lovers always have quarrels,' Ruby assured me, as if she had years of wisdom behind her. Lil nodded her agreement. They waited, eager for some girlish confidences, but I disappointed them. What happened between Harry and me was essentially private.

The next day was Sunday and Harry arrived at the hulk early in the afternoon. He brought a bunch of flowers, a bit the worse for wear, as he had clutched them while riding his bike. My mother greeted him with her usual friendly warmth.

'I've work to do,' I said stiffly.

'No, Judith,' my mother said, 'you don't have work to do. Harry has come to see you.'

I flounced into a chair refusing to look at him.

'But *I* have work to do,' she said hurriedly and left.

Harry hovered irresolutely in front of me. 'I'm sorry, Judith,' he mumbled.

I still refused to look at him.

'Really, Judith,' he pleaded, 'I am sorry. It was just ...' He stumbled. 'I loved your hair and I had bought some ribbons to give you.'

He placed several strands of blue, green and red ribbons on the table in front of me. 'And now,' he sounded desolate, 'they're no use.'

I looked at the shimmering ribbons, imagined how much money they had cost him, heard the unhappiness in his voice and burst into tears. 'Oh, Harry,' I sobbed, 'thank you. I can grow it again, you know. I'll keep them. My hair grows quickly, really quickly and cutting it will make it even thicker.' I gulped and looked up at him.

He smiled down at me. 'Friends again, Judith?'

'Yes,' I said and smiled tearfully in return.

He leaned across the table and kissed me.

Nathan spoke with his sisters and they arrived for our first meeting to organise a women's march. They wore the smug self-congratulatory air of people who believe they have been proved right. My mother had enlisted the help of Mrs Danley and Mrs Thornhill from the soup kitchen.

'I may not be right, Judith, but I think Mrs Danley will be a match for Miss Abigail and Miss Adelaide,' she said.

Mrs Danley, I knew, managed several church committees and her skills at organisation were talked about with bated breath. Mrs Danley was a good woman, a community-minded woman, even if a little overwhelming. She was also physically domi-nating with her powerful voice, stentorian tones, and large bodily presence. Beside her Miss Abigail and Miss Adelaide were small, sparrow-like women pinched into their dark clothes. I felt it was like having a galleon and two mosquito ketches in our saloon: one majestically commanded the waves, the other two buzzed in and out of small ports.

I saw Miss Abigail and Miss Adelaide glance askance at Mrs Danley and then look anxiously at each other. Clearly they hadn't expected competition. My mother had flared at them when they first suggested forming a Women's Defence Army. Now they assumed that the terrible circumstances of the wharf had subdued her.

Mrs Danley was another matter and they sensed the forthcoming battle over the pecking order. My mother, rather nervously, explained why the preliminary meeting was being held. Mrs Danley and Mrs Thornhill nodded.

'Good, Eve,' Mrs Danley said, 'well done.'

My mother looked pleased. Everyone looked pleased when praised by Mrs Danley. I was never quite certain why Mrs Danley's praise ranked higher than anyone else's, but there it was. When Mrs Danley praised my cartoons I glowed, then afterwards laughed at myself. Why some people could establish a sort of command over other people's feelings puzzled me. But then, everyone agreed that Mrs Danley was a very good soul so there was no harm in it.

My mother had introduced her to Nathan's sisters and Mrs Danley had taken it upon herself to say some words of welcome. Miss Abigail and Miss Adelaide bridled at this condescension. Good, I thought spitefully. When Harry had had the temerity to welcome them to the communist meeting they had repulsed him with equal condescension. Serve them right.

'What we need,' Mrs Danley boomed, 'is a plan of action and proposals to take to a larger meeting in the Federation Hall, and we need to enlist the support of the women in the Port. That will take some time. They'll need persuading. In the present climate we can't advertise but we can spread the word. The soup kitchen's a good place to begin. The women who come there are desperate, angry and mostly destitute. We need to tell them exactly what we plan and that the meeting is not open to men.'

Up until now Miss Adelaide and Miss Abigail had remained silent in the face of this determined onslaught. Now Miss Adelaide produced a piece of paper with careful handwritten notes. She began as if giving a prepared speech. 'This is a great opportunity,' she said, 'to rouse the revolutionary spirit of the masses.'

Mrs Danley stared at her. 'I beg your pardon,' she said, 'what opportunity do you have in mind?' The direct approach confused Miss Adelaide. She had her script and was set on proceeding.

Oh dear, I thought, sharing a look with my mother, Nathan has prepared this for them. He wasn't expecting a Mrs Danley. Then I was annoyed. Probably he had expected my mother or even me to be pushovers.

Miss Adelaide continued doggedly, 'It's not piecemeal reforms we need but the overthrow of capitalism which must be inscribed upon the banners of the working class in the struggle against the exploiters. We women must be in the vanguard of this realisation and fight against the continuing and increasing degradation of the workers.'

Mrs Danley listened courteously to this speech but I could tell by the restless way she shifted her large buttocks on the chair that her patience was limited. Her expression said clearly that they were wasting her time and again I found myself expecting that, like the Queen in *Alice in Wonderland*, she might shout at any moment in a voice of thunder: "She's wasting the time. Off with her head."

However she did not do anything as drastic as that. 'Quite,' she said. 'I'm sure there'll be time for that later but just now ...' and she returned to the details of organising the meeting in the

Federation Hall. Miss Adelaide looked offended at being dismissed and Miss Abigail bristled on her behalf.

'I'll chair the meeting,' Mrs Danley continued. 'You're too soft, Eve.'

My mother looked grateful. Earlier she had confessed to me that the thought of managing a large meeting terrified her.

But Miss Adelaide was not beaten yet. 'Our brother,' she squeaked, 'Mr Nathan Ramsay, he's well experienced and has offered to chair it for you.'

'No.' Mrs Danley did not excuse her sharp refusal.

'It's a women's meeting,' my mother said, 'a women's march. I think you, yourself, said that the police will not bash women.'

They were not mollified by her attempt to smooth over Mrs Danley's directness and they fought a rearguard action. 'If we don't have the right principles, the right political ideas, if we don't educate the workers about their plight, we cannot arouse them from their slumbers. It is the long-term goals we must bear in mind. These are just preliminary events that we must see as leading to a new socialist state.'

Mrs Danley was now thoroughly impatient. 'They know what their plight is. They don't need you to tell them.' The meeting threatened to descend into angry words and reprisals. Heavens, I thought, we all want the same thing and we can't even get along here.

Mrs Danley won the day by force of personality and despite the glowering disappointment of Nathan's sisters she organised us into ways of getting the women of the Port to the meeting in the Federation Hall. My mother walked the sisters to the gangplank, aware of their humiliation, but they ignored her soothing conciliatory comments and stalked off stiff-backed.

After they had gone Mrs Danley moved into the galley where I was making cups of tea. Mrs Thornhill who was more or less Mrs Danley's second in charge had said nothing throughout the afternoon. She thanked me for the cup of tea and smiled. Mrs Danley plonked herself down at the table, her thighs spreading over the edges of a wooden chair, and wriggled herself comfortably into position.

'Well, Eve, Judith, Ailsa, what did you make of those two ninnies? A sillier more impractical pair I've yet to listen to. Where did they get those highfalutin, outlandish ideas from?'

'They're communists,' I said.

She gave me a pained smile. 'Is that what they are? Well, if that's communism and they are communists, I don't much like their chances. Why did you invite them, Eve?'

My mother picked up her cup of tea and put her hands around the cup to warm them. The late afternoon was cool and a sharp salty wind had sprung up off the river.

'They suggested a Women's Defence Army and a women's march after the terrible fracas in Victoria Square. Their brother is a friend of Harry's.'

'Humph,' Mrs Danley said.

'I think they have high expectations of being a part of this,' my mother said.

Mrs Danley guffawed. 'Did you hear that, Ailsa?' She assumed Mrs Thornhill would share her disgust. 'High expectations. I don't doubt it. We may have to put a lid on their expectations. What was it they said? "Our hardest task will be clearing the palliative-mongers off the track of revolutionary progress."'

I laughed and my mother grinned. 'How do you remember it all?'

'If you'd sat through as many church meetings as I have, Eve, you'd probably remember it, too. It's a habit of concentration. And now, Judith, you've been very quiet this afternoon, what are you up to?'

I smiled. She did not really want a reply. She had just made a gesture to include me rather as one would acknowledge at long last a neglected child in the room.

It seemed that Nathan also had expectations and dealing with them, relayed to me through Harry, was irritating. Harry reproached me that I didn't draw cartoons in the spirit of working class liberation.

I was tart. 'And what exactly does that mean, Harry?'

He looked confused. 'I suppose like Soviet Union art.'

'And you've seen a lot of that?'

As his opinion was parroted from Nathan, he was naturally defensive. 'Nathan says it would be better if you drew the working man as nobly striding forward.'

'Flaunting a banner, I suppose? With a black hammer and sickle on a red background?'

'If you like.' He was sulky at my jibes but so discomforted I repented.

'Harry, I draw the people at the Port as I see them. Don't you think they are noble in their suffering?'

'But, Judith, they look so down-trodden and desperate.'

'They are down-trodden and desperate, Harry.'

He watched me as I worked with pen and ink. He sighed. I was using a fine nib and China ink. It was almost impossible to correct a mistake and I worked carefully. I had first made a rough pencil drawing so I had a good outline. Now I was filling in light and shade with cross-hatching. It had taken me months to learn the subtlety and control of different pen strokes.

'You do such beautiful work, Judith. For me it's enough but Nathan ...' He hesitated. 'I don't know why Nathan doesn't understand, and he's such a fearfully compelling sort of bloke.'

Harry never took umbrage at my jibes. He neither bore a grudge nor was moody. I loved him but sometimes found it difficult to understand him. When he was with Nathan he was enslaved by his fixed ideas. When he was with me he seemed to see Nathan more clearly. When I asked him if he believed in communism he quipped, 'I'd believe in anything that paid me to dance, Judith.'

Women are good at secrets and small deceptions and the poverty at the Port honed their skills and united them. In small groups they strolled along the street past the fruit stall and while one or two engaged the stallholder with chatter the others filled their bags with stolen vegetables or fruit. I knew that later they divided the spoils amongst themselves, allotting them in terms of need.

On one occasion I watched this small piece of theatre. As they casually walked away talking to each other old Ben, the stallholder, looked up and saw me watching. He shrugged resignedly. 'They think I'm too stupid to notice, Miss Judith. They're not very skilled at thieving. I'd give them the stuff but to think that they've succeeded in snaffling it from under my nose gives them a small sense of triumph. I wouldn't deprive them of that. They all have kids.'

These women and others argued with the baker, swearing that bread baked today was really two days old and badgering him into selling it at a cheaper price. They descended on the dairyman, begging for skim milk, dressing their children in old wheat sacks to convince him that their children were starving. And, of course, they were.

They invented imaginary members of the family in a ploy to get more ration cards. They queued at every food distribution and every charitable clothing distribution. They gritted their teeth and gave up any pretensions to pride. If somebody died in an unemployed camp he was often found dressed in his underwear. Someone had stolen his shoes and clothes.

They foraged for fuel. Gaunt and skeletal they were old before their time. Those who suffered most had been deserted by their husbands who, unable to find work in the Port, went on the wallaby, searching for work in the labourers' camps. Many never wrote home and simply disappeared.

Dr Banks bustled around town as usual, going in and out of houses. His clothes got shabbier, his face thinner, greyer and more lined. I heard mothers complaining that he gave them unrealistic advice.

One day he stopped me in the street and looked intently into my face. As he had done when I was a child he pulled down the lower lid of one of my eyes and peered into it. 'Tell your mother to give you some iron, Judith. You're anaemic. Some good red meat several times a week. And green vegetables,' he instructed.

I looked at him disbelievingly. *Good red meat?* Where did we get that from these days? But I didn't argue with him. There was a vagueness in his expression that troubled me.

'Rickets,' he muttered as he left me. 'Rickets. I tell their mothers to give their children milk and good food but they ignore me. Really, Judith, it's quite irresponsible of them. Now you take my advice. Young women shouldn't be anaemic.'

I walked home thoughtfully. 'Is Dr Banks OK?' I asked my mother.

She looked sad. 'No, Judith, we don't think so. I've been talking to some of the other women. He's an old man and we think his mind is going. Everyone still requests a consultation but no one has faith in him any more.'

I felt bereft. For as long as I could remember Dr Banks had been one of the comforts and supports of the Port. He had been the Medical Officer for years and operated out of our small casualty hospital. Dr Banks pronounced, like God, on the severity of an illness or accident and took the responsibility of sending serious cases to hospital in Adelaide. Well-off or poor took their turn according to the seriousness of their illness. But in addition he was a family adviser, more valuable than the local clergymen, because, as my father had once said, anyone can get a new soul but once the body has gone, pouf, that is the end. The constant changes in the Port, never for the good, were dispiriting, as one community support after another collapsed.

So the word of the meeting in the Federation Hall spread quietly. The police might watch us but they had no power over women gossiping on corners. The soup kitchen became a hive of political activity. At the thought of actually striking back against their suffering many of the women came alive again, their faces animated, their steps firm. An excited fighting spirit replaced the drudgery of endurance. In a small room off the Salvation Army hall they made and painted placards. The more literate wrote protest pamphlets, which they planned to distribute during the march. Harry took them to Nathan who ran off handfuls of copies at the *Port Beacon* hand press.

It was something of a miracle, I thought, that the police had not closed down the *Port Beacon*. It incited revolutionary activity but it was a very small operation and I supposed that the police were fully occupied in protecting the scabs.

Groups of wharf-labourers had regular running battles with the police. At the news that scabs were loading cargo onto a liner at the Outer Harbor, my father marched eight miles there to help confront them. The usual fights occurred; the usual police attacks and baton charges. My father had stopped counting the bruises on his arms, shoulders and back. My mother stoically applied iodine to the new ones and made him a cup of tea. The skirmishes and police beatings were becoming routine. As the scabs, protected by a contingent of police, marched daily to and from the wharves, the Port women and children in pathetic defiance threw stones at them. We no longer thought all of this was unusual. But to have accepted it as a way of life was frightening.

Harry and a flying squad of men from the Unemployed

Workers' Union picketed houses where women, unable to pay the rent, were threatened with eviction. Sometimes he said they tried to persuade the bailiffs to leave. 'But really, Judith,' he was bitter, 'I don't know why we bother. They're crueller and more mindless than a pack of rodents. They take everything, even the children's toys. However, sometimes we outwit them. As they load furniture into the truck we have blokes stationed there and they simply unload it again. It's strange, you know, nobody says anything. It's all done silently. They pack stuff, we unpack it. A sort of war of attrition.'

He smiled grimly. Not Harry's usual bright cheerful smile. 'Sometimes we reach an unspoken compromise. We win a bed, a table, a chair, a toy for each of the children, they take the rest. That keeps them happy. When we fight them for everything we know they'll return, like all vermin do.'

Heavy-hearted, I took his arm to comfort him. I had seen children at the soup kitchen clutching a doll or top. Once Herbie had asked, in his kindly way, if he could see a little boy's train. To his dismay the child clutched it, darted behind his mother, and shouted, 'No, it's mine. You can't have it.' Herbie had stood helplessly, distressed and finally comprehending. He poured the child a particularly large glass of milk.

Quite often we had homeless women and children camped on our deck under canvas awnings my father erected. They were transient, staying for a few days until other family members heard of their plight and either sent for or came for them. On cold nights they moved into the saloon. I offered my cabin but my father refused. 'No, Judith. Where will you sleep? You are the only one in our family who has work. You must have some private place to do it. We are all dependent on the extra money your cartoons bring in.'

He looked bleak. 'To throw you out of your cabin, my dear,

would be like killing the goose that laid the golden egg.' He patted my arm. Adversity had drawn us closer, tightening our bonds as a family.

But it was hard to concentrate on my work. Babies cried, children shouted at each other, mothers yelled at their children to be quiet or belted them, only increasing the level of noise and screaming. There was constant chaos and confusion. Try as I might I was haunted by the distress outside my closed door. Less nobly, I was exasperated and impatient and discovered to my shame that poverty remote from me was a cause for pity but up close it had all the annoyances of fallible humans.

I confessed to my mother that I felt guilty for not wanting to nurse the babies or cuddle the children and that I was only reluctantly inveigled into playing games. She kissed me on the top of my head and smiled sympathetically. 'You're a good girl, Judith. You haven't grown up in a big family. Of course you like your privacy. We all do. Just try to get on with your work. We depend on you. I can't offer these families help if you don't sell your cartoons.'

So I stuffed cotton wool in my ears and went to work as best I could but my mother's well-meant assurances had only made me more anxious. Each cartoon I did was an act of faith. What if I failed to have ideas? Or my ideas didn't sell? That others were so dependent on me was a terrible burden.

I was working on a larger cartoon with more complex and subtle figures. I drew a picket line of poverty-stricken men. Breaking through the line was a terrible skeleton riding a horse. I labelled him HUNGER. In pursuit, but halted by the picketers, were three other riders, their faces ravaged and predatory, their horses rearing threateningly in protest at opposition. One bloke on the picket line is saying to his mate, 'The first one got through but, by God, we'll stop the others.'

I knew it was powerful and well drawn but would it sell? Would readers make the connection with the four horsemen of the Apocalypse? Hopefully the *Workers' Weekly* might take it, even if the *Sun News Pictorial* refused. It had a Biblical theme but I doubted whether the *Despatch* would accept it.

The *Weekly* couldn't pay as much but they were usually a good bet. I had to bring something into the house. But then I worried. The figures of the men were not nobly transfigured by suffering. They weren't striding gloriously into the future as Nathan, and presumably other communists, wanted. They were dogged, only courageous in their determination to keep struggling against almost impossible odds.

Miss Marie consoled me when I complained that I didn't seem to fit the mould and that I was always anxious about whether my work would please. She patted my arm. 'Never mind, Judith. You are an instinctive radical but an individual thinker.'

I went to the Port Adelaide Institute to read the daily newspapers. We could no longer afford to buy them. There were regular and disturbing articles about events in Europe. The *Workers' Weekly* in particular warned of a resurgent militaristic Germany under the leadership of a fascist named Adolf Hitler. His party, the National Socialists, was gaining in popularity. I recalled Joe Pulham, who had talked to me about Hitler's book. *Mein Kampf.* It was a particularly nasty book, he commented, written by a particularly nasty bloke and if he ever got power the world would be in a fine pickle.

The *Weekly* now quoted Hitler's ominous assertion that all German people of the same blood would be united under the Reich in a Greater Germany and that 'the tears of war' would 'produce the daily bread of generations to come'. I didn't know much about Germany and I didn't know what the Reich was but the stories of Hitler's stormtroopers shooting people at political meetings frightened me. It was time, the *Workers' Weekly* trumpeted, that working people all over the world united, took notice, and were fearful. It was a long way away but I was beginning to feel its shadow looming over us.

The Federation Hall was packed. We had arrived early and found our seats, hard-backed wooden chairs near the front. Rows of these chairs filled half the hall. Behind them stretched a space for standing. The seats were quickly taken and dozens of women jammed this space behind. Prams cluttered the central aisle. Women nursed babies or held toddlers between their knees. Children who had been seated on a chair were pushed off for women arriving late. Everyone was crammed in. The hulla-baloo was deafening. The noise swept across the room in surges booming off the bare walls and from the wooden floor.

Miss Marie had joined us, thrilled, she said, to at last face the barricades. Her exhilaration was catching. I had never asked her what the Paris barricades had been or why she always dramatised them. But tonight the very sound of them had the inflaming quality of glorious and righteous martyrdom. Somewhere at some time there had been people like us who took a stand against injustice and their passion lived on in Miss Marie's memory and fiery expectations.

Mrs Danley was already seated at a table on the dais. My mother, who had agreed to keep the minutes of the meeting, sat beside her. Like all the other women in the hall they were decked with hats and dressed soberly in the dark clothes they wore for all formal occasions – church on Sundays, dinners with friends, funerals, baptisms.

Only Miss Marie looked a butterfly, scintillating in a room of ravens. Although shorter dresses were now the fashion, she wore a full-length gown of some green shimmering material, a velvet cloak of carmine embossed with emerald flowers, and a matching emerald cloche. She had floated down the aisle on a cloud of Coty's Lily of the Valley perfume when we had made our early entry.

Her steps were light and confident, her eyes sparkled over those already seated. Gasps of admiration and wonder followed us, and an occasional childish chirp, 'Who's that pretty lady?' followed by the sound of a slap and a yelp.

Feeling like a handmaiden trailing the entrance of the Queen of Sheba, I had been hard put not to giggle. If Miss Marie had indeed been born a true Aussie daughter of a South Australian grazier, then some mighty transfiguration had taken place, unless it was simply her delight in theatre.

She whispered in my ear, 'Judith, I am completely intoxicated. Just look at all these wonderful women who have come out. Aren't they marvellous?' and she beamed about her with such open inviting friendliness that her smiles were returned. 'I love them all,' she cried, waving her arms expansively to include everyone. On another occasion I might have felt embarrassed to be accompanied by someone who drew so much attention, but tonight was different.

Mrs Danley stood up and rang a small hand bell. The sound of its thin peal hardly made it beyond the first six rows. Women continued to talk. She rang the bell again and failed again. 'Ladies,' she called. A few in the front rows turned around and called shush to those behind but the noise did not abate. She tried the microphone but no sound came out. Miss Marie frowned. 'This is too bad,' she said. 'They are being naughty. They should listen. Now is not the time to chatter.'

She stood up. 'Ladies,' she called, more loudly than I had thought she could. 'Ladies, it is time for the meeting to start.'

I don't think it was her voice as much as her regal even garish appearance that stopped everyone. They gaped at her, stunned and silent, and in the temporary lull Mrs Danley called them to order. Miss Marie sat down again and smoothed her dress over her knees. She smiled at me smugly. 'That's how it's done, Judith.' I laughed. That might be her way of doing it but it was comical to envisage Mrs Danley aping her.

Mrs Danley welcomed everyone. She had fiddled with the microphone speaker and it stuttered to life. She praised us for coming out, said she knew how hard it was for mothers to come to a meeting at night with their children. She asked the children to be quiet for a little while, as quiet as little mice, she said, and put her finger to her lips. It was a gentle approach by a woman who understood other women. There was no grandstanding. I was surprised. I had expected Mrs Danley to be more domineering.

'We are here,' she told us quietly, 'to prepare for a march to defend our husbands, sons and brothers who are on strike. We are tired of them coming home bruised and injured from police beatings. We are tired of their despair at not being able to provide a decent living for their wives and children. We are tired of government handouts, charity, ration books and inferior food.'

Murmurs of agreement ran through the crowd. Women nodded, an occasional voice said, 'It's true,' and someone called, 'Hear hear!'

Mrs Danley continued, 'In case you have any doubts about the magnitude of what we are dealing with and its necessity I want you to hear first hand what happened on the wharves when our men came within a whisker of being shot by the police. Judith Larsen saw it all from the hulk. Please, Judith, will you come up onto the platform and tell us what you saw?'

Frozen with horror I stayed fixed to my chair. Surely she wasn't asking me to speak to this huge rally. I was unprepared. How dare she spring this on me? The blood flamed into my cheeks and my hands shook. I looked at my mother but she had her head bent over her book of notes, pretending to write. This was a put-up job by the two of them. I was incensed. It was like a re-run of Nathan in Botanic Park when he had dragged me to his wretched vegetable crate. Only this was much worse. This mattered.

Beside me Miss Marie squeezed my arm. 'To the barricades, *mon ami.*'

'Don't talk silly French to me,' I snapped. 'You know it's a pretence.'

She laughed. 'You can do it, Judith. You know you can. You're not a frightened little girl.'

Mrs Danley was waiting, an inviting expectant smile on her face. People rarely refused her requests. Could I be the first? How timid and churlish of me. What a disappointment I would be. The whole hall seemed to be waiting. A baby cried briefly in the silence. The minute in which I tried to decide seemed an eternity.

I stood up. 'Good on you, girlie,' Miss Marie said. I pinched her sharply on the arm. She yelped but looked pleased. My legs trembled as I walked down the aisle and climbed the two side steps to the dais.

Where to begin? What words to choose? How long to speak? I fell back on how I approached my cartoons. 'Visualise it,' Miss Marie had said, 'see your drawing in your head before you begin.' I reached the microphone, stood too close to it, cleared my throat and heard the sound blur back at me. I retreated a little and began.

It was not as difficult as I had imagined. At first my voice shook, then, as the episodes on the wharf sharpened in my memory, I described them. I did not embellish them with how I had felt, my own shock, fear and disgust, I simply told about the events as I recalled them. A hush fell on the room. Occasionally I heard an indrawn breath, a gasp, a 'no' ejected as if someone needed to push away what I was saying. Once I heard a sob. When I stopped there was silence and then a storm of wild clapping. I didn't know what to do, how to get off the dais: like a guest who needs to leave a room but can't find the door.

Mrs Danley rescued me. 'Thank you, Judith,' she said. 'I knew we could depend on you.' She turned to the now quiet audience. 'And that's a story your men probably didn't tell you.' She waited while I walked back to my seat. Many eyes followed me. Women along the aisle reached out, patted my arm and smiled. The soft sibilance of whispers ran around the room but it was not until I was completely seated that a hubbub of noise broke out.

Quite unused to such notoriety, I shrank into my seat. Miss Marie's eyes sparkled. 'Marvellous, Judith,' she said, 'very well done, indeed. A valiant tour-de-force. *Absolument.*'

'Thank you,' I said weakly.

Mrs Danley put the resolution to the meeting that there would be a street march of women, that no men would be enlisted, that it would start from the Waterside Workers' Federation Hall and end at the government offices where a petition would be presented. She explained that the petition could be signed at the door as the women left. It demanded a negotiated end to the strike; the removal of 'volunteer' labour from the Port; an increase in the dole (which was less than the basic wage of two pounds eleven shillings and eight pence a week), and the right of families to receive money assistance rather than ration cards so that they weren't always condemned to receiving inferior food. She put the motion to the meeting, calling for a show of hands. There was overwhelming support and no dissenters.

She was about to close the meeting when Miss Adelaide and Miss Abigail scurried out of their seats in the front row, hurried up the steps onto the dais and confronted her. For once in her life Mrs Danley was nonplussed. Clearly the sisters were demanding a right to speak. Mrs Danley waved her hand towards the audience, pointed to her watch, and shook her head.

But they were not to be disregarded. Ignoring Mrs Danley's angry face Miss Adelaide walked to the microphone, adjusted it to her height, and began to drone. This time she didn't read from notes but her oration sounded as if it had been learned by rote. Rather than make a fuss Mrs Danley shrugged and sat down beside my mother. They spoke briefly to each other, Mrs Danley throwing out her hands palms up with a gesture of defeat. They settled themselves resignedly.

It was obvious the women were puzzled by this new development, and restless. Resentful probably, I thought. Coming to such a meeting would have been a great effort for them. Many of their children were whining with tiredness, most of the mothers wore that harassed when-will-it-be-over-and-we-can-go-home expressions. Only a moment before they had been convinced that duty done, they could leave with a clear conscience. Now, disappointed, but reluctant to leave without Mrs Danley's blessing, they nevertheless looked impatient and antagonistic.

Miss Adelaide droned into the microphone, repeating the same words she had intoned on the hulk: 'Not piece-meal reforms but the overthrow of capitalism must be inscribed upon the banners of the working class in the struggle against the exploiters. Capitalism today cannot find markets for the commodities it produces. It can only continue its parasitical existence by intensifying the degradation of the toiling masses throughout the world.

'Just as before the Great War of 1914 to 1918 capitalist rivalry between British and German imperialism made war inevitable, so ...'

My attention strayed. From the rows behind me I heard murmurs, sighs, and the scrape and squeal of chairs as women fidgeted. I glanced behind and to my amusement saw that a baby had escaped and crawled into the aisle. The nearest woman retrieved him and he was passed like a parcel along the row to his mother.

Oblivious to the flurry of activity and the muted giggles, Miss Adelaide ploughed on, resolute and undeterred. 'So today, with the development of a resurgent Germany, the stage is set for another even greater conflict for the re-division of world markets and cheap labour.

'The continued existence of the first workers' republic in Russia and its rapid progress to communism make the situation even more insecure for capitalism, consequently the imperialist powers, lead by Great Britain, are straining every nerve to encircle and destroy by armed intervention the Union of Socialist Soviet Republics.'

The audience mood of resignation was changing. They were not interested in armed intervention against the Soviet Union. They had come out at night with tired children to help their husbands, brothers and sons. But there was still more from Miss Adelaide. Like Nathan, she didn't know when to stop. Finally she got around to what might have interested her audience – the plight of men out of work.

In a passionless voice she plodded on. 'Australia is now more and more drawn into the imperialist orbit. As a result the past two years have been marked by a savage attack on the workers of Australia.'

It was too late, her speech too abstract. They chafed at having to listen. Someone in the audience booed. A shocked silence followed, then another booed and another. Miss Adelaide struggled on, although Miss Abigail standing beside her glanced apprehensively at the audience.

Miss Adelaide rallied. 'The next war,' she pronounced, 'will be between fascism as we are seeing in Germany and communism. Don't be deceived by capitalist propaganda.'

Someone began to count. A slow remorseless chorus drowned her out. She stopped, confused. She had lost her place in the script. I pitied her. Only a short time before I had also feared being pilloried. Beside me Miss Marie stiffened. '*La pauvre,*' she said, clearly enough for those around to hear. 'She lacks judgement but she speaks truth. Indeed, we will all rue the day of a resurgent nationalist government under German Hitler.'

Already women were getting up, shuffling out of their seats. Mrs Danley tried to reclaim control of the meeting and failed. They were chatting to each other, collecting their bits and pieces, their babies, toddlers, children, prams. In haste they jostled each other along the aisle. Some stopped to sign the petition. Others just hurried out, with resentful faces, determined to make a rapid escape.

Miss Adelaide's warning words had bored them but I wondered if she had added a further threat to their lives, one they were not prepared to add to their present burdens. They weren't interested in the plight of unemployed workers in Germany or in the falsity of accusations that the misery was caused by Jewish Bolsheviks. They weren't interested in police bashings and shootings in another country half a world away. They had enough problems of their own to cope with. The communist doctrine of an international brotherhood of working people united to defeat their capitalist masters was hot air to them. They just wanted to go home and put the kids to bed.

I stood up to leave. 'Coming?' I asked Miss Marie. But she had her attention fixed on Miss Adelaide and Miss Abigail who now stood isolated on the platform. Mrs Danley and my mother had ignored them and left. Mrs Danley's anger was evident in her offended stiff-backed stride. She shepherded my mother in front of her. When my mother had glanced back indecisively at the sisters, Mrs Danley said something to her and although I could tell that my mother was discomforted, she allowed herself to be lead away. I was irritated that Mrs Danley sometimes overstepped the mark. My mother was quite able to make her own decisions.

Meanwhile Miss Marie squeezed past me and with quick apologetic murmurings to the departing women she manoeuvred herself down the aisle against the flow and eventually on to the dais. With one hand holding up her gown, she rushed across the platform and held out her other hand to Miss Adelaide. There was a brief hiatus while Miss Adelaide stared at her hand, took stock of her shining gown, and retreated a step.

I stayed in my seat fascinated to watch this small drama and the suspense of wondering who would triumph, sour Miss Adelaide or sunny Miss Marie. Miss Marie was speaking, gesticulating. She always used her hands wildly when talking. Her face was luminous and beaming and to my amazement she physically grasped Miss Adelaide's hand. I expected Miss Adelaide to snatch it away but she only looked down at Miss Marie's hand, then up at her face. Her thin body trembled, her face crumpled, and she reached out and clutched Miss Marie's hand in both of hers. She clung to her as if here was the lifeline she had prayed for.

I had never expected her to be so vulnerable. In her surliness she always seemed impervious to the feelings or opinions of others. With one arm comfortingly about her Miss Marie was leading her from the dais. Miss Abigail trailed after them. Miss Marie shepherded them through the throng and down the still congested aisle. I heard her voice, silvery and sweet but very clear. 'Excuse us,' she said several times. 'Excuse us. You don't mind, do you? I need to see these ladies out.' And they didn't mind, stepping back to allow them to pass through. Only she could have managed it with such nous, courtesy and determination. In many ways she was like Harry. They shared an ebullience, a buoyant confidence that their generous impulses would always meet with favour.

She returned at last to find me. '*Les pauvres,*' she said again. 'So desolate. So alone.' In the face of her sympathy I struggled to feel kindly towards Nathan's sisters, or if not kindly at least charitable. I failed on both counts. I could only dredge up a smidgeon of compassion. 'I can't like them,' I said.

She looked at me sharply. 'It is their timing that is at fault,' she repeated, 'not their hearts. They speak the truth, Judith.'

'But what if no one listens because they're so objectionable? They lack moderation.'

'Ah, yes,' she said, 'the wise Aristotle. But moderation is not easy. It involves compromise and to compromise what do we give up? I've lived in France. I have letters from friends. They are afraid of this Hitler. Already Jewish people are fleeing to France. These women speak truth, Judith.'

'Maybe,' I said. 'But it was the wrong time and the wrong place.'

She sighed. 'I wonder when it will ever be the right time to convince people.'

Worrying whether my cartoons would be accepted became an obsession. Frequently I awoke in the night with some vague idea and lay awake struggling to visualise an image and form the words for a caption that might fit. I discarded more ideas than those that worked. From initial excitement at my success, I now expected every piece of work to be accepted. Of course they weren't and these rejections plunged me into despair.

In actuality, I received few rejections and the reasons given often seemed odd. Some I put aside but a few bothered me. When one daily paper complained that my cartoons were 'a bit strong' and that they would only consider my work if I 'toned them down' I didn't know what to think. How could I tone down a cartoon? It was by its nature sharp and to the point. Did they want me to alter the drawing or re-word the caption? Or was it all just an excuse to put me off?

'Ignore them,' my mother said. 'Send them another cartoon and see what happens. Probably someone in the editorial department is flexing his muscles.'

I took her advice and the next cartoon was accepted without comment. But when another daily wrote me a serious letter advising me to publish my cartoons under a male pseudonym I was very annoyed. 'What do I do about this sort of nonsense?' I appealed to my mother again.

'Ignore it.'

'But if they're serious?'

'Withdraw your cartoons if they insist.'

I was horrified. 'But they take my work regularly. I could compromise and sign them J. Larsen.' I didn't like to point out what she already knew, that the money was vital.

'No, Judith. You are not going to publish under a male pseudonym, or a pretence of one. Your work is outstanding. Everyone knows that. It is yours and it should be acknowledged. You will not sacrifice your reputation. I won't have it. Nor will your father. Let that be an end to any silly thoughts you might have in that direction.'

Although incensed, I wrote a careful response, explaining that I would feel most uncomfortable with such deception and hoped they would reconsider. They did and I felt a triumphant glee at having stood up for myself. Of course, I was also vastly relieved when payment for the cartoon arrived.

Since learning about the women's march, Harry turned up at the hulk more often. For many weeks he had gone daily to the Labour Exchange seeking work but it was dispiriting and degrading and since he still had some work in dance halls and picture palaces he could get by and help his mother manage on her ration card. Given her genteel pretensions, I was not sure how she brought herself to collect her rations. Probably Harry did it for her and she went on deceiving herself with the same genteel lie that he was still working at the foundry and promoted to the office.

I wondered how many Mrs Grenvilles there were: people who were not working class like us but who had never been rich; people in the middle who now sank lower and fought their change in status by adopting small pretences and pathetic lies. And these, I supposed, were mostly women: single, widowed, deserted; poor helpless victims dependent on the charity of other family members or the pitiful state handout of three shillings to four shillings and sixpence a week for each child if they had any. The women at the meeting in the Federation Hall had had more dignity. Nathan's sisters had had more dignity. There was pride in being a battler.

There was dignity in struggle. Maybe Miss Adelaide and Miss Abigail also had to juggle ration cards. Communism was their answer to personal humiliation. And why not?

But sometimes when Harry popped in unexpectedly after a morning at the Labour Exchange he looked so subdued that I feared the remorseless struggle would dim even his bright spirit. He returned to his Sunday visits with Winnie in tow. To my mother's amusement, my father continued to greet her gallantly. Her flirtatiousness no longer shocked him and I was surprised to watch him respond rather shyly to her games. When she ogled him or flattered him he no longer stiffened, fearful that she might be taking the mickey. Now he even occasionally answered her playful advances with a light quip.

'Each time I see you, you grow more handsome, Mr Larsen.' She tilted her eyes at him.

'And you, Miss Winnifred, are a forward young woman, flirting with a man old enough to be your father.'

'I like older men,' she said, peeping at him from under her lashes.

'Winnie!' Harry was shocked. 'That is too much.'

She grinned. 'Is it "too much", Mr Larsen?' she appealed. 'Aren't you experienced? You've travelled the world, captained great ships in wild seas, seen so much more than the rest of us, had adventures.' She turned innocent eyes on Harry. 'And what did you think I meant?'

Harry frowned but sidestepped. 'Did you know, Winnie, that Mr Larsen lived with the Eskimos?'

'Golly,' she said, 'was it very cold?'

My father laughed. 'Most of the time.'

My mother indulged them but I felt a frisson of jealousy. My father had never been jocular with me. I had no memories of jokes, fewer of shared laughter, but I supposed I had been a solemn reticent child. Suddenly I longed to be like Winnie – bright, appealing, seeking and receiving affection – and all so easily.

Harry was watching me. Were my longings reflected in my face? He was astute. He jumped up. 'Mrs Larsen, Mr Larsen, we should all go out. It's a lovely day. Not too hot. This morning at dawn when I woke the sky was streaky bacon with cotton wool clouds and I thought, Here's a sizzler coming. But it hasn't. We could go to the Semaphore, walk along the jetty, buy an ice cream and forget there's a bloody depression.'

All joyousness, he was pulling me out of my chair. Winnie clapped her hands. 'Yes, please, Mrs Larsen. You and Mr Larsen please come with us.'

My mother demurred. 'No, we'll have a quiet afternoon. I've a book to read. Mr Larsen has some jobs about the hulk. You all go. It'll do you good.'

I hesitated. 'Are you sure? You don't go out much.'

She gave me a gentle push. 'Get your hat, Judith.'

Winnie took my arm as we walked to the stop to catch the electric tram that ran between the Port and the Semaphore.

Harry admonished, 'Winnie, you should be more respectful of Judith's father.'

She rolled her eyes at him. 'I'm not disrespectful, am I, Judith?'

Caught between the two of them I laughed, 'Of course not.'

Winnie looked triumphant. 'There, Harry.' And mockingly she hummed: *What'll I do when skies are blue and you're not here, what'll I do?*

'Oh, Winnie, you …' he said.

'Oh, Harry, you,' she mimicked and kissed him lightly on the cheek.

'I've decided to be happy, Judith,' she announced.

'Have you been unhappy, Winnie?' I remembered her storm of tears when we had met for lunch but had assumed that it was merely one of her short-lived moods. She shrugged. 'Well, you know what it's like, Jude. Everyone is so damned miserable these days. It's catching. You should understand. You're surrounded by miserable people, too. Do you like my hat?'

I was surprised by her sudden change of topic. 'Yes, it's very pretty.'

It was a wide-brimmed natural straw, the crown encircled by a wreath of delphinium-blue forget-me-nots.

'Sixpence in a second-hand shop.' She looked smug. 'You needn't look like that, Judith. I've discovered that some second-hand shops have the most divine clothes and all at bargain prices. Daddy gives me my monthly allowance. It's not much these days, so I go hunting. It's such fun, Judith. You ought to come with me. They usually have little cubicles, just like a doll's house, where you can try things on. Of course, I don't buy second-hand underwear. That would be a bit nasty but who needs hand-made underwear? Factory stuff is quite good enough. After all, who sees it?'

I looked at her cautiously. Any response on my part might be the wrong one. It must be a pretence, even if a brave one. Any moment I expected the sniffles to begin, followed by a storm of weeping, but she walked beside me prattling on blithely and I had to believe that Winnie, the Fastidious, had taken to second-hand clothing shops like a duck to water.

'You should come with me one day, Judith,' she urged.

'You know I hate shopping for clothes, Winnie.'

She assessed me. 'Yes.'

'Yes. You needn't say I look like that, Winnie.'

She was shocked. 'I wouldn't say that, Judith. You always look nice. But it's such fun.'

I shook my head.

'It's good works, Judith,' she wheedled, piously. 'The charity shops need the money. They are always so pleased to see me.'

There was nothing I could do but laugh. 'Oh. You, Winnie,'

I said, 'you're such a …' I hesitated. 'Darling.' I was going to say 'such a card' but that was Harry's pet expression for me and I was reluctant to share it.

It was a glittering day. The sea glistened, so calm I could have smoothed my hand across its surface as if it were a piece of stretched green cloth. Occasionally a silver leaping fish caught the sun on its back. The Semaphore jetty jutted into the sea, its long arm needed to cope with the vast tidal rises and falls of the gulf.

We strolled along it. Winnie ogled the young men, who invariably followed her progress with their eyes, and always looked back when they had passed us. Harry occasionally greeted a fisherman. Everyone was in his or her Sunday best. Some of the women even carried frivolous frilled parasols.

At the pavilion, on the sea-end of the jetty, the Port City Band played a selection of songs from Gilbert and Sullivan operettas. Harry, who had played the piano for some amateur theatricals, sang along, his light tenor voice very sweet. When he sang 'Dear little Buttercup' Winnie played up to him. She put a finger coyly under her chin, flirted her eyes, and danced a few steps to match his. A few people stopped to watch, amused, indulgent expressions on their faces. They made an enchanting pair: Harry lithe, handsome in his boyish way, the sun striking a halo of his bronze hair; Winnie, with her big straw hat, melting eyes and plump little figure.

For a moment I felt an outsider and then, as Harry smiled at me over Winnie's head, I knew a surge of love so forceful that I shook. To lose Harry would catapult me into some dreadful dark abyss where nothing mattered any more. I put up an arm to cover my eyes against the sun's glare but knew it to be an instinctive gesture to protect myself from such a black fear.

I emerged from this momentary bleakness to find an ice cream thrust into my hand. 'You were away with the fairies,' Winnie said, 'so we bought you this.'

We all licked happily, childishly up-ending the cones to catch the ice cream that trickled onto our hands. Winnie tried to wipe off the stickiness and giggled. 'Just like those posters,' she said. 'You remember how hopeless I was, Judith.'

'Yes, I remember,' I said, 'and you certainly weren't hopeless.'

It was a happy afternoon. Winnie left us to take the return train from the Semaphore into the city, Harry accompanying me back to the hulk. He looked serious.

'Judith?'

'Yes.'

'I'm very worried about the women's march.'

I was surprised. 'Why?'

'You could be hurt. The police are becoming more savage. Everything is a wild battle these days.'

'Yes, I know. But this is different. There'll be women and children and babies in prams. You should have seen them the other night. It's more likely to look like a family outing picnic day than a protest march. Nobody's going to be violent. Not even the police would attack unarmed women.'

But he wasn't convinced. 'I brought these for you,' and he handed me a brown paper bag.

I peeped inside. There were a number of little coloured glass marbles.

'Oh, Harry. We used to play with marbles when we were kids. I had quite a collection and a favourite tor. I don't know what happened to them.'

'They're not for playing, Judith.'

'I didn't expect they were. But what?'

'If you are attacked, Judith, by mounted police, throw them on the ground under the horses.'

I was shocked. 'You mean the poor horses will fall?'

'Yes, that's exactly what I mean. Anything rather than you take the beating I received in Victoria Square.'

I was sober. That memory haunted me. 'I'm not sure, Harry. It seems … We don't want to precipitate violence.'

'Whatever it seems, promise me, Judith, you'll use them if you are threatened.'

'Are you sure they'll work?'

He shrugged. 'No, I'm not sure, but it's the only thing you can carry secretly that might help you.' I assured him that I would take them, if only to lift the worried frown from his face. It all seemed unnecessarily dramatic but when I remembered the events at Victoria Square I wasn't so sure.

We had planned the women's march to begin at 10.30 in the morning. We judged that this would give the women time to feed their babies, see their children to school, perhaps start preparing their husband's lunch – that is if they had a husband to come home to the midday meal. We hoped to start on time but it was difficult because everyone would have to walk from their homes to the Federation Hall; some come quite a distance.

The night meeting at the Federation Hall had given us a picture of what the march might be like: a number of nervous, anxious, uncertain women with babies, toddlers and small children they couldn't leave at home.

The morning was cool, so my mother and I put on coats. Mine had a pocket. I looked doubtfully at Harry's bag of marbles, picked them up, let them roll around in my fingers, put them back in the drawer, jammed my hat on my head and turned to leave the cabin. At the door I hesitated. I had promised Harry. There should be no harm in carrying them. I would never under any circumstances throw them under the horses' hooves. It appalled me to think of injuring horse and rider. And yet again I remembered the mounted police in Victoria Square. I snatched up the marbles and dropped them into my pocket. They clinked so I added a couple of handkerchiefs to muffle the sound.

My mother waited for me by the gangplank. She laughed nervously as I took her arm. 'What if no one comes, Judith? None of them has done this sort of thing before.'

'We haven't either,' I said.

'No. Mrs Danley is always so confident, but you can't make people do these things.'

'They'll come, Mum. You'll see. Remember them at the soup kitchen – so thrilled to be doing something other than the daily grind to survive. For once they felt a smidgeon of power.'

She looked unconvinced. 'With a group, Judith, all things seem possible. But alone at home over the kitchen sink, sweeping floors, feeding baby, all this may seem remote. Outside their experience. Beyond their possibilities.'

She was right and it was useless to continue trying to reassure her. Neither of us knew whether they would come. The whole day and all the planning might just fizzle.

We crossed the concrete apron that backed the wharves, negotiated the web of rail lines and dodged the rail trucks that trundled and clanged perpetually along tracks that snaked everywhere. The huge stone and brick warehouses for wool storage loomed over us. We passed the dockside tavern where already a number of men lolled on outside benches, a glass of beer in their hands.

My mother pursed her lips. 'It wasn't much use closing some taverns in the Port when so many are still here.' It was her constant complaint.

My father had joked that she should join the Social Purity Movement, particularly as she now worked for the Salvation Army. She was tart. 'It's all very well for you, Niels. You have one beer and stop. Others are not so restrained. The women I see daily would break your heart.

'And don't wink at Judith,' she had snapped. 'And now don't pretend to be contrite.'

We arrived early at the Federation Hall. A few women waited

inside but most hovered awkwardly on the street. They had formed into small friendship groups, chatting and laughing. Mrs Danley bustled around. She gave me a handful of leaflets, the ones Nathan had printed at the *Port Beacon*, and I went from group to group distributing them.

The women took them gingerly and looked anxious. 'What do we do with these, Judith?'

'Mrs Danley says to give them out to passers-by as we march along.'

They were bemused. 'Should we leave the march, then? How will we get back in again?'

It seemed that they thought of the march in terms of soldiers, regimented and in place. 'Only hand them out if you can and feel comfortable but otherwise keep them for friends or relatives who aren't here.'

'Will that do any good?'

'It's important to tell people about our protest.'

They looked disbelieving. One woman, more outspoken, was cynical. 'More talk, more telling. What's the use if they don't look and see?' Her friends nodded.

I moved on. Yes, I thought, she's right. We all struggle to tell. A sort of blind faith. Even my cartoons.

The numbers grew. Mostly the women arrived in small groups, having collected their neighbours. Only an occasional woman came alone to stand lost and embarrassed on the outskirts. But Mrs Danley had eyes everywhere. 'Look after her, Judith, she must have some friends here, someone from her own neighbourhood.'

Usually I found that she did and she was rapidly absorbed into a group.

As the numbers increased, so did the excitement and the noise. Children finding friends dodged in and out between the adults, playing tag, shrieking and squealing. Mothers yelled at them, or ran to clutch them as they raced past. An occasional one was grabbed and admonished with a sharp slap. Toddlers confused by the noise and the dense press of bodies wailed miserably. Babies in prams slept on oblivious.

Most of the women wore their cheap rayon day dresses with dark coats of brown, navy or black. The idea that they could change their day dress meant for work into something smarter had long gone out the door. Once these dresses were perhaps patterned but now, washed, ironed and patched, they had faded to a uniform grey. They all wore frayed gloves with mended finger holes. Cloche hats, only a sad reminder of their former prettiness, were shabby but still worn, for to go out without a hat was unthinkable. And they all looked so tired. Was it cruel to involve them in this additional effort?

Their dark coats looked strangely nocturnal in the morning sunshine and together they had the grey of an overcast day.

Miss Marie stepped down from her taxi and made her regal path through the crowd like dawn breaking through a mass of sooty clouds. She was a gasp of radiant colour, resplendent in the red, blue and white of the French flag. All eyes followed her.

'Well, *mon amie*,' she said taking my arm, 'this is the great day, *n'est ce pas*? And they are all here. All these wonderful women. There is such power in women,' and once again she held out her arms to embrace me.

A few women giggled. Some smiled indulgently. But all who saw her nodded and looked pleased.

'You shed lustre everywhere,' I said, a trifle dryly. 'And why the French colours?'

On this occasion I thought she might have been a little less ostentatious. But from the smiles around her it seemed that nobody minded such a gorgeous contrast with themselves. And that was her magic.

She looked wise. 'Revolution, Judith, revolution.'

I opened my mouth to comment and it remained open for

pushing her way towards me was Winnie. She pounced on me. 'Judith, here you are. I thought I mightn't be able to find you. There must be hundreds here.'

I gaped at her, thunderstruck. 'What on earth are you doing here?'

She bridled at my shock. 'The same thing that you're doing.' Her little face puckered with determination.

'But, Winnie, it's not for you.'

'And why not?' She had that mulish expression I knew only too well. 'Harry said I should come. If you could do it, so should I.'

I was furious, 'Damn Harry. And who is going to look after you?'

'Judith,' she said, 'you don't go and shop in second-hand shops, do you?'

'And what has that to do with anything?'

'Not anything, Judith, everything. Experience,' she added loftily.

Miss Marie watched us with amusement. 'I'm Marie,' she interrupted prettily, 'from the Arts School.'

Winnie noted that Marie held my arm. She looked Marie up and down and took my other arm. 'I'm Winnie,' she responded coldly. 'Harry's cousin. You know Harry, her fiancé. I'm family.'

Miss Marie's mouth quirked. She had a repertoire of experiences in dealing with young students, like Winnie. 'Not to meet,' she said, 'but, of course, Judith speaks of him.'

Winnie turned to me. 'Well,' she declared, 'here I am.'

'Winnie,' I wailed, 'it could be dangerous.'

'I'm not scared,' she said stoutly. 'Well, not much.'

'She's not scared, Judith,' Miss Marie was approving. 'Of course she should come. Dear Winnie, where else would a brave sensible woman like yourself be on this day of all days?'

Winnie melted. 'Nobody thinks I have any political opinions, but I do. You'd be surprised, Judith. She thinks I'm hopeless, Miss

Marie, just because I couldn't stick up those silly posters. They were so, well, so sticky.'

'Of course you couldn't.' Infuriatingly Marie agreed with her. 'I find posters abominably sticky myself. All over your fingers, and then to get the bits of paper off, *mon Dieu*, it's impossible, and glue on your dress and in your hair.'

Winnie was amazed. 'Yes, it was just like that. Horrible.'

The two of them looked like a pair of smug conspirators.

'Damn Harry,' I hissed at them. 'He's got no right to interfere. You're not coming, Winnie. You can go home right now.'

She looked at me coldly. 'Stop ranting, Judith. Of course I'm coming.'

Miss Marie smiled benignly on her. 'Of course you are.'

I gave up. 'Very well, you can come, but see you look after yourself.'

She grinned at my surliness.

'You and Harry,' I said resignedly. 'Two peas in a pod.' Then a terrible thought struck me. 'Winnie, you haven't any marbles, have you? Harry didn't give you any marbles?'

She glanced at me sidelong, half guilty, half defiant. 'None of your business.'

'Of course it's my business.'

'He gave you marbles,' she retaliated.

I flushed. 'Yes, but I'd never use them.'

'What a Goody Two-Shoes you are, Judith. "I'd never use them",' she mimicked.

It was a vile habit. She and Harry both did it, mimicking me, often when I was most serious. 'Harry should mind his own business,' I flared.

'A lovers' tiff?' Miss Marie grinned at Winnie, who giggled. 'And I have my marbles, too, Winnie. It's an old revolutionary trick. Who knows, we all might need them. The police, they can be canaille.'

Winnie paled. She had not really thought of such an event. I waited for her to make some excuse and leave, even to sniffle, but she rallied.

'If I need them I'll use them.' She was defiant.

Cursing Harry for being so ill-advised, I felt dismayed and defeated.

It was not easy to organise the women into a procession. Rail tracks ran down the centre of some of the roads and any procession would need to split in two to let the cargo train pass. Inevitably there would be difficulties with traffic. As the start approached apprehension grew. It was obvious that some of the women now had misgivings. I saw frightened faces and shaking hands.

Mrs Danley called to me to find my mother. She looked doubtfully at Winnie but Winnie clung to my arm, so clearly she must be included in those who headed the march. I hadn't noticed their arrival, but suddenly Nathan's sisters shoved themselves to the front and positioned themselves beside us. Mrs Danley frowned in annoyance but accepted the inevitable.

There were eight of us in the front row: Winnie, myself and Miss Marie were in the middle, my mother and Mrs Danley on one side, Ailsa Thornhill and Nathan's sisters on the other.

'Fall in behind us,' Mrs Danley called through her megaphone, 'eight across each row. You know the route. Take your time, ladies, the streets are ours today. We have the numbers to command them.'

And, I thought, we did. There must have been nearly a thousand women there, many clutching or hugging the small placards they had made with such fervour at the soup kitchen. They were a pathetic collection of bits of cardboard stuck or tacked onto pieces of wood saved from the fire. After the march they would be treasured as fuel. They had made up their own messages, which were frequently misspelled, the lettering clumsy, the paintwork blotched. SCABS OUT. FOOD FOR OUR CHILDREN. WORK FOR OUR MEN.

They didn't know what to do with these placards. Mrs Danley had bullied her son into making a dozen larger more sophisticated ones for those of us in the front to carry but most of the other women seemed hesitant to use theirs. Miss Marie surveyed them. She'd had many doubtful insecure students. She took the megaphone from Mrs Danley with a 'You don't mind, do you?' and trilled, 'Lift up your placards, ladies. Like this,' as she held hers aloft. Still they hesitated, glancing from her to Mrs Danley, always their stalwart adviser.

Miss Marie was undaunted. 'I will count one, two, three and on three we will all raise our placards and shout hurrah.'

It worked. The hurrahs were faint but the placards went up.

Mrs Danley reclaimed the megaphone. 'Be strong, ladies,' she called and we all set off. Beside me I felt Winnie quiver. If she started to cry I would slap her. 'Don't you dare sniffle, Winnie.'

She was indignant. 'As if I would. Really, Judith, you know me better than that.' If she hadn't been so serious and solemn I would have laughed at her.

The crowd parted for the eight of us and slowly jostled themselves into position to fall in behind. A strange almost eerie silence had fallen. Even the children were subdued and quiet. It was as if the solemnity of the occasion possessed us all and we were awestruck by our own temerity. I was aware of this moving mass of women behind me. I could almost hear a great breath inhaled and exhaled to the rhythm of feet, slap slapping the pavement. At first the walking seemed tentative, as if a marching pace were briefly emulated and then abandoned. Now the pace was slow, steady and determined.

'They're getting used to it,' Miss Marie said. 'At first it is strange.'

'Yes,' I replied, 'I hadn't thought of it like that. I suppose they thought a march involved marching while a walk was walking, so how to decide between the two.'

Winnie giggled. 'I feel like the Pied Piper. Do you remember that poem we had to learn in third grade, Judith?'

'Of course. The Port Adelaide school had it, too. I can still recite it.' I began, '"In Hamlyn town in Brunswick ..."'

A train bisecting the road trundled towards us. The marchers split in two: Miss Marie, Ailsa and Nathan's sisters on one side, myself, Winnie, Mrs Danley and my mother on the other. Between the train carriages I saw Miss Marie diverge to lead a group of women along the footpath and under the verandas. A clothing shop advertised its sale with a large red flag. Miss Marie hoisted it from its stand and wrapped it about herself. When she returned to the road she was garbed like a flame from head to toe. She laughed with satisfaction. 'The colour of revolution, *mes amies.*'

'Harry should have told me.' Winnie looked at her wistfully. 'He knows all about revolution. I have a beautiful red dress I could have worn. And it cost me only a shilling.'

Crowds gathered on the footpaths to watch us. Most vehicles pulled over to let us through. Comments thrown from the footpath reached us. 'Good on yer, Mum. You tell the bastards. Cheers for the Bolshie women. Great stuff, girls, keep it up.' And, of course, Miss Marie drew the ubiquitous whistles and cat-calls. She responded with a beaming smile. To crass invitations to take her home any time or doing anything tonight, she threw kisses and some boys in the crowd pretended to stagger, smitten to the heart they clutched.

Slowly we became aware that there were men joining the march, falling into step behind the last of the women. Near the Labour Exchange a large group of men waited quietly. Some of them carried iron bars, others hunks of wood. I saw Mrs Danley glance at them. Her face puckered in concern. She spoke to my mother who looked worried.

'Judith, can you leave the march and speak with them? They mustn't join us.'

'No,' I said, 'I can't leave Winnie.'

'And why not?' Winnie hissed at me. 'I'm not a baby. Miss Marie is here.'

'No,' I repeated, 'I won't.'

'Perhaps Ailsa?' But my mother was doubtful. Ailsa Thornhill was a staunch foot soldier but lacked the backbone to stop any nonsense.

By then it was too late. Propelled by those behind us we had passed the waiting men and knew that they, too, had joined us and added something unpredictable. Harry told me later that they had determined amongst themselves to protect us.

And then it happened. It was all so fast that none of us had time to think. A boy burst out of the crowd on the footpath and running alongside the men shouted, 'The scabs are loading at Queens Wharf.'

Behind me some of the women halted, at first confused, then shoved forward by those behind. Mrs Danley shouted through her megaphone, 'Ladies, continue the march. We must reach the Town Hall. Be calm.'

But we were already on North Parade, approaching the wharf. Obsessed with reaching the scabs, the men bulked behind us, herding us before them in their thirst for confrontation. The crowd surged at my back and clutching Winnie I had no choice but to hurtle forward with the protesters. I searched desperately for some means of escape from what had now become a scrum of screaming, hysterical women and children. But there was no way out. We were being corralled between the warehouses and the river. The momentum precipitated us onto the wharf and there before us, lined up and immobile as carved granite, sat a row of mounted police. In unison they drew their batons from their holsters and waited.

One woman's scream topped all others and ricocheted off the stone walls of the warehouses. A flock of seagulls perched on a rooftop took off in panic. I knew that behind me prams toppled and babies were thrown on the rail tracks. The crowd concertinaed as women braced themselves against the rush to save their children before they, too, were flung to the ground. Still on my feet, I pelted forward, Winnie and Marie running beside me. Mrs Danley, still on her feet in the crush, bellowed through her megaphone for the police to back off. 'We're women and children. Back off! You're killing us!' She might have been King Canute, ineffectively and hopelessly ordering the waves to retreat.

In desperation she turned and struck the nearest horse with her placard. A baton thumped her raised arm. Men now grappled with police, struggling to drag them out of their saddles. The baton attacks became more vicious and indiscriminate.

In front of me, wedged beneath the belly of a horse, a toddler crouched, frozen with terror. In a minute he would be trampled to death. I dropped Winnie's hand and leapt forward. I smelled the horse's sweat and saw warm damp beads glisten along its belly. A baton struck my shoulder, nearly knocking me over but I reached out, grabbed the child's arm and yanked. The baton descended again but I had freed him. Beside me Miss Marie seized hold of him.

Through the excruciating pain in my shoulder I looked up and met the stoniest eyes I ever remembered having seen. With my uninjured hand I searched my pocket and felt the cold hard comfort of the marbles. A moment and I had them out. I cast them viciously beneath the horse.

Beside me Winnie screeched, 'You swine! You dirty bloody rotten swine!' And simultaneously she lobbed her handful of marbles, not on the roadway, but straight upwards at the policeman's face. I saw him rear back, lifting his baton arm to protect his eyes. Through a sick haze, I watched the marbles, a shower of glinting colour, fall about him. One stuck briefly in the horse's mane before it rolled to the ground. I noted it was a brilliant turquoise.

Faintly I heard Miss Marie gasp before she also hurled her marbles onto the road. There followed a wild skittering of hooves, a slithering, a snorting and a neighing, followed by a series of crashes. Helpless as wooden pegs in a bowling alley and almost in unison, the row of mounted police lost their balance and horses and men pitched to the ground.

The crowd, no longer penned, flowed over and around them and the three of us. Winnie and Marie helped me across the concrete apron to the side of the warehouse and an old bench. I sat down nursing my arm. 'The others,' I muttered. 'My mother?' And then I fainted.

My mother, shocked but unhurt, eventually found the three of us. She was torn between her concern for Mrs Danley, whose arm was obviously broken, and her worry about where I might be and if I were hurt. Miss Marie took over, reassured her about my welfare, and sent her back to help Mrs Danley who was stranded with Ailsa.

I was rather hazy about how I reached home but had a vague memory of Miss Marie finding a taxi. Winnie sat beside me cradling my hand and weeping hysterically. 'Don't die, Judith, please don't die.'

I managed a weak 'Don't be silly, Winnie, of course I won't die.' But she would not be consoled.

Before the march I would have been impatient with her tears but I recalled the shower of marbles, a kaleidoscope of colour in the brilliant sunshine, cascading in deadly beauty about the mounted policeman.

'Winnie, didn't Harry tell you where to throw the marbles?'

'Of course,' she hiccuped, 'but a lot of use that would have been. He was hurting you. I had to use my own initiative.'

'Oh, Winnie,' I said tearfully. 'Oh Winnie, you're such a card.'

Miss Marie ordered the taxi to take me first to the small casualty hospital where Dr Banks was in attendance. I was in such pain that he saw me immediately, although there were other women waiting, most of them distressed. He probed and pushed and made me move my fingers and open and shut my hand and finally pronounced that I had been lucky. There were no broken bones, only severe bruising.

'And where have you been to get like this?' he admonished.

'The women's march,' I said flatly. 'The police beat us up.'

Of course he had heard. 'Harumph,' he said. 'Such brutality.' He pursed his lips disapprovingly. 'What is our society coming to? Such brutality.'

He put a sling on my arm and told me to take painkillers and rest. 'No more marches,' he ordered as if I was still a child engaging in naughty practices. He stumped off and called his next patient from the long line of battered women.

Fortunately for me my left arm was damaged, not my right, so I could still draw. It was a miracle that in the mayhem on the wharf no one was killed. Babies, although tipped from their prams, had rolled harmlessly and been retrieved, crying but uninjured. One five-year-old boy had his front teeth broken but I heard his mother had been philosophical: they were baby teeth and he would lose them soon anyway. But many of the women were severely bruised from falls, batons and horse kicks. All were shocked and terrified by what might have been a more disastrous outcome.

The mounted police were constabulary enlisted from outside the Port. As it was useless to vent rage on them, the local police became the town's target of jibes and abuse. In shops and bars they found themselves jostled and harangued.

There may have been abuse of women at home but public abuse was seen as an outrage, a threat to everything society said it held dear – the sanctity of women, children and the home. From my experience at the soup kitchen I no longer believed that all the homes in the Port were sanctified but it was always good in a cartoon to appeal to what people thought they valued. So I worked on a cartoon entitled *The hand that rocks the cradle* and beneath the hooves of horses, and under the batons of police, women and babies were heaped on the road. Underneath it I penned the caption *Great Expectations: Women & children first.* And in a second cartoon I drew a woman bandaged from head to foot in a hospital bed while her skeletal child weeping beside her says, *But, Mummy, the nice policeman said the horse did it.*

Although I heard the story from Harry, who heard it from Nathan, it was all over town that an incensed Mrs Danley, impressive with her broken arm in a sling and her face purple and swollen with bruises, stalked into the premises of the *Despatch* newspaper and demanded to see the editor. When he scuttled in she commanded him to print in full the petition we had been prevented from presenting at the Port Town Hall.

Unwisely, he demurred, even having the temerity to suggest that the women had brought the trouble on themselves by lacking 'political wisdom'. It would have been better for him if he had kept a still tongue in his head. Enraged by his attitude, Mrs Danley told him roundly that if he refused he would be blacklisted by the congregation of St Paul's Anglican church and not one church-goer would dare speak with him again.

Faced with her threat, he buckled, and the petition appeared in large print on the second page. In addition there was a state-ment about the number of people who had signed it and a grovel-ling sentence or two suggesting that the younger members of the police might have 'over-reacted'. After all, they were dealing with women and children, not burly wharf-labourers.

But from then on he ordered his staff to keep watch for Mrs Danley, and, on the few occasions she went to place an advertise-ment in the column for church news, he fled out the back and hid in the lavatory.

Of course the *Despatch* and the *Register* had proclaimed a victory for the police in preventing the illegal attack on volunteer labourers who were merely doing their job loading wheat onto the *Van Spilbergen*. The women marchers were ill-advised in allowing themselves to be used by gangs of hoodlums who came armed with bottles and chunks of wood to throw at police also doing their duty. And it was disgraceful that some women were heard to use the sort of foul language only heard in bar rooms.

The *Workers' Weekly* on the other hand hailed it as a triumph for working-class action. Women who had previously been politically dormant had now erupted into a major force to be contended with. All hail the mothers of the revolution, it proclaimed.

A meeting of the Port Adelaide Trades and Labour Council passed a motion that 'We protest strongly against the action of some mounted police riding down inoffensive citizens under verandas and along footpaths and using batons in defiance of British law and the Constitution which says a baton should be used only as a last resource and the Commissioner of Police is not under law an infallible authority to deprive citizens of their rights'.

When my father read this he hawked up a rich globule of yellow saliva and spat into the river. It was always his way of dispelling his disgust. 'Feeble, futile bastards. Couldn't they come up with something better than that? Like supporting us to get the scabs off the wharves and back into our own jobs?' He spat again.

When Harry visited we sat together quietly, often not speaking while he held my hand. I asked him if Nathan's sisters had come out of it unscathed.

'Yes,' he said, 'not like you. They were unharmed, but Nathan said they were very distressed and quite affronted. He didn't seem to feel that their comment was strange so I said nothing.'

But I told my mother that they had been distressed and affronted. She guffawed. 'Affronted? That's a good one. What next? Women chasing their babies all over the wharf, terrified that they'd be trampled to death or knocked into the river, but

Nathan's sisters are merely "affronted".' She slammed the lid on a saucepan of stew she was cooking. 'Affronted? Go and have a good spit over the side into the river for me, Niels.'

Of course, Miss Marie also visited and after she had inquired about my health we discussed my work and I told her that cartoons were my compensation for not being physically able to change the course of things and I needed this emotional consolation.

My father said, 'She's a very pretty woman, although maybe a little flamboyant. And what's this Froggy stuff she talks?'

I laughed. 'Memories, I suppose. Like you occasionally recall a phrase in Icelandic.'

'Mm,' he said. 'I suppose so.'

Part 3

Political Cartoons

Harry and I decided to marry in the spring. We needed somewhere to live in the Port. I refused to move to Adelaide, so far away from my parents and the river. To leave my cabin on the hulk and all its memories was difficult enough for me. So we went house hunting – somewhere suitable to rent – not too costly, but not as cheap as the hovels in Timson Street, renowned for housing the destitute.

It was easy to find available places. But although we searched together for our future home, and it should have been a joyous adventure, it was in fact sad and dispiriting. Many of the abandoned houses had stood empty for months. We saw miserable reminders of past tenants: a broken toy, a half-cleaned saucepan, a torn cushion, a tatty rag mat. More than likely the previous tenants had been evicted, forced out by lack of money. I wondered where they had gone.

'I feel awful,' I told Harry. 'It's as if I'm a vulture picking over the carcase of someone's life.'

He put his arm about me and kissed me. 'Don't be sad, Judith. It's only a house. We'll make it ours.'

I did my best to match his cheerfulness. But there was more and more evidence that the Port community was wounded. Protests and beatings continued and the strikers and their families continued to struggle with grim-lipped determination. They had no alternative, proud people refused to crawl into holes and die. They fought not only the public battles and brawls on the streets but the petty pinpricks of government officials determined to show their power over people less fortunate and more helpless than themselves.

Everyone knew it was coming but this didn't relieve the anger and dismay when beef was removed from the ration cards.

Mr Mountford, our butcher, rebelled in a small manner against the regulations. I had waited in his shop with my ration card while he dispensed the usual ration of chopped up bits of fatty mutton to the tight-lipped women in the queue ahead of me. Mostly he handed over the meat with a shamefaced apologetic murmur, but that day he singled out a woman more desperate than the rest.

'Why, Mrs O'Brien,' he said, his tone bluff and kindly, 'how are you? And that brood of lovely kiddies you have? Seven, isn't it?'

She was a small haggard, anxious woman, thin to the point of emaciation. He chucked her meat on the wrapping paper and by a quick sleight-of-hand reached under the counter for something extra. Hurriedly he wrapped it all together and handed it to her.

'A little something to give it extra flavour, missus. That'll put roses in the kiddies' cheeks.'

He winked at me, knowingly. I smiled back. We all knew that he regularly secreted a few pieces of good gravy beef in Mrs O'Brien's rations.

None of us had noted the two strangers who had entered and were standing at the back of the shop. I think I saw them first. In their dark suits they smelled of officialdom.

'Quick, Mrs O'Brien,' I said, 'put the meat in your basket and leave.' I gave her a little push but she was confused and still clutched the parcel in her hand.

One of the officials shoved through the waiting women to stand in front of the counter. Before Mrs O'Brien realised his intentions he snatched the parcel from her, flung it down on the counter and proceeded to unravel the paper wrapping. All chatting in the shop ceased abruptly. All eyes were riveted on Mrs O'Brien, who, red-faced and desperate, tried to rewrap and reclaim the meat.

He pushed her hand away and she burst into a storm of weeping. He looked her over, his eyes thin and rapacious. 'Now, madam, that's enough of that. You know your entitlements.'

He poked around in the small heap of fatty mutton and discovered the few bits of gravy beef. 'And what have we here?'

He turned triumphantly to his companion. 'Beef, I'll be sure.'

Mr Mountford remained silent but there was hatred in his eyes as he looked at his accuser and shame as he looked at the weeping Mrs O'Brien. 'Judith,' he appealed to me helplessly.

'You're a pair of curs.' I glared at them. 'A pair of rotten curs, hunting down the starving. This woman has seven children to feed. What's it to you if she has a few pieces of gravy beef?'

'None of our business, girlie. It's regulations and we're here to uphold them.'

Incensed by the 'girlie', their contempt and heartlessness, I raged at them. 'Give her back her meat right now. Can't you see that these women go home to starving children?'

They both shrugged. 'None of our business, girlie, and none of yours. And any more lip from you and we'll close down this establishment, pronto. This parcel of meat is evidence. What do you all expect on the susso? Tell your husbands to get a job and pay for your keep and all your brats'.'

They turned to leave the shop but the silent women now blocked their way.

'Move aside, ladies.'

No one budged. Someone hissed, a soft sibilance that escalated and then crescendoed into a sinister threat that filled the shop.

'Let us pass, ladies.'

But now their strident command held a note of panic.

'Not likely', Mrs Rawlings said.

'We'll take that meat,' Mrs Pole said, and reached for the package.

They tried to back away but were trapped by the press of bodies.

'It's evidence!' They tried belligerence.

'Evidence?' Mrs Rawlings snarled. 'We'll evidence you. Hand it over and now or we'll take it.'

The two of them shrank. Their belligerence had turned to squeaking. 'You'll be sorry for this, all of you. The police'll be here. Threats to government officers.'

'Oh, shut up,' Mrs Pole said. 'We'll tell you what threats are. Come here again and we'll tar and feather both of you. There's plenty of tar down the timber yards and plenty of local chooks we can pluck. You leave Mr Mountford alone, because if he closes we'll come for you and your kind. You pass the word around.'

They stuttered. 'Threats won't g-g-get you anywhere, ladies.'

With a jeering laugh the women half carried, half-shoved the two officials out the door and flung them onto the roadway. They lined the footpath, watching their victims scramble to their feet and then, as they made a last effort to stand their ground, Mrs Rawlings grabbed a broom leaning against the doorway and rushed at them.

They fled before her down the street. She returned breathless but triumphant. Of course, when it was over, they feared reprisals but no government officials came again to Mr Mountford's shop and his right to dispense rations in exchange for ration cards continued. It was a small victory, much talked about and it cheered everyone. But it was only local. As for the bigger picture, the beef marches and the hunger marches began.

I penned my cartoons as a response to the incident: two dogs, wearing hats of government officials, sniffing around a butcher's shop and one saying to the other, *Can you smell beef? I'm certain I can.* And a second one, more vulgar: two dogs with official hats on their heads outside a butcher's shop, one with his leg cocked against the doorway and the caption, *How many now have we had to mark for giving out this beef? I'm running out of pee.*

My father chortled at this, but my mother was a little shocked. 'Judith, do you have to be vulgar?'

I was tart. 'Not half as vulgar as starvation, Mum.'

'Leave her alone, Eve,' my father said. 'The blokes will love that one.'

Harry and I found a suitable house. It was a small working-man's cottage in Divett Street with a central hallway, a bedroom and living room, and a small kitchen and bathroom at the rear. The bathroom had a chip heater but there was a newer gas water heater above the kitchen sink. When I turned on the hot water tap the pilot light ignited the gas and there was a delightful popping sound. I turned it on and off a couple of times just to amuse myself.

'Listen to this, Harry,' I said.

He grinned and hugged me.

There was a small enclosed veranda, which might have been a child's bedroom. In a lean-to shed out the back there was a copper and a trough and clothes mangle. The backyard was a narrow ribbon of unkempt grass and weeds.

The house had served as a shop as well as a home and had been extended at the front to include a small room with shelves and a counter. It seemed to have been used for serving fruit and vegetables, for in a corner were a few old crates labelled SOUTH AUSTRALIAN TOMATOES. I recalled Nathan's stump in the Botanic Gardens. What an awkward green girl I had been – so shy, so clumsy.

'Does Nathan still speak at The Stump?' I asked Harry.

He was roaming about the room, inspecting and prodding the woodwork for borers.

'Sometimes, I think, but his main job now is to educate the comrades.'

'He always had a book in his hand at the Chew It.'

'Still has. And expects us all to do the same. Could you believe it, Judith? But I'm now struggling with Lenin's *The State and Revolution* and Jack London's *The Iron Heel*. There's not much humour in either.' He chuckled. 'But I tell Nathan that I prefer Jack London. At least he makes some pretence of writing a story.'

'I read Jack London years ago. Joe Pulham introduced me to his *White Fang* and *Call of the Wild*. They weren't political but they were marvellous tales. He killed himself, Harry.'

'Not Joe. I never heard that.'

'No, Jack London.'

'I don't think there are borers in this counter, Jude, but we'll get rid of it just in case.'

I smiled lovingly at him. Harry lived in the present. It was rare that memories from the past saddened him with any sense of time passing. Once he said to me that he liked the communists because they concentrated on the future and it was such a hopeful future.

'When you'll be paid to dance,' I had gently teased him.

'Of course,' he replied. 'You know that's my chief motivation.'

But I wasn't certain that Harry really understood himself. Sometimes he seemed to be seeking something, rather like now, with head down and eyes peering for the tiny telltale holes left by borers.

To my amazement and consternation the *Workers' Weekly* rejected my cartoon of the two government officials dressed as dogs urinating on the butcher's wall. I had been certain that they would share my sense that its nastiness aptly matched and countered the beastliness I had witnessed in the butcher's shop. Those officials had shown a personal and vindictive malevolence and deserved nothing better than the way I had portrayed them.

The reason for rejecting my cartoon was brief and abrupt. It was in bad taste. Too vulgar for their readers. It would lower the tone of the paper that aimed to be uplifting.

I read and re-read these cold comments. Had they come from the editor or some office boy? I was angry but also discomforted, finding it hard to shake off an uncomfortable feeling that somehow I had committed an indiscretion. I showed the rejected cartoon to Miss Marie. I was in class practising my pen strokes. I still had much to learn about hatching and scribbled strokes. Sometimes I found it hard to create the decisive but fluid strokes so telling and so necessary.

Miss Marie constantly admonished me, 'You are too tense,

Judith. Relax. Feel the stroke flow first in this direction then in another.'

I liked working in pen and ink and had a collection of various nibs, some fine, some coarser, and occasionally I collected a dropped feather from the deck of the hulk and fashioned it into a quill. It was easy to carry several pens, a pad and a small bottle of ink in a bag and make quick sketches outside. As well as my cartoons I had a collection of drawings of people and scenes from the Port. One day I would develop them into larger more complete works.

But at the minute I found myself obsessed with not only my disappointment but also a sense that what I had assumed I knew and understood had no reality. I had discounted Harry's comments that the *Workers' Weekly* wanted my cartoons to reflect more nobility, believing it a piece of nonsense. Now I could see that my view of what was true didn't suit the party line.

'What do you think of it, Miss Marie?' I asked while I drew a line so wobbly that I threw the paper aside.

She read it and laughed. '*Ma pauvre* Judith, and what did you expect?'

'Respect for my work. It's a good cartoon. Good cartoons should offend.'

'But you didn't expect it to offend the comrades?'

'No, of course not.'

'*Ma pauvre* Judith,' she repeated. 'You perhaps haven't realised how straight-laced the comrades are. They are not, you know, so different from everybody else. Little things can discomfort and offend them and they'll make the most of it.'

I put my pen aside. It was useless to continue to grapple with graceful fluid lines. I was too incensed. 'And what price, then, their passion for revolution to change society?'

She smiled wryly. 'That's an entirely different matter, Judith. That is in the head, not in the sensibilities. You should not expect people to be consistent. It's at odds with your cartoons, which are built on a clever awareness of the inconsistencies, banalities and even venality of people. The comrades are puritans, *mon amie*, modern Cromwellian Roundheads.'

I recalled Nathan's extreme embarrassment at finding me dishevelled in Victoria Square after the 'riot'. 'Mmn,' I said. 'That fits.'

She gave me an odd look but I didn't explain.

'Send your cartoon to *Spearhead*,' she chuckled. 'Tell the editor ...' She scrummaged around in her handbag. 'I have his address here somewhere. Tell the editor that I recommend you. And,' she threw me a naughty look, 'that the *Workers' Weekly* has rejected it. That should tickle their fancy. I think you'll be pleasantly surprised.'

'They're anarchists,' I said.

She was off hand. 'Of course. *Naturellement.*'

'Are you an anarchist, Miss Marie?'

She avoided my eyes. 'There are many paths to a perfect state, Judith. I jump in and out of ideas. Now take my advice and send your vulgar cartoon to *Spearhead*. I can guarantee your instant acceptance.'

She was right, of course. I sent the cartoon and a letter came back post haste with acceptance and effusive thanks. They had seen my cartoons in the *Workers' Weekly* and the *Sun News Pictorial* and admired them for some time. They had even hoped that I might offer them an occasional cartoon. But now I was so well-known, so acclaimed, they had hesitated to ask me because they could not pay me as much as the daily papers or the *Workers' Weekly*. They hoped humbly that I would accept a smaller payment. The letter ended with an enthusiastic comment that it was a jolly good cartoon and they had all split their sides laughing over it, despite its serious intent.

So, it was a letter from a young person, like me, and its

enthusiasm warmed me. I had not realised that my work was so widely known and it was delightful to have it sought after even if I was not so well paid for it.

When Harry arrived at the hulk waving a copy of *Spearhead* at me he looked agitated and distressed. 'Judith, I've seen your cartoon. It's here.' It was almost an accusation.

'Yes.' I was non-committal.

'Judith, it's in *Spearhead*.'

'Yes. They accepted it and paid me. Not a lot but they've contracted me for a weekly cartoon. It's regular money and they like my work.'

'But, Judith,' he protested.

In the face of my cool response to his agitation, he looked at a loss. 'Judith, they're on the other side. They're anarchists.'

I sighed. 'Harry, they're on the left. We all agree society needs to be better. We all look at things that are wrong. How can they be on the other side? The *Despatch* is on the other side and the *Register*.'

He looked nonplussed. 'They hate the communists.'

I grinned. 'And vice-versa it would appear. What a waste of time.'

He looked unhappy. I stood up and kissed him. 'Come on, we'll make a pot of tea. Are you out tonight?'

Harry's work was mostly at night. His small band continued to play regularly at the Semaphore and he rode his bicycle there and back to save us money.

He still looked uncertain as he followed me into the galley. I took down the teapot, cups and saucers, and found some biscuits, filled the kettle with water and put it on to heat. Then I sat down opposite him. 'Harry,' I said, 'these newspapers, whether they're communist, anarchist or capitalist, buy my cartoons. They do not buy me. They are free to accept or reject my work and I am equally free to send it to whoever I choose. Whatever the news-paper, my work doesn't change.'

'You're so determined, Judith. So strong,' he said miserably and I felt that unfortunately his comment was not praise but a sort of reproach.

My mother made us curtains for the windows of our house. They were blue-check gingham, cheap but bright and clean. She had tried to make a seamstress of me but I had always preferred to draw. Sometimes with a new piece of cloth in my hand I imagined myself making something beautiful but usually after this first flush of pleasurable anticipation the long haul of cutting, stitching and hemming bored me and my mother would reproach, 'Judith, you never finish anything.' Eventually she gave up expecting me to sew.

'Do you like these?' she asked, holding up the neatly hemmed oblongs of cloth. I think they'll brighten your rooms and they'll be easy to launder and won't require a lot of ironing.'

I looked at them, speculating on how long it would be before I had to do either of these tasks. Washing and ironing didn't appeal to me any more than sewing. My mother understood and laughed. 'You'll have to do a little housework, Judith, if you have a house. You can't live in a pig sty.'

I grinned at her. 'Of course, I'll do a little – as little as possible. And don't say "Poor Harry" as if the absence of a wife devoted to his domestic comfort will somehow leave him deprived.'

She chuckled. 'Harry's so sweet-tempered I doubt he'll ever criticise you.'

And I didn't tell her that I baulked at the idea that I should be grateful for Harry's sweet temper. As far as I was concerned our marriage was a marriage of equals.

Harry and I did the rounds of second-hand shops searching for a wardrobe, chest of drawers, kitchen table, chairs and a food-safe. We found two old wooden rocking chairs for the parlour and my mother made us some cushion covers, which I stuffed with kapok.

We had found an old iron bedstead but we had been extravagant on a new mattress. It was cheap but clean and firm.

Harry continued to be assiduous for any telltale signs of borers or bed bugs. Bed bugs were particularly hard to detect because usually the furniture had been wiped over and there were no signs of smeared blood. They were cunning little blighters that slid into the smallest interstices where they hid and thrived before their nightly attacks. Often children at the soup kitchen arrived with ridges of raised welts across their legs and arms, which they scratched frantically. We always had a bottle of bicarb-soda and regularly dabbed the sufferers with a gluey mixture of soda and water. Afterwards they looked like little spotted clowns.

We were very excited to see our purchases installed and went from room to room hand-in-hand exclaiming how nice everything looked and how clever we had been to manage so cheaply. Harry cleaned and polished the front windows and I swept and scrubbed the old linoleum floors. Its pattern was faded and it was cracked in places but we couldn't afford to replace it so in front of the parlour fireplace, where there was a large hole, I decided to put the rag mat which had always been in my cabin on the hulk.

It was the mat more than anything else that made me realise the complete change that was about to take place in my life and when I took it up I burst into tears. My mother put her arms about me. 'My little cabin,' I sobbed. 'I won't ever sleep here again when I'm married. I won't smell the sea or hear it lap against the wharf. I don't like our new house. It's horrible.'

She consoled me. 'No, my dear, of course it's not. You can come back here to sleep whenever you want. Your father and I aren't going away. Your house in town is only a little change and you'll love it. So much to look forward to.'

I hiccuped, miserably certain that she was deceiving me and that I wouldn't enjoy my future life one jot.

However Harry's enthusiasm for the mat lessened my misery.

'It looks grand, Judith,' he said, 'and it's so generous of you. I'm sure you didn't like taking it from your cabin.' He touched it lovingly. 'It'll be our special treasure. I love hand-made things.'

Darling Harry, so many of his feelings matched mine.

Winnie and I went shopping for my wedding outfit. Winnie was ecstatic.

'No, Winnie,' I forestalled her, 'don't give it a moment's thought. I'm not going all in white, done up like a wedding cake. I need a nice dress that I can wear again for best.'

She looked disappointed but accepting. 'I suppose that's sensible. You won't have much money.'

'No.'

'A second-hand shop? They've usually got great bargains.'

'No, Winnie, something brand new, from Myers I think. One of the new rayons.'

'OK.' She looked resigned. 'It won't be much fun. Myers is so very staid.'

I took her arm. 'How you've changed, Winnie. We're a bit like the two bears – one got better and the other got wuss.'

She giggled. 'I suppose it's thinking about marriage that has sobered you.'

I poked her jokingly. 'Shut up, Winnie. Don't tease me.'

She giggled again, then glanced at me seriously. 'What do your parents think about your marrying Harry?'

'They expected it.'

'Yes, but are they happy with it?'

'They love Harry.'

'Yes, everyone loves Harry. But let's face it, Judith. He isn't much of a catch, doesn't have many prospects. And fewer now because he's mixed up with all those bolshies. Doesn't it worry you that he may never get a steady job?'

'I'm not marrying a prospect, Winnie. I'm marrying someone

I love. He has his band and we'll always have his piano playing.'

She sighed and said, sententiously, 'Love doesn't pay the bills.'

This is just what I'd heard my father remark, quietly to my mother, when he thought I couldn't hear.

'I'll pay the bills,' I asserted. 'It doesn't matter which of us brings in the bacon.'

'You probably will have to, Judith.'

'It's not like you to be so cynical, Winnie. You've always been so romantic.'

'Not really. At heart I'm a practical shop-keeper's daughter and this depression has taught me a lot about reality.'

'And you're afraid that I've lost both my heart and my sense of reality?'

'Yes.'

'And you'd have me refuse Harry because of what might happen in the future?'

She looked unhappy. 'I don't know.'

I hugged her. 'I couldn't do that, Winnie.'

'No,' she said, resignedly. 'I can see that. It would be quite impossible for you to do that.'

'Yes, quite impossible.'

We found a dress I loved. It was turquoise and rayon as I had planned, with a nipped-in waist and a full flowing graceful skirt. I also found a natural straw hat, decorated with a matching turquoise ribbon. Summer gloves and a pair of new black shoes and I was set.

'You know, Winnie, this turquoise is the exact colour of one of the marbles you threw at the policeman.'

'Heavens, Judith, don't go remembering all that.'

'It's hard to forget. It was just one marble and it stuck in the horse's mane and trickled down its neck. It was this blue.'

She shuddered. 'I thought he would kill you.'

'So did I, Winnie. Thank you.' She flushed and looked teary.

'No, Winnie, please don't cry.'

She laughed shakily. 'A coat. Have you got a coat, Judith? It may be cold. Spring days are unpredictable.'

'My old coat'll have to do. I can't afford a new coat.'

'It might spoil the effect.'

'I'll hope for a warm day. And no, Winnie, I won't search the second-hand shops.' I didn't tell her that my skin crawled at the idea of wearing someone else's cast-off clothes. I'd rather go in rags.

We were lucky. It was a beautiful spring day for our wedding. The breeze was a little cool and I might have been more comfortable wearing my coat but for the occasion I preferred a few goose bumps on my arms.

We had decided on the Adelaide Registry Office. Harry's mother had complained vaguely that a proper church wedding would be nice, more like a real marriage. She maundered on about her own wedding and how exquisite it had been and how she had worn a lace gown and veil and had three bridesmaids and at the memory of past happiness wiped tears from the corners of her eyes. Harry did his best to cheer her with promises that the Registry Office was very pleasant. He reminded her, perhaps unwisely, that things had changed since she married and we all had to be careful about money. We were all in a depression he said.

'Well, dear,' she was concerned. 'If you are depressed about getting married you should call it off. Are you also depressed, Judith?' And she looked anxiously from me to Harry.

'Not a bit,' I said and grinned at her.

'There, Harry,' she reproached. 'Judith isn't depressed, so you should cheer up. No woman wants a depressed husband.'

His mother, Winnie's parents, Winnie, my parents and Miss Marie all attended the ceremony, which was brief. Harry was nervous and I hoped that Winnie's father hadn't given him a ponderous lecture on responsibility.

When the Registrar asked him if he would take an oath of affirmation on the Bible Harry got confused and said yes.

We had decided not to swear on the Bible because communists didn't believe in religion and I was indifferent to it. But in the confusion the Registrar ruled a large black line across the secular part of the marriage licence. He handed the Bible to Harry. 'It's unusual for people to object to taking the oath but these days it happens and I have to ask.'

Since Harry had taken the oath and that large black line looked so daunting I did similarly.

Later Harry said to me apologetically, 'I couldn't retract it, Judith. Did you mind?'

'Not at all. It was really quite funny. Your uncle and aunt looked so bemused. They thought we were heathens to get married in the Registry Office anyway.'

Afterwards we all returned to our new house. My mother had made the best cake she could with the ingredients available to her. I had asked Miss Marie to bring her nasturtium-leaf sandwiches and she arrived with a huge box of chocolates. Winnie's mother contributed a box of delicacies, some ham, cheese, dried biscuits, fruit, and two bottles of white wine from the Barossa Valley.

For a wedding present my mother and father gave us their piano. When the carriers had brought it a week before, Harry had been speechless. Crimson with joy, he opened the lid with shaking hands and reverently played a few notes. 'Now,' he had breathed, 'I'll learn to read music and play something really worthwhile. It deserves the very best. My own piano. I never dared dream.' I had secretly contributed money to having it tuned and I shared my parents' happiness in his awed delight.

Miss Marie gave us a hand-painted tea set. She must have worked for months on its intricate flower design. Winnie's family gave us a cheque for 200 pounds. It was twice the amount Joe had left me and I had eked out that money for years. Glowing with pleasure, I kissed and thanked them both. What could Harry and I do with 200 pounds? I had once boasted to him that we could live like kings on two pounds a week and now we had before us the magical possibility of living like kings for two years. I need no longer lie awake at night worrying about the success of my cartoons. Whatever they brought in would be a bonus. Marriage, I decided, draining the last dregs of wine from my glass, was a very happy state.

Harry sat opposite me at our own little kitchen table, staring at the cheque and looking thoughtful.

'Isn't it marvellous, Harry? Blessings on your uncle. Now we can live like kings for two whole years and after that there'll probably be no depression, you'll have a job and I'll be a successful cartoonist.'

What with the wine and our good fortune I floated in a euphoric pool of well-being and a belief that now anything in our lives was possible. He continued to finger the cheque, unresponsive to my enthusiasm.

'What's the matter, Harry? Are you concerned that your uncle couldn't afford it? Is there something I don't know about Winnie's family? Something you're hiding? We could give some to your mother.'

Now I was anxious, guilty to be so overjoyed by our good fortune.

He laughed awkwardly. 'No, darling, I was only thinking. It's nothing.'

'We ought to talk about "nothing". You are worried about something.'

'Not at all.' He jumped up. 'How about a tune?' and with a sort of strange desperate defiance he lifted the lid and plunged into 'If you knew Susie like I know Susie'. Puzzled, I cleared the table. It was now quite late. After eating we had all had a sing-song around the piano, Harry revelling in the company and the music.

'We should think about turning in, Harry,' I said casually. Perhaps this was what was worrying him.

I went to have a wash and put on my best nightie. When I returned to the bedroom he had changed into his pyjamas and was propped up in bed waiting for me.

'Shall I put out the light?' I asked.

'No. I want to talk to you, Judith.'

'Yes.' I jumped into bed beside him. 'Fire away. Spit it out. I'm listening.'

I cuddled up to him. I was relieved. Now, perhaps, I would hear what had worried him. It couldn't be all that serious. I waited.

He fumbled for words. At last he got it out and it would have been better if he had remained silent.

'Judith, I want to give some of that two hundred pounds to the Communist Party.'

All the breath sucked out of my body. 'You what?' I was surprised that I could speak and that my words were so steady and cool.

'I want to give some of the two hundred pounds to the Communist Party.' But he wouldn't look at me.

'No!' I said, so violently that I even surprised myself. 'No!'

I pulled away from him and he cringed. He reached out a hand to me. I shoved it aside and he flinched.

'Half of it is mine.' He was surly. 'You can have a hundred pounds and I can have a hundred. That's fair. And I can do with my share whatever I like. We're supposed to donate to the Party. How else can it keep going? And I'm ashamed because I never have anything to give.'

'And you've nothing now.' My voice was tight and furious. 'We have to help your mother and my parents and we have to live. You give your hundred away and then we have to live on mine.'

'I don't plan to give it all away, Judith, just ...'

'I don't want to know about "just". You're not giving one penny to the Communist Party.'

Beside myself with rage and a sense of betrayal, I threw back the bedclothes, sprang out of bed, and stood trembling on the bare floor.

'Look at me, Harry!' But he refused.

I could hear myself, strident, screeching. I knew that I should stop, be quiet and reasonable, discuss whatever Harry wanted, but I was seized both by disappointment and panic. I knew that Harry had joined the Communist Party and that he admired Nathan. I had even jibed, 'Simon says,' when he repeated Nathan's dictums. And Harry had always side-stepped my comments with his: 'A socialist state will pay me to dance, Judith.' It had all seemed light-hearted, but now it wasn't. It was a serious intrusion into our newly married life and I wasn't prepared for it.

Bugger Nathan, I thought. This was his doing. His and his two poisonous sisters. 'Let's get this clear, Harry. Our money is our money. We don't halve it so you can throw yours away uselessly and then live on mine. We share everything and decide together what's important. If you don't want that then we have no marriage.'

I stormed out of the bedroom and slammed the door behind me. Shaking with fury, I pulled the hanging switch for the light in my workroom. It was only a pale yellow effulgence. Feverishly I dragged some pages of unfinished cartoons and drawings from the press, plonked them on the table, picked up my pencil, and prepared to work. If Harry was going to give our money away, then I'd better start supporting us in earnest. But, of course, I couldn't work. I just sat there, shivering with distress.

Half an hour later Harry found me. 'Judith,' he whispered from the doorway, 'I'm really sorry. I can't imagine what a fool I've been. Of course you're right. Please, Judith, forgive me. I've always been an irresponsible idiot but I'll try to do better.'

He came to my side and stroked my hair. I stiffened. He bent and kissed the nape of my neck. 'Please, darling, come back to bed.'

'And you won't give our money away?'

'No. Of course not.'

'Never?'

'No, never. I promise.'

He put his arms about me and sang softly, 'What'll I do when skies are blue and you're not here, what'll I do?'

'Don't, Harry,' I said wearily. 'Please don't always sing that song. Sometimes it makes me sad.'

'And I've given you enough sadness for tonight.'

He pulled me to my feet and cradled me. 'There,' he said. He had come in without his pyjama top and his skin was smooth and creamy. I touched it and found it warm. He looked down at me. My nightie had slipped off my shoulder and he bent and kissed my breast.

'You're so beautiful, Judith.'

And as his body was warm and urgent against mine I recalled the Indian boys leaping into the sea, and laughing Ganesh with his cotton garments clinging about the little knob between his thighs, and Joe Pulham's reluctance to explain to me about Aristophanes' *Lysistrata*. 'Not yet, Nearly-Twelve,' he had apologised. 'When you are older.' Now I thought with secret amusement I could say to Joe, there's no need to explain anything to me. I'm no longer Nearly-Twelve and I've discovered it all myself.

The following day our happiness of the previous night was tinged with a little constraint. Neither of us could completely put aside our dreadful row. I felt ashamed to have been so harsh. Harry, I knew, felt a degree of resentment. I made us some breakfast and we were awkward with each other. We had been friends for years. We had shared happy experiences and some terrible ones but today it seemed that we were strangers, meeting for the first time. The night's events had made us closer but at the same time more distant, plunging us into a foreign country where we were wary of the unfamiliar language and its hidden meanings. Expectations, once casual, were now entangled in intimacy; stronger, yet at the same time, more fragile.

I had strolled confidently into marriage, expecting only a continuation of what was familiar. Now I knew it to be a state more complex, more delicate and more easily broken.

I looked across the table at Harry. Seemingly he was absorbed in his porridge but his eating was automatic and his face so usually merry and confident looked sober, even worried.

'If you haven't any plans for today, Judith,' he said cautiously, 'I should go to the Labour Exchange and see if there is any work.'

Immediately, with a rush of guilt, I knew that he was doing this because I had shouted about money. I didn't know how to handle this. 'We should be together for the day,' I mumbled. It was another lovely sunny morning.

'We could go in to Adelaide perhaps. Stroll through the gardens. Or to the Semaphore. Take tea at the pavilion. We could go out,' I said humbly.

He looked at me gratefully. 'You'd like that?'

'Yes.' I smiled at him lovingly. 'We can't afford a honeymoon.' I stopped, confused. Here I was talking about money again.

But he rescued me. 'No,' he was firm. 'We can't. No one can these days. But we can go out. Put on your best dress, darling. Where will we go? I'm at your service, ma'am,' and he jumped up and bowed to me with a grin.

'Oh, Harry, you ...' I laughed. He hugged me.

I put on my wedding dress once more and my pretty hat and we caught the tram to the Semaphore. At a little cafe overlooking the beach we ordered tea and cakes. It was low tide and the sea had receded leaving pale green threads of water between mauve sand banks. How tranquil it was. Why had I no longings to be a painter? Why did I choose to always comment on the turbulence of political life, which in the end was more ephemeral than this?

Thousands of us, not only from the Port but from all over Adelaide and its surrounds, joined the march of protest against the removal of beef from the food rations. Later it came to be known as the Beef March, but I called it the Hunger March. Harry agreed. He said that to call it a hunger march described it accurately and united us with all the other poor starving sods in England and Europe taking to the streets.

It was eight miles from the Port to Treasury Place in Adelaide. All along the route police harassed us: for walking on the tram lines or train lines, for obstructing the traffic. When they diverted us onto footpaths they pestered us for causing congestion and inconvenience to the general public.

We ignored their petty irritations and complied with instructions. We gritted our teeth and refused to be provoked into reprisals. However we persisted in shouting our slogan from the Free Speech Movement: THE STREETS BELONG TO THE WORKERS and WORK OR FULL-MAINTENANCE.

By the time our Port contingent arrived in Adelaide the roads leading to Treasury Place were overflowing. It was both inspiring and dispiriting to see such a show of strength but know it was strength derived from desperation – so many battles behind us, so little hope or expectation for the future.

From the back of the crowd we could neither see nor hear the speakers. I think there were several Labor Party politicians, probably, as my father growled, trying to gain mileage for their electoral hopes. In reality they never offered us more than anyone else. I thought bitterly of the spate of letters to the *Despatch*, particularly the one that expressed nastily the opinion that government should put an end to the 'irritating exactions of meeting the cost of the dole'.

The crowd was becoming tired of trying to listen. Frustrated and exhausted by a long and seemingly fruitless march, they were ripe for immediate action, an outlet for their rage. I felt the wave of restlessness surge around me. Harry, who had shinned up a lamppost to see better, now dropped beside me.

'There's the usual contingents of mounted and foot police guarding the front of the Treasury building. I don't like it, Judith.' He glanced behind us. The crowd there was less packed in.

'Come,' he said, 'quickly. Before we are trapped.'

He grasped my hand and we edged our way through the people behind us. They gave way. No one was interested in us. Their attention was directed towards the front of the march.

'What's happening?' The urgent question was repeated over and over, but remained unanswered.

A couple of boys followed Harry's example and climbed lamp-posts. From above some people leaned out of the windows of buildings. They were called to: 'What's happening?'

'Looks like a fight,' someone shouted.

Around us people started to sweep forward. Harry dragged me off the road to the footpath and we squeezed against the wall of a building, resisting the headlong rush until once again a space opened before us. We broke through into a quieter open street.

'We're not going to be beaten up again,' Harry panted. 'What is the point?'

It was sickening to think of another defeat for all these poor people and not be part of it, but Harry was right. To end up injured again would serve no purpose. And yet, what did serve any purpose?

I looked down at Harry's hand holding mine. It was strong and comforting. 'Oh, Harry,' I wept, 'it's awful to be always defeated. Will it always be like this? It's so unjust.'

We walked quietly and he continued to grip my hand. 'I don't know, Judith. I'd like to believe it isn't so. The communists assert that these are the death throes of capitalism and that given another ten years it will collapse.'

Ten years, I thought. In terms of history this was nothing, a tiny dot on the map of time. Aristotle had written on moderation

2000 years ago but in my life span ten years seemed forever. How queer our personal measurement of time. So would we go on squeezing our lives through the narrow jaws of poverty for another ten years? And then what? A brighter future? A brighter communist future? It was a remote dream.

But not to Harry, it seemed. 'Think, Judith,' he said. 'The Russian Revolution took place barely fourteen years ago and look what changes that has brought about. And now we are seeing a successful socialist alliance in Spain. It'll be the second communist state in the world. You'll see.'

I knew that the second Spanish republic was on the verge of coming to power. It was an alliance of several left-wing groups, including the communists, and its success would herald a victory over the powerful organs of the Catholic Church, the conservative conclave of rich landowners and the army. For the workers to defeat these mighty Goliaths through the ballot box would be a triumph reminiscent of the overthrow of the Russian state. No wonder Harry and his comrades had stars in their eyes.

As he spoke, his face flushed with enthusiasm, I realised that he really did envisage and believe in a socialist utopia. For Harry none of the contradictions of fallible humans sullied his great dream. To him it was like the rhapsody of a piece of music that leads inevitably to a great and satisfying resolution. And was I the poorer for my doubts? My cartoons were grounded not in some great faith but in a more savage awareness of what I saw as the gap between dream and reality.

As usual the police bashed up the marchers, a number of whom were jailed for defending themselves.

Winnie, of course, had seen our house while we were in the process of furnishing it, and later at our small wedding celebration. But now she bounced in asserting that she had come to really see it. 'As it is lived in, so to speak.'

She brought a large bunch of flowers and immediately fussed around in the kitchen searching the cupboards for a vase. 'You must have one, Judith. Everyone has vases.'

'Use a milk bottle, Winnie. There's one on the sink.'

She picked it up, looked at it distastefully, rinsed it, tried to arrange the flowers and failed. 'Haven't you got anything else?'

'For heaven's sake, Winnie, try the laundry.'

She went out and came back with a second bottle and a tin. She halved the bunch and arranged some of the flowers. 'Scissors, Judith.'

I found them. She shortened the stems of the remainder of the flowers and arranged them in the tin. Then she looked around for a place to put them all. Finally, with a deep sigh, she gave up and left them all standing on the draining board.

I grinned at her. 'I'm sorry my home is so inadequate, Winnie.'

She grinned back. 'It's like you, Judith.'

'Not inadequate I hope?'

'Of course not, silly. You know I didn't mean that. I mean you just think about other things.'

'I have geraniums.' I pointed to a pot on the window ledge. 'I like geraniums. They're tough and Mum always kept a few on the hulk.'

Winnie perched on one of the kitchen chairs, her elbows on the table. 'Wasn't it Mrs Spicer in the Henry Lawson story who always kept geraniums? That was such a sad story. She had lots of children, I think. Do you and Harry plan to have children, Jude?'

'Not yet. Some time in the future, probably.'

'Not yet?' She looked coy and I was tempted to smack her. 'How will you manage that?'

'None of your business, Winnie.'

'Just interested.'

'No, Winnie, just curious.'

'Aren't they the same?'

'No. You're prying.'

She laughed. 'And you've put me in my place.'

'Nicely, I hope.'

'Always, Jude. We're old friends and now we're family.'

I made her a cup of tea and put out some bread, cheese and apples. We munched companionably.

'Speaking of marriage, Winnie, have you met anyone you liked?'

She rolled her eyes. 'None of them has any money. And I'm not like you. I need to be supported. You know second-hand shops for my clothes were a great novelty at first, but now it's worn off. I don't want to do it forever. Courting isn't much fun these days when I know the swain is penniless. I haven't the slightest intention of being a Mrs Spicer. Harry's also a bit of a bore these days, isn't he? So earnest.'

I was affronted. 'He's certainly not a bore.'

She shrugged. 'He used to be so full of fun, always joking and laughing, dancing and loving music. Marriage has sobered him, Jude.'

I was defensive. 'It isn't me. It's the Communist Party.'

'I thought it might be.'

'They're terribly serious, Winnie.'

'Sort of believe in joy deferred.'

'That's hit the nail on the head.'

She looked thoughtful. 'Maybe it's only a short-lived enthusiasm. Harry always had intense but brief passions. Except in your case, of course. You're not a brief passion.'

'Thanks for the reassurance.'

She chuckled. 'Don't mention it. And I daresay that his devotion to the Communist Party will be as short lived as all his other enthusiasms.'

I felt uncomfortable. I didn't want to believe that Harry couldn't stick with anything. Although I also wished that he was a little more moderate I felt the need to defend his devotion. Steadiness, I thought.

'He really does believe in their ideas, Winnie, and he is working for them. I think the experience in Victoria Square changed him. On the surface he has been the same ebullient Harry, but underneath he has always been searching for the why. Like it or not, the communists have given him an answer and a purpose.'

She took a bite of her apple. Her teeth were small and white and even. A writer of romances would have called them pearly. So were Harry's. Those shining teeth made their mouths particularly attractive and their smiles healthy and young. So many children at the soup kitchen had blackened, broken and decaying teeth.

She munched thoughtfully, extracting with her fingernail a piece of apple skin from between her front teeth. She placed the piece on her plate and licked her fingers. 'I'm sure you're right, Judith. These days you know him better than I do but it doesn't augur well for his future or yours.'

'Winnie, you're always harping on this theme. Our times are very uncertain. Harry and I have both given up thinking of the future, which I suppose is contradictory because the communists dwell all the time on what the future holds and Harry never stops talking about it.'

'The great and glorious state?' she grimaced.

'Yes, and they take heart from every small triumph in Europe: at the minute the success of the Spanish republic in establishing a workers' state.'

'And they ignore every defeat or failure?'

She was right. Winnie had very little of what might be called a social or political conscience, but she had developed a fund of common sense and a down-to-earth grasp on what went on in politics.

I recalled the recent statement in the press about the evil threat of the Bolsheviks. They were 'slyly and insidiously worming their way into the citadel of the labour movement in order to use its forces to preach violent class war, to take control of the unemployed, force demonstrations, foster discontent, and prepare a revolutionary situation'.

It had been savage, but Harry had found in it, not a warning of defeat but a hope of victory. He had been jubilant. 'We're winning, Judith. Every night when I go to a meeting of the Unemployed Workers' Union and talk to them about communism they listen. I know we're succeeding. Nathan's right. Give us another ten years. You'll see. If we weren't effective they wouldn't fear us. It's wonderful to confront the conservative forces of capitalism. I feel like a soldier in the field, scenting victory.'

And Harry's face had glowed with pride and a sense of achievement.

But I couldn't explain any of this to Winnie for she was such a bread-and-butter girl.

Harry's work in the Unemployed Workers' Union was planned by the Communist Party. Nathan visited regularly, staggering in under a pile of books. Over the kitchen table he and Harry talked well into the night discussing Harry's strategy of instruction. Harry assiduously took notes.

I retired to my work room at the front of the house but caught the occasional word. 'Bourgeois' was often repeated and 'proletariat' and 'exploitation' and, of course, 'capitalism'. Nathan's voice was now stronger than I would have expected from such a slight man. Harry told me, admiringly, that after his failure as a botanic park stump orator, Nathan had set himself the task of developing and training his voice. It couldn't be called stentorian now, but it was robust and full-bodied.

To show Harry that I bore Nathan no ill will I usually made them supper. It amused me to see Nathan rock back in his chair, fold his hands across his stomach, and assume a parsonical manner. Though frequently overwhelmed by Nathan's intellectual confidence, Harry retained his sense of humour. 'They call him Einstein, Jude. Or The Professor.'

'He's not an old man,' I said, 'but he looks like one.'

He chuckled. 'You know Jock, from the wilds of Glasgow? Nathan's offsider? He says that Nathan's eloquence never matches his sense of injustice. He's too ponderous, long-winded and deadly serious. I was having a beer with Jock in the Newmarket pub the other afternoon. He'd had a couple too many, Jude. "You know, Harry," he confided, "Nathan is a nine-carat left-winger but despite what the comrades joke about his eyes being whoppers behind his thick spectacles, they don't stick out like a bulldog's balls".'

I shrieked with laughter. 'Oh, Harry, did he really say that? And the comrades objected to my dogs cartoon.'

'I'm sure Nathan thinks,' Harry continued to laugh, 'that all young people are in danger of being frivolous and a good dose of communism will educate them. I don't think any of them have had much opportunity to be frivolous. They have usually carried the weight of families with an unemployed or absent father. I'm trying to form a group of young communists in the Unemployed Workers' Union. Nathan calls it a cadre and the Communist Party aims to infiltrate lots of organisations and form similar ginger groups. He says mine will be ground-breaking. I'm to be given a Party name – Comrade Sullivan.'

'What on earth for, Harry?'

'I'm not quite sure. But I think it has something to do with the police not being able to identify us. We expect to be targeted very strongly by them as we progress.'

'But, Harry, everyone in the Port knows who you are. Most know you are a communist. You sell copies of the *Port Beacon* on the streets. What is the point? Isn't it rather silly? A bit extreme?'

He shrugged. 'It's Party policy.'

I looked at his notes lying on the table. 'And what sort of things do you teach these frivolous young people? We're not much older ourselves.'

He picked up a sheet of paper and read to me: 'We are in the last stage of humanity's march towards a classless society. Labourers will overcome capitalism and bring in a new society which has no classes. It is the capitalists of the world who are banded together against the working class.'

He looked at me eagerly. 'They, too, are labourers, Jude. That is if they ever get work. They'll be keen to bring in a classless society.'

'Oh, Harry,' I said, 'how is this received? Don't they find it rather ...' I was going to say airy-fairy, but settled for 'abstract?'

He looked deflated. 'They do get bored pretty quickly.'

'Yes,' I said and avoided his eyes. In the face of his earnestness I couldn't show him I was laughing. 'What do you do then when they get bored?'

'I give up and bring out my violin. We have a sing-along.' He grinned. 'They all know the words of 'Waltzing Matilda' and 'The Wild Colonial Boy' and then there are Irish songs like 'The Wearing of the Green'. Nathan was a bit taken aback when I told him what I did. The trouble, Jude, is that he doesn't know when people have had enough talk.'

'Perhaps he lacks a little moderation? Even judgement?' I was cautious about making any critical comments about Nathan having found that Harry tended to take them personally. But now he only nodded wisely.

'You're quite right, darling.'

And I was comforted. My fear, that his belief in communism would entirely consume him, evaporated. He would believe, but not as Nathan wanted or expected. Nathan might go fishing for converts but just when he thought that Harry was safely in the net my husband would slip away, a bright sliver of inextinguishable light.

'Oh, Harry,' I said, 'I do love you.'

'And what part of me, ma'am, do you love the most?'

'Well,' I pretended to consider.

'And while you're deciding ...' He enveloped me in his arms and we didn't clear the supper dishes away until the next morning.

I continued submitting my cartoons to the *Workers' Weekly*, *Spearhead* and occasionally the *Sun News Pictorial* and I suppose that it was as a result of these that I received a letter from a magazine called *Women Today*. I noticed that it was published by the Forward Press, which also published the *Workers' Weekly*. The editor, a Mrs Edna King, sent a warm courteous letter explaining that she had seen many examples of my cartoons in the papers and asking if I would be interested to contribute regularly to her new magazine. She was looking for 'strong, independent, forward-thinking women who were politically aware but also interested in the everyday lives of women in the community'.

Already a number of well-known and highly respected women, such as Nettie Palmer, Katharine Susannah Prichard and Jean Devanny, were interested in writing articles or sharing their novels to serialise. She hoped that I might be willing to contribute the occasional cartoon but also some drawings of women, particularly those affected by the depression. She felt that my cartoons showed a deep compassion for those suffering women and any drawings I could contribute on this theme would add to the strength and message of *Women Today*. She understood that I was doubtless in much demand, but sincerely hoped that I might find the time to join them in their new enterprise. I read the letter several times.

I had never thought of myself as being much in demand although I worked hard every day, regularly walking to the Port Institute and searching the newspapers for ideas so that I might keep up with the politics of the day and comment on their bitter outcomes. In the face of draconian government cuts to spending on the unemployed I was working now on a cartoon of Sir Otto Niemeyer, head of the Bank of England. I drew him at the Melbourne conference offering the Prime Minister, state premiers and treasurers a minute slice of Christmas pudding with my caption: *Have an Empire Christmas pudding.*

I hoped my audience were sophisticated enough to recall the Empire Marketing Board's slogan to persuade the British to buy Canadian flour, Indian spices, and Australian dried fruit. And I hoped that they could see that Niemeyer's pressure on the Australian government would leave the poor with a very minute slice of the pudding.

I loved my work but it involved hours of planning and then drawing the cartoon and a considerable amount of time in matching the drawing to an appropriate brief and biting comment. Frequently I offered up a silent thank you to Joe Pulham, who had educated me through books. There was a fund of material in literary references and a wealth of learning about words and language. I always worked with a large dictionary beside me, and a Thesaurus, a bible for shades of meaning, for catching the exact word I needed.

And then, of course, there were my time-wasting failures. Sometimes what I envisaged in my head didn't work out on paper and no matter how I tried I inevitably threw it in the dustbin. Perhaps the figures weren't right; I had failed in a caricature of the face; or the pen lines were clumsy; or the ink had run and despite constant scraping left a nasty smudge on the page. Technically it was unforgiving work and I had dozens of incomplete experimental sketches before I settled on a final drawing – and even then something could so easily go wrong.

Mrs King's letter was fishing. It was not clear how many drawings she wanted or how often nor, most importantly, whether she could pay me. I was flattered to be in the company of such women as Nettie Palmer. The communists spoke of her and her husband

Vance with bated breath. But doubtless they had more money than I had. They could afford to make a life's work of their ideas. But I had to support three families.

Together we had decided that Harry should make a regular donation to the Communist Party because I now understood that this was a part of his self-importance and his beliefs, not only in the comrades, but his own work as a member. But we could not both afford to make that sacrifice.

It wouldn't be difficult for me to send a couple of my drawings of women at the soup kitchen. My press overflowed with drawings I had made that weren't cartoons although frequently I would use one of them. I lifted a couple out and laid them on the table. They would surely suit. This was clearly a left-wing magazine, although Mrs King had made no point of this.

I could send them. It was pleasing to be sought after.

I was still holding them in my hand when Harry came in. He looked over my shoulder. 'Poor Mrs Gill. We tried to save her from eviction months ago. I was so angry, Jude. She sat on the one remaining kitchen chair they left her, her apron over her face, and wept, and her children, all four of them, stood around her howling also. I resolved then that the way our present society runs is shit.'

'She never came to the hulk with other homeless women. Do you know where she went, Harry?'

He shook his head. 'I think her sister may have come. We passed around the hat but none of us had much to put in it. Reminded me of that Henry Lawson story about the mate who always passes around the hat to help everyone. And I thought it good to be kind but kindness needs to be a political way of life to really help. I hope the communists will be kind, Jude.'

'Yes, I hope so, too,' I said.

I put the drawings back in the press. I didn't think that my kindness need extend to a gift to the Forward Press.

Harry spent the afternoon digging up a plot of soil in the

backyard. It didn't look particularly fertile – a lot of sand and gravel – and probably wouldn't grow the vegetables he planned. While he worked I penned a careful and, I hoped, tactful letter to Mrs King. Yes, I was interested in her magazine, and flattered. I crossed that out and put 'honoured' to be included. I was delighted that my work pleased her and that she judged it worthy of inclusion. Could she, please, be a little more specific about the terms for using my work? How many drawings might she require and at what intervals? And did she, as yet, have any thoughts about an appropriate payment?

I told her how much I was paid by the *Workers' Weekly*. There was not much point in trying to wrap that up in euphemistic words. Payment was payment and that was all there was to it. I added that I would be most interested to see any published copies of the magazine.

It was an opportunity and I hoped that I had not closed the door on it. I felt guilty that I was becoming mean and mercenary. After all, these women were trying to do something worthwhile. But I looked at our meagre bank balance and the few shillings in my purse; only an idle dream our 200 pounds would last two years. I looked at the calendar to anxiously assess when I might hope to receive some payment from the *Workers' Weekly* and *Spearhead*. When it came it would be little enough.

Harry had lost part of his small but regular income when the silent films became talkies. We all went to the Ozone Theatre to see the first of them and were amazed to hear voices emerge from the screen. But Harry's excitement was tempered by gloom. 'Nothing I can do about it, Judith. The writing's on the wall for all of us who played the piano for the silent movies. It's very hard on you.'

'It's not your fault, Harry,' I consoled him as stoutly as I could.

But he was miserable. 'It's not fair. It's like the Industrial Revolution in Britain. Every time some new piece of technology is introduced into the workplace a few profit and the poor suffer.'

There was not much I could say. The pity of it was that most of the musicians who played for the silent films were anonymous. They were always there. But they might have been the chairs or other furnishings. No one took any notice of them as workers and in the excitement of the new no one noticed that they had disappeared. I wondered how many other people felt worthless and unappreciated because their jobs had vanished without notice.

The little cartoon I sent to the *Sun News Pictorial* was accepted. I had drawn a theatre with a talkie film and the ghost-like apparition of a musician departing down the centre aisle. An actor from the talkie looks out. He peers across the audience and asks: *Is someone unhappy with our performance?*

The editor wrote me a brief but personal note. 'Dear Miss Larson, This is a sad state of affairs. You might be keen to know that the celebrated Sir Bernard Heinze is giving a special concert for musicians now unemployed by the theatres.'

I hadn't told him about Harry but perhaps he guessed that in this instance my work was intensely personal.

I didn't show Harry the letter from Mrs King. I knew that his instant reaction would be that I must accept. If my work were published by the Forward Press then it would be for the good of the cause. Sometimes his generous impulses were a burden to me. He admired my cartoons and drawings but I knew that, despite often watching my labour, he still had a tendency to discount the effort it cost me.

I complained of this to Miss Marie but she only shrugged. 'It is the same all over, *ma pauvre*, every country, so many think the same, the labour of the arts is not real work, and we should always be willing to give not sell our endeavours. Now if I were a bricklayer or a wharf labourer ...'

'You don't look the part but you'd have a union.'

'And then people would pay me?'

'It wouldn't do you much good these days to belong to a union,' I said sourly.

'No, Judith. Not even bricklayers or wharf labourers these days. What chance musicians and artists?'

Sometimes when Harry went to his meetings with the young unemployed workers, I visited my parents to share their evening meal. My father had picked up irregular work on a shell-grit ketch. My mother now worked at the soup kitchen only one day a week. The poor of the Port still needed its help but a younger group of women had taken over.

Mrs Danley's broken arm had taken months to heal and she had been forced to let go the reins. The new group of women had their own way of organising the kitchen. Without Mrs Danley, Ailsa Thornhill was lost. My mother often felt that she was by-passed and given only the housekeeping jobs of peeling vegetables and washing up. She could no longer enjoy the warmth of serving the women and chatting with them.

It was sad, she said, to see Herbie being driven away, his help discouraged, even discarded. 'Perhaps,' she said, 'it is better organised, but I don't know. It is certainly more regimented.'

Now there were fewer waifs and strays seeking a bed for a night or two on the hulk. Often, when I visited, there was no one there except my parents and it was like old times. We sat around the galley table after our meal and talked in a desultory fashion. I told them about Mrs King's letter and my hesitation. They agreed that I should be paid for my work.

My father growled that the country continued to go to the dogs and that Labor Prime Minister Scullin had been a useless bastard and that, although he crawled to Sir Otto Niemeyer, the workers of Australia wouldn't be bullied by an imperialist power. He fumed that all the state premiers and treasurers had genuflected to the Bank of England and grovelled that they'd all been bad boys who had spent more than their pocket money. They would have to learn to save – on the backs of the poor, of course.

'The *Workers' Weekly* was right, Judith. Scullin is a shit-all labour man. He's just a lackey of capitalism.'

I had heard it all often enough from Harry but it rang truer every time I heard it.

'Bloody Thomas Bavin,' my father said in disgust. 'Thirty women from women's organisations all over New South Wales begged him to help the poor and he had the gall to tell them that it would be disastrous if the state accepted responsibility for the unemployed. There's another cartoon for you, Judith.

'*"Nothing ever matters and nothing ever fails*
As long as nothing happens to the bank of New South Wales."'

My mother had been quiet during this diatribe. She looked exhausted these days and I worried that she wasn't well. 'I suppose, Judith,' she said with the ghost of a smile, 'that if we had a peaceful, equitable society you'd be out of a job.'

I grimaced. 'Gosh, Mum, that's an irony. To think that I should be grateful for all this misery.'

Later in the evening Harry came on his bicycle to collect me and we walked home together through streets fitfully but gently lit by electric lighting. There were always a few people abroad but sometimes when they merged with the shadows as only indistinct shapes I was reminded of my childhood fears of those shadowy creatures that skulked along the wharves and still occasionally haunted my dreams.

'You know, Harry, I often recall a line from Shakespeare that conscience makes cowards of us all. But I always change it to imagination makes cowards of us all.'

'That is if you have imagination, Jude.'

'Everyone has imagination, Harry.'

He demurred. 'Some have a lot more than others.'

'And I guess,' I said, 'some have a heavier dose of conscience.'

He held my hand as he always did and we didn't hurry. The darkness was a soft and private world.

A month later Jock hammered at my front door. It was mid-morning. I was working as usual and Harry had gone to the Labour Exchange. I ran to answer the urgent summons.

'For heaven's sake, Jock, what is it?' And then in a panic: 'There's been an accident? Harry? My father? My mother is ill?'

'No, Judith,' he panted, 'it's the police. They're raiding all our premises. They've closed down the *Port Beacon* and confiscated our printing equipment. And now they're searching the homes of anyone they suspect of being a communist. Have you any stuff that might incriminate you and Harry?'

'Stuff?' I was bemused. 'Only my cartoons. Surely not them? This is terrible, Jock. Nothing else?'

'Are you sure? What about newspapers? Books? Letters?'

I was indignant. 'But we have freedom of the press.'

'Not any more. They're activating the 1926 Crimes Act.'

Frightened, I said, 'We probably have a few copies of the *Workers' Weekly* and *Spearhead*. My cartoons appear in both. But everyone knows that. I throw out-of-date newspapers into the laundry for fuel for the copper.'

He pursed his mouth in grim humour. '*Spearhead*! That'll set them on their toes. They won't like that. What an irony it'd be to be arrested for the bloody anarchists.'

'I'll look,' I said. 'A parcel came for Harry last night. He said he'd put it in the laundry until he could open it.'

We ran outside and into the laundry. I was fearful. It was only recently that I'd read in the daily papers of Hitler and his thugs shooting down their opponents on the street. My horizons had widened and I had begun to search the newspapers assiduously to glean what I could of European affairs. I experimented with drawing caricatures of Hitler. I had re-borrowed copies of Will

Dyson's cartoons, about the expanding imperialist Germany, and studied them. I had seen that a good cartoon could both foretell and warn of future events and such a warning entered our visual memory and was never forgotten.

If the brutality in the Port were only a microcosm of the world then I shuddered to look into the future. Was this the outcome of the hysterical anti-Bolshevism in the press, the calls for a private army to defend citizens against us?

In my anxiety I had started to warn Harry to be careful when he left home for his meetings and he would look at me oddly. 'I just ride my bicycle, Jude. The roads are pretty quiet at this time of night.'

'Yes,' I said, hugging him, 'but be careful.'

'What over, Jude?' He was puzzled.

I laughed uncomfortably. 'I don't really know, Harry. It's just a feeling.'

'Silly old you,' he said and kissed the top of my head.

Jock and I found copies of the *Workers' Weekly* and *Spearhead* lying on the floor. They were torn and covered in dirt marks.

'Do you think the police might take it that I've tried to disguise them?' I felt a little hysterical.

'The parcel, Judith.' Jock sounded frantic. 'It has a German postmark.' He tore the wrappings. 'My God, copies of *Imprecor*. The official journal of the Comintern. From Germany but published in English. Have you any more copies in the house?'

'No, I've never seen it before. Surely the police won't know what the Comintern is. They're pretty dumb.'

Jock guffawed. 'Dinna kid yourself, lassie. They'll know. We must get rid of these. And the *Workers' Weekly* and *Spearhead*.'

'We can burn them.'

'Not enough time. Besides it'd be suspicious. A fire in the middle of the day and no washing?'

'Then I'll take them to the hulk. My father will help. We can chuck them in the river. You go now. Better you're not seen here.'

'Yes,' he said, but hesitated. 'Harry wouldn't like me to leave you alone.'

'Go, Jock. You're too well known. I've got my bicycle. Harry found me an old second-hand lady's bike. '

Still he lingered. 'You'll be OK, Judith?'

'Of course. No one will stop a girl on a bicycle. I'll put all this stuff in my art bag. Now, for God's sake, go.'

He went.

I grabbed the copies of *Imprecor*, the *Workers' Weekly* and *Spearhead*, raced about the house, snatched up notes Harry had made, shoved copies of *Ten Days That Shook the World*, *The Iron Heel*, *The State and Revolution* behind some other books at the back of the bookshelf, threw my drawing gear out of my art bag, and stuffed in all the incriminating material. It was bulky but I couldn't help that. To help conceal it, I put my sketch book on top. With my bag slung across my shoulder I wheeled my bike onto the street and mounted. Lipson Street was busy, cycling on the road difficult and slow. I got off and wheeled my bike along the footpath.

Two policemen blocked my way. 'Got something interesting there, miss?' one of them asked.

I batted my eyelashes at him, tried to look a little tremulous, and wished I could do it as meltingly as Winnie. If I hadn't been so scared I would have felt a complete idiot. 'Really, officer,' I said, 'that's not a nice thing to ask a lady.'

He blushed. 'I meant your bag, miss.'

'Well, I hoped that you did … otherwise …' I left the sentence unfinished.

He studied me with a puzzled frown, his eyes fixed on the bag. I felt sick.

Suddenly he said, and his face broke into a grin, 'Aren't you the girl that does those cartoons? Remember I asked you out one night.'

I recognised him and knowing him, however sketchily, made the situation a little less frightening. Relieved, I beamed at him, 'Of course, I was sorry to refuse.' I hoped that I didn't sound too effusive.

'Well,' he said, 'if it isn't too late.'

I made my left hand obvious.

'Oh,' he mumbled, seeing my wedding ring. 'Sorry. You've married.'

I continued to smile.

'And the bag,' he persisted.

'Art bag,' I said and made as if I intended to show him. I hadn't the slightest idea what I would do if he insisted on looking. 'It's such a beautiful morning.' And I began to wheel my bicycle past them. 'The river calls.'

Yes,' he said, 'it would. You must have a lot of equipment there.'

'Yes.' I tried not to sound breathless.

His companion, who had stood by silently, pulled his arm. 'Come on, Bill, we've work to do. Stop trying to chat up a married woman.'

Bill touched his cap to me and they moved on.

The sweat trickled under my arms and slid coldly down my sides. I remounted my bicycle shakily. Better to be on the road. I didn't want any more face-to-face meetings with the police.

It was a relief to burst onto the wharf area and see the river open out in front of me, the water winking brightly and companionably in the morning sun, the few ships at rest, the gulls squawking and squabbling.

I wheeled my bicycle over the rail tracks and the uneven planking of the wharf. Our hulk looked solid, secure and familiar. My breathing steadied and my panic subsided. I left my bicycle on the wharf and hurried up the gangplank.

My mother came out of the galley wiping her hands. 'Judith,' she said questioningly, 'you don't usually visit us in the morning. How are you, darling?'

I kissed her. 'No. Is Dad about?'

She looked around. 'Somewhere, Judith. He's been doing some painting. The wood work, as you know, the salt. It needs constant repair.'

She noted my bag and then studied me. 'Is something wrong?'

I didn't want to worry her. 'I need Dad to help me get rid of some stuff.'

She was quick. 'What stuff, Judith?'

'Some newspapers and journals.'

'Newspapers and journals?'

'Yes.'

'It's urgent?'

'Yes, I think so.'

'Niels,' she shouted, hurrying along the deck, 'Niels, Judith is here and needs you.'

He came quickly, cleaning his hands with a rag and smelling of paint. 'What is it?'

'The police,' I said. 'They're raiding houses. They've closed the *Port Beacon*.'

His face darkened. 'The dirty rotten bastards.'

My mother gasped. 'Where's Harry?'

'I don't know. Jock came to warn me. He helped. I came on my bicycle. I need to dump these.'

My mother looked in the bag and paled. 'Could we be searched here, Niels?'

'Don't know, but first things first. I'll need a sack I can weight.'

He hurried off and returned with a hessian bag. He pulled out the newspapers, grunted when he saw the copies of *Imprecor*, and stuffed them all in the sack. He had brought a short heavy iron bar and he forced this down on top of the papers. Then he twisted the top of the sack and wound a rope tightly around it, knotting it, as only a sailor could.

I watched his quick efficiency with relief. Years of crises on windjammers and the need for instant decisions had honed his responses. He had a cool head. He lifted the sack and we followed him across the deck. He hurled the sack into the river.

We saw it float a moment, ballooning as the air inside swelled, then this collapsed and slowly the water consumed it. My father dusted his hands and grinned at me. 'Goodbye to bad rubbish, daughter.'

'No,' I said soberly, 'not bad rubbish, Dad. Freedom of the press, respect for the ideas of others.'

He patted my shoulder. 'Don't worry. I'm sure Harry will be safe.'

'I hope so.' My voice trembled.

'He's a good boy. Far better that he didn't come home. He'll be OK. He's a quick-witted lad. Let's make her a cup of tea, Eve, and some of those scones you made this morning.'

My mother, white-faced with shock, had sunk onto a seat at the stub of the old mast, cut down and never now used to fly a sail. I looked at her anxiously. I hadn't meant to frighten her.

'Judith,' she wrung her hands, 'this is sinister.'

'No,' I said stoutly. 'It's just a foolishness, a stupidity. It'll pass.'

Tears welled in her eyes. 'I'd like some peace, Judith, like in the old days.'

I took her arm. 'A scone would be nice, Mum, and a cuppa.' She rallied and managed a weak smile.

I left after the tea and scones. I needed to get home in case there was some news of Harry. It was dreadful that our home should, today, be a dangerous and threatening place for him. Home should be a haven, or else there was something seriously wrong with the world.

Although distracted, I cycled carefully. I had enough worries without injuring myself. I let myself in the front door and called his name hopefully. But the house was silent and smelled empty. I went through to the backyard and into the laundry but there was no Harry. I wandered back inside and stood irresolutely in the kitchen. Should I stay home or should I go out and search for him? But where might he be? Where to begin searching? Would my searching seem odd? Might there be police spies watching me, following me?

Bizarre scenarios of conspiracies, spy rings, people disappearing off the streets, prison beatings, and other imagined horrors all opened out in front of me. My search for him might alert someone, anyone who meant him harm. Memories of Harry's injuries after Victoria Square haunted me.

I sat down at the kitchen table, clutched my head in my hands and rocked back and forth in an agony of fear and indecision. Was this how people felt in a police state? Helpless?

The knock on the door, although a mere tap, seemed thunderous. I leapt to my feet. Should I answer it? What if it were the police? Had I got rid of everything?

The tap was repeated. Now it was more tentative. The police wouldn't be tentative. Maybe it was Harry who'd forgotten his keys. No, Harry would call out. I heard a third tap, a rustle of paper and then retreating steps. I waited until I could no longer hear them, then ran to the door. There was a note on the mat, thrust under the door.

'Darling,' he wrote, 'I've got some business in town. I'll be home for tea.'

So he was OK. I sank onto a chair and cried with relief. I needn't start preparing the tea for another three hours. I tried to work but couldn't concentrate, so I set about cleaning the house. After this I prepared some vegetables. I looked at a piece of fish in the safe, a good-sized snapper my father had caught, but it was too early to bring it out. At a quarter to six I guessed that he would be home soon. In the main Harry was punctual. I put the vegetables on the stove and set the table.

Six o'clock came and went. Half past six. The food was cooked.

I went to the front door and looked along the street. No Harry. I returned to the kitchen. Should I start my meal without Harry? Serve him right if his was cold.

I served myself, sat down, looked at the food miserably, and pushed my plate aside. I'd rather wait. It didn't matter if it were cold. Why did he not come?

Time went by, minutes became hours, and my anxiety grew. Harm must have come to him. He would send a message if he could. I wished for a telephone but that expense was beyond us. There was no way I could contact anyone. If I left the house Harry might return and find me gone. Then he'd panic about my whereabouts. I couldn't go to bed. To behave normally would seem like abandoning him.

I wandered from room to room, my awareness of Harry sharpened by anxiety. His shaving soap was left untidily on the wash basin. His razor strop hung behind the bathroom door. He had just cleaned his dancing pumps and they shone with the smell of shoe polish. His Brilliantine sat on our dressing table where he had left it. No matter how vigorously he applied it to his hair in an effort to flatten it, like Harry it always sprang up again ready for life.

At last, cold and shivering, I huddled in one of our rocking chairs and wrapped a blanket about me. Eventually, distraught and exhausted, I dozed fitfully.

Dawn edging around the curtains on the window awakened me. For a few seconds I couldn't recall where I was or why. Then memory flooded back again, overwhelming me. I got up stiffly and struggled into the kitchen to make a cup of tea.

The small amount of sleep and the new day had restored some of my strength and while I made a hot drink I forced myself to review the situation calmly. Harry hadn't come home but it didn't necessarily mean he was in prison. Not contacting me needn't be sinister, just an insurmountable difficulty. If he had been hurt or detained surely one of the comrades would have told me. After all,

Jock had come to warn me.

Despite my memories of Victoria Square, we didn't live in a lawless state. But, and I knew this for certain, I couldn't sit helplessly in the house all day, taking no action, a prey to out-of-control fearful imaginings. I forced down a piece of toast, took a bowl of hot water from the kitchen into the bathroom and stripped down for a thorough wash. I couldn't face the effort of lighting the chip heater over the bath.

After a wash, clean clothes, a hot drink and some food, I felt stronger and saner. I would go to the Federation Hall. Surely someone there would have news or if not news, advice. I wouldn't go to the hulk. My mother had had enough worry.

I waited impatiently until it was close to nine o'clock. No one would be at the Hall before nine. Then I set off on my bicycle. How bright and normal everything looked in the morning sunshine, how clean everyone in their fresh working clothes.

The Federation Hall was surprisingly quiet. Given Jock's panic of yesterday I had expected turmoil, frantic comings and goings, a bustle of people like myself desperately seeking news. I went down the empty passage to the union organiser's office and knocked.

'Come in,' he called.

When I did he looked up startled. 'Judith, Mrs Grenville, you're an early bird.'

He hurried from behind his desk, found me a chair and pulled it forward. He was a burly man with a thick body and short bowed legs. He was new to the job having replaced Matty Gibbs. Recently I had drawn a caricature of him lumping a three-bushel bag of wheat on his enormous shoulders while his legs bowed beneath him with the weight. I had many such drawings, all unpublishable, but together a graphic representation of life at the Port.

'Is something amiss?' he asked. He was a bluff but kindly man. 'Your father, is he ill? Does he need some help?'

'No,' I said, 'it's my husband, Harry.'

He looked puzzled. 'Your husband? He's not one of us, is he? Not a watersider?'

'No, he's a musician.'

He wrinkled his brow. 'Then how can I help?'

'He's missing.'

He smiled benignly. 'Judith, Mrs Grenville, husbands often go missing. It's a usual mishap in marriage. Have you tried the pubs?'

'No.' I was indignant. 'It isn't that. Harry doesn't drink. Or very little. It's …'

He interrupted me, continuing to smirk, and I supposed that many women defended their husbands' reputations by denying their heavy drinking.

'Mrs Grenville, if your husband is really missing, and you should probably wait a day or so to make certain, you should contact the police.'

'No,' I pleaded. 'The police are the problem.'

He looked stern, then cleared his throat, preparing to give me a homily. 'If your husband has done something wrong, Mrs Grenville, we can't involve ourselves.'

I interjected impatiently, 'You don't understand. The police have been raiding the houses of the communists. My husband is a communist. He may have been picked up and taken into custody. Have you heard nothing of all this?'

He pursed his mouth. 'A communist? Oh, my dear, how unfortunate. Yes, we have heard something, Mrs Grenville, but we don't involve ourselves, either in what the communists do or what happens to them. Our responsibility is to our union members.'

I glared at him. I was beginning to see red at his glibness. 'But I've attended communist meetings in your Hall.'

He shrugged. 'A business arrangement. We hire out the Hall to many organisations. It doesn't mean we support or approve of them. It's a free country, Mrs Grenville.'

I mocked him. 'Is that so? Not if you're a communist it seems.'

He looked at me pityingly. 'I'd like to help you, Mrs Grenville, but there's nothing I can do.'

He stood up and held the door open for me. I went out feeling so lonely and isolated I could have wept again. That the communists were an integral influential part of the community was only an illusion. I knew now that in reality they were small, unpopular and vulnerable.

I rode my bike home and, because I still fulminated from the interview and was now infuriated with Harry for not contacting me, I stopped at a milk shop and bought myself a threepenny double-headed ice cream.

There was a wooden seat on the edge of the pavement and I leaned my bike against it, sat down, and licked my ice cream in the sun. Nobody took any notice of me and that I thought bitterly is how society really is: all of us individuals intent on our own concerns, quite separate from each other. So what price communism? Or any other messianic ideal to save the human race?

Sitting in the sun, eating an ice cream, minding my own business was the way to go. I was still hopping mad with Harry for being a member of the bloody Communist Party, for not telling me where he was, for causing me a night of misery and a humiliating session with a union organiser who thought me a deceived hardly-done-by little woman. I was fed up with all this cloak-and-dagger stuff.

Late that afternoon Harry arrived home. I heard his key turn in the lock and rushed to the door. He looked unhurt. He even smiled at me. He dared to look normal and smiling. He had barely set foot inside when I screeched at him, 'Where have you been?'

And I hit him.

He grabbed my arm. 'Whoa, Judith, whoa. What's all this?'

'Don't whoa me,' I yelled at him. 'Don't you dare.' And I tried to hit him again.

'Stop it,' he said, 'stop it, Judith. What's the matter with you?'

'Matter!' I shouted. 'Matter? You've the front to ask me what the matter is. You've been missing for nearly two days. No message to me. No reassurance that you were OK. Jock here in a panic. Your bloody communist papers, *Imprecor* of all things, and I had to race to the hulk to get my father to chuck the lot into the river. No help from you. My mother sick with terror. All of us frantic about you. And you ask me what the matter is.'

He was quiet. 'I sent a note.'

'Oh yes? And that told me a lot. And you didn't keep your promise. I waited for you all night imagining ...' I choked, 'imagining Victoria Square.'

'Oh,' he said. 'I never thought of that. Never dreamed that might occur to you.'

Suddenly the anger drained out of me, leaving me empty and weary. 'Where have you been, Harry? Didn't you know about the police raids?'

'Yes. But we had a more important matter to deal with.'

'More important than one or both of us being arrested?' Disbelieving, I glared at him.

'Yes.'

'Tell me again, Harry, so that I can grasp it. I can make neither head nor tail of all this. You disappear for nearly two days. I'm distraught with worry that you've been arrested and beaten to death. You don't tell me where you are or why. And now you inform me that there was something more important than all this.'

He looked uncomfortable but unrepentant. 'I'm sorry, Judith, that you've had a difficult time but the police have put out a warrant for Bernie-Benito's arrest. And if they catch him they'll deport him to Mussolini's Italy and we all know that the Black Shirts will murder him. We had to hide him and spirit him away.'

'Bernie-Benito? Deport him? Can they do that?'

'Of course. He's not an Australian citizen.'

'But there's lots of people here who aren't Australian citizens and no one bothers them.'

'They're not communists, Judith.'

'No,' I said. 'Oh, Harry, how awful. How bloody awful.'

'Yes, it is awful.'

'Where did you hide him and where has he gone?'

'At my mother's at first.' He gave the ghost of a grin and I realised that until now there had been no real humour in his smile. 'My mother thought he was charming and asked him if anyone in his family were an opera singer. He didn't fully understand her but he caught the word opera and sang a few bars of Puccini's 'Your tiny hand is frozen' and then he took her hand and looked into her eyes as soulfully as only Bernie can and she was entranced. Actually, Jude, he has a really fine tenor voice and I never knew.'

He had followed me into the kitchen and now sat at the table while I boiled the kettle and put out some food. 'Have you eaten?'

'Not recently. I'm starved.'

'And after your mother's, what then?'

'Pat had brought him to Mum's in his car and he went off to a saleyard and picked up a second-hand Ford pretty cheaply. The Party paid for it. Lots of cars have been turned in for a song because of the depression. There's another young Italian in the Party and he agreed to drive Bernie to Mildura where they can lose themselves amongst the Italian fruit-pickers. I waited until they left.'

I poured our tea and sat opposite him. 'Was all this raiding and searching because of Bernie-Benito?'

'No. He's just a part of it. Jock said you got rid of the copies of *Imprecor.*'

'Yes. Or my father did.'

'Thanks, Judith.'

'Jock came. He helped.'

'Yes, he said he would.'

'You sent him? So he knew about Bernie?'

'Yes.'

'And neither of you told me?'

'No. We decided not to. Sometimes, Jude, it's safer not to know.'

I took a deep breath but remained silent. I smarted from a feeling of betrayal but put it aside. What he said made good sense. I hadn't the faintest idea how I would have reacted if the police had questioned me about Bernie and I had known his whereabouts.

'Will he be safe in Mildura?'

He shrugged. 'We can only hope so, Jude. He's not very good at being in the shade. There's nothing more we can do.'

For the next couple of weeks every knock at the door sent my heart racing but no police visited us. I had been terrified that if they came searching for Bernie I might, through sheer nervousness, betray that I knew where he was. But gradually things returned to normal and the police raids, although still gossiped about with excitement and indignation, became events of the past with no more importance than all the other police confrontations.

I received two copies of *Women Today* in the mail and as it was a mild morning I took a chair into the backyard and sat in the sun to read them. I liked them. They were intelligent and without pretension. Harry would be delighted if I contributed because the magazine was the official organ of the women's committee of the Unemployed Workers' Union. Now I thought, with some amusement, there was no escape for me. I would have to send them some work.

The magazine emphasised women's interests and problems. There were recipes and advice on how to feed a family of eight on two shillings and sixpence a meal. There was an article on the need for equal pay for women who were sweated in the clothing factories as cheap labour on one pound eighteen shillings a week. But aside from domestic issues there was international news: articles about the new Spanish republic and what it hoped to achieve; pleas to women to boycott Japanese goods because of Japanese imperialism in China; praise for the efforts of the League of Nations to secure world peace. And overall there was an emphasis that women should unite against war.

The enclosed letter from Mrs King expressed her delight at my interest and offered me a small payment for each of my drawings. She asked if I could send two each week. I wasn't sure whether they expected my sketches to illustrate a particular article but as no mention was made of this I took from my press several of women at the soup kitchen. If they accepted these then I could send others of women in the march.

It was a comforting feeling to be sought after. The more established I became the less I worried about my work being accepted and the less I panicked when I received a rare refusal. Recently I had expressed my fears to Harry and he had looked amazed.

'Heavens, Jude, why do you always worry about people accepting your cartoons? Everyone knows you're famous.'

I took this with a grain of salt. Being known at the Port didn't make me either famous or known to everybody. But little by little I came to realise that my work was known and respected well beyond the confines of Port Adelaide. And *Women Today* was another step in that direction.

I arranged with Winnie to have a day out with her in Adelaide. Lunch at a small cafe on North Terrace and then take in a movie. I was fed up with being frugal and resolved to have more confidence that my work would bring in a secure income. I took the train and Winnie met me at the station. As always she gave me a huge hug. With her arm linked in mine she said, 'I've brought the newspaper program of films that are on in the city. We can decide over lunch.'

'Anything,' I said, 'except a horror movie. They are so ridiculous and I can't get involved.'

'I love them,' she said. 'It's great to get a thrill and know that all the time it's make-believe.'

'Well, then, a compromise.'

We crossed North Terrace outside the station and walked slowly on.

'I saw Harry a couple of weeks ago. I called in to see my aunt. Dad likes me to visit her occasionally to keep an eye on her.'

'You're good with her, Winnie. I know Harry's grateful.'

'He had a friend with him, Jude. The most gorgeous man. I think he was Italian. He had that smouldering sombre Rudolph Valentino look. And when I introduced myself – Harry's so neglectful, I even suspected that he hadn't wanted to introduce me – that lovely man looked at me with eyes like liquid chocolate. Really, Judith, I could hardly breathe. I had to tell you. Do you know who he could have been? And Harry looked so shifty.'

I tried to sound casual. 'He's a friend of Harry's.'

She was impatient. 'Yes, but do you know him?'

'Yes.'

'Well?' Eager-eyed, she waited.

I would have to tell her. 'His name is Bernie. Bernie-Benito.'

'Why that?'

'Because he shares a name with Benito Mussolini and isn't a fascist.'

She giggled. 'You're talking in riddles, Judith.'

'He's just a friend of Harry's, Winnie.'

But she was alerted. 'Come clean, Jude. What's the mystery?'

I hesitated for a moment but the incident was over, Bernie-Benito was gone, I needn't say where, and the police were off our backs.

'Bernie-Benito is a communist and the police were chasing him. They want to deport him. Harry was hiding him.'

'Goodness, Jude. Don't you mix with anyone but communists these days?'

I grinned at her. 'Them and their sympathisers.'

'And Harry was hiding him?'

'Yes.'

'At my Auntie May's?'

'So I understand.'

Winnie had begun to laugh. 'But, Jude, Auntie May couldn't keep a secret. She doesn't understand anything. She's quite dippy.'

I caught her merriment. 'Yes, I know she's quite dippy. I suppose that's why Harry took him there.'

We both rocked with laughter.

'Oh, Jude,' Winnie gasped, 'Auntie May brought out some tea and cakes for him and I'll swear the cakes were a month old because they had little specks of grey mould on them. Harry wasn't fast enough to stop him and your Bernie took one and ate it and didn't show by so much as a flicker that it must have tasted vile.'

We shrieked with laughter again. 'Poor Harry,' I said.

Winnie choked. 'What a pity the police didn't come. Auntie May could have offered them some mouldy cakes, too. So that's why the old car was parked outside. I wondered. I knew it wasn't Harry's or yours. Knew my aunt didn't have visitors who drive a beat-up old Ford.'

More sober now, I said, 'They got him away.'

Her eyes still twinkled. 'I think so, although at the time I didn't expect the old Ford to make it beyond the next corner. So Bernie-Benito's a communist? And Harry was shielding him?'

'Yes.'

'My brave and foolish cousin. That Harry. One day he'll really get himself into trouble.'

'Thanks for that, Winnie. I like to be reassured.'

'Well,' she said, 'you do like to hear the truth. You'd know if I pretended. And I am family.'

We had reached the cafe. There were chairs and tables outside.

'A-la-Parisian style,' Winnie said and plonked herself down. 'What'll we have? They make delicious chicken sandwiches here and the best Ceylon tea.'

Several pots of tea later, and some cream cakes to top up the sandwiches, we were still gossiping and it was too late to go to the matinee.

Later that week Harry and I, my mother and father, and sundry members of the Port Communist Party arrived at the Empire Theatre in Adelaide to hear an address by Ted Sloan who had just returned from a visit to the Soviet Union.

Harry was euphoric, excited and restless. 'Do you think that now we'll really know how a communist state works and what it's like to live in one? I wonder if they really pay people to learn to dance. I've heard, Jude, that any poor person can now go to the Bolshoi Ballet for next to nothing. We can't do that here.'

But I detected in him a certain anxiety, even fear, that what he heard might dispel his beautiful dream.

'You go,' he said nervously. 'You and your mum and dad. I've work I really must complete.' But I was adamant. I didn't tell him that I had guessed the cause of his reluctance, but if there was an illusion to be lost then he'd better get over it now.

The building, once used for theatricals, was now better known for holding boxing matches. It seated over a thousand people and it was packed. We were lucky to find some seats. Nathan was fussing on the platform, organising a row of chairs behind the speaker's podium and ushering an entourage of guests on to them.

'Who are they?' I asked Harry.

'I don't know their names but I think a good few come from Sydney and are literary coves.'

My father eyed them speculatively. 'Toffs from Sydney,' he muttered to my mother. She put a reproving hand on his arm and he winked at me.

Nathan spoke at length with one of them.

'Ted Sloan?' I asked Harry.

He was tense. 'I suppose so.'

I studied Ted Sloan with his round babyish face and small mouth. He was neatly dressed and of medium height and didn't look particularly radical – but then neither did Nathan nor Harry. Somehow the innocence of their ordinariness made even more nonsense of the vitriolic newspaper attacks on sinister Bolsheviks secretly conspiring to overthrow the state. Ted Sloan looked more fitted to an accountant's office with ledger and pen in front of him.

Nathan cleared his throat into the microphone and called the audience to order. He mumbled his words of welcome and turned away from the microphone so that his speech introducing Ted Sloan only reached us in isolated words.

I grimaced at Harry. 'Did you say that Nathan has improved at public speaking?'

He shook his head. 'Heaven only knows why he doesn't let someone else do it.'

Ted Sloan was both competent and assured. He adjusted the microphone to his height, thanked Nathan and the Adelaide Communist Party for inviting him, made a couple of flattering comments about the beauty of the city and a disparaging joke about Sydney which went down well. The row of disciples behind him smiled and nodded. It was a trifle patronising and insincere because none of the well-dressed visitors on the platform would have given a moment's thought to living in Adelaide, no matter how clean and beautiful it was. And, communist sympathisers or not, they wouldn't have lived in the Port in a month of Sundays. But I had learned from sending out my cartoons how parochial Australia was and how stupidly competitive our capital cities were.

Ted Sloan spoke for an hour. His speech was very long, very dry and thick with statistics – which I lost track of as soon as he uttered them. What I recalled was sparse. He began with a brief history of Russia since the revolution in 1917; the effects of four years of what he called 'the imperialist war'; and the disastrous drain on the country of the three years of intervention as Britain, France, Japan and America conspired to overthrow by force the new Soviet state. It was important to realise, he insisted, how exhausted the infant state had been and the mammoth efforts required to restore the economy. The wars had completely dislocated industry; mills and factories were at a standstill; mines wrecked or flooded; antiquated iron and steel industries in a state of collapse; agricultural production pitiful.

The people of the Soviet suffered acute food shortages and queued for bread, fats and meat. Clothing, kerosene, soap and other basic necessities were simply not available. Rumblings of social discontent threatened the very basis of what had been so dearly won.

He irritated me. I supposed that we had come to hear about Russia, but, even so, he set my teeth on edge. Where did his awareness of his own country come into it? A speech like this at the Port would have been given short shift. The Russians might have been hungry but we, too, knew all about starvation. No doubt they rumbled with discontent but our battles had been fiercer than rumblings. Why didn't he look about him in Australia?

I glanced around me. With a few exceptions, the people near me were better dressed and better fed than those at the Port. It was clear that hunger hadn't brought them out.

I appraised him cynically as he continued with his idyllic overblown view of Comrade Lenin and Comrade Stalin overcoming the insuperable obstacles in their mammoth task to lead the way forward. He said he had seen, with his own eyes, the inspirational developments during the first five year plan. Comrade Stalin had roused the nation with his call to patriotism and loyalty to communism: 'We are fifty or a hundred years behind the advanced countries,' he had declared. 'We must make good this distance in ten years or they crush us.'

'He has inspired his countrymen,' Mr Sloan asserted, 'by making the working people the heroes of the new Soviet state.'

I could almost hear the jeers and cat-calls of our workers in the Port at accepting any more sacrifices for the state. I, too, was suspicious of the state and of heroism demanded for any state. For what purpose? I wondered. This sacrifice? To inspire us to do what the Russians had done? To hold the line against capitalism? Perhaps even fascism? It seemed a utopian dream.

'There is a great spirit of hope abroad in the Soviet,' Sloan claimed. 'I have seen the new industrial expansion,' he boasted. 'The huge hydro-electric schemes, the magnificent iron and steel works, the locomotive and chemical works, and all this progress has exceeded what was expected.'

It was all too pat, too easy, I thought. What was he leaving out?

But his praise grew even more lavish. 'The collectivisation of the numerous small uneconomic farm holdings has tripled agrarian output and the enthusiasm of farmers for new methods and new agricultural machinery is astonishing. From being ignorant peasants they now all strive to acquire a technical intelligence. Schools are being built, education, the arts and science flourish.'

I shook my head in disbelief and glanced at Harry. He was attending but his mouth was pursed reflectively.

The phalanx of supporters behind Sloan failed to give him their full attention. They wriggled on their seats, glanced at their watches, polished their spectacles and whispered to their neighbours. It was obviously a speech they had heard many times.

And, to me, Sloan's enthusiasm seemed rehearsed as he climaxed grandiosely, 'And believe it or not, comrades, I saw, actually witnessed, strawberries under special scientific conditions growing in frozen Siberia.'

The audience, which up until now had sat in increasingly bored politeness, came alive at this detail and I supposed that it would be the one fact they constantly quoted about Russia's progress. My thought was proved correct when a small article in the next day's *Despatch* was headlined RUSSIANS GROW STRAWBERRIES IN SIBERIA.

At the close of his speech he urged us all to support the Australian Soviet Friendship Society, emphasising that now the time was ripe to unite in peace and brotherhood and resist all further imperialist wars.

As we made our way out of the theatre through the crowded aisle someone called my name. I turned around to discover that one of the entourage from the platform was pushing his way towards me.

'Miss Larsen,' he called. 'Miss Larsen.' He reached my side breathless. He was a tall, well-built man, nattily suited, and his skin wore the gleam of good food and money. How different from so many people at the Port whose skin was muddy or grey or blotched with sores.

He smiled at me engagingly. 'Miss Larsen. Well met.' And he held out his hand. I shook it.

'I'm Kevin Han ...' In the noise I lost the last part of his surname.

He kept on shaking my hand enthusiastically. 'I've been an admirer of your cartoons for several years. Just when I think there's nothing good in a newspaper I turn the page and there is a Judith Larsen cartoon to delight and challenge me. You will join our Soviet Friendship Society, won't you? I know that everyone would be thrilled if you honoured us with your patronage and perhaps,' his eyes twinkled, 'we can inveigle you into doing some drawings for us. Have you ever tried to draw a strawberry farm in Siberia?'

We both laughed. Overcome by his effusiveness I was flattered but also wary. 'Thank you,' I murmured. `

But just as I turned to introduce him to Harry someone grabbed his arm and pulled him away. He glanced back at me ruefully but was swallowed up in the crowd.

Harry was quiet during the train ride home. We walked with my mother and father from the station to see them to the hulk. My father was silent. Finally he said, 'Neat little bloke, wasn't he? Wouldn't go far as a lumper.'

'Oh, Niels,' my mother laughed, 'he'll have brains not brawn.'

'Humph,' Dad snorted. 'I'm always a bit suspicious of people who swallow all they're told. They've sure dished it to him. And he dished it to us.'

'And you think he hasn't actually seen it at all?' Harry was thoughtful.

'Can't say, lad. But he wouldn't admit it.'

'It would be dishonest,' my mother said, 'if he hadn't actually seen it.'

'Maybe he believes he's seen it,' I suggested.

'Fairies at the bottom of the garden.' My father was cynical.

'I would have liked to ask him if Nathan is correct and they pay people to dance. But it seemed such a naïve question,' Harry said.

My father slapped him on the back in a comradely style. 'And that's the problem, Harry. He mightn't be prepared or able to answer a simple question. All these falderal statistics – anyone can cook those up.'

Harry was silent.

Later when we went to bed he said to me out of the darkness, 'People need to believe in something, Jude.'

'Maybe. It depends.'

'On what they believe in?'

'And who judges the value of that?'

He sighed. 'Do you really believe that they're growing strawberries in Siberia?'

'I suppose it's possible. Science is doing more and more for us all. But I think it has a magical flavour to it as if the Soviet is a modern-day Camelot. The notion that something is ideal always troubles me, Harry.'

He didn't answer me immediately and I thought he had gone to sleep. Then he said, 'I don't know whether I care all that much for this deification of Comrade Stalin or the Soviet Union. I thought communism was about people being equal, not big bosses. It's great that even poor people can now go to the ballet but that's there and we're here and I wonder if we need to find our own way, Jude. What do you think?'

But I was too nearly asleep to answer him intelligently.

Our lives fell into a more or less peaceful routine. It was a relief to have no dramatic events to cope with, no major demonstrations, no direct confrontations with police. The poverty of the Port was unremitting but we had even become accustomed to that.

Harry worked every Friday and Saturday night at the dance hall in the Semaphore and, sometimes with Winnie, Ruby and Lil, I also went to the Saturday night threepenny hop. Harry's small dance band was lively and he was always popular as a pianist. But to Ruby's disappointment he no longer joined the girls on the floor for a quickstep. 'See what marriage has done,' she mourned. 'Now he's just an old sober sides.'

'Don't tease, Rube.' I defended him but I was aware that the flirtatious Harry had been replaced by a more serious man. I got tired of asserting that it was not marriage but devotion to the Communist Party that had sobered him. They really never understood.

Sometimes Miss Marie came to supper. She always brought food to help with the meal. My mother would have been mortified if one of her visitors contributed something to the table but I accepted gratefully and without embarrassment. There was rarely enough food in my larder to feed extra people. They understood because most of them were in the same boat. We had what we called a share-as-you-go system.

I always called her Miss Marie although these days she responded, 'Dear Judith, please call me Marie. I'm not your instructor any more. We are friends, *n'est-ce pas?*'

'*Oui,*' I replied teasingly.

'Or,' she added, 'you could call me Stella, which is my real Aussie name.'

'Stella,' I mused, 'it's a pretty name and suits you. But no, I think you'll always be Marie to me.'

'And so, how is communism these days, Harry?' she quizzed him, and although her tone held a gentle mockery he neither took offence nor tried to argue with her. And together they would sing a duet: *Sur le pont d'Avignon, l'on y danse, l'on y danse,* as she had taught him the French words.

'Do you know any Spanish?' he asked her on one occasion.

She was surprised. 'Not a lot, but a *soupçon,* from brief visits. Enough to get by. Why, *mon ami?*'

'No reason,' he was vague.

Later he said to me, 'She's such a pretty woman, Jude, and has a very sweet voice.'

I agreed. 'I miss my classes with her now that my course is finished but I still frequently call on her opinion.'

'She's not a communist, is she? But I feel there's something there, perhaps some hope for her.'

'Oh, yes, Harry. I'm sure there's something there. But I wouldn't hope too much.' He knew I was laughing at him but as always took it in good part.

Mrs King was pleased with the drawings I sent her and they appeared regularly in *Women Today.* The article about the exploitation of young women and girls in factories had taken my attention. For years I had concentrated on the destitution and despair caused by unemployment. It had not occurred to me, and I took myself to task for this, that in the present climate of lowered wages girls would be particular victims.

Given my hated work at the Chew It when I was fifteen I should have thought about others like myself. Many of the young men in the Unemployed Workers' Union had sisters and I asked Harry to inquire if any of them worked in the local flour mill. His answer was startling. Many did and often their pittance kept families afloat.

He arranged for me to speak with three of the girls one Sunday afternoon. They arrived shy and uncomfortable and dressed in what they had of Sunday best. They were younger than me but looked older by twenty years. They had the dead white skin of people imprisoned away from the sun for most of the week. Their bloodshot eyes were red-rimmed and stained beneath with heavy purple shadows. They coughed persistently. They were thin.

I asked them about the flour mill, what it was like to work there. They hesitated, fearful that any criticism might endanger their job.

'What is it that you really want from us, Miss Larsen?' the oldest and sharpest of the three asked. 'We know you do wonderful cartoons and we have seen some of your drawings. Do you want to ask us questions about our work in the flour mill or is it that you want some drawings of us?'

Her bluntness left me tongue-tied. I had not thought that I would be exploiting their misery by drawing them but now, in the face of her direct question, I realised that was my intention. Mesmerised by my belief that a portrayal of working class suffering would help everyone, I had insensitively assumed that my drawings would be acceptable to these girls.

One of the girls flushed. 'It is very kind of you, Miss Larsen,' she said, 'to think of us but we are not very beautiful these days.' And the third girl added, hastily, 'Our families wouldn't like to see us looking so poorly. They feel guilty. It's hard, Miss Larsen, to see ourselves in mirrors, still young but looking so ugly.'

I grew hot with shame, pity and embarrassment. 'Of course,' I said. 'I wouldn't think of drawing you without your permission. Please forgive me. If you are unhappy I never would ...' I floundered to a stop. 'Let me make you all some tea.'

They accepted but in the main it was a silent stiff uncomfortable afternoon. I was afraid to ask any questions in case they suspected my motives and they were shy and diffident.

When Harry returned home he asked, 'How'd it go with the girls, Jude?'

'It was terrible. So sad, Harry. I couldn't draw them. All they want is to be pretty and young again.'

As usual Nathan visited regularly and occasionally Jock and Frank joined us. Jock could only listen to Nathan's ponderous lecturing for a short time before he became restless and ended the sermonising with, 'Give us a break, laddie. My head fair aches with stretching itself around these ideas. How about a tune, Harry?' And he strode to the piano, opened the lid, and before Nathan had finished his last sentence thumped a few loud notes to silence him.

Harry grinned at me behind Nathan's back, went to the piano, pulled out the stool, settled himself comfortably and played a few bars of 'Glasgow belongs to me'. And Jock puffed out his chest, looked surprisingly sentimental, and sang, *I'm only a common auld worrrking chap, as anyone here can see, but when I gets a coupla drinks on a Saturdee Glasgee belangs to me.*

And if Frank was there he would demand that Harry play 'The Wearing of the Green' and we would all beef out: *Oh, Paddy, dear, and did you hear the news that's going round? The shamrock is by law forbid to grow on Irish ground. Saint Patrick's day no more we'll keep, his colours can't be seen for there's a cruel law against the wearing of the green.*

And then, because we had made ourselves sad by the losses of the left, in tribute to Bernie-Benito we all sang 'Bandiera Rossa': *Avanti popolo alla riscossa, bandiera rossa, bandierra rossa.*

But Nathan never joined in our singing. When he had gone home I asked, 'Do you think he can, Harry?'

'What? Sing?'

'Yes.'

'Probably not. Or not well. Nathan wouldn't like to do anything he wasn't good at.'

'That must be restricting.'

'I suppose so. But he seems contented enough.'

'He never has longings?'

'Longings, Jude? He wants a communist state. I suppose that's a longing.'

'No. I meant personal and private ones.'

He grinned. 'None I've ever heard of. But, of course, he did have tickets on you.'

'That's past, Harry, and you know it. And I'm not sure it was ever really true.'

'Oh, it was true all right. Sometimes I wonder ...' he hesitated. 'I feel a bit uncomfortable because he talks of you as if he has some special knowledge or understanding of you hidden from me.'

I raised my eyebrows. 'Indeed? Then the poor man's deluded, Harry.'

'Yes, I know this. But it still makes me feel uncomfortable. It's a strange part of his character that he can't always face the truth.'

My thoughts lingered over the girls from the flour mill and I drew two cartoons to send to *Women Today*. One was a drawing of a baker's shop with rows of bread in the window. Under it was an advertisement for the wares: WE CAN GUARRANTEE THAT ONLY 5 GIRLS FAINTED MAKING THE FLOUR FOR OUR BREAD. A second cartoon featured a flour mill as background and in front of it a fat factory owner holds a loaf of bread announcing, *This is the staff of life*. A thin hollow-eyed girl beside him protests, *I wish flour wasn't the stuff of our lives.*

I sent them off explaining that the working conditions for girls in the flour mills were appalling and suggesting that perhaps *Women Today* might like to look into the situation.

A couple of editions later there were my cartoons and a full-page article. I felt much better about how I'd treated the girls.

Usually Harry and Nathan and other comrades who came to meetings at our house discussed Party affairs amongst themselves and then went home. I was happy not to be involved and usually worked at my drawings in the front room. But this night Harry asked me if I would join them because there was something they wanted to talk over with me.

I didn't know why the thought of Nathan wanting to talk something over with me made me jumpy but it did. Instinctively I knew that whatever he might propose I would baulk at it. As always he seemed nervous with me and far from initiating the conversation he deferred to Harry. Cunning, I thought. What does the slippery rat want now?

'Well,' I asked, and was none too friendly. Harry hesitated.

I knew my antagonism to Nathan was a constant source of embarrassment to him and that I had put him on the third point of a very awkward triangle. But to put it bluntly I didn't trust Nathan. He and his sisters used people. Once I was direct about it with Harry.

'He may, Jude, but it's for the bigger cause.'

'It doesn't matter,' I snapped, 'whether it's for himself or for what he believes is some greater cause. He still uses people and I don't like it.' And for good measure I added, 'And so do his sisters.'

He grimaced. 'And you accuse the comrades of being puritanical. Listen to yourself, Jude.'

'Oh, you, Harry,' I joked.

He grinned. 'Oh, you, Judith. You're such a card.'

Now I looked suspiciously from Harry's reluctant face to Nathan's bland and uncommunicative one.

'OK, boys,' I said, attempting jocularity, 'out with it. What's up your sleeves?'

Harry relaxed but Nathan compressed his lips. Objectionable prune, I thought.

'Would you like a little holiday, Jude?'

'Holiday?' Now I was even more suspicious. We couldn't afford a holiday. My God, I suddenly thought. Images of Ted Sloan's speech sprang to my mind. My God, they're proposing we go to the Soviet Union. Ted Sloan's inspired them to some stupidity.

'No,' I protested violently, 'I'm not going to Russia. You, Nathan, can keep your fantasies to yourself.'

'Russia?' Harry was bemused. 'Why would we go to Russia?'

'Oh,' I said, feeling foolish. 'I thought … Ted Sloan …'

He shouted with laughter and hugged me. 'No, Jude, Mildura.'

'Mildura? Why Mildura?'

Harry couldn't resist it. 'Because it's not as far as Russia.'

Despite Nathan's sour look at our levity, we both rocked with laughter. At last I said, 'What's going on in Mildura?'

Nathan thought it time to intervene. This wasn't being treated with the solemnity it deserved. 'We want to set up a branch of the Party there.'

Still laughing I said, 'And can't the Mildurians or the Mildurianites …?' Once again Harry and I shrieked with mirth. 'Can't they do it for themselves?'

'No.' Nathan was terse. 'They need our guidance.'

'Mm,' I said, still chortling. Once Harry and I got into this hilarious mood it was hard to break out of it. 'So they need guidance? And Nathan here,' I threw him a provocative look, 'is just the person to do it? Why do you need Harry and me, Nathan?'

But Harry, catching Nathan's disapproval, made a good job of being serious again. 'I'm going there to learn, Jude, how to set up a Party cell. But I said I'd only go if you'd come, too.'

I guessed from Nathan's expression that there'd been an

argument and Nathan had met that unexpected streak of stub-bornness in Harry. I had my mouth open to say, 'That was brave of you, Harry,' but shut it. I was learning that there was only a certain tactful distance I could go in criticising Nathan to Harry.

'How long for?' I asked.

'Just a couple of weeks.' Harry was eager. 'You'll come?'

'Of course,' I smiled at him lovingly, 'but only because it's not as far as Russia.'

He chuckled. 'You are a card, Jude. There, Nathan, I told you she'd come.'

Nathan smiled, one of his habitual tight smiles. How Harry managed to get on with such a humourless man always astonished me.

We left the Port very early. Jock and Nathan sat in the front to share the driving, Harry and I in the back. Jock had borrowed Pat's car for the couple of weeks we'd be away. I thought it very generous of Pat and remembered how he'd ferried Harry and me home after the fracas in Victoria Square. It was an old car that squeaked and rattled and jolted over potholes. I had packed a basket of food for our journey and hoped Jock and Nathan had done the same. I had also borrowed from Miss Marie and Winnie a couple of vacuum flasks, which I filled with weak black tea. Milk I couldn't carry.

The electric streetlights mounted on ornate lamp-posts dropped rings of hazy brightness but beyond them the shadows were long and dark. Few were abroad and we passed only a couple of other cars. Briefly their headlights pierced the darkness and long shards of light momentarily illuminated what had been secret and forbidden. Then the night flowed in again and the shadows seemed even blacker.

Then we were through Adelaide, travelling north on the Sturt Highway. We passed through Gawler in the darkness. I peered out the car window trying to see something of it. 'It's no good,' I said, 'I can't see a thing.'

'Wheest, lassie,' Jock snorted, 'dinna fash yersel. There's not much to see. There used to be industry here but the depression's killed that.'

The sky glowed a soft grey. A few streaks of pink colour tentatively eased over the horizon and in a burst of enthusiasm the sun leaped up and the whole sky, suffused in red and gold, shouted to us that it was day.

In the darkness the road had been mysterious; the air from the part-open window cold on my face; the scrubby trees mere silhouettes in our headlights. Now it all opened up, a flat, dry monochromatic landscape of browns, golds and ochres, stretching away on either side, while the road straight ahead and receding smaller and smaller was a perfect lesson in perspective.

Several kangaroos bounded out of the bush, keeping pace with the car. The power and rhythm of their easy levitation thrilled me. Then, for no apparent reason, the largest of them swerved across our path. Jock braked furiously. The car slithered dangerously and the kangaroo shot past in front of us, the others following.

'Stupid bugger,' Jock swore. 'Heads the size of peanuts. No wonder there's no brain inside.' I was shaken but amused. Kangaroos wouldn't be a road hazard in Glasgow. We disturbed a large lizard on the verge of the road, immobile and sunning himself, head cocked in our direction. In the flick of a moment he was gone, back into the bush.

We stopped for breakfast, which we ate either sitting in the car or standing around in the morning sunshine. I needed to spend a penny but there were no penny-in- the-slot public toilets here. Harry warned me to be very careful of snakes, so I crept over the dry crackling leaves and grass, suspiciously inspecting every black twig before I stepped on it. I found a conveniently large tree stump I could hide behind and, having carefully checked the area, cautiously squatted down. The only thing I disturbed was a nest of large red ants, which rushed frantically from their hole, comically reared on their back legs, and waved their antennas belligerently. I was quite sure that they'd give me a nasty bite and kept clear of them.

The day grew hotter. There were some sheep, poor grey dusty creatures and ahead of us the road shimmered like the shifting of light over water. It was my first experience of a mirage. It was an eerie desolate landscape. The small towns we passed looked as if most of the life had been drained out of them.

'God, it's monotonous,' Harry grumbled.

But I didn't think so. An endlessly pastel landscape, yes, but there were subtleties of colour in the tones of brown and the silver-grey of the eucalypts. It was all new to me and I was fascinated. The very size of it left me awe-struck. Until now I had had no visual concept that I lived on the edge of such a vast continent. For a moment, in the face of such timelessness, I wondered why we were heading for Mildura and so taken up with the transient affairs of people.

However I had risen very early and as the afternoon wore on the heat and the dust exhausted me. It was difficult, because if we shut the car windows we suffocated and if we opened them we swallowed dust. Eventually I fell into a doze.

Harry shook me gently. 'Wake up, darling.'

I stirred drowsily. My head had fallen against his shoulder and he leaned down and kissed me softly. 'Wake up, darling, we've reached Renmark. You must see the Murray River. It's grand.'

I sat up, smiling at him. From the front seat Jock grinned at us. 'You two canoodling lovebirds, don't you know we're on serious business?' He glanced slyly at Nathan and winked at us. 'How about a leg stretch, Nathan? And a beer at the local pub? I could do with a pint to wash down all this dust.'

We were all covered in a film of it. I shook the skirt of my dress and was immediately enveloped in a cloud. 'Sorry,' I apologised between sneezes. 'I'll have a good shake when I get out.'

'We all will, darling.' Harry's face had little rivulets of ochre sweat. 'Pull over, Nathan.'

Nathan drew the car into a dirt siding beneath gigantic red gums.

'Before beer,' I said, scrambling out, 'I must see the river first.' And without waiting I ran along the dusty path which, crackling with leaves and twigs beneath my feet, led to the river bank.

'Watch out for snakes,' Harry called after me. 'They like water.'

And there it was. I gasped at its immensity. I stood on a coarse sandy beach and before me a vast volume of brown water, at least half a mile from bank to bank, made its slow and inexorable way to the sea. Its grandeur overwhelmed me.

In the shallows of the sandy beach the water was palely golden and lapped gently. Further out the current pulled twigs and leaves and other debris into its flow and spun them around in curling eddies and tiny whirlpools. It smelled quite differently from the river at the Port. At home there were always traces of salt in the air; often mixed with fumes of coal, the dry mustiness of wheat bags, or the rancid smell of wool fleeces. Here there was only the warm foetid smell of water shifting a cumbersome load of earth in its bowels.

I kicked off my shoes and crept into the water to my knees. It was cool and I bent and washed my arms and gathered some in my hands and splashed my face. The three men had followed me but still stood, stuffy in their shoes and socks.

'Come on, Harry,' I called. 'Come and join me. It's lovely.'

He laughed at me. 'I'll wait for Mildura, darling. It's the same river.'

'But not the same water,' I said wisely. 'See those leaves? They were swirling about a minute ago right here. Now they're yards downstream.'

'She's a father and mother of a river, all right,' Jock said. 'You keep out of that current, girlie.'

I came out reluctantly. Harry gave me his handkerchief to dry my feet but it was so hot I just shoved them into my shoes. I looked along the bank where the mighty roots of the eucalypts knotted and twisted and twined themselves into gargantuan shapes. 'My sketchbook is in the car, Harry. Would I have time?'

'No, Jude, the boys want a beer. You'll have oodles of time in Mildura.'

Regretfully I followed him.

At the pub Nathan and Jock leaned on the bar. As women weren't permitted in the bar room Harry joined me in the lounge. He brought me a long glass of ice-cold lemon squash.

'They've tried quizzing the barman about Mildura but he doesn't seem to know much.'

'Is it far, Harry?'

'Probably a couple of hours, depending on the road.'

'Where are we staying?'

'I'm not sure. But Nathan says it's a bit out of town. There's a camp there for the telegraph men and they have permanent housing.' He looked anxious. 'I hope it's OK, Jude. Nathan said it's suitable.'

'But he hasn't seen it?'

'No, of course not. But he said the Party man in Mildura was reliable. He's assured me, Jude.'

'How do we find our way there?'

Nathan says that Bernie-Benito's meeting us at the first petrol station we come to as we enter the town. He'll show us the way.'

I had always been fond of Bernie-Benito and my spirits, which had taken a tumble, revived. 'Bernie's OK? He's found work? The police have left him alone?'

'Yes, so I understand, and he's been doing some great Party work amongst the Italian fruit pickers. He's been Nathan's contact with other members. I gather it's a pretty rough hillbilly sort of place and they have to hold meetings in secret.'

This news didn't appeal to me as much as it seemed to do to Harry. The thought of the excitement brightened his eyes. I was puzzled. 'If Bernie has the Party situation well in hand why does Nathan need you and Jock here?'

'It's support, Judith. Keeping up connections. Educating the workers in the role of the proletariat. Making them aware of the importance of the Central Organising Committee.'

'In other words,' I said dryly, 'keeping a grip on them in case they slide off the path into anarchism or socialism or reformism.'

'Really, Jude,' he protested, 'you're always so cynical.'

'Not at all, Harry. It's just that my stock in trade is a keen sense of irony and I have a responsibility to keep your feet on the ground.'

He blew the froth off his second glass of beer and looked at me wickedly. 'I much prefer our other responsibilities. I hope our hut is very very private. An idyll by the river for a delayed honeymoon.'

As he had tried to look lascivious, I laughed. 'Oh, Harry, you.'

'Oh, you, Judith. You're such a card. But I'll always love you no matter how much you laugh at me or ...' For an instant he was solemn. 'Maybe because of it.'

'Well,' I responded, 'I never intended to add Nathan and Jock to our honeymoon. But I guess we can get rid of them somehow. Do you think we could frighten Nathan by inviting him to come swimming *au naturel*, as Miss Marie would say?' I pretended to look coy.

Harry chuckled. 'We could try. But we might have to hatch another plot for Jock. He's made of sterner stuff.'

Bernie-Benito was waiting for us. He lounged against the side wall of the small petrol station with its twin bowsers. Nathan pulled up and Jock jumped out. 'There's me little mate,' he said, and rushed to grab Bernie's hand. He shook it vigorously and slapped him on the back. 'How are you, you little fascist bastard?'

Bernie sloped towards us with Jock's arm draped about his shoulder. He grinned at Nathan and Harry and shook hands. 'Judith,' he looked soulfully at me, 'lovely Judith.'

As I gave him my hand he bent and kissed it gently. 'Dear Bernie,' I said and reaching up kissed him on the cheek. 'And you're OK?'

'OK and my English much better.'

I winked at him. 'Don't try to trick me, Bernie. Your English has always been much better.'

He smiled slyly and flicked his hand across his throat. 'You like my ...?'

'No,' I said. 'You know that and you only do it to tease. It's all a big pretence, Bernie. You've never killed anyone.'

His eyes grew distant. 'Lovely Judith, you think not? Italy under Mussolini – another country.'

Jock drew him away and I stood by the car on my own while the garage attendant filled the petrol tank. Bernie talked quietly to Jock but gesticulating wildly with his hands he once or twice glanced at me, then back to Jock shaking his head.

He doesn't want me here, I thought.

Harry was talking to Nathan and he, too, looked anxious. The garage man went over to Nathan who paid him. I got back into the car.

A few minutes later the four men joined me and we squeezed Bernie into the back seat with Harry and me.

'We're going to the telegraph men's camp,' Harry said.

I was suspicious. 'How well ...?'

He interrupted me. 'It'll be OK, Judith. Nathan has fixed everything.'

I thought it better not to respond.

Jock had had his directions from Bernie and he told Nathan

who turned the car around and headed out of town. We reached a turn-off along a dirt and gravel track. The car jolted violently.

'Poor Pat,' I said to Harry, 'there may not be much of his car left.'

'She'll be right,' Jock said. 'These old crates are tougher than they look.'

'Or feel.' My laugh shook as we crashed through another series of potholes.

The track wound between looming eucalypts for about a quarter of a mile. Finally we emerged into a cleared area, the telegraph men's camp. Through the trees I saw the glint of water and knew we were again close to the river. There were half a dozen galvanised-iron huts and in the centre of the area a brick fireplace.

Nathan pulled up and we sat silently, viewing our accommodation. Harry took a deep breath; Bernie whistled a few bars of *'Avanti popolo'* and stopped; Jock cleared his throat; and Nathan got out and stood irresolutely.

A tall shambolic man carrying a bucket of water ambled through the trees from the river. He put the bucket on the ground, stared at us, and then hurried forward. 'Gooday, comrades,' he greeted us, eagerly shaking hands with the men. Then he saw me. 'Christ!' he exclaimed. 'A woman! You didn't tell me you had a woman with you.' He scratched the back of his neck helplessly and repeated, 'A woman. Jesus Christ, this is no place ... We weren't expecting ...' He stopped.

'She's my wife,' Harry said tightly and with a mixture of consternation and anger he turned on Nathan. 'You said it'd be comfortable. You said you'd fixed everything. I trusted you.'

Nathan looked embarrassed.

'Steady, laddie,' Jock said, 'he couldn't have known.'

Harry was not to be soothed or quietened. 'Then he shouldn't have been so bloody confident,' he shouted.

Now Nathan was angry. 'I didn't want you to bring Judith. You insisted.'

I was tired of being the centre of their conflict and argued over like an inconvenient parcel. 'Stop it all of you. Let's see where we are to sleep tonight and tomorrow we can discuss it.' I was very weary after the long day's travelling and they, too, were exhausted.

'Oh, Jude,' Harry was remorseful, 'I'm so sorry.'

'It's not your fault,' I said. I glanced at Nathan who also looked uncertain and unhappy. 'It's not anyone's fault. It's just been a big misunderstanding.'

I smiled at our host, who stood helplessly, awkwardly shifting from one foot to the other. 'Have you two separate huts?' I asked. 'One for my husband and myself and one for Nathan and Jock?'

He was gruff but polite, clearly relieved that I had broken in on the dispute. He led the way to one of the huts. I followed him and Harry walked beside me, swearing under his breath.

'Ssh,' I said. 'That poor man. Having me here has made him completely miserable. This is a men's camp and I'm the intruder.'

'I could kill Nathan,' Harry said savagely. 'He never thinks of anything except the bloody Party. He's not human, just a walking set of dogmas.'

I took his arm. 'Ssh,' I said again. 'It's only for one night. We'll find something better tomorrow. Mildura's a town. There must be a reasonable pub.'

The huts were one-roomed, built only for sleeping in. The beds were a pair of single camp stretchers with a thin mattress, a ticking pillow, and a grey blanket. Folded up on the end of each stretcher was a set of cheap sheets, a pillowcase and a small rough towel. Somebody had made some basic arrangements for our arrival. There was a shelf and a few hooks on the wood uprights of the wall to hang clothes. A couple of windows were holes in the wall with a wooden shutter that swung outwards and upwards. I could hear the zing and whine of mosquitoes, but there were no nets.

Harry took one glimpse of the two stretchers and snorted

disgustedly. 'So much for our romantic idyll. A second honeymoon was it, Judith?'

I laughed and kissed him.

'Where do we wash and toilet?' I whispered.

He groaned. 'God knows. Let's leave here at once, Jude. I'll make Nathan and Jock find a pub for the night.'

'No, it's too late, Harry. Just ask him.'

Harry went outside. I sat on one of the stretchers. The night was cooling. I hugged my cardigan about me.

'He says there's an earth lavatory on the far side of the clearing and he'll give you a torch but we need to bring a bucket of water from the river for washing and we need, if we want to, to have a bath in the river.'

At his dismay I chuckled. 'We meant to go dipping together, Harry.'

'But not this way.'

'Is there another?' I pretended to be arch. 'After all the river is on our doorstep.'

'Oh, Jude,' he repeated. 'I do love you. You have such sterling resilience.'

The telegraph man waited anxiously for us outside. Harry had found out that his name was Andy.

'It's very nice,' I lied, 'and looks quite comfortable.'

Relieved, he grinned at us. 'I'll make you a cuppa and a biscuit. Billy's on the boil an' I bought some clean china mugs. Thought you city types mightn't like tin mugs. Glad I did now we have a lady.'

Around the fire sat two old lounge chairs with broken springs and torn fabric, several old wooden seats, and two stools. The telegraph man offered me a lounge chair and I sank onto the creaking uneven springs, trying to shift my weight so they didn't stick into me.

It was a glorious night, still, clear and cool. I had never before seen such a host of brilliant stars. It was as if they were appliquéd on an ebony cloth. At home stars shone and sometimes glittered in the sea but often streetlights dimmed and diminished their radiance. Here such light sprang from them that I had the illusion of a kaleidoscope of rubies, sapphires, emeralds and topazes, and each star flashed at me with its individual colour and its individual beauty.

Andy handed me a mug of tea, sweetened with condensed milk. I leaned back, sipped it and while the fire warmed my feet the darkness enfolded me. It was a beautiful place, redolent of euca-lypts. Maybe we could manage to stay here. But as I swatted at mosquitoes I knew that at least we would need to chase protective nets before a second night.

Later two men in an old tin lizzie rattled and clanked along the track into the clearing. We had just finished a plate of rabbit stew, prepared by Andy, and with my hand in Harry's I felt very peaceful.

Nathan and Jock and Bernie, who had been sitting with us around the fire, got up to meet them. Harry looked up. 'Better see what's going on, Jude.'

'Mm.' I was sleepy. 'Don't forget you have a date with me in the river.'

He squeezed my hand. 'A bit cool, Jude.'

'Mm,' I joked, 'but you promised.'

Sometimes he wasn't quite sure about how serious I was and he looked at me uncertainly.

'Of course it's too cold, Harry,' I laughed. 'Go and meet the men.'

I picked up my torch and found my way to the pit lavatory. It was primitive but adequate.

Andy had left a bucket of water outside our hut and a piece of soap on the grass beside it. I ladled some over my hands, looked doubtfully at the slightly discoloured water in the bucket, decided that others used it, and cleaned my teeth. Heaven only knew how long Harry would be, so I made up our beds, put on my pyjamas and lay down on my stretcher. Immediately the mosquitoes began their nightly torture. I pulled the sheet over my head and cocooned somewhat airlessly fell asleep. I didn't even hear Harry come in.

Flocks of screaming galahs and corellas woke me at sun-up. I unwound myself from the sheet and peeped out the door. An idyllic morning greeted me. I dressed, took one of the rough towels and prepared to creep out. Harry still slept. I studied his face. It had grown thinner. Even in sleep his lips were compressed as if still disapproving of Nathan's arrangements. His nose jutted more and his cheekbones were sharper. I had once known him as an ebullient carefree boy. Now I looked at a mature man. Only his mop of bronze untidy hair still made him look youthful and vulnerable because of it.

Had I similarly changed? I supposed that I had, from the rough fifteen-year-old slinging hash and giving lip in the Chew It. I was now a young woman, no longer feeling the need to be rough to assert my independence but still an intensely individual person with no talent for compliance.

Harry's fluctuations between asserting his own individuality and complying with Nathan's drive to submerge every personal difference in Communist Party policy frequently caused conflict, not only between us, but these days in himself. It was only a couple of weeks ago that he had commented to me rather sadly, 'I once thought that being a communist was a simple belief, that they'd pay me to dance and be a musician, and that I'd happily go on doing both for the rest of my life. Now I know that Nathan doesn't think dancing or music are important and sometimes I get the feeling that he is just indulging me, or worse, patronising me, and I search around for something in myself to tell me what it means to be a good communist.'

I understood that what he believed in or didn't believe in troubled him and as I had no addiction to any system of belief I remained silent. Whatever I said might appear dismissive of his worries. After all, he wasn't asking me my opinion, he was merely sharing his doubts with me.

I closed the door gently and wandered across the clearing. A yellow-crested black cockatoo spread his huge wings and took flight. A flock of tiny green budgerigars had settled on the grass for a feed. They carpeted the edge of the clearing. The occasional flashes of azure on their wings looked momentarily as if tiny fragments of the sky had fallen amongst them.

A short track led to the river bank and ended as usual in a narrow beach of coarse sand. Here was a tiny cove where the water lay still and benign but further out I again saw debris swept into the surging current. There was no one about, so I slipped off my clothes and entered the water to my thighs. There was no pull of the current so I floated a little and swam a few strokes. It was cold but not as chill as I had expected. I came out, dried myself on the rough towel and put on my clothes. When I emerged from the trees I saw Andy and two other men preparing breakfast on a grill over the open fire. I could smell bacon. They saw me and stopped awkwardly. I grinned at them. 'I've had a swim.'

They relaxed. Obviously young women who went for an early morning swim weren't as delicate as they had imagined. I received a warning to be on my guard in the current, which was a 'real nasty bugger', and I promised I would.

'Like some brekky?' Andy asked.

They handed me a tin plate, a knife and fork, and ladled several strips of bacon and a couple of fried eggs onto it. Bacon and eggs were almost unheard of these days in the Port. How could people in Mildura live in such an idyllic world?

Tousle-headed and sleepy Harry found me and skewered himself a piece of my bacon. 'Mm,' he said, 'when did we last taste bacon?'

'You haven't had your early morning bath,' I teased. 'You don't deserve it.'

'In the river?' He shuddered.

'Yes, in the river.'

'Ah, well,' he was resigned, 'save me some bacon.'

'Plenty here,' Andy said.

With mock amazement, Harry sighed. 'Did you hear that, Jude? Plenty here and he means it.'

When he returned breakfast was in full swing and Nathan and Jock had appeared. Bernie had returned to Mildura with the two blokes who had come in the tin lizzie.

'What did they want, Harry?' I asked.

He hesitated and glanced at Nathan as if for approval in telling me.

I was sharp as I so often was when I felt Nathan's influence shadowing us. 'What did they want, Harry?'

'They want us to help set up a branch of the Communist Party.'

'But you came here to do that. It isn't a surprise, is it?'

'No, not entirely.'

'What do you mean "not entirely"?'

He hesitated again, throwing a how-much-do-I-tell-her look at Nathan, and then said, 'It won't be as easy as we thought. That's all, Jude.'

After breakfast Harry told Nathan bluntly that we wouldn't sleep here another night and that he could cough up enough funds for our hotel accommodation. Nathan demurred and grew sulky, saying that Harry came to do a job and that the Party was short of money. After all, it was only for a few nights.

Harry was belligerent. 'It's your mistake, Nathan. You fix it.'

Once again I interrupted their dispute. 'Let's go into town and see if they've got any mosquito netting and we can look at the pub. But it's not too bad here, Harry.'

'Not too bad?' He looked stunned. 'Not too bad, Jude? It's

dreadful. Two camp stretchers, an earth lavatory, and the river to wash in?'

'Yes,' I responded dreamily, recalling my morning swim and my bacon and eggs. 'Quite lovely, actually. And the whole place smells of eucalypts. And the sweet smoky fragrance of burning wood from the fireplace. And the birds in the morning are glorious.'

Harry was speechless and Nathan smirked. For that I could have smacked him. He deserved a reminder of how far he could stretch my endurance. 'But if there are no mosquito nets, then it'll have to be the pub,' I snapped at him.

This compromise didn't appeal to Harry. 'I want a proper room, Jude, and a proper bed. This place isn't right for you.'

But I didn't mind it as much as Harry did. Harry had grown up in a genteel house in Adelaide. I had been reared on a hulk. A hulk wasn't a telegraph men's camp but maybe it had prepared me for more adventurous accommodation. 'Come on,' I placated him, 'let's see what's available.'

So Nathan drove us in to Mildura and parked in the main street. It was a sizeable, seemingly prosperous town with wide roads and shaded footpaths beneath overhanging verandahs. We found a general store that seemed to sell everything from clothing to hardware. Harry, still determined, said he'd go in search of a pub, and I could look for mosquito netting if I wanted to. He marched off, offended that I had seemingly rejected his care. His stiff back told me that he considered himself betrayed.

Nathan and Jock went off together, saying rather mysteriously that they wanted to meet a friend. It was a perfectly normal sunshiny morning with quite a few people busy about the street and I sighed at the continued secrecy of the Communist Party. Nathan always trailed a sense of conspiracy that seemed to create its own threat. I wished Harry were free of it.

I wandered through the store searching the shelves but

eventually had to appeal to the shop owner. He led me to a shelf where there were rolls of green netting and asked me how much I wanted. Of course, I didn't know. Helplessly, I said, 'Enough to drape over two camp stretchers.'

He pursed his lips. 'How you goin' to do that?'

Once again I didn't know. He looked me up and down. 'From down south, are yer?'

'Yes, Adelaide. Actually Port Adelaide.'

He assessed me. 'Where yer stayin'?'

'At a camp out of town. The telegraph men's camp.'

'Strange place for a lady to stay.'

I was defensive. 'I'm with my husband.'

He smirked. 'Husband, eh? What's he do?'

I would have preferred not to answer but I was cornered between him and the shelf and I needed the netting. 'He's a musician.'

'Plays in bands, eh?'

'Yes.'

'Lookin' for a gig?'

'Yes.'

That seemed to satisfy him. 'You'll need some long bamboo poles to fix crosswise at each end of your stretcher and then you pull the nets over them. But you want made-up nets, not this stuff.'

He led me to another shelf. 'How many do you want?'

I hesitated. Should I say two or four? 'Four,' I said.

He raised his eyebrows. 'Other band members?'

'Yes. That's right.'

'Play yourself?'

I allowed myself to be confiding. 'No, I'm tone deaf.'

He looked me over. 'I'm sure you've got other assets.'

I ignored his leer.

'Better watch yer step out there.'

'Snakes?' I asked.

'Yair. Two legged ones. A lotta red raggers camp out there.'

'Really?' I pretended shock.

'Yair. Regular commie bunch. Red raggers. We don't care for them much in this town and we know how to deal with them.'

My hackles rose but I didn't look up from counting out my money.

'What do you do to them?' I continued to search in my purse.

He snorted. 'Whatta we do with them? Shove 'em on the first train outer town or throw 'em in the river. After we've roughed 'em up a bit. Just to stop 'em from comin' back. That gets rid of 'em. Good riddance to bad rubbish I says.'

He dusted his hands. 'Don't want that sorta riff-raff here. You and your musician *husband* ...' he leered at me again. 'You take care out there. You don't wanna get mistook for a red ragger.'

I took the nets and hurried out, knowing that his eyes followed me to the door.

Harry was waiting gloomily by the car. He noted my flushed face. 'All OK, Jude?'

'No.' My voice was tight. 'I've got the nets but I've just had a conversation with the most sickeningly abominable man. I don't know how I kept a still tongue in my head. This is not a safe place, Harry.'

'No?' he jibed at me. 'But only a short time ago you told me it was quite lovely.'

I was impatient. 'Don't be spiteful, Harry. I wasn't talking about people.'

He relented. 'No, you weren't. The bloke in the pub wasn't friendly, either. Quizzed me within an inch of my life. And advised me not to associate with the red raggers at the telegraph camp or I might end up dead in the river one night. How's that for hospitality, Jude?'

I had a lazy day at the camp reading a book and sketching the red gums by the river. Bernie arrived later in the afternoon and he,

Harry, Jock and Nathan spent the hours conferring while Nathan took notes. We had purchased some food in town and I left the men to muck around preparing it but none of our group was very adept at camp cooking so Andy did most of the work and didn't seem to mind.

As darkness approached Harry sat down beside me anxiously. 'I'm worried, Jude, and don't know what to do.'

'Why?'

'We have a meeting in town tonight.'

'Yes, but you expected this.'

He grasped my hand and held it tightly. 'I don't like it, Jude. I think this is a nasty town.'

'But we're not in town, Harry. We're out at the camp.'

'But I don't know whether it's safe, Jude. I can't leave you here tonight on your own and I don't like to take you with us. There could be trouble.'

He still clasped my hand so I squeezed his. 'Don't be silly, Harry. We've met trouble before. It'll be simpler if I come with you and then you can keep an eye on me.'

He groaned. 'A choice between Scylla and Charybdis.'

I laughed. 'Honestly, Harry, that's far too dramatic. It's only a meeting. You're making too much of a few threats from some loud-mouthed roughnecks. What are they going to do? Shoot us up? It isn't the Wild West.'

But he was silent. At last he said, 'I need to go to the meeting, Jude. It's expected.'

'Of course it is. Stop worrying. You don't want me to stay here, although I'm sure I'd be quite safe with Andy, so I'll come with you.'

His response was strangely violent. 'There's no way I'm going to leave you here, hoping someone else will look after you.'

So that's it, I thought. Nathan has been needling him, trying to persuade him to leave me at the camp.

'Well, then,' I said quietly, 'if you feel like that it's far better if I come.'

I had no idea what he said to Nathan and Jock that evening but they each greeted me pleasantly as I got into Pat's car. Bernie, who had stayed to eat with us, again squeezed into the back between Harry and me. At the end of the track we turned towards Mildura and he directed us through now quiet streets to a small wooden house with an iron roof. It was set back from the road amidst some straggly dried-up shrubs.

No light showed from the windows so I was startled to enter and find a well-lit room with a dozen men. A couple sat at a central table, the others ranged around the walls. I hadn't been able to see any lights because heavy blinds and some rigged-up dark sheeting shrouded the two windows. There was an eerie claustrophobia about the room that made me uneasy. Instinctively I looked back to the door as an escape route.

At my entrance a train of startled glances ran around the room. Then, as one, they stood and raised their hats to me. Overcome with embarrassment, I halted.

Nathan was impatient. 'Sit down everyone.' And he waved his hand around the room. 'It's Judith, Harry's wife. We had to bring her.'

'Rude bastard,' Harry snarled in my ear, his comment thank-fully lost in the murmurs of greeting.

Extra chairs were found for us and I drew mine into a corner where I could sit as inconspicuously as possible. Nathan appro-priated a chair at the table and laid out all his material. Jock, meanwhile, was full of conviviality. He shook hands, asked names, quipped and joked. Harry stood irresolutely beside Nathan, thoughtfully watching Jock. After a moment he spoke to Nathan who briefly looked up at him, then at Jock, who was deep in conversation with one of the Mildura men. Nathan's glance was short and uninterested before he returned to his papers. It reminded me of his earlier visits to the Chew It, where, embedded in his book, he had no awareness of me or the people around him. How, I wondered, did he ever hope to persuade anyone to agree with him.

He grew restless. It was clear he wanted to start the meeting. He took up one of his papers, showing no sign of introducing himself nor of speaking words of greeting or thanks. Jock was quick and fully aware of his ineptness.

Before Nathan could launch into his prepared speech, Jock took over. He spoke briefly of his impoverished childhood in Glasgow, his hard life in the ship-building yards and the struggles of unionists. His message was simple: united we stand, divided we fall. This his audience knew or they wouldn't have been secretly at this house in the middle of the night. They grimaced at some of his story, shook their heads, and finally nodded wisely in agreement. Jock, by his understanding, held them in the palm of his hand.

Nathan lost them. He droned on about Marxist economics and the role and importance of the industrial proletariat. At first they listened courteously and then finally with impatience. At last one of them could endure the lecturing no longer.

'Look, mate,' he said, 'you come here to a farming place and talk to us about the industrial proletariat changing the world. Do you see a lot of industrial proletariat around here? We're fruit pickers, mate, and poor farmers. I've read a bit of your Marx and Lenin. Which one of them was it that called the peasants 'ignorant dolts'? Well, mate, he got it wrong and so have you. We want a say in how we run things, not some bloke from the Central Committee ordering us about.'

Nathan was squashed. He had no redress. He wasn't flexible in his thinking and that was his trouble. He sat down and his glance at Jock appealed for rescue. But even as Jock opened his mouth we heard cars rocketing down the road outside and a voice blaring through a megaphone. One of the men leaped to his feet and immediately doused the lights. I had never liked complete darkness. Out of it always emerged those furtive shadows, figures of undefined and therefore terrifying evil. My heart accelerated and if I had known where the door was I would have leaped to it and dashed outside.

I felt around me and called Harry's name but the noise from outside drowned my voice. A scream rose in my throat.

'Ssh, girlie, ssh,' a voice hissed beside me. 'Ssh.'

Terrified I bit my tongue, shut in the cage of my own silence. The noise outside escalated. Now chanting, bawling voices abused and threatened us, clamouring for red raggers to get out of town or they'd be chucked out. A barrage of rocks bombarded the iron roof. Glass splintered in a window and a thunderous deluge of sound went on and on. A hoarse voice sang through the megaphone, 'Run rabbit run.'

I covered my ears and shrank in my chair. This was worse than a police baton charge. In the Port the community didn't hate us.

At last they left. After they had gone no one spoke or moved for some time, then someone put on the light and we all looked around. No one was hurt. Harry rushed to my side and enclosed me in his arms. I was shaking and immediately became the centre of attention. It was as if having a target for their concern deflected their fear and provided an outlet for their anger.

'To do this to a woman,' someone muttered.

'But they didn't know I was here,' I said later to Harry.

'I doubt whether it would have made any difference to those hoons, Judith.'

Back at the camp we made a cup of tea on a primus and discussed the events. Nathan was shocked, Jock furious, Harry tight-lipped, and Bernie continually flicked his throat with a pretended knife.

'It's the train for you tomorrow, Jude, and no argument,' Harry said.

'No. While you'll stay I'll stay. Go home and worry myself sick. Not likely.'

'You're a good girl, Judith,' Jock said, 'but Harry's right. We can't do the job while you're here.'

I rounded on him. 'Bugger your job. Mind your own business. And you, too, Nathan. And don't either of you dare tell me what I can or can't do. I'm not going on the train and that's flat.'

Bernie smiled at me sweetly. 'Lovely Judith,' he crooned. 'I knew a girl in Italia ... just like ...' and he became dreamy.

Diverted, I said, 'Did you, Bernie? What happened?'

He didn't answer but I guessed. He had fled and left her behind. How little I really understood about dear Bernie and his life.

Harry looked miserable.

'You're not going to be some sort of sacrifice, Harry, not for a set of ideas.'

'Ideals, Jude,' he said unhappily, 'not ideas.'

'It's the same thing. Pie in the sky.'

He sighed, defeated, and looking at him I felt awful. I couldn't go on the train and leave him to be injured in some political brawl but in refusing to go I had somehow deprived him of something important to his manhood. It was all too much for me and I did what I usually scorned: I burst into sobs of distress. And it was all muddled up with Harry's and my dream of a honeymoon and the beauty of the river and the burly timeless eucalypts and the birds at dawn and the gentle water on my skin.

I sobbed pathetically as Harry helped me to put on my pyjamas. Then he squeezed onto the stretcher beside me and held me tenderly. 'Don't weep so, darling. We'll both go home tomorrow.' But I knew that I exploited his love and was blackmailing him into a decision he hated and I cried even harder.

He continued to try to soothe me and the warmth of his body against mine was a comfort, but neither of us thought of love-making: I, because I was too distraught, he because his thoughts were troubled. In an emotional trap of my own making, I eventually hiccuped myself to sleep.

The emotional turbulence of the night before left its scars on us all. Next morning Harry was so withdrawn Nathan glanced at him warily and Jock being overly cheerful did not help. Andy served us breakfast breezily. He looked us over with amusement. 'Shock, eh? Didn't expect it?'

As the three men remained silent I replied, 'Yes and no.'

'Forget it,' he said cheerfully. 'Happens all the time. One of our blokes got chucked in the river. He'd been giving out some pamphlets about a union meeting. Not even Communist Party stuff. They roughed him up and pitched him in the Murray. Broke his nose. Luckily we were there to pull him out. Poor bastard, coughing up blood and water. Nearly drowned.'

He slapped a piece of bacon on my plate.

'Another time they grabbed one of the pickers and flung him on a goods train bound for Melbourne. He had a wife and kid here so he jumped off and walked back. Collected his family and high-tailed it out on the next train. Reckon he'd had enough. Right scared he was. Then, of course, commitments weaken a man. He had a wife and kid.'

I flinched and poked the bacon around on my plate. My egg had congealed. Was that what I was to Harry? A commitment that weakened him? I had always believed, perhaps wrongly, that we gave each other strength. I tried to think rationally. Was this sort of violence really any different from the police beatings at the Port or the wars between scabs and unionists? Why did I feel it was? Why did I feel that a menace hung over this town?

But Nathan wasn't sensitive to nuances. Andy's stories frightened me but they seemed no more than water off a duck's back to him. He finished his plate of eggs and bacon, scraped it clean with a piece of toast, drank his mug of tea, and put plate and mug neatly beside him on the ground.

'I'll wash those later,' he said to Andy.

He had been punctilious in doing his share of the jobs. He

polished his glasses with a clean handkerchief and then looked up at us all. The morning sun caught his spectacles and for an instant the light dazzled across the lenses so that it was impossible to see his eyes.

'While we drove around yesterday,' he said, 'I took careful note of where we might hold our street meeting. There's a store on the corner of two of the main streets and it has a large plate-glass window. Jock, you can speak from a platform in front of the window and that should prevent any missiles or attacks. I'm certain the store owner would be most unhappy to lose such an expensive piece of glass. He's doubtless influential in this town.'

Jock raised his eyebrows in disbelief. 'Och, laddie,' he responded, his Scots burr rich and cynical, 'is that your plan and all? And what do you think will happen afterwards? Yer daft. They'll slaughter us and Nathan, you bloody dolt, I canna swim.'

Nathan was not put off. 'It takes time and sacrifice to educate people.'

'They don't want us!' Jock was short. 'Didn't you understand what they said? They don't want a Central Committee ordering them about.'

Nathan persisted doggedly, 'Another meeting might persuade them. Maybe they didn't understand the first time.'

'Did ya hear that, Andy?' Jock was scornful.

Andy smiled quietly and went on drinking his tea. Bernie whittled away at his piece of wood and the sun danced along the blade. As always he whistled '*Avanti popolo*' but when he looked up at Jock his eyes were understanding. I wondered if, of all of us, only Bernie had experienced the complexities and pain of sacrifice. Certainly Nathan hadn't. He burbled on about the necessity of doing the job we had come to do, that the Party expected us to form a branch in Mildura, that's why they had financed our trip.

Now, incensed, Jock snarled, 'Well you can tell the fuckin' Party we're not going to be martyrs. I'm not putting myself out in front at some street meeting so that Harry and Judith here can drag my body out of the river. I wouldn't expect you to be around when there's real trouble. You need guns to fight fascist bastards. Right, Bernie?'

Bernie smiled secretly and his knife flashed as he continued to whittle.

'He who fights and runs away lives to fight another day,' I murmured sententiously.

Nathan looked daggers at me. Offended and defeated he sulked. Finally he said, 'Will you all compromise with another house meeting tonight? There may be a few brave lads there who are willing to carry on when we leave.'

Jock snorted. 'OK. If that's all you have in mind.'

Andy had heard us out. 'I'll look after your wife,' he said quietly to Harry. 'She can stay here with me.'

'No,' I said, 'I'm going.'

But Harry was adamant and belligerent. 'I'm staying here with you.'

That night after dark the three left in Pat's car. We heard them jolting down the track and then the quietness of the bush fell around us. Occasionally a restless bird settling for the night reawakened and cried out. There were gentle rustles. Now I was certain I could hear the river pushing and pulsing towards the sea. The day had begun with an early greyness and although I had bathed, the water, with no sun to penetrate it, had looked and smelt dank and threatening. Its appearance had compounded my mood of dark unhappy thoughts.

Now that Jock had also defied Nathan I felt happier. Harry had his support and the weight of opposition to Nathan didn't rest solely on my shoulders.

After Nathan, Jock and Bernie had left we sat on in the firelight. Andy brought out his guitar and strummed happily. He and Harry talked about music. Harry tried to play Andy's guitar and laughed at his own ineptness on a new instrument. At about ten o'clock we decided to turn in but it was hard to sleep. We both wondered and worried about what was happening at the meeting in town.

It was close to midnight when we heard Pat's car tearing along the track. It slewed to a stop, skidding on the grass between the shacks. Nathan, Jock and Bernie piled out.

'They're coming,' they panted. 'Pursued us out of town. Quick, into the huts.'

Awakened by their shouting, Andy loped out, rubbing his eyes sleepily. He looked back along the track, saw the advancing head-lights, retreated into his shack, and re-appeared with a rifle. 'Get inside,' he ordered sharply. 'I'll deal with this lot.'

We hesitated to leave him alone.

'Do as I say.'

We ran back to our huts. Harry put the bolt across the door and would have closed the shutters but I stopped him. 'I can't. It'd be like a cage. I must see.'

Of course I could see very little through the small space but there was plenty to hear. Half a dozen trucks screamed into our camp, hurtling at breakneck speed in a circle around the fire. Grass and dirt spattered from beneath their wheels and I smelt the scorch of hot rubber tyres as they braked then accelerated. They carried an army of men, all bellowing abuse and threats.

As they charged past the ground shook and the walls of our tin shack trembled. Once again I felt the sick terror of being trapped. Far better to be on the street or on an open wharf if I was going to be murdered.

Finally they scudded to a stop. Their leader appeared, a burly ugly bloke.

'Come out, you rotten commie bastards. We're waiting for you. Or are you going to die like rats in a hole?'

He jumped down from his truck and lit a brand from the fire. It flared.

'Christ,' Harry gasped.

Andy, who none of them had noticed, walked casually into the middle of the ring of vehicles. He pointed his .303 rifle straight at the leader with his burning brand.

'Drop it!' we heard him say. 'Tell your fascist mates to get back into their trucks and piss off. You stay here. If you move an inch or they make a wrong move I'll shoot your balls off. And it'll be self-defence. Make no mistake. We still have a few law courts in this country.'

The gang leader dropped his brand, which sputtered and then went out. He turned as if to join his mates but Andy's cold voice stopped him. 'I told you to wait. And just so you know I mean it ...' He aimed a single shot on the ground in front of him. Grass, twigs and dirt sprang up and there was a sharp smell. Quick as a flash he reloaded.

Trucks revved violently, horns tooted, and six tried all at once to get out of the clearing. At last they sorted themselves out and sped back down the track. Their gang leader roared after them uselessly, 'Don't leave me, you bloody cowards!'

He stood cravenly in front of Andy. There was complete silence, the trucks could no longer be heard, but still Andy waited. 'Just in case,' he said, 'any of those bastards decide to sneak back.'

An hour later he released his prisoner and ordered him to walk back to town.

'It's ten miles,' the fellow whined.

'Yes.' Andy was amused. 'Good exercise for you. And don't come here again. Next time there'll be more than me with guns.'

We joined Andy outside. I gave him a big hug. Our thanks embarrassed him.

'That's it,' Jock said. 'I draw the line at being burned alive.'

Nathan was silent. Jock poked him in the ribs. 'Feel like being a bit of cinder for the Party?'

But Harry took pity on Nathan's discomfort. 'Dry up, Jock.

He's only trying to make things better for working people. Don't jibe at him.'

Jock raised his eyebrows. 'Support comes from unusual quarters.'

Harry flushed.

'And what about my little 'fascist' mate Bernie-Benito? What'll happen to him now?'

Bernie patted his arm and flicked his knife across his throat.

'They'll kill you, Bernie.' Jock was distressed.

'No,' Bernie said, 'not me. Mussolini couldn't even kill me.'

Not convinced, Jock glared at Nathan.

Nathan capitulated, 'We'll go home in the morning. We can't always win, it seems.'

Jock snorted. 'And we'll take Bernie?' Nathan said nothing to this. After all, it was only recently that they'd got Bernie out of Adelaide.

However next morning Bernie was gone. Andy didn't know where and we had to pack up and leave without him.

Our return trip was a quiet one, everyone absorbed in their own thoughts. Harry, who never brooded over perceived injuries, tried a few cheerful comments but neither Nathan nor Jock responded. We were relieved to get out of the car and be home.

'Phew,' Harry said, 'I never expected to see a parting of the ways between Jock and Nathan. I suppose they'll get over it in time.'

We lit the bathroom chip heater and shared a delicious hot bath.

'It's a lot better than the Murray.' Harry sighed with contentment and luxuriously rubbed his soapy hands into my back and shoulders and gently around my breasts.

'Mm,' I said. 'Intimacy is delicious and our own bed heavenly. Never, never again will I sleep on a camp stretcher.' And bending to kiss the tips of his fingers I added, 'It's far too narrow.'

We arrived home at the end of November and Christmas was approaching rapidly. Until our trip to Mildura Colonel Campbell and his New Guard of right wing warriors had meant nothing to me. Now I recognised their menace.

Harry was quite certain that the hoons who had threatened us were part of his army. 'They were too organised, too confident, to have just been a loose rabble. The Party has been warning about them for some time and even the Laborites are concerned – and they're conservative enough.'

I had thought a cartoon about the events would be futile because it wouldn't resonate with readers but now I changed my mind. On the banks of the Murray I had recalled Banjo Paterson's 'Clancy of the Overflow', that romantic nostalgic hymn to the beauties of freedom and the bush. Perhaps I could turn it on its head and use it in a cartoon.

So I drew a drover being kicked into the river by a gang of hood-lums and headlined it, The New Guard. They were shouting, *Sink you red ragger!* Beneath the picture my caption read: *In my wild erratic fancy visions come to me of Clancy gone a-drowning down the Cooper where the western drovers go*. Appreciating the cartoon depended on knowing the poem but I hoped that most Australians would.

The *Sun News Pictorial* rejected it but the *Workers' Weekly* gobbled it up and I felt better for having targeted the New Guard.

Harry and I were to have Christmas dinner with my parents. Harry's mother and Winnie would join us for tea on Christmas night. I invited Miss Marie, but she was making her once-a-year visit home to see her parents and brother and sister.

'The gathering of the clan, Judith,' she joked. 'And all political discussion is banned. Such a pity because it so enlivens a boring family reunion.'

My mother always insisted on attending the Christmas Eve service at the Anglican church. Neither Harry nor I found comfort in religion but my mother hovered on the edge of belief and Christmas, with its cordiality and community feeling, engulfed and soothed her. Briefly she escaped into a benign world where, as the songs of the day told us, love ruled supreme.

My father, whose 'mean old bastard' of a father had cured him early of any belief in religion, never argued with her about the Christmas service. He always put on his best suit and meekly accompanied her.

Harry loved the music and joyfully joined in all the carols: 'Hark the herald angels sing', 'The first Noel', 'We three Kings', and his lovely tenor voice soared above those around us.

'Sing up, darling,' he nudged me, but I was always too shy.

We heard the oft-repeated story of the birth of Christ and the arrival of the shepherds and the wise men and I wondered, as I had often done at past Christmases, what three wealthy, sophisticated, and, presumably, learned kings of the Orient made of a baby in a stable. Were they really impressed or were they bitterly disappointed and regarded the whole affair as a complete fizzer? And to make matters worse, they probably didn't live long enough to see what came of it all. I didn't know why talks of birth inevitably led me to conjectures about time and mortality.

At the close of the service the organist played 'Jesu Joy of Man's Desiring'. The congregation filed out but Harry sat transfixed, his eyes rapt, as the full-throated notes of the organ resonated and rolled around the church. I waited quietly beside him until he was ready to leave.

'Oh, Jude,' he marvelled, 'have you ever heard such miraculous fabulous sound? One day I'll learn the organ and play Bach. The piano merely tinkles beside those great chords. Isn't it awe-inspiring? The sound of the organ beggars description.'

We had a happy Christmas and later, as we kissed and sang 'Auld Lang Syne' to welcome the New Year, we briefly hoped that 1933 would be better.

But it wasn't. Better years were not our lot. Perhaps if we had been happy to close our doors on events outside the Port the year might have seemed more hopeful. As early as January the axe fell. Adolph Hitler became Chancellor of Germany. Immediately he rounded up all opposition to his power. He would 'smash Bolshevism' he trumpeted, and communists, socialists, Jews and Gypsies were incarcerated in concentration camps. It didn't require a lot of imagination for me to envisage Germany in terms of the hoons of our New Guard let loose on a community to terrorise and kill. Joe Pulham's predictions of 'that nasty bloke Hitler' had become frighteningly real.

'Even the conservative forces in Australia are alarmed, Judith,' Harry said, throwing a copy of the Melbourne *Argus* on our kitchen table. 'We've been warning for years that Hitler threatens the peace of the world and that the League of Nations is a paper tiger. Anyone who reads *Mein Kampf* knows his plans for a Greater Germany. It's a choice now between fascism or communism.'

Harry was always tired now. He was constantly absorbed into urgent Communist Party meetings and hardly ever at home. They were working frantically, he said, to formulate their policies.

I had lunch with Miss Marie in Adelaide. She greeted me soberly. 'This is terrible, Judith. I have many friends in France and they are very afraid. They write that the Versailles Agreement is now no more than a bit of useless paper. This monster will trample Europe. The barbarians are at their gates.

'How lucky we are to live in Australia with the beautiful sea for a boundary. So many of my friends have experienced armies marching across their frontiers. It's so easy there if anyone has a mind to do it. And this Hitler person certainly has a mind to. We'll see his marching hordes within a few years.'

She was despondent. 'Mind you, if we hadn't brought Germany to its knees after the last war maybe … Well, it's all too late now.'

She drank her coffee and was silent for a few minutes. At last she sighed. 'You'd better get busy on those sharp cartoons of yours, Judith. Your specialty is biting satire. Thank heavens. I get so sick of puerile jokes, masquerading as cartoons, that feed on stereotypes about women being gold-diggers and the working class being drunken slobs who keep coal in their baths. You'll always be a lone voice, perhaps, but you'll make people think.'

So I went home and drew the cartoon that had been shaping in my mind for several days. I drew a monstrous dog with Hitler's head. Two portly gentlemen struggle to hold him on a straining leash. In front of the dog is a bowl of food and the meal a collection of small human figures labelled Socialist, Communist and Jews. One of the portly gentlemen speaks to the other: *Do you think we'll be able to hold him after he's eaten his breakfast?* For good measure I decorated the clothes of the two gentlemen with some British, French and American symbols. And to be really provocative I added a small kangaroo.

Looking exhausted, Harry came in late from the night's meeting. He slumped into a chair and watched me pen the finishing touches. 'That about sums it up, Jude. The communists are as busy as bees. There's a whole lot of buzzing to and fro, much talk and a lot of opinion. I'm afraid that amongst ourselves we believe our own bombast and our own propaganda. I don't really know whether the workers of the world will unite against this monster. He has power, Jude, a power we can only dream about and such is the miserable plight of the German people that many see him not as a barbarian but as a messiah.'

He picked up my cartoon, studied it and smiled bitterly. 'You've hit the nail on the head as always. He'll gobble up his opposition and the rest of the world will sit around hoping it won't turn out too badly.'

He laid it down. 'You should send this to the *Argus*. Try again to break in on the main press.'

'They won't take it, Harry.'

'I don't know about that. A lot of people are very worried.'

'That's what Miss Marie says but she's talking about her friends in France.'

'Nevertheless, Jude, I'd give it a try if I were you. You deserve a wider audience than the *Workers' Weekly*. After all, there you only preach to the converted.'

So without much hope, for it was a very conservative newspaper, I sent my cartoon to the *Argus*. They responded within the week and surprisingly were enthusiastic but cautious. Could I, they suggested, delete the communists from the food bowl and just have Hitler devouring the socialists, Jews and Gypsies.

My experience of the New Guard in Mildura had toughened my stance against bullying. I was short in my reply. Either they took it as it was or I withdrew it. They capitulated and featured it as a large item on page two above an article warning of Hitler's threats to extend the borders of Germany. They paid me more than the *Workers' Weekly* and *Spearhead* combined paid me for a single cartoon. Apparently it delighted their readers and there was such an overwhelming response to it that they requested more work.

On the same theme I produced a cartoon of Cerberus guarding the door to the Underworld. I depicted each of his three heads as the slavering face of Hitler. He crouches at the door to Hell and the caption reads: *Don't be mistaken. I'm only Cerberus in disguise. All living beings, especially communists, socialists, Jews and Gypsies are welcome here.*

There was no argument about the communists this time and presumably readers of the *Argus* recognised how I had turned the Cerberus myth on its head. I was commissioned to produce a weekly cartoon on the same theme. Readers were buying the paper for my cartoons. It was hard work coming up with a fresh idea each week and often I lay awake at night pummelling my poor head but usually I managed something. And, at Harry's further urging, I sent one of my Hitler cartoons to the *Daily Herald* in London.

The Communist Party ran large public meetings at the Port and we attended even larger gatherings in Adelaide. Speakers came from Melbourne and as far away as Sydney. They accused the Labor Party of shilly-shallying: it had no answers to fascism, Nazism, poverty or unemployment. It was just a lackey of capitalism. Communism had the answer. It alone stood strongly united. It alone could meet the challenge of fascism and Nazism.

Party membership grew by leaps and bounds and Harry was even busier. He became organiser of our local branch. The international threat of a resurgent Germany led by a ruthless fascist united members of the Communist Party and buried all previous personal differences.

They still argued, Harry told me, about how to persuade people, how to present their policies, but they were as one in agreeing what the policies should be. Nathan, with his wisdom and impressive knowledge of communist theory, was an inspiration. Jock's practical experiences amongst the workers of Glasgow were invaluable. Everyone, Harry said, was now steadfast.

We were all caught up in the emotional turmoil. Stories emerged of Jewish people fleeing Germany with terrible tales of persecution. If we did nothing, a second world war would be the inevitable outcome of our failure.

The world was now divided into two camps, Harry said, fascism versus communism, and we must all choose which side we were to fight on. Spain, he said, had led the way. There the people had thrown down the gauntlet to their capitalist oppressors and formed the second Republic – in contrast to Austria where Englebert Dolfuss, the dictator, had crushed the workers. The Spanish Republic stood firm as an inspired front of the left.

Harry was on fire with a messianic belief and hope. But I still read copies of *Spearhead* and knew that the anarchists in Spain were organising revolts against the mine owners and calling for a general strike on behalf of striking railway workers. Their opposition to the Republic resulted in terrible reprisals: thousands of unionists were arrested and those peasants with the support of the anarchists who tried to seize land from the land-holders and establish an egalitarian community were shot. Who were the top dogs in the Republic, I wondered. Were they like Nathan at the meeting in Mildura, set on imposing from the top something the people didn't want? Who was being sacrificed in the name of unity, and what principles?

But Harry continued to view the Republic with stars in his eyes. Only once I dared comment that maybe it wasn't all it was cooked up to be. He looked bemused. 'What are you talking about, Jude?'

'*Spearhead,*' I said.

He scoffed. 'What would they know? A tin-pot little paper in Australia hundreds of miles from Europe? Pure propaganda.'

'No, Harry,' I said quietly. 'I don't think so.'

He kissed me cheerfully before dashing off. 'Well, that's OK, so long as you don't draw any cartoons about anarchists being all right. We can do without them splitting the ranks.' I sighed and kissed him back.

He left the house and I enjoyed the peace to think my own thoughts. These days it was always full of his exuberant and loud excitement. For like all the other comrades he fed his anger on daily stories of disaster as evidence that the communists must triumph.

So it was an appalling shock to him when later that year the Spanish Republic collapsed and in the following election a right-wing government took control. He was disbelieving. 'It can't be so, Jude. How could it happen? It's those bastards of anarchists. They've betrayed us. They've messed it all up.'

'Is that what the comrades say?' I asked.

For the first time ever he snarled at me. 'Don't call them

comrades in that mocking way. They're my friends and they're good communists working bloody hard. Sometimes I could do without your smug I'm-the-great-cartoonist style.'

Horrified, I stared at him. This was a nasty Harry I had never known. The conflicts in Europe between people we had never met over issues remote from us were not our personal business. Harry's fanatical beliefs were unreal. To thrust those fantasies in my face with such bitterness was madness.

I was hurt. Of course, I was hurt. But more than hurt I was shocked and afraid. Something dark had opened up between us. Had he for years concealed some resentment of my work? Did my success threaten him? Did he need to believe utterly in a cause? Did he need to dream that it would succeed and he bask in its glory? Had he transferred his disappointment at never being a great musician to a hope of finding ultimate satisfaction in the Communist Party? Had playing Bach on the great organ seemed an impossible achievement, while a significant role in the Communist Party was an easier, more attainable one?

These thoughts jostled together in my mind as I silently looked at him. Eventually he flushed and hung his head.

'Do you really feel that way about me and my work, Harry?'

'No,' he mumbled, 'of course not.'

'Look at me, Harry.'

But he refused.

'I'm sorry,' I said humbly. 'I didn't know you felt like that. I meant nothing by calling them comrades. We've often done so before between ourselves.'

'Yes,' he mumbled again. 'I know. I'm sorry, too. It was all such a shock, the collapse of the Republic. We had dreams and expectations. It's such a grievous disappointment.'

I knew better than to rub salt into the wound by pointing out that what happened in Spain really had nothing to do with us, for clearly it meant something personal to Harry.

But when he had gone my earlier instinct for reconciliation turned to resentment. I flung the cartoon I had been working on into the press, tossed my pen on the table, grabbed my coat and slammed out of the house. I'd go to the hulk and tell my mother and father and Dad could spit over the side of the boat when I told him how fed up I was with communist claptrap. And what's more, in future, Harry could take his fair share of bringing money into our home. He could start thinking of me slaving over each bloody cartoon while he brought in a pittance for being an organiser for the Communist Party.

He had even given up playing his piano at the dance hall and we had to do without the small amount he had earned from that. Well, he could get that job back again.

By the time I reached the hulk I was in such a stinking mood that I spilled out all my resentment. My mother clucked sympathetically but told me not to take it to heart – Harry was obviously over-tired and not himself. I snorted at this.

Harry was a warm-hearted boy, she said. (To them Harry was always a boy.) But he became easily involved. His sweetness made him naturally impressionable. She was sure that when he returned home he would be full of repentance for being so rude to me.

Only partially mollified, I continued to grump.

'Let him alone, Judith,' my father advised. 'He's suffering from hot-house fever. A too-concentrated dose of the Communist Party and their angst. Of course, his conscience is over-loaded, too. Too much belief that you are right and that the responsibilities of the world rest on your shoulders alone gives you massive indigestion, confusion and bad temper.

'He'll come around. Even Harry will see that eventually too much conscience makes you self-opinionated. And that's the comrades all over. A surfeit of conscience is their specialty. No one else has one, unless they believe as the comrades do. He's a good boy and not nearly as stupid as he appears to be at the minute. Give him a little time to come around.

'And now, how about using that spare fishing rod of mine and we'll see if we can catch your supper?'

I went home with a good-sized flathead wrapped in a wet cloth and a determination to ignore Harry's words.

As my mother had predicted, he came home full of misery and repentance and with a large bunch of flowers. I kissed him warmly and was pleased to see his mood lighten. That night we didn't say one word to each other about the problems of the world. There were happier things we could do.

But, despite the sweetness of our reconciliation, the bitterness in Harry's words rankled. I dwelled on them and wrestled with how much I was to blame. I felt guilty for feeling resentful about how little money Harry earned. My thoughts should never have turned in that direction. They were mean thoughts.

I recalled Winnie warning me in her practical manner that Harry was 'not much of a catch' and I'd better get used to the idea of being the family provider. I had dismissed her comment angrily. 'I'm not marrying Harry to provide for me. I can do that myself.'

And she had annoyed me with her look of pity. Had I really so changed that I could now complain about him in just that way to my parents? I felt ashamed. And yet, as I tried to honestly confront my faults, I didn't think it was money that separated us. Harry could simply not understand why I wouldn't join the Communist Party and support it as whole-heartedly as he did.

'I can't fathom you, Jude,' he said. 'You produce such biting political cartoons and publish them quite happily in the *Workers' Weekly*. Our paper. But you won't join us – although everyone in the Party wants you.'

I squirmed at the 'our' and 'us' but replied equitably, 'I don't think I could belong to anything that imprisons my ideas, Harry. It would be like putting fetters on myself.'

He shook his head in disbelief. 'We don't do that, Jude. You are very contradictory. One minute you seem to believe one thing, the next you have other ideas.'

'No,' I said, 'I'm not contradictory at all.' And at his incomprehension I was tart. 'I can't fathom why you must have all your ideas presented to you ready made.'

Suddenly he grinned. 'Tit for tat. But I do not. I agree with the opinions I agree with and disagree with the ones I disagree with. But at the minute, with all this business in Germany, what the communists are saying makes sense and I see no point in arguing. If you won't join us, maybe we could enlist your help?'

His face was solemn but his eyes laughed.

I responded cautiously, 'OK, but it depends.'

He pretended to give the matter much thought and I didn't know whether or not it was a joke.

'What we need, Jude, is a dirty-big cartoon glorifying Comrade Stalin. Perhaps you could do a very big man with a large star on his chest confronting Hitler, who has shrivelled to a tiny creature.'

I looked at him uncertainly. Did he really mean it? Previously we had argued about Comrade Stalin. 'He's a dictator,' I had said. 'He has too much power for one man.'

And Harry had returned, 'A great communist leader.'

But I hadn't been certain whether there was a sardonic inflection in his tone. Was he in earnest now or merely teasing me?

At my confusion he shouted with laughter and hugged me. 'Oh, your face, darling. You'd think I'd offered you a poisoned chalice.'

'Oh, you, Harry,' I said. 'For a minute I wondered if you had.'

He stopped laughing, suddenly. 'Did you really?' And I knew that once again I had overstepped the mark.

'I love you, Jude,' he said, 'and would never, never, never do anything to harm you.'

Of course I hadn't meant to hurt him. It had only been a silly joke. Why did our political sparring always take a personal tone?

It seemed that what we really argued about was ourselves. The Communist Party might give Harry his sense of worth and importance, but it was the bane of my life.

Miss Marie visited and teased him without mercy about the Communist Party. She even dared to call it the Comical Party. She advised him, quite outrageously, to give up the communists and join the anarchists, who were, on the whole, a happier bunch, more relaxed, friendlier, and a damn sight more egalitarian. They did not regard themselves as the saviours of the world but were content to be the labourers in the fields, humble still in their role as human beings.

And he took it all from her without ire and joked at her in return. And during her visits he played his favourite tunes on the piano and they sang together cheerfully and I felt a sad outsider. Why couldn't I bring him such joy? Why couldn't I find again the old Harry, the merry young man I had married?

Miss Marie felt my unhappiness and when we were alone she became serious. 'It's harder, Judith, when two people are very close. They fear anything that might separate them and fear is like a big snake around their necks, squeezing the joy out of them.'

'So,' I said testily, 'we are afraid because we are separating from each other? But it's not the separation we need to be afraid of but the fear of it. That doesn't make any sense, Marie.'

She sighed. 'I suppose not, *ma pauvre*.'

'We can't even talk to each other,' I burst out. 'Any serious conversation always ends in accusations. I watch every word, guard my every expression in case I hurt him and I think he does the same to me. So we only speak of the superficial and even that's not always safe. It's driving me crazy. Perhaps I ought to join the Communist Party. Would it help? Would he be happy? I've reached the point of not caring one way or the other. I can accept Communist Party philosophy and put up with all the rhetoric that goes with it. After all, I like quite a few of the members – Jock, Pat, Frank – and I can tolerate Nathan. They'd welcome me with open arms.'

'Of course,' she said. 'Judith Larsen, cartoonist par excellence, even of international fame now the London *Daily Herald* features your work.'

'Well?' I asked. I was impatient. My international reputation couldn't have seemed more remote to me. My immediate concern was Harry. 'Well, should I join? What do you think?'

She studied her nails, which were always finely filed and polished to a pearly sheen. 'I think, Judith,' she looked up at me searchingly, 'I think you have to be honest and Harry can't expect you to be otherwise. He, too, has to be honest, and realise that insidiously he is blackmailing you and causing you much anguish. He is a very naughty boy to put the Communist Party before you. Ah, the stupidity of converts whose beliefs are frequently as narrow as a coffin. Which, of course, eventually buries them.'

Her metaphor, although apt, disturbed me. That Harry should be completely subjugated by a set of ideas frightened me. How could one fight ideas?

But Miss Marie must have spoken with Harry, although how she managed not to upset him was a mystery to me. The tension eased between us, helped, I suppose, by my quiet resolution neither to join the Party nor to be defensive nor apologetic about it. For a time we tacitly accepted our differences and sometimes the old Harry would sing softly to me *What'll I do when skies are blue and you're not here, what'll I do?* And I was so grateful to reclaim something of his former self that I didn't tell him it made me sad.

It was strange but as the international situation worsened we grew closer. I came to accept his total commitment to the Communist Party as the only way he could see to combat Hitler's terrible fascism and he came to accept that my way of protesting was to draw cartoons that alerted people. We were both, he told me one night, happily heading in the same direction and as I curled up comfortably against him in our warm bed he held me fiercely, almost as if he feared to let me go.

Workers' Weekly and *Imprecor* regularly reported the news from Spain. The right-wing government now in power would soon be hand in glove with Hitler. Spanish workers lived in terror. The band of socialist youth were preparing for bloody revolution. Harry avidly followed the news. Because he had been such a dedicated leader in the Communist Youth League he had a fellow feeling, he told me, for our young Spanish brothers, as he called them.

He now fervently argued with Miss Marie that the anarchists were splitting the left with their different aims. With some asperity she pointed out that it was the Spanish anarchists, not the communists, who had tried to set up a truly libertarian society. And it was the anarchists who had been slaughtered by the military at the hands of the great Republican Government while it had lasted, and the communists had been a part of it. I listened to both their arguments and was troubled because in my work I had to try to make a judgement, not in political but in human terms. I searched the daily papers for any news of Europe but it was mostly the *Workers' Weekly*, *Spearhead*, *Daily Herald* and *Imprecor* that reported events.

So for want of certainty I stopped doing cartoons about Europe and concentrated on the events in Australia. Harry was disgusted. 'You've lost your fire, Jude,' he reproached me. 'How can you do such pussy cartoons when such huge events need comment?'

In one regard he was correct. I couldn't ignore the threat of fascism. Hitler's regime was becoming a monstrosity. But after several cartoons about him I had no fresh ideas.

'I don't know what is happening in Spain, Harry. It's such a mixed-up picture.'

'It's not, Jude. You only have to read the *Weekly*. That gives you all you need to know.'

I had wrestled with the problem of whether I should take my opinions from the *Weekly* and decided not to. 'No,' I said wearily, 'it doesn't. And in any case no one here wants a cartoon about Spain. It's miles away and is not alarming like what's happening in Germany. Everyone has heard of Hitler.'

'Not alarming? Spain is the melting pot of the future. If fascism takes root in Spain we'll all be ruined.'

So once again, we started to argue. Now my cartoons really did lack fire. I worked doggedly but without inspiration. What had been an exciting challenge now became drudgery. I felt listless, bone weary, from what seemed to be years of political fighting, drained by never winning.

We were both unhappy. Harry was so miserable that my heart went out to him. It was a special sort of pain, knowing how he felt but being helpless to solve whatever was troubling him. I didn't even know what it was. And if I had known I wondered whether I would have the energy to deal with it.

Did he want to leave me? Probably. I felt ill at such a thought. But when he caught me studying him in bafflement, he assured me that he loved me. I had to cling to the hope that something else bothered him and made him so distant.

At night I cuddled up to him but he was restless and held me absently. When I sang his favourite song 'What'll I do when you're far away' he responded quite violently. 'Don't, Jude. I'm tired. I've got a lot on my mind.'

Hurt I pulled away and turned my back. I knew he didn't sleep. I heard him tossing and turning for much of the night. But I was damned if I'd ask him what the matter was. If he told me it was a Party matter I mightn't be able to stop myself screaming at him.

The coolness between us seemed to go on and on. Harry avoided looking at me and I tried falsely to be as cheerful as possible.

Finally, one evening after dinner, one of the rare evenings he was home, he remained seated at the table. 'Jude,' he said, 'I need to talk to you.'

'Yes?' I was uninviting.

'Please sit down.'

I went on scraping the dishes and assembling them on the sink.

'For God's sake, Jude, sit down. I need to talk to you.'

I turned to face him. 'Is that so, Harry? A bit late isn't it?'

He flushed and I saw him grit his teeth. 'Please,' he said quietly, and there was something so urgent in his tone that I left the sink and sat down.

'Well?'

He took a deep breath. 'I want to go to Spain.'

All the air in my body left me in a great gasp and I seemed to float dizzily. It was both a shock and a huge relief, a bit like finding out that he'd only wanted to go to Mildura and not Russia. He only wanted to go to Spain, I thought hysterically. He didn't want to leave me. Well, for a short time, I supposed, but not forever.

Overcome with relief, I jumped up, ran around the table and hugged him. 'Oh, Harry, thank you.' I sat down again and burst into tears.

Bemused by my reaction, he stared at me. He had returned my hug but was now silent. 'It'll only be for a few weeks, Jude. Just to talk to the communist blokes there. To get some first-hand knowledge, a grasp of it all, to pass on to the Party members here.'

'Yes,' I said, gulping back my tears, 'yes, of course.'

'You don't mind?'

'Not so much,' I replied.

'Not so much?'

'Not as much as ...'

'Jude, you make no sense.'

'No,' I said, 'but Spain's OK.'

'It's OK for me to go to Spain? You don't mind?'

I beamed at him. 'No. It'll be a wonderful adventure. Much better than Mildura. I've never been overseas. When do we leave?' Then I stopped. If I hadn't been so euphoric with relief I might have thought more clearly about practical matters. 'How do we pay for it, Harry? It'll be very costly.'

I raced into the bedroom and snatched our bank book out of the bedroom drawer. We had some savings, so that eventually we could buy a home. Oh, well, I dismissed that future. We could begin again. I could work harder. My work was now accepted.

'We've got enough, Harry. Plenty.'

I put the bank book in front of him and eagerly kissed the top of his head. He took it up but didn't look at it. The old misery was back in his face.

'Jude,' he said quietly, 'I'm going with Nathan.'

'Yes. Well, we did in Mildura. I more or less expected that.'

'No, Jude, just Nathan. The Spanish Communist Party has invited us and the Party is paying.'

'Well, that'll be a help. We only need to find my fares. I'll come home with lots of ideas for cartoons. I need the stimulation. I've been feeling dull lately. Maybe I'll even be able to do some that satisfy Nathan and the Communist Party.'

I laughed, but he didn't join me. Why was I so dense, so uncomprehending? I thought afterwards.

'Jude,' he pleaded, 'please understand. This is a Party matter. You can't come with us. You're not a paid-up member of the Communist Party. The Spanish communists haven't invited you.'

If he'd chucked a bucket of ice water over me I couldn't have felt colder. All the joy drained out of me and I sat looking at him in frozen silence. Finally I stammered, 'You're going without me?'

'Yes.' He looked mulish.

'With Nathan?'

'Yes. I told you.' He was defensive.

'For the Party?'

'Yes.'

'Without me?'

'For God's sake, Jude, don't look like that. You said Spain would be OK.'

'Yes,' I said, and I was afraid to say anything more. I mightn't be able to stop.

I got up, filled the sink with water, and began the washing up.

He grabbed a tea towel to help me. Neither of us spoke. When he had put the dishes away he put on his hat and coat, said he had a meeting and might be late home, and left.

I sank onto the kitchen chair in the empty kitchen and hated Nathan, the Communist Party and Harry.

Part 4

A Separation

I STOPPED WORKING. There didn't seem to be much point in it. This is the end, I thought. Why should I struggle to support us? I may as well use up our savings, and I started to withdraw, bit by bit, from our account for household expenses. It was restful, not having to drive myself to a routine every day. Requests from newspapers for my work I threw in the dustbin.

Harry found them. He was horrified. 'Jude, what is this?'

I shrugged. 'None of your business.'

'None of my business? Aren't we married?'

'Are we?' I was scornful.

'Jude,' he appealed, 'why are you doing this?'

I shrugged again.

'But it's your career.'

I was silent.

'It's Spain, isn't it? You don't want me to go? It's not forever. Just a few weeks and then we'll be back together again. I'll be quite safe.'

'Quite safe?' I mocked. 'Spain is in a state of insurrection. This much I know. Haven't you been reading the *Workers' Weekly*?'

He ignored my jibe and repeated, 'I'll be quite safe. Nathan has contact with Party members there. They're going to supply an interpreter. It's all arranged. I'll be safe as houses.'

I was cynical. 'Safe with Nathan? You're a fool, Harry. Nathan will be as useless as always. They'll probably murder you in Spain. Why is it, do you think, that Nathan has never been beaten up in any of our demonstrations? And no one has ever wondered about this. Somehow no one expects that Nathan will ever get hurt. It wouldn't do for the big Party intellectual to show a few bruises. But the rest of us, the poor foot soldiers, we can get injured – you can nearly get *killed* in Victoria Square – but Nathan, he was OK. He didn't even lose his glasses.'

And I recalled how even in my dazed state of terror I had seen the light reflect off his perfect spectacles still on his nose and quite unharmed. At the time I had been grateful to see him. I had never dreamed then that he would become the Mephistopheles in my life.

'You go to Spain with Nathan. By all means go. But if there's any trouble you'll be on your own. Look at Mildura. He would have hung Jock out to dry with his damned street meeting. But Jock's tougher than you. Jock can tell the Party to get fucked. But not you.'

So I berated him. He didn't respond and when he had left I tormented myself with both loving and hating him. Sometimes his dedication appeared strength. At other times I believed that it was the weakness of an impressionable man tossed this way and that by anyone stronger. And beneath it all were the unworthy thoughts that I was ashamed of: that it was my work that paid for our life together, our meals, our rent, our gas and electricity bills. But now I was the one to be left at home to keep working while Harry had the overseas adventure – with Nathan, of all people.

Harry was attacked from all sides. If my thoughts about him hadn't been so painful I would have pitied him. My mother reproached him for deserting me. 'I'm disappointed in you, Harry. I wouldn't have expected it of you.'

My father scowled, 'Much better to see the world before you marry, not after.'

'I'm not going to Spain to see the world, sir.' Harry was defensive.

'Nobler purpose, eh?' my father scoffed. 'And don't call me sir. Communist, aren't you? All men equal and that sort of fantasy? Niels's my name, as you very well know, Harry. You're being irresponsible.'

Miss Marie refused to succumb to his cajoling to sing with him while he played the piano. 'No, Harry,' she said, 'I'm not in the mood. I don't care for what you are doing. You won't find your ideals amongst the Spanish communists. Better if you continue to search for them here.'

'I'm not searching for ideals,' he denied.

She raised her eyebrows in disbelief.

Accustomed to her usual merry, light-hearted responses to him, he looked confused.

'I didn't expect ...' he stumbled.

'Expect what?' She was cold.

'That you'd take it all so seriously.'

She laughed shortly. 'Then you don't know me well, Harry.'

I looked at her sharply. There was an unusual bitterness in her voice but she only laughed awkwardly, as if caught out expressing some intimate knowledge.

To Harry's dismay she turned her back on him.

Winnie had heard and rushed around to see us. She screeched at him, 'Going to Spain with that horrible man with the huge glasses? The one that looks like a dumb owl? Just as well you're not taking Judith.'

At her apt description of Nathan I choked with laughter and Harry looked daggers at me. But Winnie hadn't finished. 'And who's going to look after Auntie May, your mother, while you're away?'

'She manages quite well on her own and I won't be gone long. Everyone seems to think that I plan to leave for a lifetime.'

'She only manages,' Winnie shouted at him, 'because I call in all the time and do her shopping and Judith helps. What do you do?'

Guilt, I thought, doubtless fuelled Harry's anger and Winnie's reproaches were the last straw. He turned on her. 'Well, you can keep on doing it, can't you? You lead a pretty frippery useless life. Good for you to do something useful.'

Winnie spat at him, 'What a rotten rat you are. Swanning off to Europe and leaving Judith destitute. You don't care for Judith, your mother or me. Just your stupid old Communist Party.'

Enraged, she threw her cup of tea at him, cup, saucer and liquid. The tea spilled down his shirt front, an ugly, brown dribbling stain. The cup and saucer smashed on the floor scattering bits of broken crockery.

He was so furious that I thought for a moment he might strike her. But he stormed out of the room. I heard him crashing open drawers as he looked for a clean shirt and then he was gone, slamming the front door behind him.

Winnie giggled. 'Sorry, Judith. I'll replace your cup and saucer. Was it a valuable one?'

I picked up the pieces. 'No, just for the kitchen. But really, Winnie, you went a bit too far.'

'Not at all. He deserved it.'

She took the mop from me and made a sketchy job of cleaning up the mess. 'Harry always had a quick temper.'

'I've never seen it.'

'Really?' She opened her eyes wide. 'Never?'

'No, never.'

'My,' she grinned, 'you must have him tamed.'

'That, or I don't torment him, as you do.'

She chuckled irritatingly. 'Don't know about that, Jude. I'd think that at the minute anything I dished out would be mild in comparison with what he's getting from you: the terrible silent reproach and withdrawal. He wouldn't know how to cope with that. It's too subterranean. With Harry, everything's on the surface. I don't mean he's shallow. It's just that … Well … Hard to explain. Any more tea in the pot?'

She helped herself to a clean cup.

'And he really is leaving you for Spain?'

'Don't put it that way, Winnie. He's not leaving me. Just going away for a short time.'

'Well,' she said, in disgust, 'I hope for your sake he comes back.'

Amused, despite myself, I replied, 'For my sake and his.' As she left she gave me a smacking kiss.

It was odd, but Winnie had done what I secretly longed to do – throw something at Harry and feel the release of some violent physical action; something simpler than our obscure changes of mood and carefully guarded words; something clear and in the open. I couldn't have thrown anything at Harry but Winnie had done it for me. She felt no guilt and I felt none on her behalf and as I went around the house doing a few chores I found myself singing to the tune of 'If you knew Susie' the words *If you knew Winnie like I know Winnie, oh,oh,oh, what a girl.*

Maybe Winnie's action also cleared the air for Harry. He could be angry with her in a way he couldn't with me. I said I was sorry that Winnie had been like that and ruined his shirt. He replied, 'No matter. She'd always had a quick temper. She'll get over it.'

So we reached a sort of truce and managed again to talk to each other, even laugh occasionally, and if I pretended not to be sad while we made love I don't think he noticed or if he noticed he didn't say.

Nathan who had often come to meetings at our house now never came and that was a relief. My tolerance could only stretch so far. I had started working again and Harry was careful not to criticise my cartoons although I knew that they had lost their political bite. I abstained from critical comments about the Communist Party. Neither of us discussed Spain and what was happening there, although when I had the house to myself I read the *Workers' Weekly*, S*pearhead* and *Imprecor* gleaning what I could. None of the news from Spain cheered me and when Harry was not around I sometimes succumbed to despair and fear for his safety. At those times, if I were working, I would lay down my pen and just sit staring at nothing in particular, unable to concentrate or think.

Harry and Nathan sailed on the new P&O liner *Oronsay*,

which docked at Outer Harbor. We all went to see them off –
my parents, Winnie, Miss Marie, Jock, Frank, Pat and Nathan's
sisters. I kissed him goodbye, struggled not to cry and failed. He
held me fiercely. 'I'll write, Jude. I'll be back soon. Please don't
worry.'

What stupid advice, I thought.

Winnie wept. 'Oh you, Harry … You always do these things.
I don't know why.' And these things must have filled her memory
to the brim.

He hugged her. 'Take care of Jude for me, Winnie.'

He kissed my mother, who was also tearful, and shook my
father's cool hand. 'Take care, boy,' he growled.

We threw streamers from the dock to the ship but as the
tug began to tow her from the wharf the streamers broke and
strands of abandoned coloured paper fluttered into the sea. The
band played 'Waltzing Matilda', the ship turned and we could no
longer see Harry. We watched for a long while, and then, desolate, turned to leave.

My mother spoke kindly to Nathan's sisters who had stood
apart from us. 'They are distressed,' she said, 'poor things. An
only brother. But they wouldn't come back with us.'

My mother and father took me home that night and I lay on my
narrow bunk even more lonely than I might have been at home,
where at least Harry's presence was all about me. I thought of the
night before he left. He had held me passionately.

'Don't pull away, Jude, please. I know you are hating me and I
can't bear it.'

Overcome with pity at the misery I was causing him, and his
anguish, I returned his kisses with equal fervour and loved him.
And if he detected how much our love making now saddened me,
he gave no sign of it.

Afterwards, as we lay in the dark, with his hand resting across
my breast, he said, 'I know you think that I believe utterly in the

Communist Party, but it's not so, Jude. Somehow I couldn't tell you before. It sounded like giving in.'

'To me?'

'No, not you. To all the vitriolic attacks on us that seem to come from every quarter. If I disagree it can't appear to be because I have succumbed to all this external hatred of us. I'm hoping Spain will clear my head. That I can see whether international communism has any hope. Whether people who have achieved power and lost it are good people. Whether we are fantasising about the whole thing and so much more.'

He laughed uncertainly. 'Even whether communism will pay me to dance. I don't know what I expect to find but perhaps ...' He stopped. 'But that's enough for tonight. I just wanted you to know.'

'Yes,' I said. 'Thank you, Harry. It helps.'

The first few days were the worst. Stupidly, I rushed to the mailbox every morning but, of course, there were no letters. I shouldn't have expected any. Peter, in the Post Office, had told me that even if Harry wrote from Perth I couldn't expect anything for up to a fortnight and if he wrote from foreign ports then the time the mail took was in the lap of the gods, or the lap of foreign postal services, and that was more unpredictable and unreliable than the gods.

I didn't seem able to curb my agitation and took to going for long walks to exhaust myself so that I would sleep at night. Even then I woke frequently and reached out for Harry and finding him not there lay miserably alone until light crept through the curtains. Then for some reason I felt peaceful again and returned to sleep.

Mind you, I was not alone. In fact, I scarcely had a daytime moment to myself to think or to mourn. Most days Winnie called in, telling me bluntly that it was to cheer me up. Her assumption, that I must always be down in the dumps, and her harping on how thoughtless Harry was to so desert me, eventually became more annoying than consoling.

'Shut up, Winnie,' I said in exasperation. 'For heaven's sake give it a rest. He's only gone for a few weeks. That's all there is to it. He'll be back.'

But then her eyes filled with tears and she hugged me. 'I know how you must feel, Jude. You're just being as brave as you always are. I wish I could be as understanding. I think he's mean and I'm scared he'll die there and we'll never see him again.' And she sobbed so hard that I ended up comforting her.

'He's my favourite cousin,' she hiccuped.

'Have you any others?' I was diverted.

'No, only Harry.'

'Then how can he be your favourite?'

'And why not?'

'You have no others to compare him with.'

'This is a stupid conversation, Jude.' She was grumpy. 'You know what I mean.'

And for the first time in several weeks I laughed. 'Oh. Winnie,' I chuckled, 'you're such a card.'

'And you're a card, too, Jude. Harry always says that about you.'

'Yes, I know. How sweet he is, Winnie.'

She blew her nose but continued to sniffle. 'Are you afraid for him?'

'No, not really.'

'But there's a lot of terrible things happening in Spain – strikes and things.'

'There are plenty of strikes and things here, Winnie, but no one's got killed. I suppose Spain is the same. Now, if Harry were in Manchuria or China I'd be really worried. Japan has taken over Manchuria and a part of China. There's war there.'

'No one's interested in what Japan does. They're Asians and we're British.' Winnie was dismissive.

'A lot of people are interested, Winnie. If Japan and Hitler ever get together the world'll be in a nasty pickle, as my old friend Joe Pulham might have said.'

Up until that moment I hadn't thought of a cartoon to comment on Japan's military expansion, although tales of their appalling cruelty had started to creep into the news. Now I thought I might be adventurous and a few ideas began to run through my head. Although, rather than ideas, they were visual images that I played with: the Japanese Emperor sitting astride Cerberus, or the Emperor's face replacing one of Cerberus's, or Hitler and the Emperor shaking hands over the dead body of China. They were all possibilities.

Jock, Frank and Pat also called in regularly, asking if there were jobs to be done about the house: electric bulbs replaced, anything broken in need of repair, gardening – although our pocket-hand-kerchief backyard required little weeding and I could easily do that. They were so eager that I found myself searching for jobs I might give them to do. If I ate with my parents on the hulk my mother always insisted I stay the night and would not take no for an answer.

All this attention was a comfort but at the same time I felt like a child blocked from any independent move for fear harm might come to me. I became a little dependent on all this cosseting. I was content to indulge myself into believing that it was my due, since Harry had abandoned me.

Miss Marie took me to task. 'This is no good, Judith. You must face the fact that Harry won't be back for several months, not weeks. Where is your strong character? You have work you could do. You should get on with it.'

And so I shook myself and got down to some drawing. First I considered my cartoons about Manchuria, the Japanese Emperor Hirohito and Hitler, and eventually found one that satisfied me. This time the *Sun News Pictorial* accepted it. They had been running apocryphal articles on Japan's imperialist ambitions and asked me for a series of cartoons on that theme.

Harry's letters, when they began to arrive, were sketchy but I read and reread them avidly. The trip across the Australian Bight had been rough. The ship rolled in the heavy swell. He had been amused by the English sailor's comment that it wasn't really rough at all, just a very *uvvy swoll*. Nathan had been seasick and spent most days lying down in his cabin. (I was delighted to read that Nathan was having a miserable time.)

It had been a relief to dock at Fremantle, Harry's letter continued, a small white, clean port. He had taken a bus into Perth. The road was lined with coral trees. They weren't in flower, which he thought was a pity because in spring they would be a glorious show. The Swan River was attractive with lots of little yachts bobbing around. Nathan had felt better but didn't want to tour. There weren't any comrades in Perth he needed to see.

The Indian Ocean was warmer than the Bight and it had been good to put the grey skies and rain behind them. There were plenty of jolly things to do on the ship and sometimes he joined in the deck games. People sat in deck chairs in the sun or strolled around the deck to take exercise. The meals were quite good.

Nathan had gained his sea legs and was more cheerful. (That was a pity, I thought. I had enjoyed imagining him being laid low.)

Colombo had been a shock. The first thing that struck him was the heat and humidity. The port was dirty and there were hundreds of skinny little men loading cargo onto ships with strange Asiatic names. 'We have foreign ships coming into Port Adelaide, Jude, but nothing like the size and number of these. They tower over the wharf and their hulls are so rusted that I wonder how they make it across the ocean, particularly in a very *uvvy swoll*.

'I saw a funny sight. A couple of English people all dressed in white. He even had a white suit and she a sort of floating dress and a big frilly umbrella. They were boarding one of the ships and behind them trailed at least twenty porters all carrying a load of their luggage on their heads. Imagine having enough of this world's goods to need twenty porters to carry it. I wondered if they had left anything at home.'

'Bombay,' he wrote, 'had the same atmosphere: terribly hot and humid. Tropical seas have a pearly quality as if the heat has sucked all colour out of the water and left only a thin silver skin. And the smell in Bombay was strange. It reached us even on the ship. I think, maybe, it was the smell of spices. And the porters who rushed on board to pester us for work had a close smoky odour, rather like you get if you sit around a bonfire, but subtly different. They are a poor ragged lot. Desperately and sadly insistent. Of course, we weren't getting off, so they left us to pester other passengers.

'We haven't had any extra money to take tours, so usually I just wander around the port. Behind the Bombay port there are rows of tumble-down shacks put together with bits of junk. People live in them. And there are beggars – poor creatures with twisted or missing limbs or filthy bandages around their hands or white sightless eyes. We've often talked of poverty, Jude, but I've never seen anything like this.

'The Suez Canal is amazing. It's just a narrow stretch of water where two ships can pass each other but it's lower than the land on either side, so we could see strings of camels and their riders plodding above us along the sand dunes. Port Said was even dirtier than Bombay and Colombo. Nathan refused to go ashore. He said the filth horrified him and he was afraid of contracting some dreadful disease. I wondered, Jude, whether or not he saw these people as part of the international working class that somehow or other he hoped to unite under communism. I asked him but he just shrugged impatiently. "Of course not, Harry," he said. "They are far too ignorant to comprehend." Doesn't their poverty move you? I asked him. And I found his response quite strange. He replied, "Really, Harry, you must grow out of just being an emotional revolutionary. It will get us nowhere. I'm grooming you for better things."

'His comments were so unexpected that I laughed at him and he was quite miffed. I didn't pursue the matter but it made me think, Jude. I wondered where these desperate people might fit in under communism and whether they would be better off than they are under capitalism. And there are so many of them to consider. And I suppose I only see a few.

'I know it sounds naïve but I have never before realised how many people there are in the world.'

Always his letters ended with how much he loved and missed me and although he found travelling stimulated his thoughts he would prefer to be home. Obviously, Nathan wasn't much of a travelling companion and simply did on the ship what he did at home: immersed himself in a book of communist theory.

But Harry was different. The personal miseries of the poor had always affected him. From the time he had tried to stop evictions his commitment to communism was really a search to find a system that relieved his sense of impotence at not being able to help enough. When, after the hunger march, I had wept that it was awful to be always defeated, he had said, yes, it was, and that was why we needed to find a political way to help people to live decently. 'I'll never forget, Jude, the despair of those evicted women, weeping while their few possessions were taken away. It was the anguish of those who have learned to be content with little and then lose even that.'

Dear, sweet Harry, who had a heart full of feeling. I should have been more understanding and probably I might have been if Nathan hadn't always been a presence in our lives, pushing, pushing, a 'compelling bloke' as Harry had said. But to me, Nathan was too damned compelling, too damned dictatorial.

His next letter told me he had arrived in England. The ship docked at Southampton and they caught the train to London. There was a thick yellow fog and the air was foul with the acrid smell of coal. Nathan told him that the English kept warm by burning coal, hence the smoke and smell of the terrible fog.

'It's nothing like a sea fog, Jude, which is beautiful and strangely mysterious. This is nasty and eerie because disembodied footsteps follow and pass you and people are just like ghosts. You see them suddenly and then they vanish.

'We are staying in a cheap hotel near Hyde Park. Our room is on the third floor. It's cavernous and cold and the bathroom is one floor below. It is a bathroom and I emphasise the bath, Jude. It is a truly noble structure and stands on a plinth in the middle of the floor. We pay a shilling to fill it with lukewarm water and to get light in our room we have to put a shilling in a meter. Everything seems chill and dank. Even my clothes feel damp all the time. I can't imagine why so many Australians talk of the glories of "home", meaning England. Obviously they haven't stayed in this pub.

'Nathan had a meeting with Harry Pollit, the head honcho of the communists here. He was overcome by the importance of the occasion and bitterly disappointed in me because I had a stomach upset and couldn't get out of bed for two days. However, although he was very impressed with Harry Pollit, he was a little put out to be joked at for being a colonial communist. They treated him very well but he wasn't certain whether he was being patronised for being Australian or treated as a celebrity for being unusual. Poor Nathan. He finds it so hard sometimes to get a grasp on what is going on in a conversation.

'I love you, Jude, and miss our cheerful little bathroom, the chip heater and someone to share a bath with me.'

In his letters I heard more about Harry's reactions to Nathan than he had ever before expressed to me but I supposed that this was the first time he had an opportunity to closely observe him. Or maybe the rarefied atmosphere of travel and change brought him new perspectives. Or maybe he could speak to me in a letter while I wasn't present to put a damper on his opinions.

I had come to see that little by little Harry had avoided arguments with me. Horrified to think such a thing, I asked my mother, 'Is he afraid of me?'

'No, no,' she consoled, patting me on the arm. 'It's just that you're so strong- willed. But he's always known that.'

She hadn't really answered me. Did my strong will overwhelm Harry? And if it were so, what the hell could I do about it? I couldn't become without will.

Winnie was no use either. She just giggled. 'He needs someone to boss him around. I've always done it.'

'But I've noticed, Winnie, that it doesn't always work when you do it.'

'Well, I don't expect it to.'

'And what if I do it?'

'Oh, that's different,' she said airily.

Miss Marie was similarly useless. 'Of course you're strong-willed, Judith. How else could you become such a fine cartoonist?'

'But with Harry? Isn't that different?'

'Well, yes. But we can't change ourselves, Judith, to make others comfortable. Has Harry told you he doesn't like your strong will?'

'Really, Marie,' I grimaced, 'he's hardly likely to do that.' And I mimicked, '"Jude, I really hate your strong will. I think you ought to change."'

She laughed. 'Yes, Judith, it's as silly as that. Now what new cartoons have you in mind? I think something about Spain should be next on the menu. Spain is like a lady in waiting. For Hitler to gobble her up. The left appear to be in disarray, all fighting amongst themselves. Since the communists expelled the anarchists from their ranks I think the anarchists have all congregated in Spain and are setting a fine example to the world on how to run a libertarian community without the support of a big brother. What a delightful headache for the comrades.

'*Spearhead* could do with a little more help from you, Judith.'

'Harry wouldn't like it. It looks like doing something behind his back.'

She raised her eyebrows. 'He isn't here, Judith.'

'No,' I grinned. 'He isn't, is he? Nor is Nathan. And these days Jock has a pretty breezy attitude about it all. Sometimes he swears about the anarchists but he was raised in the slums of Glasgow. Marvellous leveller in political thinking, real poverty.'

'Yes. And cuts through the hocus-pocus of men like Nathan.'

We agreed.

'And Frank,' I added, 'he's first and foremost Irish. I don't think Nathan has ever caught on that he's less interested in the views of the comrades on international brotherhood than in Ireland being for the Irish.'

So I worked at a couple of cartoons for *Spearhead*. I drew a big Stalin with exuberant moustache in his full uniform, a huge star on his chest. Stepping out of his plane, he looks down on a crowd of anarchist workmen in overalls, and says to them: *This is Spain. We don't want any workers' state here.*

Spearhead loved it and rejoiced, as they put it, in reclaiming me. I waited for the barrage of abuse from the comrades but they said nothing. Jock rolled his eyes at me and snorted, 'Bloody anarchists. Part-time revolutionaries. Want to begin the revolution at eight o'clock in the morning and knock off at five o'clock.' Frank smirked but added, 'Darlin', when the cat's away the mice come out to play.'

I hoped he meant Nathan, not Harry. Whatever either of them meant, I was both amused and irritated. I would have composed it, I told myself, whether or not Nathan and Harry were away. I had supplied *Spearhead* with cartoons before this. If I were going to be a gadfly in my work I'd better have no favourites and I had come to wonder whether Stalin were a larger edition of Nathan – another compelling sort of bloke.

But I also had to confess privately to the less worthy motivation of wanting to retaliate against Nathan. As I had once said about his sisters, I found it very difficult to subscribe to a set of ideas when I disliked the people who pedalled them. Then, maybe, I reflected, there was some justice in my viewpoint. Were ideas really bigger than the people who held them? When Harry returned home I must discuss this with him.

My father didn't believe in being sick. He regarded illness as either a personal affront to his manhood or a weakness that should be ignored. That was until my mother had a heart attack one afternoon. Suddenly she collapsed into a chair, complaining of pains in her arm and an unbearable pressure on her chest. 'As if a horse has stepped on me, Judith,' she gasped, panting and sweating in distress.

Fortunately I was visiting and sent my father running for the doctor while I did what I could to comfort and calm her. My own heart pounded in fear and it seemed an age before my father rushed back accompanied by the new doctor who was now the Medical Officer for the Port. He was a slightly built man who looked pathetically young but there was no doubt about his competence. He examined my mother and sent my father to call an ambulance from the nearest phone booth.

'Adelaide hospital for you, Mrs Larsen. You'll get good treatment there. Better than we can provide here at the Port. Our casualty hospital is not fitted out to manage heart attacks.'

My father, who had been so cool and capable on windjammers, panicked. He managed to control himself until after the ambulance had left and then he burst out, 'She's going to die, isn't she, Judith? They only take people in an ambulance if they're going to die.'

I tried to soothe him but none of my assurances, that she would live because the doctor had said that he thought it was only a mild heart attack, consoled him.

'How will I live without your mother, Judith?' He was lost in bewilderment and plunged into the deepest gloom and despair. Since I was more worried than I'd admit to him it was hard to be patient.

Reluctantly, he came with me to Adelaide to visit her in hospital, but when we got there he said he'd wait outside. 'Can't abide hospitals,' he muttered. 'All those sick people. Some don't seem to know what day it is. Their heads have gone as well as their bodies.' He shuddered. 'I look at them and know they're dying. Can't stand it, Judith.'

'What a lot of rot, Dad.' I tried to be bracing. 'They're here to get better. You just see them at a very bad time.'

He was disbelieving. 'That's what all those doctors want us to believe. None of them would have a job if they told us we wouldn't get better. It's all a con. You go in, Judith, your mother will want to see you.'

'And she'll want to see you, Dad.'

It's hard to tell a father that he is being both stupid and selfish so I settled for suggesting to him that he was being a little irrational, which, I assured him, was quite understandable, given that he was so shocked.

To my surprise he admitted that I might be right and with a shame-faced grimace plodded after me down a long white corridor smelling of disinfectant – that clean impersonal smell so peculiar to a hospital.

In my mother's ward there were three other women; two of them looked very ill. A nurse bustled in and pulled the curtains around one of them. She did something mysterious, we heard a slight moan, and she bustled out again.

My father looked askance at the closed curtain. 'I told you, Judith.'

I ignored his silliness and taking his arm directed him to where my mother lay propped up on pillows and smiling brightly at him. 'Why, Niels,' she said, 'dear Niels.' And she held out her arms.

He embraced her awkwardly and then stood helplessly beside her bed – a large lumbering man completely at sea – although, I reflected, if he had been completely at sea he'd have had a lot more ideas on how to manage.

She smiled lovingly at him and took his hand. He clutched it. 'It's all right, Niels. I'll be home very soon. The doctor says I'll need a little rest but will make a complete recovery.'

He looked at her doubtfully. Irritated I thought that he should be the one reassuring her.

'I'm not trying to deceive you, Niels,' she insisted. 'You know I'd never do that. I really will recover.'

His mood lightened slightly and he sank into a chair beside her. I left them to have some time to themselves and wandered outside. There was a seat in a small garden and I sat in the sun and watched a bee bury his nose in the bosom of a flower while he worked his back legs in a sort of ecstasy. Maybe the nectar was particularly delicious. Maybe he was excited at his new discovery or maybe he was just rejoicing to be alive on such a lovely morning.

It was a relief to see my mother so improved and without pain. I wondered where Harry was. I couldn't tell him how ill she'd been. With no forwarding address I was unable to reply to his letters. He'd be sorry to hear about my mother. She'd always been so kind to him. He loved her, I knew that. In some ways her motherliness was more real to him than his own mother's. Mrs Grenville seemed so emotionally absent most of the time. Once he had said to me in sad resignation, 'For a long time it's been hard to make any real contact with her. Sometimes I wonder if skating on the surface with her has crippled my ability to have deeper relationships. I've failed so often to reach her that I've given up. No matter how I try she just flits away from me into a set of fantasies.'

'Darling Harry,' I had consoled him, 'you're certainly not some kind of cripple. A man more quickly involved in other people's suffering I've never met. You're warm and lovely.'

'Dear Jude,' he had replied, 'when skies are blue whatever would I do without you?'

'What'll you do?' I had laughed. 'You'll cuddle me.'

'Mm,' he said, 'that's a very good idea.' And he did just that.

Although Harry's letters had come at reasonably regular intervals, I wasn't overly worried to not receive one for several weeks. My mother needed help and I spent much of my time on the hulk.

His last letter had told me that the Communist Party in England was organising their trip through France and in to Spain. They would take the ferry from Dover to Calais where they would be met. There would be plenty of contacts to help them. Nathan, he wrote, was confident and pleased but in many ways, 'I just tag along'.

'It may be difficult to post letters, Jude, but I'll do my best. I have been learning from my French phrase book to ask: Where is the post office? How much is a stamp to Australia? Tell Miss Marie I could really do with her help. Once again, all my love, Jude. This is the really important part of the trip and it's a relief to know that it's coming up because it helps me to see the end of our journey and with the end I can again think of coming home to you.'

Little by little Jock fell into the habit of looking after me. At first it was just the occasional job but now he sometimes dropped in to drink a cup of tea with me, ask for news about Harry, discuss happenings in the Communist Party, or comment on my latest cartoons. It was a comfortable friendship. I was grateful for it and always pleased to open the door to him. I knew he was a lonely man and sometimes cooked him an evening meal. He ate his meat and vegetables with the serious concentration of a child, saying very little. But he lingered over his sweets, eventually resting his spoon in the empty plate, and remarking with wistfulness, 'I always enjoy little delicacies like stewed fruit.' So I always cooked some apples or pears for him just to watch his eyes light up.

Sometimes he had bursts of rage at the latest political event but at other times he reminisced about his early days in Glasgow: the gangs he joined as a young man and the street battles; his father putting him on the mat one day and ordering him to find work or leave home; his early days as a unionist in the shipyards and eventual rise to union organiser. 'I learned to be a hard man, Judith, a varry tough negotiator, an ultimatum man. Then of course I joined the Communist Party.'

I asked him why.

He shrugged. 'They were organised. I liked their ideas and they didn't compromise. Suited me. I'm not a shilly-shallying man. If you don't have one road to travel, because you're always wondering about the other tracks and where they might lead, you won't get anywhere.'

One evening as we finished our meal I asked, 'And why did you leave all this, Jock, and emigrate?'

He didn't answer for a few minutes and his eyes had a distant sad expression. I waited, concerned that I had clumsily intruded into something painful in his life.

At last he said quietly, 'I had a wife, Judith, a poor wee lassie. She was never strong.'

I remained silent, sensing that he needed no response from me.

He went on, 'She died. Consumption. It's the scourge of the poor in Glasgow. Very few families escaped it. Many lived with it but eventually ...' He stopped, then added, 'In Glasgow in the winter the sun only shines, if at all, for maybe two hours a day and then it is darkness. The streetlights come on at four in the afternoon. And the cold, Judith, it eats into your bones. Poor Jean. We would sit together in front of a few bars of the gas fire and she would talk of the sun. "Imagine, Jock," she would say, "of having a whole day, a whole working day from eight o'clock in the morning to six at night, of sun. What an indulgence that would be. What a luxury."'

I knew my eyes had filled with tears, imagining the young woman dreaming so piteously and uselessly of the sun, the sun that is free to everyone if they can find a place where it shines.

Jock continued, 'So when she died I packed up and came to Australia. The blokes in the union reproached me for leaving them. I told them to get fucked. I'd had enough of the bloody country.'

I jumped up to take his empty cup to the sink. There I dabbed my eyes. It wouldn't do to let Jock see my tears, which were not only for poor Jean who died in the cold but also for Harry somewhere in Spain. Neither Jock nor I wanted to succumb to our loneliness.

When he visited during the weekend he was keen to help me in the garden. Often he was disappointed in the small plot of earth he and Frank had dug over. 'This is no good, Jude,' he said, 'I think we need to buy better soil to get plants to grow. It'd be nice to have a wee bit of garden.'

'Yes,' I agreed. 'Perhaps when Harry …'

He looked at me quickly. 'Of course, lassie, I've no mind to intrude.'

'You haven't.'

He kicked a bit of the soil and dust rose in a cloud. 'Dry and useless,' he said.

'Well, if you like, Jock, a wee bit of garden would be nice and Harry isn't much of a gardener.'

'That's OK,' he growled. 'He can play the piano. I canna do that.'

'Like you canna swim, Jock?'

He laughed at me. 'Many things I canna do or canna abide, Jude.'

It was Jock who brought me the news that Nathan had returned home. He arrived at the front door flustered and stricken with anxiety. The only other time I had seen him in such a state of perturbation was the day the police raided communist headquarters and the homes of comrades. Recalling my panic on that occasion, I once again felt ill. Something terrible must have happened.

'What is it, Jock?' And my unsteady voice squeaked with apprehension.

He blurted out his news, his face a deep guilty crimson as if what he had to tell me was his fault. 'I must tell you this, Judith. You will hear it from others. Before you ask, I havna spoken with Nathan. I didna know what to do. I didna want to frighten you, but you should know.'

All of this was said in a rush and I could not make head nor tail of it. 'What are you telling me, Jock?'

He looked blank. 'I'm telling you, lassie, that Nathan's come home.'

Bemused, I stared at him. 'Nathan's home?'

'Yes.'

'But where is Harry?'

He looked distressed. 'I canna say, Judith.'

I didn't seem able to take it in. 'Harry hasn't come with him?' I stopped. 'No, of course he can't have. I'd be the first to know.'

I was still trying to understand, to take in the suddenness of it all.

Jock's self-control worried me more than if he raged. The tension in his body made me feel that at any moment he might explode. That he was holding himself in so tightly so as not to scare me made me even more terrified. Something dreadful had happened and he was keeping his rage over it to himself.

'Where is Harry?' I repeated. My brain didn't seem to be able to ask anything more complicated.

He didn't reply.

I put my hand on his arm and shook it. 'Jock, where is Harry?'

'I dinna know.'

'But Nathan is here? In Port Adelaide?'

'Yes,' he snarled.

'And what does he say?'

'I havna seen him. I couldna. I was frightened I would kill him. I couldna speak with the fucken bastard.'

'So no one has asked him where Harry is?'

'No.'

I took a deep breath. 'Might he be dead, Jock?'

He flinched. 'No, Judith, no, I'm sure not. Even Nathan wouldn't have concealed that.'

'Then?'

'It must be a Party matter, Judith. Some bloody Party matter.'

'But Harry's not home, and Nathan is.' I didn't know why I kept stupidly repeating this. He understood my confusion but had no more to add. As calmly as I could I said, 'Then I must go to see Nathan. He's the only one who knows what all this is about. Will you come with me, Jock?'

He shook his head. 'I canna, Judith. You know my hot temper. I canna be responsible for what I might do to him.'

His large calloused hands worked nervously. They were powerful and so were the muscles in his arms. He was a short man but had probably been a pugilist in his youth.

'Yes,' I said, understanding and amazed at my own self-control and apparent detachment. 'Better if you don't come then, Jock. We don't know what the news might be. Nathan may not be to blame.'

He snorted contemptuously. 'He has no personal loyalties, Judith. I found that out a long time ago. He's just a fucken bastard and that's all there is to it. But I could walk with you some of the way.'

'No,' I said, 'I'll ride my bike. It'll be quicker. But thank you.'

I gave him a light kiss on the cheek. 'It's not your fault, Jock, that you have always been the bearer of bad news to me.' Imitating his Scots accent I added, 'Ya canna help it.'

He returned my smile gratefully.

I made myself concentrate on my bike riding. It would not help my missing Harry if I got injured on the road. It seemed to be a particularly busy morning on Commercial Road. The traffic congestion was more bothersome, the clanging train bells more strident, the shouts of horse and cart drivers more aggressive, the actions of pedestrians leaping in to the traffic more reckless. Everything about me seemed exaggerated and, like my feelings, blown up to an hysterical dimension. But I managed to reach Nathan's small cottage at the far end of Nile Street in half an hour.

Shaking with apprehension, I knocked on the door. Miss Adelaide opened it. She looked surprised. 'Why, Mrs Grenville, this is ...' She halted. Something in my face warned her. 'What do you want?' She barred my way. An aggressive little hen, devoid of feathers but bristling nonetheless.

I kept my temper. 'I need to see Nathan.'

'I don't think ...' She paused. Was she going to lie that he wasn't home? I could see his hat lying on the hall table. She knew I had seen it. Nathan never went out without his hat.

'He's busy,' she said flatly.

I stood my ground.

She moved to shut the door. I placed my hand firmly on it. 'Miss Adelaide, I need to see your brother urgently. He went to Spain with my husband and has now returned without him. Do you really think it unreasonable of me to want to know where my husband is?'

She flushed, hesitated, and finally held the door open for me. I followed her down the short passage to a small sitting room. At the door she stood to one side to let me enter. Nathan, as always, sat at a table, a book in front of him. He didn't look up when I entered, although I knew, by a nervous tick in his cheek, he was aware of me.

Miss Adelaide hovered silently in the doorway. She had not introduced me. I crossed the room and stood in front of him. His eyes remained fixed on what he was reading – or pretending to read.

Suddenly I was sixteen years old again and he was the strange young man at the Chew It who had refused to look at me. The eight years since then flashed through my memory, like a set of cinematic images which, although brilliantly clear, never linger. And although so real, these images were neither orderly nor sequential, because each one was a precious recollection of Harry.

'Where's my husband, Nathan?' My voice was tightly controlled.

He ignored me.

'Look at me, Nathan. Where's Harry?' I demanded, my voice rising.

He glanced up but it was a mere flash of his glasses and his eyes didn't focus on me before he resumed his reading.

'Look at me, Nathan,' I shouted. 'What's the matter with you? Where's my husband? Where's Harry? Is he dead?'

I heard Miss Adelaide gasp and now he did look at me.

'No,' he mumbled, 'of course he's not dead. Well, I don't think so.'

I could hardly believe what he was saying. He didn't know whether Harry were dead or not. The world around me darkened to a murky fuzz. God, I thought, I'm going to faint. I took a deep breath and clutched the edge of the table.

'What do you mean, you don't think so? You either know or you don't know, you rotten coward. Have you left him in some sort of trouble? Run out on him? That would be your style, wouldn't it?'

He was defensive. 'No, of course I didn't run out on him. He ran out on me. Harry's not steadfast. He's not a good Communist.

We argued and he mated up with some anarchist and they went off together. He was supposed to come back to Madrid but he didn't keep the arrangement. So I came home. That's all there is to it.'

'That's all there is to it?' I screamed at him. 'You came home without inquiring about where he was?'

'Harry's a man, not a child. And don't yell at me, Judith. I wasn't his keeper.'

I tried to be calm. 'No,' I said savagely, 'just his friend. Where do you think he went with the anarchist bloke?'

He was casual. 'Probably to the Asturias. He was talking about it. I told him not to.'

'The Asturias?' I shrieked. 'The Asturias, where the big mine strike ended in thousands being shot?'

He dared to shrug. 'Harry was always reckless. Too easily involved. Too addicted to drama.'

'You loathsome bloody bastard.' I was breathless. 'You left him without even discovering if he were alive or dead or in need of help.'

'Harry made his own choices.' His voice was flat and dismissive.

Terror overcame me. The reports of the miners' attempt to set up a commune in Asturia and their bitter strike, which ended in tragic disaster, had filtered through to even our mainstream press. Of the 8000 striking miners 3000 had been shot. The army had even dragged the wounded out of hospital, asked no questions about who they were or what side they were on, and shot them. Franco was dubbed 'Butcher of Asturias'. What if Harry had been wounded and shot, no questions asked?

A violent nausea racked my body. Only by vomiting up the entire contents of my stomach could I rid myself of the excruciating pain that gripped me. I threw up all over myself, Nathan's table, Nathan's book and Nathan. Shaking and sweating, I continued to convulse.

Through a sick miasma I felt Miss Adelaide's arm about me. 'Sit down, Mrs Grenville,' she was urging. 'Sit down, my dear. Really, Nathan, I warned you before about being so tactless. You've worried Mrs Grenville. Now stop being so useless and bring me some towels and warm water.'

If I hadn't felt so ill I would have laughed at her idiocy. She was reproaching Nathan for being tactless but not for abandoning Harry.

I suppose he must have done as she ordered because I felt her wipe my face and do her best to clean my clothes. I wept hysterically.

'Do stop, Mrs Grenville. You'll make yourself ill. I'm sure your husband is all right. We would have heard. The Spanish authorities would have notified someone – the Australian or perhaps the British Ambassador. We're not at war with Spain. Calm yourself. An Australian couldn't be shot and no one know. Please calm yourself.'

She held some water to my lips and I sipped thirstily.

Half an hour later I was still weak and distressed but able to step into the taxi she called for me and paid for. 'We'll arrange to send your bicycle home for you tomorrow,' she said. 'Now, please don't worry, Mrs Grenville. And please don't come again. Nathan has told you all he knows.'

I knew that this was not so and only had contempt for her fatuousness. But I was too sick to argue. Maybe Jock or Miss Marie might be able to delve deeper into the labyrinth that Nathan called his mind.

When I reached home I was too exhausted to do anything but drop my soiled clothes on the floor of the bathroom, drag a dressing gown about myself and curl up in the sitting-room chair. I was cold and I shivered. I saw myself cringing there, cowed and waiting for some further blow to strike me. Soon I must have a bath but lighting the chip heater was too much of an effort.

I had sat like this in this same chair, similarly despairing and afraid, when Harry failed to come home after the police raids. At that time I had vented my fury on him for his careless neglect in not letting me know where he was. But now I had no strength for rage. Despair drained my spirits and left only the terrible dregs of helplessness. My past worry over the police raids seemed laughable. If Harry had been mislaid then, how easy it would have been to find him or to discover news of his whereabouts.

But Spain! Thousands of miles away! What could I do about a lost husband in Spain?

I had prepared several cartoons about Spain while Harry was away. They had gone to the *Sun News Pictorial* and *Spearhead*. I had read about the slaughter of the Asturia miners by the Foreign Legion troops and pinpointed the mateship between Hitler and Lerroux, the leader of Spain's right-wing coalition. Lerroux had come to power against a backdrop of the rise of fascism in Europe and he seemed too comfortable in Hitler's company.

I had penned a pair of cartoons sitting side by side. One I had captioned *Spain* the other *Germany*. Both cartoons figured a line of men fronting a firing squad, each with a label about his neck. For Germany the labels read *Communist, Socialist, Anarchist, Gypsy*. For Spain each label read *Communist, Socialist, Anarchist*, but also *Asturias*. On the German side an officer addresses Hitler: *Are these all you want, sir? I have others.* On the Spain side an officer of the Foreign Legion addresses Lerroux: *We've cleaned up the Asturias. When do you want us to start on the rest?*

I had also sent this cartoon to the *Daily Herald* in London. They had grabbed it and asked for others. 'Events in Spain' they wrote, 'are becoming headline news in England'. So I composed another: four crosses on a hill and over each crucified figure the captions *Justice, Tolerance, Compassion* and *the Asturias*. At the foot of the cross Lerroux is saying to Hitler: *A little crucifixion cures every trouble.*

The efforts of the combined left-wing groups in Spain to launch a general strike had collapsed because of factional in-fighting and only the miners of the Asturia had attempted to carry it through. In true anarchist style – and in the spirit of the 1871 Paris Commune, as Miss Marie had sadly said – they struck and marched on the capital Oviedo. Along the route they took control of the towns, redistributed land to the peasants, seized mines and factories and set up Workers' Committees to run them. They bucked the centralist control of the Communist Party and pleaded with the socialists to help them obtain arms. But they were hung out to dry. When the troops of Franco's Foreign Legion landed on their coast it was all over. It was another failure of idealism in the face of guns.

And how futile my cartoons. I was merely some poor sheep bleating that there were wolves out there. Some of us bleated louder than others but in the end we were just carcasses for vultures to pick over.

Had Harry, I worried, marched with the miners to Oviedo? Had he been swept along by the inspiration of actually witnessing a new political system? One so close to what appeared to be pure communism but rejected by the communists? If he had been there, how confused he must have felt. How disenchanted. Was this what he and Nathan had rowed about – Harry's determination to find out for himself? If he were still alive.

At one stage the communists at the Port had put up candidates for the state election. But despite Harry's hopes it had all come to nothing.

Was their talk of revolution just hot air?

How casual we had been in our belief in violent revolution, how stupidly euphoric in our dream that it would all end in our victory. Now it seemed only youthful zeal, the result of the hubris of ignorance. The end of such dreams was death. Even if the miners of Asturia had been armed, their deaths at the hands of the crack troops of the Foreign Legion would only have been delayed.

Despair had soaked into my bones and like some corrosive acid dissolved my strength. I continued to just cower in my chair, cold and lost.

Jock returned and at his insistent hammering on the door I let him in and returned to my chair. One look at me and he asked no questions. He made me a cup of tea and sat while I drank it. But I left the biscuits on the plate.

He must have phoned Winnie because she also came banging on the door.

'Oh, it's you, Winnie,' I said tiredly. 'I'm really not up to a visitor.'

'Nonsense.' She was brisk. 'You smell awful, Jude.' Winnie was never one for niceties.

'I suppose.' I shrugged. I didn't care.

She went into the bathroom, kicked my clothes to one side, wrestled with the heater, and eventually had the bath filled with hot water. 'Come on,' she ordered. 'Up you get. You'll feel better after a bath.'

'It's Harry, Winnie.'

She pursed her mouth. 'Jock's told me. We can't do anything about Harry at the minute. Now off with your underwear and in to the bath.'

She picked up my clothes and disappeared with them, I assumed to the laundry. I obeyed her, vaguely surprised that she wasn't weeping all over the place.

The bath helped. It was warm and comforting. She had left me a clean towel on the stool and a set of fresh clothes on the floor nearby. Feeling a little more normal I crawled out when the water began to cool, towelled myself and dressed.

In the kitchen Winnie had heated soup and made toast. I looked at it doubtfully. My stomach still churned.

'Don't be a duffer, Jude. Get this into you. You'll feel a heap better.'

'Harry,' I started to say again, but she interrupted me firmly.

'We'll talk about Harry later,' she said. 'Not now.'

'It's Nathan,' I persisted.

'Bugger Nathan,' she said. 'Miss Marie's gone to talk to him.'

'Oh,' I said. I was surprised. 'I tried, you know.'

'Yes. So I believe.'

'He couldn't tell me much.'

'We'll see. Miss Marie is a marvel at extracting information.'

'Even Marie might fail.'

'Have you ever known anyone deny her?'

'But even so, if there's nothing he can tell us …'

'There'll be something. Now you're to lie down and rest and I'll come and sit with you. Maybe you'll be able to sleep a bit. I'll wake you when Marie comes.'

'I'm so worried, Winnie. He might be … He might be …'

'Yes, Jude. He might be dead.' Her voice shook but she controlled herself. 'But it's no good dwelling on what might be. Harry always dared to climb the tallest tree but he always managed to clamber down again. Have some faith in his toughness. I've seen plenty of it.'

So I allowed her to tuck me up in bed as if I were some distressed child and with her hand in mine I fell asleep.

It was dusk when Winnie woke me. The clock said nearly six o'clock. Miss Marie was in the kitchen drinking tea. She jumped up, hugged me, and looked me over critically.

'You have done a grand job, Winnie. Jock told me she was quite done in.'

Winnie flushed with pleasure. Everyone revelled in Miss Marie's praise.

'She was quite done in but our Judith is tough.'

'And Winnie's tough, too, Marie. She hasn't cried once.'

Winnie reproached me. 'I never cry when things are really serious, Jude. You should know that.'

I didn't but I smiled at her. 'Of course, but you know if I hadn't forgotten that I might have been really frightened by your composure.'

She chortled. 'It's such a relief to have the old sharp Judith back again, Marie. I thought for a bit she'd lost her fighting spirit.'

'Never,' Miss Marie said. 'That indeed would be a tragic day.'

I knew all this cheerful play-acting was for my benefit but I went along with it and found it comforting. Neither of my friends seemed to be plunged in the bleak pessimism that afflicted me.

'Could Nathan tell you anything more?' I asked Miss Marie.

She grimaced. 'That man is a master of obfuscation. He dodged and feinted and side-stepped like some mediocre boxer but eventually I pinned him down. Of course, he feels guilty as hell. I'd say he rushed out of Spain in a fit of rage. Oh, yes, he experiences a lot of repressed anger. He tries to hide it but I saw it at once.

'Of course, having started on the homeward journey he couldn't return. He must have been tortured by what he had done. Even Nathan has some realisation of what others might think of him.' She added cynically, 'Some sense of obligation.'

'So his sisters didn't shut the door on you?'

'No, *ma pauvre*, of course not. People don't usually shut the door on me. I never let them do that. Besides Miss Adelaide knew me from the meeting and I felt she had some hope that I might make things easier for her as I did then. They are guilty, Judith, and ashamed and very frightened.'

'They're frightened?' I was outraged and scornful. 'That's rich.'

'Oh, yes, Judith. *Mon Dieu*. Harry is dearly loved around the Port. Everyone recalls his brightness and kindness. While Nathan and his sisters just hang on to the edge of acceptance. This could topple them off completely. And what a fall that would be: to face the opprobrium of the entire community. It would be unbearable for them.'

'Serves them right,' Winnie spat viciously. 'I hope to see them driven out of town.'

Winnie, I knew, would have no hesitation in blackening Nathan's name. She hated him.

Miss Marie was more diplomatic. 'Careful, *ma chere*. We may yet need some help from him. He still has connections. Do not sink the goose with the golden egg.'

'Kill the goose,' Winnie automatically corrected. And then laughed as she caught Miss Marie's twinkling eyes. 'I'll be good but not too kind. Under the circumstances that would be quite impossible.'

'Then, *ma chere*, we must not ask the impossible. Only a little discretion.'

'So,' I said, interrupting them impatiently and accepting the second cup of tea Winnie put in front of me, 'what did you manage to get out of Nathan?'

'Well, Judith, as you probably know, Harry went to the Asturias with a Spaniard he met in Madrid. Nathan swears the Spaniard belonged to the Anarcho-Syndicalists and that he did his best to talk Harry out of getting embroiled with him. But Harry would not listen.'

'Sounds frighteningly like Harry,' I said bitterly.

Miss Marie continued, 'This Spaniard's home village is in the Asturias and Harry was "hell-bent" – Nathan's phrase, not mine – on discovering how these anarchists planned to set up a workers' commune. At this point in our discussion, I think Nathan could barely contain his anger at the memory. And really in telling the whole incident he went livid and his hands shook.

'He said the communists had rejected the anarchists and thrown them out because they were just a leaderless rabble who wanted to conduct a private revolution on their own terms. I'm afraid that this made me a little angry, too. And I said, rather sharply, "You mean they rejected communist leadership and instructions from the USSR?"

'It was unwise of me. One of those moments when unfortunately

I lost control of myself. Luckily Miss Adelaide came to my rescue: "Calm yourself, Nathan," she ordered. "Miss Marie isn't here for a political argument. She just wants any information you can give her about Mr Grenville."

'I must admit that I found it odd to hear Harry referred to as Mr Genville. It was as if he was some stranger to them but afterwards I realised that it was a form of self-protection aimed at distancing themselves from him. How strange people are, Judith, in the way they use words to protect themselves.'

Winnie snorted in disgust.

'As Miss Adelaide had calmed Nathan I asked him if the anarchist had a name. At first he said he didn't know, couldn't remember, but I persisted and eventually he said he thought it was Garcia. He only knew that people spoke of him as Garcia from Sama in the Asturias. Sama, he thought, was a village not far from Oviedo, the provincial capital. He had no desire to go there and Harry should have taken his advice.'

Miss Marie looked resigned. 'He was quite petulant, considerably sorry for himself, and full of self-justification, and that's all I could get out of him.'

'It's more than I did,' I said quietly.

'Yes, *chérie*, at least we have the name of the Spaniard he went with and the name of the village where perhaps he went. It's a good start for our search.'

I looked at her hopelessly. 'But where to start? Who to contact? I've not heard from Harry for weeks. Nathan took maybe six weeks to get home. What has happened in that time?'

'No, Judith. Nathan managed to get home in three weeks. Miss Adelaide told me. He got on board a British patrol boat in the Mediterranean and when it docked briefly in the Suez Canal he boarded a P&O liner from Port Said. At Perth he took the train to Adelaide. It's only three weeks since he left Spain. So his news of Harry is relatively recent.'

'Recent, but not better. The miners' strike in Asturia must have taken place in those three weeks. We've all heard of the slaughter there. What can any of us do from here? The last letter I had from Harry was posted in England. I've not even received a letter from France.' I choked at the memory of that letter. 'He wrote that he was learning French phrases to help him find a post office or buy a stamp when he got to France. Oh, Marie, what am I going to do?'

'You're going to come to Spain with me. That's what we're going to do.'

I gaped at her. 'Spain? With you?'

Winnie squeaked, 'Spain? Oh, no. Haven't we had enough of Spain?'

'I have no money for that, Marie. Only a little in our bank account. So much went on my mother's medical expenses. It would barely get me to Sydney or Melbourne. Europe's out of the question.'

'Not at all. I have money.'

'No,' I said abruptly. 'I can't take your money. Can't involve you in this. You've done enough.'

'No, Judith, not enough. You think about it. If you don't hear from Harry shortly then we should go and look for him. And I don't think we should let too much time elapse.'

I was speechless. Winnie's eyes fixed on Marie were wide and scared. 'Please,' she whispered, 'please don't take Judith to Spain. She might never come back.'

'Nonsense, Winnie. Of course I'll bring her back and we'll find Harry and bring him back, too. Courage my friends. *Le diable est mort.* I've been to Europe. It's not such a big thing. Not at all.'

There was no way I could keep the distressing news about Harry from my mother. If Mrs Danley hadn't rushed already to tell her, it would only be a matter of time. Gossip spread like wildfire in the Port. Far better, I thought, if I were the bearer of bad tidings because then my mother could see immediately how I was taking it. I knew her concern for me would equal her concern for Harry.

So I rode my bike to the hulk and wheeled it carefully up the gangplank. Our little banana boat bobbed up and down on its mooring rope and I recalled Harry hauling me out of the river while I shrieked in terror at the thought of a shark. My soaked clothes had clung to me and when he clutched me against him I smelled the damp sweetness of his body. We had both laughed in embarrassment when he released me, hiding from each other what we had discovered about desire.

I found my father in the galley where surprisingly he had taken to cooking. When I had showed my amazement he reproved me. 'And, Judith, how do you think boys like me survived in Iceland? There were no la-di-da servants to cook for us. If we didn't make our meals we starved. I learned very early to not only catch fish but how to prepare and fry them.

'Frying fish became my speciality,' he added, his eyes twinkling with pride. 'It hasn't been difficult to progress from there. Cooking is just a matter of following the rules. Any fool can do that.'

I didn't laugh at him. It would have hurt his feelings and it was endearing to watch him pore over a cookery book, carefully following the instructions and snorting with disgust if they were not exact. 'Such haphazardness at sea would get us all ship wrecked. What do they mean here, by half a teaspoon of spice? Or cook for an hour to an hour and a half? No teaspoon has exactly the same measurement.' And he would go on grumbling. Then he would grin and say, 'The greatest difficulty, Judith, has been chasing your mother out of the galley. She still doesn't think I'm competent and keeps sneaking in on any feeble excuse to check what's on the stove.'

Today he was making scones. He looked up as I entered. 'You look very tired, Judith,' he said. 'Been working late?'

'Yes, Dad,' I answered. 'I am tired. But no, I've not been working late.' I hesitated and he looked at me searchingly.

'Something troubling you, girlie?'

'Yes, Dad. Something serious. And I don't know how to tell Mum – or even if I ought to. But if I don't someone else will.'

He was quick. 'It's Harry?'

'Yes.'

'Very serious?'

'I think it may be.'

'He's not hurt?'

'I don't know. And you may as well ask, Dad, and not pussyfoot around. He's not dead, as far as we know.'

'As far as you know? What do you know? Sit down. Far better you tell me first. Your mother is having a nap. We can decide what and how much to tell her between us.'

He poured me a strong cup of tea from the pot, which now always rested on the side of the stove. The tea, which brewed there all day, was a dark bitter tannin, but it represented to me a happier change in our circumstances. I could never stomach weak tea and shuddered to remember those desperate poverty-stricken years when my mother dried the used tea-leaves and re-used them until the tea became no more than a pale wash. We still needed to be frugal but my father now managed to find occasional work on the river. I gratefully sipped my tea and told him.

'And this Nathan bastard left him in Spain?'

'Yes.'

'Because he didn't return at the exact time decided on?'

'Apparently.'

'What sort of no-good idiot bastard does that?'

'Nathan, it seems.'

'And wasn't there anyone else in Spain to stop him?'

'I don't know, Dad. All Nathan's mates, if you could call them that – colleagues, acquaintances – were communists. If Harry went off with someone reputed to be an anarchist ...' I looked at my father hopelessly.

He exploded. 'Bloody reckless fool. Hasn't he any political nous? What fool tinkers with political factions in a country like Spain?'

'Dad,' I said wearily, 'don't go on about Harry. It doesn't help. Don't you think I, too, have cursed his foolishness?'

'Yes, yes.' Admonished, he stopped. 'And now what to tell your mother?'

My mother spoke from the doorway. 'Yes?' she invited. 'What is it that you both need to tell me?'

She came and sat at the table. 'Don't leave those scones too long, Niels. They'll dry out. Scones should go into a hot oven as soon as you've made them.' Then she looked from him to me. 'Pour me a cuppa, please, Niels. And since I suppose it's Judith's news I need to hear, what is it, darling?'

She was smiling at me and I dithered. 'I don't want to worry you, Mum. It's difficult. I don't want to alarm you.'

'For heaven's sake, Judith.' She was impatient. 'Just tell me. All this shillyshallying is making me more anxious than your news probably will.'

'Yes,' I said, a little uncertainly. 'Imagination does make cowards of us all.'

Briefly I remembered how Harry and I had walked home together from the hulk in the soft comfortable darkness, his arm about me. What had we discussed? I thought it must have had something to do with conscience because I had paraphrased the Shakespearean phrase *Conscience doth make cowards of us all*.

Now, maybe, imagination was something I needed to be afraid of. I didn't know what had happened to Harry and in the absence of facts imagination could destroy me.

'Nathan has returned from Spain but left Harry there.'

She looked bewildered. 'Nathan's home but not Harry?'

'Yes,' I said.

'But why? Didn't he go with Harry? Why would he leave him in Spain?'

'I don't fully know. But he did.'

'Then Harry must be following on a later ship.'

I was silent.

'You haven't heard from Harry?'

'No, not for many weeks.'

'Oh, Judith,' she said. 'You must be frantic. My poor darling. Has someone spoken to Nathan?'

'Yes, I have and Miss Marie.'

She smiled slightly. 'I suppose Marie got more out of him than you did.'

'Yes.'

'And of course it has been some political issue?'

'Yes.'

I had told neither of them that Harry had gone to the Asturias where under the orders of General Franco so many of the miners had been murdered.

But my mother was astute. 'You've only told us half the story, Judith, haven't you?'

I was never good at lying to my mother but I was cautious in my reply. 'I think he may have gone to a mining district in north-west Spain where a general strike was being organised.'

My father nodded. 'A rotten life being a miner. Good luck to them. The miners nearly starved during our depression. Mind you starvation might be quicker than coughing your lungs out with coal dust.'

'But Harry was never a miner,' my mother persisted.

'No, but the anarchists were organising it and he went with an anarchist.'

She sighed. 'And they're going to bring in their brand of a perfect society.'

I gulped. 'They tried.'

'What do you mean "they tried"?'

'Some of them,' I couldn't tell her 3000, 'have been shot.'

'My god, Judith. This gets worse and worse.'

I was struggling not to cry and she knew it.

My father burst in, 'And that rotten miserable bastard Nathan knew he'd gone there.'

'Where is it again?' my mother asked.

'The Asturias,' I said.

'That piece of shit ran out on him,' my father growled.

My mother looked shocked but strangely calm. 'What do you plan to do, Judith?'

I took a deep breath. 'Miss Marie suggested that she and I go to Spain to try to find him. He may be wounded or ill, Mum. The fighting was terrible. Crack troops from northern Africa, the Moors and Legionaires, against unarmed miners.'

My father snorted. 'Franco's mob. Fascism is more than a sleeping lion in Spain these days.'

At my mother's dismay I added hastily, 'But we can't go at once because I need a passport and visas. So I'll wait and hope that I get a letter from Harry.'

'Yes,' she said. 'Yes, of course.' And then quite calmly she patted my hand.

'If a letter doesn't come you must go. Can you pay for it? We have a little put by. I suppose your inheritance from Joe Pulham was spent years ago.'

I nodded, tears in my eyes. Dear Joe, who had so enriched my young life.

'Miss Marie is so insistent about helping me that I know I'll eventually agree. I have a little in savings and some money owing to me but I'm worried about leaving you, Mum.'

She smiled gently. 'I'm quite well now, Judith. Your father does our cooking.' She gave him an impish smile. 'And I've many friends in the Port who'll always lend a hand. Brenda Danley would be happy to take me over entirely. And, my dear, oddly, although my heart attack gave me my first taste of mortality, it has also made me calmer about life. It would be impossible for you to envision a future without Harry. So if it becomes necessary you must go with Marie and find him.'

A week later Harry's letter from Spain arrived. I saw his writing and the Spanish stamp and a wave of relief swept over me. He was safe. Probably he had written about his plans for coming home. Maybe with the elapse of time he was already on board some ship. I needn't go to Spain to find him. All was well. I gripped the letter basking in the rapture of fulfilled hope.

Yet I hesitated to open it. I suppose, at the back of my mind, there was a frisson of anxiety that my confidence might be shattered. To hope and have hope dashed could be more terrible than not hoping at all. So I just sat there clinging to the precious letter, half-glad, half-fearful.

At last I forced myself to search for the date of posting on the envelope but it was indecipherable. Far better to face what was inside. I tore open the envelope and unfolded two single sheets of writing paper. Harry rarely wrote lengthy letters. I was used to gleaning tidbits of news. Two sheets was unusual but the sight of his scrawling handwriting, so familiar and now so dear to me because it was all I had of him, renewed my faith that he was alive and well.

I glanced at the date heading the letter. It couldn't be right. The last week in September? It was now nearly November. After my first dismay I tried to reassure myself. A letter could take that long to reach me. A normal trip on a liner would take at least five weeks. How stupid I was to worry.

Just let me read the letter. But I was apprehensive. Something was not right. I felt it almost as if the paper on which the letter was written breathed some warning of disaster.

He had begun cheerfully. He had met a bloke in Madrid. His name was Garcia, nicknamed 'Little Lorca'. They called him this because he wrote poetry and hoped one day to be as great a poet as his hero, the celebrated poet Garcia Lorca. Hence he was Little Lorca and not Big Lorca.

I shook the page impatiently. 'Get on with it, Harry,' I said aloud. 'You're prevaricating as usual. What's your real news?'

But it was still delayed. Little Lorca had taken him to a musical evening with some of his mates. They were all playing the bagpipes.

'Such a din, Jude. The squealing, moaning and whining of the bagpipes is OK outside in one of the street processions, which seem to happen everywhere and all the time. Very colourful and bright with national costumes. But inside the noise of the bagpipes is ear-splitting and unbearable. They invited me to try blowing one but I ran out of puff.

'We had a jovial night because they had the traditional wine skins filled with the local booze. These wine skins have a spout and they are expert at tipping the skin so that the wine squirts from the spout directly into their mouths. Of course, I had to take part and naturally drowned myself in wine. They bellowed with laughter at my ineptness and made some pretty crude jokes about whether I always had trouble finding where to put my snout.

'There were many nods and winks and a lot of backslapping and hilarity at my expense. I have found that being a foreigner who makes mistakes over local customs is a source of endless fun to them but there is no malice in it.

'Luckily Garcia speaks pretty good English and he interprets for me. I heard them ask him if I were a communist. I know he said yes because they all looked at me assessingly. "An Australian communist," I said hastily. They looked relieved. "Not a Russian bastard?" "No," I said, "Australia is a long way from Russia." They nodded. "A very long way. You are lucky."

'It turned out they are anarchists and Garcia is from north-west Spain. An area known as the Asturias. It's coal-mining country and has a number of political groups: communists, socialists and anarchists but most of the miners are anarchists. It would seem that what is agitating them are the plans of the Madrid Government to include three representatives of a fascist group. They are alarmed that this is a dangerous step towards further repression.

'Garcia is full of enthusiasm that I should see how the working people of Spain organise themselves to resist. "We do not have your education," he said to me, "or your knowledge of democratic government. The English have had so much practice at governing themselves. But we know what we want." It's useless for me to protest that I'm not English. Australia is unknown and unknowable to them. They continually tell me that I am lucky to live in a green country with boundless supplies of rain and water. Once I corrected them and said that much of Australia is dry like Spain but they just scoffed at me and assured me that I needn't save them from being envious. They knew England was a much pleasanter country to live in than Spain.

'I've had many conversations with Garcia and, Jude, it's not that I want to become an anarchist but that their ideas have made me see some of the weaknesses in communism. People do need to manage their own affairs. And in the Asturias the workers aim to set up their own committees to run the place, Garcia says. Like the men in Mildura told Nathan, although of course he wouldn't listen. But I'm prepared to listen, Jude, and I'm coming to the realisation that there is not just one answer for social change and a better fairer community.

'It will be very interesting to see whether these people succeed in launching a general strike. The communists in the Port talked so much about a general strike to overthrow the government but we never got it off the ground. Here it's treated as a real possibility and they discuss having arms to defend themselves. Remember how we always said, rather blithely, that without arms we would always be defeated? But now, here, I don't know whether I'm sold on the idea of arming people. I get the feeling that politics here is much more serious, more bitter and more dangerous than in Australia, that behind the miners' strike is a nasty history of repression and violence and probably a poverty incomprehensible to us. As I said in my earlier letters I've been appalled at the level of destitution in some ports, some countries.

'But then, maybe, an effective revolution can't take place without violence. Who knows, Jude? I spoke of this to Nathan and he turned white, called me a fool and said if I got myself mixed up in an armed skirmish in Spain he couldn't be responsible for me. I was annoyed and told him that I needed neither him nor anyone else to watch over me and as he had always preached the need for the violent overthrow of the state he was being a bloody hypocrite.

'I simply wanted to know as an observer how the Spaniards went about things. Wasn't that why we had come here? Of course, he dished out the usual, that we had come to get advice from our communist brothers. Anyway we settled that I would be back in Madrid in a week.

'I suppose you got my other letters from France and the previous one I sent from Spain.'

Of course, I hadn't. And it had been useless for me to attempt to contact him with no fixed forwarding address.

He went on: 'It's such an incredibly old country, Jude, with ancient castles, churches and monasteries dotted everywhere. People like Garcia (who comes from a village called Sama) seem to consider themselves citizens of their town or province. It's a bit like you or I thinking of ourselves as citizens of Port Adelaide rather than Australia. Garcia says no one likes being controlled by a central government and all the anarchists are federalists.

'All this new experience has sent my mind running in different directions and when I come home I think you'll find my attitudes changed. I'm still searching for some new political answer to the horror of the depression but I think I'll be more patient and more contented to keep searching and questioning. Altogether, a great eye-opener, Jude, darling.

'In a week I'll leave here with Nathan. I can hardly contain myself at the thought of seeing you again and holding you in my arms. As I go to sleep at night I dream of the blissful privacy of our little house and of lying beside you and feeling the warm silkiness of your skin against mine.'

I placed the letter on the table carefully, almost as if I might injure it. I would read it again later. Now I needed to cope with the realisation that Harry had not returned from the Asturias, that he could well have 'got involved in an armed skirmish'. I grimaced at Nathan's understatement and shuddered. Three thousand dead was rather more than a skirmish. And the news from Spain had continued to filter through into our newspapers. The cruel repression continued. Franco's Moors and Legionaires occupied the cities of Oviedo and Gijon and inexorably rounded up and shot the miners.

I knew Miss Marie had already begun my application for a passport and visas and that a P&O liner was due at the Outer Harbor in a few days. I would need her magic to get my papers and book a cabin for both of us in time. But we must go. My decision was made. Harry, alive or dead, was somewhere lost in the Asturias and I needed to find him.

Part 5

The Search

OUR ARRANGEMENTS FOR LEAVING Adelaide were so hurried that I had little time to dwell on the miseries of parting. Miss Marie said my clothes were inadequate for the European winter. I must have a new coat. Winnie concealed her unhappiness in the ecstasy of taking me shopping. The price of new wool coats appalled me. 'I'll wear it for only a few short weeks and never again, Winnie,' I protested. 'I can't afford one.' Finally I yielded to her advice to do the rounds of second-hand shops. She took over gleefully and I let her search the racks until she found one that might suit me. It was a little frayed on the cuffs and had a moth hole or two but it was heavy and warm, in fact, so suffocatingly hot on that early November day in Adelaide that I couldn't imagine ever wearing it.

My passport and visas for France and Spain arrived and our bookings on the SS liner *Orsova*. My father rudely called it the Arse Over. It was a sister ship of the *Oronsay* on which Harry had sailed.

I had a last evening meal with my parents. My mother was very quiet but as she bustled around the galley I was comforted to see the return of healthy colour in her face. My father smoked his pipe on deck. The doctor had warned him not to smoke near my mother and while she finished preparing the meal I joined him. Night was settling and the lights from the shore gleamed in the water.

'It's many years since I left Europe, Judith,' he reflected. 'Before you were born. Many years. I've never really wanted to go back. My home's here with your mother and you and my mates at the Port. It's strange to think of you, my daughter, travelling the route I took in a sailing ship. Makes you wonder about time and what it means to any of us. Looking back I can remember years of my life in a few brief minutes, sometimes even seconds. How odd that the time it takes me to recall them is so brief in comparison with the years I took to live them.'

He put his hand on mine. I looked down on it. The sinews and veins were sharp ridges, the skin fallen away between them was dry and pockmarked with liver spots. I curled my fingers so that I clasped his. 'Mum will be waiting,' I said.

'Yes, we'd better go in.' He knocked out his pipe. 'You'll find Harry, you know, Judith.'

'Yes.' I said. 'I'm sure I will.'

My mother wanted me to spend that night on the hulk but I insisted on going home. I knew that it was an effort on her part to let me go and that she wanted to cling to every final moment with me but I needed to be where Harry was.

My father walked me home and I held his hand as I had done as a child although I was no longer fearful of the shadows that loomed over the wharf from the enormous warehouses. He kissed me at the front door and I hugged him.

'See you tomorrow at the wharf, daughter.'

I gulped. 'Yes, Dad, of course. Thank you.'

It was a long time before I fell asleep. Memories of Harry wouldn't leave me. Before going to Spain he had told me excitedly, 'I feel a little like John Reed, going in to Russia at the time of the revolution to write his *Ten Days That Shook the World*. Such an adventure, Jude. Perhaps I, too, might see the birth of a new society.'

Dear Harry, I thought, the incurable romantic, hooked on the fantasy of a glorious new world and always, as I now knew from his letter, always searching. John Reed had died in Russia and that had been the end of his idealism. It wouldn't, I determined, be the end of Harry's. I would find him and he would have his future life to go on dreaming and searching. Strangely, the lines from Robert Browning's poem 'Andrea del Sarto' came in to my head: *Ah, but a man's reach should exceed his grasp or what's a heaven for?* These words, so hauntingly beautiful in their truth, reassured me and I slept.

I believed that we had all faced and overcome the pain of departure until next day when the ship actually pulled away from the wharf at the Outer Harbor. As the faces of my mother and father, Winnie, Jock and Frank receded to miniscule indecipherable blurs, and as the ship turned and they finally disappeared completely, a sense of loss overpowered me. My eyes dimmed with tears. I couldn't see them but the shore was still visible and I clung to the rail straining for a last glimpse of even that.

Our cabin on the *Orsova* was well above the waterline. Miss Marie stated that she had no intention of being buried in the bowels of the ship and we should be comfortable. Harry's cabin, I recalled, had been on a level with the sea and the porthole would have been impossible to open except in very calm weather. He had written with amazement that a flying fish had landed on their cabin floor, flip flapping frantically. He had flung it back into the water. 'I think I would have gone to hell, Jude, if I had destroyed something so beautiful that wanted to fly.'

Shipboard life struck me as an ephemeral artificial world where people I neither knew nor was likely to meet again became my temporary companions. Propinquity demanded conversation; boredom thrust us together in social activity. But despite the superficial friendliness there was no real engagement. We met and parted easily. Passengers who disembarked left without regret or sorrow on our part. We were simply going on and would eventually leave in the same manner.

The days passed slowly and I needed something to do. Marie was always happily occupied. I played the occasional deck quoits and each morning as the weather in the Indian Ocean warmed I swam in the pool. But most of the day I sat in a deck chair, either in the sun or, if it were cool, protected from the wind. The lounges always smelled of cigarette smoke and I preferred to be outside.

To amuse myself I sketched the faces of the people who marched past, zealously taking their exercise in turns about the deck. It was not long before curiosity drove one of them to stop and look over my shoulder. I hesitated in what I was doing, always embarrassed to be watched and now anxious about the possible annoyance of the person I was sketching. But I needn't have worried. My skill spread like wildfire. My peaceful isolation disintegrated and I was besieged by requests for caricatures. I demurred. There was bound to be someone who felt insulted by my take on their face.

However, as usual, Miss Marie smoothed the path. She told them in her charming manner how talented and well-known I was, what a celebrated cartoonist, recognised in Australia and England as well. And, of course, they must tolerate my taste if they wanted a sample of my work.

I reproached her for such exaggeration but she scoffed at me. 'Judith, you are naïve. I think you do not know the world at all. They are quite prepared to risk being insulted by an important artist but they would not stomach an insult from an inferior one. Now you should put a price on these portraits.'

I was horrified and mortified. Was Marie suggesting that I should use my abilities to help pay for our trip? It would be quite fair of her to do so, but I cringed at the thought.

She saw my confusion and guilt and responded quickly. 'No, Judith, of course not. You are taking me the wrong way. But the ship has its own charity. If you ask for a small payment for the Mission to Seamen it may help some poor lone seafarer and it will certainly weed out those who only want a free ride on your skill.'

It turned out to be a happy solution to what was becoming a deluge of requests. It lessened the demands on me and at the same time comforted me with thoughts of my father and his boyhood at sea. I also recalled Ganesh with his mouthful of brilliantly white teeth, the Indian boys skylarking on the bosun's chair and the starving swimmer who stuffed a crust of soggy bread into his mouth. They were all men lonely and adrift in foreign lands and perhaps I could help them a little.

That night I dreamed of the shadows skulking along the wharf. As always they were faceless and nameless figures, drifting out of nothingness and disappearing into nothingness. They weren't threatening figures and they did not frighten me but I always awoke from this dream deeply sad.

Miss Marie had, as usual, been cunning, for while I was occupied in drawing the caricatures I briefly forgot Harry and my worry about him. Her cynicism about the other passengers had shocked me a little but she only gave me her whimsical smile.

'Such innocence, *ma pauvre* Judith. You have survived street battles and you draw such incisive cartoons – and yet,' she shook her head at me in mock regret, 'some people never lose their innocence. I suppose it is because of their expectations.'

Falling into her jocular mood, I replied, 'My cartoons are the dark side of me.'

'The dark side? You have no dark side, Judith.'

'Oh, yes,' I asserted, 'I do. A very dark side. You can see it in my cartoons. Isn't there always a tragic gap between expectation and reality? Maybe I'm not as innocent as you believe.'

She laughed. 'How philosophical you are becoming, *ma chere*.'

'Sometimes. Joe Pulham introduced me to Aristotle and Aristophanes when I was nearly twelve.'

She gave a shout of merriment. 'Aristophanes at twelve? How absurd.'

'Not absurd at all. A very good lesson about the idealist and the comic satirist. The dark and light locked together, perhaps a bit like life.'

She eyed me, gently derisive. 'You're too smart for me today, Judith.'

'Nonsense,' I grinned at her. 'You just don't like to lose an argument.'

'And who says I have? You look much happier already.'

Always she managed to divert my attention from Harry and her sunny optimism brightened the long days and kept me hopeful.

At night I often stood at the stern of the ship and looked at the sea. The screws throbbed louder and more persistently in the darkness. The wake from the ship radiated outwards in great wings of plumed water, touched with green phosphorescence, and above me, undimmed by city lights, the icy stars shed their own cold blue light. As we crossed the equator and entered the northern hemisphere the stars of the Southern Cross slid further down the sky. Each night I strained to see them but eventually they disappeared over the horizon leaving me feeling strangely alienated and bereft.

We passed through Colombo and Bombay and eventually the Suez Canal. I, too, saw the oddity of camels plodding along sand dunes while the desert rose above the level of the water. They had the illusion of a dream where we see but cannot hear and perspective goes askew.

As we passed through the Straits of Gibraltar and entered the Atlantic Ocean the weather grew colder and the winds were biting. We docked at Southampton and it was bitterly cold. I clutched my warm coat about me and felt my feet freeze in my stockings and thin-soled shoes. Our passports and health cards were checked and we were on the train for London.

I looked out of the window at a sunless landscape of skeletal leafless trees with frost whitened branches, hedges and rooftops. Narrow winding roads hedged on either side traversed a gently rolling countryside with an occasional village. Southampton had been a big crowded port but now the countryside emptied. I had expected more houses but found it rural. After the congestion of Colombo, Bombay and Port Said the spaciousness pleased my eye.

Because England looked so small on the map, not even the size of South Australia, I had expected congestion and I was surprised.

The joy of being able to look into the distance rested me. I relaxed in my seat, more at peace than I had been for a month. The ship journey had been a time of waiting. Now action was within our reach and with that knowledge I felt resilient and confident.

We booked into a small hotel in Kensington, a short walk from the gardens. London passed in a whirl of names familiar from my reading but unfamiliar in reality: Trafalgar Square with its statue of Lord Nelson, Piccadilly overhung by the flying figure of Eros, Regent Street, Fleet Street, Westminster and its soaring Gothic cathedral, and the ornate Houses of Parliament fronting the broad dark reaches of the Thames.

As soon as we had landed at Southampton I had grabbed a collection of newspapers and pored over them for news of Spain. There was very little. Only a tiny article in the *Manchester Guardian* reported that the repression in the Asturias had continued with unionists in the strike being searched out and arrested. The Asturias now was an armed state and the populace very frightened. Some of Franco's troops had been withdrawn but enough remained 'to keep order'.

'How long must we stay here, Marie?' I was anxious and urgent, sick with worry.

She did her best to calm me. 'It is necessary to find out as much as we can from here. Perhaps make some necessary contacts. We must not rush off half-cocked. I need to send cables to friends in France to request help with a car and arrange meetings in Paris. Please try to be patient, *ma pauvre*.'

'It's agony, Marie,' I burst out.

'Yes, Judith, I know.'

She took charge bustling me in and out of taxis and the red double-decker buses passed by on the road in a blur. At Marks & Spencer, a huge store, we shopped for fur-lined boots, scarves, gloves and woollen hats.

'Now think, Judith,' she queried, 'what clothes did Harry have with him? What warm clothes?'

I thought of his suitcase lying open on our bed. In Adelaide his clothes had seemed adequate for his trip but now, as the cold stabbed through my heavy coat and a raw wind burnt my nose, I imagined him shuddering in a wintry blast, freezing as well as injured.

'Is Spain as cold as here?'

'No. The cold doesn't cleave you so intensely but there will be snow on the mountains and the wind off the Atlantic, *mon dieu*, it's like a knife. We must think ahead, Judith, of spiriting him out of Spain into France and the long journey back to England. That will be cold.'

'Yes,' I said, 'of course. I hadn't thought as far as that. Only of finding him,' and my voice caught and trembled.

She took my arm and asked a shop assistant for directions to the men's clothing department. I bought Harry a heavy jumper, a flannel shirt and warm socks. For travelling in the car we bought knee rugs.

Marie determined to visit the headquarters of the Communist Party on her own. 'I will be very discreet and not tip them off about Harry. But there may be communists in the Asturias who are safe to contact. These terrible events may have driven them into the arms of the anarchists. Perhaps even united them all. It's worth a shot.'

We parted and I took a taxi to the office of the *Daily Herald*.

'Do not reveal too much, Judith,' Marie warned me. 'When you don't know people well it is better not to trust them. Just say you are going to join Harry in Spain.'

But I had never been a convincing liar. The editor, a tall, spindly, middle-aged man with thinning hair and a long face, peered at me through his spectacles.

'Mrs Grenville?' He was questioning, confused, surprised by my sudden appearance. 'Mrs Judith Grenville?'

'Yes.'

'From Australia?'

'Yes. I think you will know me as Judith Larsen.'

He leapt up, rushed around the table, and grasped my hand. 'Judith Larsen? All the way from Australia? My brilliant cartoonist?'

I flushed, overwhelmed by the warmth of his welcome.

'Sit down Mrs Grenville, Miss Larsen …' He floundered. 'Sit down. Well, I never.'

He shouted for someone called Em and a plump middle-aged woman hurried in.

'Em,' he said, 'Em, this is Judith Larsen from Australia and she never told us she was coming.'

'Em is my secretary. Emily Cruikshank.'

Em smiled at me quietly and shook my hand with composure.

'Tea, Em,' he said, 'and cakes. That shop over the road. They have those nice little things.'

'Strawberry tarts,' she said.

'Yes,' he beamed. 'Now, Mrs Grenville, tell me all. When did you arrive? How long are you staying? Have you any new work to show me?'

I hesitated, painfully uncertain. Marie's warning hung in the air between us. I felt that of necessity I was becoming suspicious of everyone, afraid of making some terrible mistake and endangering Harry, but this was England, not Spain. This man with his open generous manner would surely be no threat. I needed his friendship. I took a chance and plunged into my story.

He listened and his delight turned to concern. 'The Asturias,' he said in an angry repressed tone. 'So that is where those cartoons of yours came from.'

'I didn't know then about my husband. Only later.'

'No, of course not. And what do you want from me?'

The tea and strawberry tarts arrived. He poured me a cup,

allowing me time to think, then he handed me the tarts. 'These are very good. Try one.'

'Have you any up-to-date news?' I asked.

He looked up and pursed his lips. 'Not much. We don't have a reporter there and our sources are pretty much the same as the *Manchester Guardian*'s. Spain is still a sideshow to an English audience.'

I drank my tea while he regarded me thoughtfully. 'You know, Mrs Grenville, your cartoons are excellent.'

'Thank you,' I said. Biding my time I knew what I wanted to ask and only needed to be bold. 'Would it help me or us ...' I started again. 'I have a friend with me,' and at his enquiring look, 'a woman friend. Would it help if I had a press pass?'

He didn't answer for a minute or so and I thought he was assessing me, probably amazed at my presumption. After all, I was not a journalist, and the *Daily Herald* had only published a few of my cartoons. Possibly his praise had been excessive, offered because I was an Australian visiting England, a flattering piece of courtesy.

At last he answered me. 'Mrs Genville ...'

'Judith,' I suggested absently, all my attention concentrated on what he was about to say.

'Judith, then. I would willingly offer you a press pass if I thought it would help you, but I think it may bring danger. Spain is volatile. Like all civil conflicts, brother is against brother, friend against friend. There are bitter divisions between left and right and within the left the factions fight each other like Kilkenny cats. A press pass would tell officials – and anyone else interested – that you plan to report on doings there. And many people have too much to conceal. It would not protect you and I doubt if it would open any doors to you. And dare I say, without insulting you, that you are inexperienced in these matters. Some journalists have spent years in Spain and learned the ropes. In these complex situations you must know how to play your cards. It would be much better if you and your friend went in as lady tourists. A couple of quiet innocent artists enjoying the beauties of Spain.'

He broke off and looked a little whimsical. 'Of course, it would have been more convincing if you were enjoying summer or spring beauties, but the English are known to be eccentric, so you can be two eccentric ladies.'

He warmed to his theme, enlarging on the possibilities of deceiving the Spaniards. Then he stopped abruptly. 'You must think me insensitive, Judith. It sounds almost as if I'm expecting you to have fun.'

I laughed in spite of myself. 'No, of course not. It's very sound advice.'

'Yes,' he said. 'How long are you here?'

'Only a day or two. We must get on.'

He nodded. 'I don't know what the phone service is like in Spain but I'll give you my home, not my office, telephone number. If you are ever in real trouble, please call me and I'll do my very best to get you some help.'

I thanked him and stood up.

'Good luck. Safe travelling – and success, Judith. I hope you find your husband well.'

'And alive,' I said abruptly.

'I won't even think about that, and nor should you. It would be an unbearable burden to carry on your journey.'

I returned to the hotel cheered. It had been a relief to talk to a sympathetic listener and although I supposed that his phone number would not be much use to me it was comforting to tuck the piece of paper into my purse.

Marie arrived back at the hotel in a state of deep gloom. 'I have failed, Judith,' she mourned. 'Failed. And I could kick myself. I made a big mistake. I pretended to the comrades that I was French. Usually it works and opens doors but whether they saw through my deception or simply do not trust the French, they refused to talk with me. They appear to be very cautious, and extra apprehensive about people they don't know. Of course, I understand they are helping communists who are trying to escape Germany and this makes them more paranoid than usual. I suppose I could have been some sort of German spy. It would have been better if I had confessed honestly to being an Aussie from Down Under.'

She sighed dispiritedly. 'But at all costs I wanted to avoid any connection with Nathan and any reference to Harry which they might use against him in Spain for turning to the anarchists. This labyrinth of suspicion is very disheartening, Judith.'

It was my turn to console her. On the following day we caught the ferry from Dover to Calais.

We left Dover in a misty rain. The famous white limestone cliffs rose pallidly out of the sea and slowly disappeared into a grey blur. The wind left a film of dampness on our coats and hats. The ferry lounges were a blue fuzz of cigarette smoke and smelled of stale beer.

It was still raining when we docked in the crowded harbour of Calais. Suddenly all the notices were in French: loud hailer announcements, port directions, customs queries. I produced my sketchbook and pens as evidence of my work and intentions. Marie did the same. At my English and few halting French phrases the customs officer frowned superciliously but at Marie's effortless French and melting eyes he beamed and waved us through.

We needed no porters because most of our heavy clothes were on our backs and our cases were light. The train station was a hubbub of noise, frantic with travellers all rushing about in a frenzied search for their seats on the Paris train.

Dragging our cases behind us we climbed two steep steps into our carriage and negotiated our way along the corridor to our compartment Two elderly men rose, doffed their hats, and helped us push our cases onto the overhead racks. Our seats faced the engine, one by the window. But there was not much to see. The rain was heavier. Lights gleamed in the wet surface of the platform, now roofed by dozens of umbrellas.

We pulled out slowly, the wheels grinding and grumbling, smoke from the engine mingling and clouding with the rain. I gazed at a flat grey wet countryside. So this was France. Despite my continued anxiety about Harry, a small part of me had anticipated feeling some excitement at actually stepping foot in Europe. England had seemed only a comfortable extension of Australia, a corroboration of things I already knew, but I had expected something different from France. What, I wasn't sure.

Beside me, Marie hummed happily under her breath, and occasionally tried to peer out the window. Piercing the gloom outside was impossible and she relaxed back into her seat with a sigh of regret. I felt her joy at returning to a place she had known and loved but to me it had neither the pleasure of recapturing something once known nor the exhilaration of experiencing something new and promising. It was simply wet and grey and flat. The train smelt old and dusty and the smell of sour urine from the toilet wafted along the corridor into our compartment.

I tried to sleep. Paris was some hours away. Maybe I was tired. Maybe it was impossible to sustain feelings not related to my fears about Harry. I dozed, stirring only when the train jolted to a stop at platforms with unfamiliar French names. There was the same anxious rush to find seats. It still rained. Marie slept beside me.

When we entered the outskirts of Paris Marie awoke and looked eagerly out the window searching the darkness for something familiar. Now as the train pulled in she was excited.

'The Gare du Nord, Judith. Paris. I can hardly believe that I am back. Dear, shabby, glorious, dirty Paris. In all the world there is no city like it.' In a flood of French she spoke to the two middle-aged men with whom she had exchanged a few words during the journey. They smiled on her benignly and lifted our luggage down. Once again they doffed their hats and stood aside to let us precede them.

The corridor was packed with people jostling each other eager to leave. Why, I wondered, did travellers display such a sense of urgent importance? I had noticed it in South Australia, even on our local trains. Their actions said we must get on at once, or we must leave at once.

There were taxis outside the station. Marie negotiated our fare, gave instructions and bundled me inside. I was relieved she had not hired a car for Paris. The traffic was far worse than Diamond Corner at home at the Port. With Rafferty's rules, cars shot out from all directions, and cut in on each other to sweep around corners. People leapt into the traffic in foolhardy attempts to cross the huge squares, dodging vehicles as they ignored the cacophony of squealing horns.

For a confused moment I panicked as our taxi swung into the right lane. I clutched the seat.

'It's all right, Judith. Don't fear. We are in France. It is all correct.'

And of course now I recalled that the French drove on the right-hand side of the road.

Awestruck by this commotion in which amazingly no one was killed, I asked anxiously, 'How will you manage to drive, Marie?'

She patted my hand. 'Courage my country mouse.'

I smiled at her ruefully. 'You mean colonial country mouse.'

She grinned and with her beret pulled over her brow and her coat collar turned up about her gamin face she looked more French than Australian.

Our hotel was a skinny three-storey pension jammed in a row of similar grey-stone buildings. A creaking lift took us to the top floor. Our room had a washbasin, a small balcony overlooking the street, and two single beds. There was a tiny wardrobe and a small table. It was so cramped that we needed to squeeze ourselves around every piece of furniture. One of our cases sat on the table but I looked about helplessly searching for some place to put the other. Eventually I slung it on the bed.

Marie watched me with amusement. 'Space here is not like space in Australia, *ma chere*.'

The noise of the city – a continuous drone, so like the roar of the sea at night – accompanied my sleep, but the clamour, clatter and clang of morning activities woke us early.

The hotel didn't provide breakfast so we dressed and walked down the street to a small cafe where we ate croissants and drank coffee. The rain had stopped but the slimy cobblestones gleamed treacherously and we had negotiated our way with slithering caution.

Over breakfast we discussed plans for the day. Marie said that she would try again, this time at the French communist head-quarters. This time her French would not be a handicap but an advantage, for the French always warmed to those who spoke their language. 'They must have met Nathan and Harry when they passed through France,' she said. 'It would be unusual to find an Australian communist in France. Hopefully they will remember Harry as a communist and will have heard nothing more of them after they left here. I don't want to alert them to what has happened. I doubt if they'd be sympathetic. But maybe I can worm a little information out of them that might help us.'

'I should come with you.' I was eager. 'Perhaps they might recall Harry and speak to me of him. There would be some comfort in their recollections.'

She hesitated. I could see that her pity for me warred with her doubts.

'Perhaps not, Judith. If you can bear it, I should go alone. It might be hard for you not to show your worries and our real intentions. The truth might emerge and, my dear, we can't even be sure that among the communists there are not fascist spies with links to Spain. In Australia I have laughed about the paranoia of the comrades but, believe me, in Europe these days there is reality in their fears. Here persecution ends in death or a concentration camp. For protection they have learned to squirrel information away. I do not want to betray us.'

I was disappointed but determined not to show it. 'No, of course, you are wise.'

'Perhaps you could fill in time with a visit to the Louvre. It might take your mind off things.'

I doubted whether I was in a mood for an art gallery, however great, but it was kinder to reassure her and pretend some enthusiasm.

As we walked back to our hotel we stopped briefly and leaned on a parapet overlooking the Seine. A girl sat on the parapet swinging her red-stockinged legs against the wall. They dangled there like a shock of scarlet creepers. She wore a red coat and hat and was alone. Beside the water a couple wandered arm in arm along the concrete walkway below us. Two little boys floated tiny boats of walnut shells in a shiny puddle. They were intent, immersed in their game just as I had seen children at home. I thought of the children Harry and I might have. It would be good to watch them play like this and talk about them growing up. I needed to believe that Harry and I had a future and that Marie and I were not too late.

We returned to the hotel and collected what we needed for the day. I looked rather doubtfully at my French money and Marie explained the value of the coins. Then she called two taxis and we parted.

The Louvre was a huge labyrinth of art galleries with arched ceilings. I was in no mood for concentrated and planned discovery and just wandered. At another time I might have revelled in the glories of the past but not today.

It was the 2000-year-old Winged Victory of Samothrace that arrested me. It stood at the end of a long gallery at the top of a flight of stairs and it dominated by its power and size. The goddess Nike stood on the prow of a ship. She thrust into the wind, her billowing carved draperies sucked between her legs and taut over her breasts and belly. The enormous pinions of her wings were bared for flight and the illusion of the sea rippled along the sculptured flying draperies. It was a woman's figure, powerful but headless. She could be any victory or a particular one. It didn't matter. Anonymity suited her. She was Nike, a symbol of triumph.

I stood in front of it and wept.

Victory was an illusion, a tale told by an idiot to lead stupid children to dusty death. None of us was fit or ready to cope with the evils of the world. How dare some artist centuries ago sculpt such an image of soaring inspiring beauty when its message was a lie. Artists should be truthful, not inveigle us into fantasies that would destroy us.

Before leaving London I had had a brief visit to the Kensington Gardens to see the statue of Peter Pan. It was a small work and whimsical. A pigeon had perched on his head as if he owned this fairytale character. Even James Barrie had depicted Peter as noble in death. To die, Peter had said, would be a big adventure. How glib from a boy who knew nothing about adulthood, nothing about the pain of love and the fear of separation. Another deception.

Only Wilfred Owen, whose poems about war had shocked so many people by their harsh realism, had written bitterly of the uselessness of noble death, the emptiness of victory. He had mourned the death of a young soldier in his words 'Was it for this the clay grew tall?'

Artists should be truthful, not wrap us in impossible dreams.

So I stood with tears streaming down my face. I saw myself as another Winnie, and didn't care. Let whoever passed think whatever they liked. My sorrow and fear were my business. I couldn't bear to look at any more lies and left the gallery to sit outside on a bench. It was cold and the cold matched my desolate mood.

I returned to the hotel by taxi, having had the forethought to make a note of our address. Marie came in shortly afterwards. She looked tired.

She washed her face and hands in the basin and perched on the bed. I was resting with my feet up.

'I've had a mixed day, Judith. First of all the arrangements for the car are OK. It'll be delivered here tomorrow morning and we can set out.'

'And the comrades?' I asked. 'Could they help you?'

'No. They were vague. Deliberately so, I thought. They avoided answering me. Yes, they had met Nathan and Harry but after that they shrugged as only Frenchmen can. What is it to do with us? their expressions told me. I felt very dispirited.'

She sighed. 'But there was no use pressing them when they had determined not to talk. I left them, at first unaware that one had followed me. He passed me casually on the stairs as if he were hurrying home. But his eyes met mine and I sensed they invited me to follow him.'

She giggled. 'I felt a bit like someone in a spy thriller. He walked to the river and stopped, leaning on the parapet as we did this morning. I did the same a short distance away and he spoke quietly but without looking at me. It was an odd sensation to stand near someone who talked to the river when his words were for me. He remembered Harry, a happy young man, and Nathan very earnest. A good Party member. They had taken the train. Madrid was their destination.

'Of course, Judith, I knew all this, but I didn't hurry him. I hoped there was more to come. He went on. He had heard later, on the grapevine, you know, that the two Australians had parted company in Madrid. There had been harsh words between them and the young bright one had stormed out. Shortly afterwards the other had left Spain. Everyone in the Party was talking about it.

'Why would a young Australian remain in Spain after his comrade had left? It seemed suspicious. Then it was discovered that he had gone into the Asturias to Oviedo. Now the comrades were really concerned. What if this young Australian were a spy, reporting on Communist Party business to the anarchists? Everyone was worried. He had seemed such a nice chap. So friendly. Everyone had liked him. Was this his disguise?

'I asked him what happened after Oviedo, Judith, because that was the news we wanted, and he hesitated. "I'm not sure," he said. But he knew Harry was staying with one of the anarchists in a small village in the foothills. The Party kept track of him for some time. Then he mentioned the October 4 massacre. As you can imagine, Judith, I held my breath. I was cautious. I didn't want to frighten him. I asked him if there were reports of an Australian being shot. "I don't know," he said again. "But a couple of weeks later we heard there was an Austrian in one of the villages. Sometimes our comrades are uneducated and we deduced that it wasn't an Austrian but an Australian".

'He said that was all he could tell me. It is not much but it was something. We do know that Harry was alive a couple of weeks after the massacre. It is a soupçon of hope.'

'Yes,' I said. 'It is the first piece of news we've had and it is a lot better than nothing. Thank you, Marie.'

It was amazing how that minuscule piece of news that Harry had not died in the massacre revived my hope. And with hope my spirits rose. Somehow it seemed that Marie's good luck in meeting the one man who was prepared to help augured well for our search.

We would find Harry and we would find him alive. I cast off my despair.

But she still looked tired. I realised guiltily how difficult this was for her, what a burden she had taken upon herself for me and for Harry. She had made a lot of her happiness in returning to Paris but there were shadows under her eyes and worry lines on her forehead. I was aware that I had been driven by an urgency as if I were constantly setting my watch by what she did. I had begun to take her good-heartedness, her generosity, and her courage for granted.

'I'm sorry, Marie,' I burst out, 'so terribly, terribly sorry.' I felt like weeping again as I had in the Louvre but controlled myself. I had leaned on her enough. She didn't need an hysterical woman in addition to all the practical issues she was coping with. 'I'm sorry,' I repeated.

She looked at me surprised. 'Whatever for, *ma pauvre*? None of this is your fault. We must do what we must do. It's as simple as that.' And I wondered why in the past I had ever thought that Marie's behaviour was more play-acting than reality.

She spread a map on the bed. 'We will take the road down the Loire Valley to Tours and then head towards the coast through Poitiers and Bordeaux. That way we avoid the Pyrenees in winter. Our Citroën is old and I would not risk the steep climb over the pass. There is the danger of being snowed in for days. The road through the Loire Valley is flat and the coastal plain will be more temperate. The road around the coast will wind and may be slow but I do not have so much fear of the weather there. From Biarritz it is only a short drive to the frontier. And then Spain, Judith.'

'Yes,' I said. 'Spain.' And my heart skipped a beat. 'How many days do you estimate?' I knew I shouldn't press her but anxiety drove me.

'I cannot say. It's rural. I don't know the condition of the roads and we may be slowed by flocks of animals or slow-moving carts and horses.'

Next morning a young man delivered the dark-blue roomy Citroën. He grinned at Marie and ogled her. She was amused when he told her in halting English that she 'pleased' him. 'So hard to reject such an enticing invitation,' she chuckled, 'but he was rather too young and green for me.'

I laughed with her and wondered what lovers Marie had had in France. She was no longer young and her charm often eclipsed her face. I surprised myself by seeing her as if for the first time as a beautiful woman. Her brown hair was lustrous and curled about her cheeks and brow. Her eyes were long and deep and of that extraordinary blue which is almost black. Her generous mouth drooped a little at the corners, so that in repose her rather long face reminded me of a Modigliani Madonna, but when she smiled the sadness of her face vanished and the sudden metamorphosis to a charming gaiety surprised and captivated.

She drove carefully, skilfully negotiating the morning traffic and then we were on the highway heading south along the Loire River.

'You'll see many chateaux along the way, Judith. The Loire was the holiday resort for aristocrats before the revolution. Now they're retained for their heritage and tourist potential. If we had the time we could explore. You'd be bowled over by the luxury.'

The fields around us were barren and cold with an occasional stand of skeletal trees, leafless and bare-armed against the sky. There were no fences and this feel of unoccupied land increased the sense of desolation. I had never before seen a landscape that slept through winter. Marie said that I'd be surprised to see it in summer with the crops of grain, the grape vines heavy with fruit, the peaches, melons and strawberries. It was hard to believe her as I looked at the acres of gnarled writhing, leafless vines.

Marie couldn't drive for hours at a stretch without rest and I struggled not to urge her on when I knew she was exhausted. So although I fretted I concealed it from her with a reasonably placid exterior. I don't think she was deceived but tactfully she said nothing.

We bought some bread and cheese at a local market and ate our lunch in the car. Marie said she felt revived and we continued. At times the road ran side by side with the river and where we met a village the road squeezed between homes and water. Sometimes we needed to slow down for people who stepped out of their front doors directly onto the road. There were no front gardens or pavements. At other times mobs of sheep, or goats, or horse- or oxen-drawn vehicles lumbered ahead of us blocking our way. The slowness frustrated me but Marie remained calm.

As night approached we stopped at a small village and found a room over a cafe. Marie lay down to rest and I wandered out onto the street and strolled along it in the dusk. There was a small church I discovered. Inside it was very dim and cold from the stone walls and floor with a faint smell of wax from candles burning at the altar. My footsteps sounded hollow and echoed slightly.

I approached the altar and looked up at a painting of the cruci-fied Christ. The candles lit the bottom reaches of the work but the rest remained shadowed as if the painter had intended the face to be lost in the dimness. But even in that light I recognised its rich beauty. It was not the work of an amateur. Over the years I had visited the Adelaide art gallery to glean what I could of painting and drawing skills. This painting had composition and skilful brush strokes. How strange to find such a thing of beauty in this poor village church.

Out the back I could hear the comforting domestic sounds of crockery clattering and I smelt the aroma of cooking meat. A priest appeared, flitting towards me like a comfortable bat in his long black robes. He spoke in French but I didn't understand.

'I'm Australian,' I said, 'just visiting.'

'Austria?'

'No. Australia.'

He looked puzzled.

'I don't speak French. Only English.'

'Good evening,' he said carefully and stopped. This was the

extent of his English. He hesitated and smiled benignly on me. '*Joyeux Noel*,' he said before drifting away. I had forgotten that it would soon be Christmas.

I sat for a few minutes. I did not believe in the God that was supposed to inhabit this church but it was tranquil and I appreciated that it was a place of refuge for many who, like me, wondered if life might get too difficult for them.

It was good to be peaceful and pretend, if only briefly, that the affairs of humans, and that included their politics, were ephemeral matters we could discard for higher things. I don't think I would have had these thoughts in a great cathedral. It was the comfortable domesticity of this little church that prompted them.

Marie found me and sat quietly beside me. She, too, studied the painting. '*Mon Dieu*, Judith,' she said, 'I do believe it is a Rubens.' She glanced about. 'What a country this is. A Rubens here. Now you must come and eat.'

The villages we passed through were all the same with flat-faced, two-storey, steep-roofed cottages with dormer windows. Marie constantly worried about finding petrol and whenever we stopped at a garage to fill up she anxiously asked how far it would be to the next one.

After Tours we left the Loire Valley and headed south to Poitieres and Bordeaux, a city with wider streets but narrow cobbled lanes between stone buildings. In the distance the conical towers of chateaux reminded me of inverted ice-cream cones. The cathedrals we caught glimpses of took my breath away. I had never before seen the lace work of Gothic decoration, such gargoyles and flying buttresses, but there was no time to linger.

Three days and we reached Biarritz and the Atlantic coastline. My first sight of the sea breathed the familiarity of home. The towering lighthouse reminded me nostalgically of the lighthouse at Port Adelaide.

'We're coming into the country of the Basque people,' Marie said as she negotiated a narrow winding street. 'The Basques are a separate national group and their territory actually straddles France and Spain. They are proudly independent and consider themselves neither French nor Spanish. The people of the Asturias also consider themselves separate and independent and they, too, are reluctant to accept the dominant control of the Madrid government. It is one of the problems of the Asturias.'

'Ah,' I said. 'Hence their anarchist ideas. No central government, just workers' committees to run the place themselves.'

'Such a dream, Judith. But, *mon Dieu*, they are unlucky, because the Asturias are rich. Mines, you know: coal and gold. Lots of people want a piece of the Asturias. There's money there.'

'Isn't it always the way? I suppose that if they were poor they'd be left alone to live in happy poverty and no one would give a damn whether they had workers' committees or not. But whatever dreams Harry might have had I doubt whether their home-grown anarchist ideas would suit Port Adelaide. They certainly wouldn't suit the ship owners.'

She grimaced. 'Money makes the world go round, ma pauvre.'

'And my husband had to get himself mixed up in someone else's political struggles.'

We savoured our shared cynical feelings in silence.

Once again she was intent on the road, which wound around the steep cliffs. Below us, beneath jagged outcrops, lay the Bay of Biscay. Inland we could see the saw-teeth snow peaks of the Pyrenees that at times floated ethereally above the clouds. On the slopes of the foothills grew pine trees and since they weren't deciduous the countryside looked greener, less dismally cold.

The wind that swept in from the Atlantic threatened to sweep us off our feet when we paused for a rest. I hugged my coat around me but gratefully breathed the sour smell of salt. We stopped at St Jean Pied de Port only a few miles from the Spanish border. 'We must eat,' Marie said. 'I don't think that we'll have any difficulties at the border but just in case we are held up, better to eat now.'

Anxious excitement tightened my stomach. I knew that crossing the border would not solve the problems we faced in finding Harry but Spain meant I was nearer to him and all that I hoped for. We were approaching that time when we would know what we could or could not do.

I had dodged thinking of the possibility that during the weeks we had travelled Harry might have left Spain and was now journeying home. If this were the case, who would tell me? Would I take the long journey back to Australia tormented by a lack of news of him, suffering again the agony of doubt, always wondering, always conjecturing? I had never confided my fears to Marie that the whole trip might be futile but I supposed she, too, had known this; even perhaps feared it.

St Jean Pied de Port was a pretty little town with wooden fishermen's cottages and a small cafe on a narrow cobbled street that wound down to a protected cove. Marie ordered minced veal with spicy peppers, rice and potatoes. 'Basque food, Judith,' she said with satisfaction. 'Enjoy it. Harry won't be helped by you not eating. Crossing the frontier is only another step on the road. It is not something to fear. No one will interfere with us.'

'No,' I said, more to reassure her than myself. 'Of course not.' I spoke a little shakily, ashamed to admit that each difficulty we came to filled me with a fear that we would fail to hurdle it, that at this point something would happen to baulk us. I even dreamed at night those vague frustrating nightmares when I struggled helplessly to do or find something that was nameless but terribly important.

Marie ate calmly, savouring every mouthful. 'I haven't had such delicious food for many years. I had forgotten, it's so long since I was here.'

'You? Here?' Amazed, I stared at her.

'Oh, yes, in some by-gone era.'

'You never told me.'

'Didn't I? I suppose I thought you knew.' She laughed. 'It was oh so long ago.'

'So long? And now you're an ancient woman, Marie.'

She chuckled.

But the discovery that none of this was new to her reassured me and I tucked into my veal mince. With full stomachs we walked back to the car.

At the border two French guards looked plump and bored. One leaned negligently against the side of the hut which was the frontier post. Marie pulled up and he drifted over to our car. She wound down her window and smiled. His spirits visibly lifted at the sight of a pretty woman. Later Marie commented with amusement, 'He probably gets sick of peasants and animals and fishermen. I was a nice change.'

He checked our passports cursorily, glanced in the back seat, noted our artists' easels, and burst into a flood of French conversation with Marie. I heard the word *Anglais* several times and gathered by his surprised expression that Marie had delighted him; an Englishwoman answering in fluent French.

A fisherman in oilskins, carrying rods and a basket, came through from Spain. Without more than a glance the guard waved him through.

'He has a girl on the French side,' he smirked and winked knowingly at Marie. 'Says they are prettier in France.'

He was in no hurry to let us go and lounged by the car, one hand resting on the door. Eventually he sighed, stood back, and waved us on, all the while urging us to return and spend an evening with him. Spain was no place for pretty women. But he had eyes only for Marie.

The Spanish officials were less friendly. They had guns slung across their backs, wore heavy leather boots and patent leather caps. Their faces were dark and saturnine. One, unsmilingly, inspected our passports with diligent attention.

'English?' he questioned.

'Yes.' Marie's Spanish was fair but she didn't try to explain that we were Australian.

'Here? Now? Visiting?' He looked surprised.

'Yes.' She produced her engaging smile. 'We're artists. Painters.'

'But this is winter.'

She looked mournful, full of regret. 'Yes, I know. They told me Spain was sunny even in winter and very beautiful.'

He was slightly mollified to have his country praised.

'Besides,' now she was confiding, 'when I was young I visited here and I never forgot. You know how it is when one is young.' She even managed to blush on target. 'He'll be as old as I am now. An old man.' And she flirted her eyes at him.

He allowed himself a small smile and again checked our passports slowly and thoughtfully, looking from the photos to our faces. He turned over our belongings on the back seat, paused at our cases, his hand hovering, but he didn't open them. He stepped back and waved us through.

Marie's shaking hands clutched the steering wheel and she trembled as she translated what had passed. 'I was afraid, Judith,' she gasped, 'that he'd open our cases and see the men's clothes for Harry. I tried to think up a lie to cover that and my mind went quite blank.'

'Marie,' I said fervently, 'you constantly amaze me. I am filled with admiration. And all this for me and Harry. How can I ever repay you?'

She grinned at me. 'Just once in a while, Judith, I am scared, but mostly I am having fun. This is the greatest adventure of my life.'

I looked at her disbelievingly. 'I understood that your youth was full of adventure. Full of hairy escapes.'

'Ah, yes, certainly. Those hairy careless years. But this one, Judith, is the great adventure of my mature years. It has purpose. The only adventures that are worthwhile have purpose. Then they are never forgotten.'

I smiled at her lovingly and a little tremulously and then I looked out the window so that she wouldn't see the tears in my eyes. Surely in the whole world no woman ever had a friend as courageous and loyal as Marie.

The Spanish Atlantic coast was, of course, the same as the French one. The road wound narrowly around steep cliffs. Sometimes I feared to look down as the drop turned waves into mere lines of frothy ripples about jagged rocks. Marie chatted easily, driving skilfully, honking the horn on bends. Sometimes we trailed a cart drawn by horses or oxen, waiting for a slight widening in the road to squeeze past. Occasionally a rider on a mule or an overloaded doleful little donkey drew to the side and gazed at us curiously as we went by.

'I'm guessing – because again the road's unknown – but I'm estimating that it should take us only a couple of days to reach Gijon and Oviedo and from there we can begin our search.'

Eventually the road left the coast and we headed inland towards Bilbao to find accommodation for the night. A set of craggy lime-stone peaks made jagged lines in the sky as if some giant had incised the rocks with a huge knife.

'The Picos de Europa,' Marie said.

I stared at them wonderingly as, never out of our vision, their dominance followed us along the road.

We drove through Bilbao, an ugly industrial town, and found a small hotel on the outskirts. The proprietor was curious about our destination but when we said Oviedo he shook his head.

'Don't go there, ladies,' he warned. 'It is not a nice place. Franco's dirty soldiers from Africa have taken over. They prowl the streets like packs of wolves.' He spat into a bronze spittoon. 'Women are not safe and men they shoot. Even children they shoot.' He spat again. 'The navy shelled Gijon and planes dropped bombs on Oviedo. I believe the cathedral is destroyed. A heap of rubble. What barbarians destroy the house of God? No respect for our holy church. The dirty Moors. Let them come here. We Basques know how to deal with dirty Moors. Don't go there, ladies.'

We collected our bags from the car, put them in our room, and walked out to find a cafe for our evening meal. We were subdued and silent. We had read of the atrocities in the Asturias but now they were much closer, more personally threatening. We were both, I think, worrying about Harry and apprehensive about the dirty Moors who roamed the streets like packs of wolves.

'Maybe not Oviedo,' Marie said. 'Maybe somewhere smaller and quieter.'

The next morning we left Bilbao very early. We soon met the coast road, strung with numerous small towns and villages that either clung limpet-like to the cliff face or nestled in sheltered inlets with groves of pine trees behind them. The sun shone and occasionally there was the curving dazzle of a yellow sandy beach. We crossed bridges; some were stone structures with supporting arches slimed with the green damp of ages.

Sometimes the road swung inland and the folds of the countryside looked green and lush. Later that afternoon we reached Llanes, a busy fishing port with terracotta-roofed stone houses.

'It's still early,' Marie said, 'but if you don't mind I think we'll stop here for the night and make some inquiries about where we might stay close to Oviedo. There is a large town La Felguera a short distance from Oviedo but it is industrial and may have suffered as much from Franco's Moors.

'On the other hand we should plan to be close enough to the village Harry mentioned in his letter. What was it, Judith?'

'Sama, I think, or Sami. I memorised it because I was afraid to carry his letter. His friend is Garcia.'

Marie snorted, 'That may not be much help. I have a feeling that Garcia is probably a name as ubiquitous in Spain as Mary is in Ireland.'

'He also had the nickname 'Little Lorca'. Harry said he aspired to be a poet.'

'That might narrow it down a bit.'

My spirits sank. Once again our task seemed dauntingly impossible: such a huge place; so many cities where people slid into anonymity; so many dispersed villages where it was likely that outside their small world little was known. And then there were the mountains and their inaccessible villages where there would be no roads for a Citroën; only tracks for mules or donkeys.

Marie glanced at me and read my thoughts. 'Have you ever ridden a mule, *ma chere*?'

'*Non*, Marie.'

'An experience, Judith.'

'*Oui*, Marie. But it will be very slow. How many miles an hour does a mule do?'

She began to laugh. 'Depends, I suppose, on whether it's a farmer's Deux Cheveaux or a Peugeot mule.'

Her laughter was infectious and if there was a little hysteria in our joking there was also relief in our merriment at the ridiculous.

Marie appealed to the proprietor of the hotel in Llanes for advice. As always, I marvelled at her ability to charm and deceive. We were English ladies on holiday, requiring help, preferably from a man wise enough to give the right advice to naïve English gentlewomen who dabbled in the arts.

Time and again I had seen some man puff out his chest and succumb to the melting helplessness of Marie. That she was no longer young seemed only to increase her charm. With none of these enticements and little capacity to play a part, I kept in the background, and although I was always treated courteously men did not usually show the same desire to protect me.

The beaming proprietor fondled his small moustache and passed a hand over his thinning hair. He suggested the small town of Sotrondio. A village would be impossible for us, he said. We wouldn't find a suitable hotel and there would be no petrol for the car. And we should not venture into the mountains. The roads were bad and there were bears.

Marie squeaked in English, 'Bears! My goodness!' and then in Spanish, 'I don't want to meet a bear.' She turned to me as if needing confirmation of her terror of bears and her eyes twinkled. 'We don't want to meet any bears, do we?'

I shuddered. 'No, Marie, no bears.'

She turned back to the proprietor. The twinkle disappeared and her eyes were now fearful. 'Will there be bears in Sotrondio?'

'No, no,' he assured her indulgently. 'You ladies will be quite safe from bears there. But do not go out in the street at night. There are wolves.'

'Wolves?' Marie squealed again.

'Yes, two legged wolves.' He hesitated, then added, 'There has been trouble in Oviedo and Gijon. It needn't concern you. English ladies will be respected. But stay inside at night.'

We retired to our room to rest. 'Should we ask him about Sama?' I heard the note of urgency in my voice but knew that there was nothing we could ask him except where was Harry.

'No, Judith.' She looked at me earnestly. 'Not yet. We mustn't rush in asking questions that might arouse suspicion. I know the waiting is agony now we seem so close. But we need to go slowly. People need to get used to us being about. We need to convince them that we are harmless, even perhaps a little silly, enthusiastic holiday-makers. Enquiries must come gradually and seem inno-cent curiosity.'

Of course she was right. To come all this way and mess it up by being impatient would be downright stupid.

We found a cafe for our evening meal and ordered the local

dish of beans and sausage. It was heavy and neither of us liked it much.

'What do you think, Judith? Should we make Sotrondio our base? I think there is a cluster of villages quite near there. One of them could be Sama.'

I considered. 'Well, I suppose villages invite sketching. We could be seen as seeking local colour.'

She nodded. 'And if people are curious about us, then all the better. If we are a novelty we'll be discussed.'

'Maybe,' I was eager, 'maybe Harry might hear about us and try to contact us.'

She nodded again. 'There are many possibilities. Little by little we'll explore them.'

After Llanes we followed the coast road before turning inland to Oviedo, La Felguera and Sotrondio. Fortunately it was not the road to the port city of Gijon, which had been shelled from the sea and bombed from the air and where we might expect to meet soldiers.

However, our comfortable assurance was shattered as Marie, negotiating a web of roads on the outskirts of Oviedo, drew up abruptly. In front of us was a military checkpoint. Several dark-skinned soldiers with rifles waved us down. We both took a deep breath and waited. I placed my hand over Marie's and squeezed it. 'It'll be OK,' I whispered. 'We are English ladies.'

'Innocent English ladies,' she whispered back.

We wound down our windows. Two soldiers, more harsh-looking than the border guard, strolled to our car. They rested their hands on the car doors. With one on either side we felt uncomfortably hemmed in. They leaned in the windows and ran their eyes over us. Their bodies smelt heavy and their breath stale.

I gritted my teeth and smiled through them. Marie managed to appear confused and puzzled.

'*Pasaportes*,' one rasped. We searched our bags and produced them unhurriedly. Instinct told me that speed or anxiety would be dangerous.

We waited patiently while the soldier at my door assessed them, however he was more interested in running his eyes over me. I longed to smack his smirking face. I wondered what we'd do if they ordered us out of the car. Here were two-legged wolves without a doubt.

He handed my passport to his henchman and managed, reaching across us, to touch our breasts. I stiffened. The soldier on Marie's side handed our passports back again. 'Going far?' he asked. 'To Oviedo?'

'No,' Marie appeared relaxed. 'Somewhere further on. We'll look for a hotel when we're tired. We're artists, painters. Oviedo!' She shrugged. 'We don't like big cities. And I believe there has been trouble there.'

He preened himself. 'You'd be safe in Oviedo now. We've cleaned up the troublemakers. English ladies needn't be afraid.' He leered.

Marie smiled at him. I don't know how she managed it. 'But for artists the countryside has most appeal. I don't suppose we'll find troublemakers there. And we'll be quite safe.'

He shrugged and the two of them stepped back from the car.

Marie revved the engine and miraculously, because she shook so much, didn't stall it. Then the soldiers were behind us. In the rear mirror I could see them watching us.

'Don't look back, Judith.'

'My God, Marie,' I gasped. 'That was close. Did you ever see such an evil-looking bastard? If they are the wolves that hunt at night, heaven help the women of Oviedo.'

We reached the small town of Sotrondio late that afternoon. Oviedo was behind us and the cluster of villages that might hide Harry was close. My spirits rose.

Our hotel was a pleasant two-storey grey-stone building. Our room on the second floor was tiny. I slept fitfully that night. There were so many unknowns in my life that I couldn't relax or find peace. It was dawn before I dozed off, so the next morning I was heavy-eyed.

'No sleep, Judith?'

'Very little.'

'Some fresh air will buck you up. It's a beautiful morning and we'll permit ourselves to enjoy the sun.'

We made a point of carrying our easels downstairs so the proprietor would notice them. He looked up from his bookwork. 'Painting, ladies?'

'Perhaps.' Marie beamed at him. 'We may or we may just look at the beautiful scenery. And the road inland, how is it?'

'Quite good. A bit rough in places. But don't go up into the hills. There are bears.' It was a relief that he could speak English.

It seemed everywhere we went someone warned us about bears but was silent about the soldiers.

After breakfast we decided to look for Sama in the nearby cluster of villages. The countryside was a series of gently rolling foothills. In the distance trees forested the higher slopes. The car hummed along happily. We passed through a couple of villages that straddled the road and finding a siding parked the car and set up our easels and artists' stools.

It was a windless morning and warm in the sun and for a time I just sat and gazed at the distant crags rising above the trees. There were probably dozens of villages tucked away in sheltered gullies and valleys or clinging to the walls of gorges; mining villages and rural villages, perhaps shepherds' huts.

'Marie, do you think Harry might be hidden there?'

She looked up. 'Begin to draw,' she said. 'Some villagers are curious.'

A group of women stood a little way apart watching us. They huddled together like a small school of fish seeking safety in their numbers, protecting their circumference and all within it. After observing us for a few minutes they drifted back into their houses. Marie's eyes followed them thoughtfully.

'We'll come here again, Judith. We should cultivate their interest. Women know things. And now we must work. Word will get around if we behave oddly.'

For the next three days we drove to the siding and set up our gear. The women came each day at about the same time. They were a motley group, some old, some young, some bare-headed, others wearing scarves. They were dressed in winter skirts and home-knitted sheep-wool jumpers.

Each day they drew a little closer. On the third morning they showed more confidence. '*Inglés?*' one asked tentatively. '*Artista?*' She was middle-aged with a scarf over her head. Marie smiled at them companionably. '*Australiano*,' she corrected. They looked puzzled. '*Inglés?*' the woman repeated. 'Yes,' Marie said, giving up the battle to explain our Australian-ness. 'We are artists.'

At her Spanish they looked relieved. 'The English, they are good. A good people.'

Marie returned the compliment. 'Spaniards are good people also.'

Their faces closed. 'Not here,' one said, and then, as if having said too much, she stopped abruptly.

Marie looked innocent and inquiring, but they were afraid and started to leave. She plunged in, and later told me that she felt panic stricken that she would lose the opportunity to question them.

'I came here when I was young,' she rushed in. 'There was such a lovely young man.' She sighed romantically.

One or two in the group smiled. 'The young are like that,' one murmured. 'Always lovely young men.'

Marie appeared to be searching her memory. 'I think his name was Garcia.'

'Ah, Garcia.' One laughed.

The hope on Marie's face was not feigned and my heart flopped around in my chest.

'So many Garcias,' another said, 'and all romantic. Imelda, here, she knew a Garcia.' She poked her. 'Eh, Imelda?'

Imelda looked resigned, presumably at the fickleness of all men.

'And did he write poetry to you?' Marie asked. 'Beautiful poetry, like Garcia Lorca?'

Imelda looked blank. It seemed she had never heard of Garcia Lorca and couldn't imagine why any young man would waste time writing poetry. They thought it a huge joke and went off chuckling. Marie said that she heard one woman comment that perhaps young English men wrote poetry to their girlfriends, the English were a very polite people.

We felt depressed that evening and in an attempt to cheer ourselves sampled too much of the local cider, brewed each year from the apple crops. It was delightful, and quite strong enough to make us feel relaxed and a little light-headed.

There seemed to be no point in returning to the same village, so next day we drove further. None of the villages were named on our map so this made finding Sama almost impossible. We asked a shepherd herding a small flock of sheep if he knew where the village of Sama was, but he only scratched his head and pointed vaguely along the road towards the hills. Clearly he didn't know but, as Marie said, he probably felt that it would be impolite to seem unwilling to help.

'In any case,' I said, 'it's probably useless to pin all our hopes on Sama. We may as well find another village and have a shot.'

The village we chose to explore was larger and some way off the main road. It was tucked into a fold in the hills and there was a small orchard of bare-branched apple trees. I knew they were apples by their peculiarly twisted and gnarled growth. Some of the houses had vegetable gardens and a few women worked in them.

There were two-storey barns attached to some of the houses and I assumed that the cattle were kept on the ground floor and grain on the upper. There were no men about and no children. Perhaps the men were employed in the mines.

We had left the car parked outside the village and now we strolled in, carrying our easels, collapsible stools, sketchbooks and pencils. Immediately we felt unwelcome intruders. It was as if we had impertinently walked into someone's home because the front door happened to be open. Beneath the lack of welcome I sensed suspicion and fear.

We knew that it was rudeness to set up our easels and intrude into these people's lives but we ignored any delicate feelings. Finding Harry was our priority, and if we seemed to impose ourselves on people then so be it. We set up and worked determinedly, appearing absorbed. Perhaps familiarity might reassure these women. Perhaps they might speak to us.

A small child came out of the door of one of the houses. Her mother, stooped over her garden patch, straightened, stretched her back and shouted angrily at the child who immediately scuttled inside. The woman glanced at us but we could not read her expression. She resumed her work.

We had been there a couple of hours and were puzzled. There were only a few women working in their garden plots, no children playing outside, no old men strolling or basking in the sun, no young women talking and laughing in groups. The emptiness was eerie and disturbing.

We heard its grinding engine before we saw the truck and turned in curiosity to look. It was a military vehicle, one of those with a canvas back flap. Over the dashboard we saw the faces of uniformed soldiers.

I clutched Marie. 'What do we do now?'

'Ignore them if we can. We have nowhere to hide.'

All the garden plots were now empty. The women had

disappeared inside. Ignorance and being English must be our protection so we kept working nervously. My pencil wavered along the lines, and the folds of my valley looked more like the billowing crests and troughs of the sea. I tried to rub it out, smudged the lot, and giggled tensely.

'If they look they certainly won't think us great artists.'

'Probably don't know anything about art anyway,' Marie whispered.

Our bravado was false and we didn't deceive each other.

From the corner of my eye I saw half a dozen men jump down from the truck. They conversed for a moment and then strode towards us. They were in pairs and each of them carried a brace of guns. Two of them hovered behind us. What they said in Spanish I couldn't understand but although Marie stiffened she composedly filled in the scene she was drawing. However she was white about her mouth and I was afraid.

They came closer and peered over our shoulders. One pointed to Marie's sketch and then to the distant view. They spoke together again. This time Marie looked up, feigning surprise. She smiled disarmingly and amazingly the one who had pointed to her sketch smiled back.

'*Artista*,' he said, 'good.'

'English,' she nodded and he looked pleased as if she had confirmed what he had already guessed.

'*Inglés*,' he repeated to his companion and the other nodded, also comfortable in their discovery.

They moved on.

I put down my pencil and clenched my hands together to stop them shaking. 'That was close.'

Marie slumped on her stool. 'My imagination, Judith. *Mon Dieu*. What I didn't think of. And behold it seems they are friendly. Only doing some routine task.'

We watched their progress down the road. Marie poured us a

cup of coffee from our vacuum flask and we sat in the sun confident and relaxed.

Then it happened. Two of the soldiers stopped at one of the houses. There were no fences so they simply tramped across the small garden, kicking aside the plants. They hammered on the door and when there was no response butted it open with their rifles. There were shouts and screams from inside and they emerged dragging a young boy between them. He was gangling and thin and must have been no more than fifteen. Several women pursued them sobbing and pleading. One clutched a soldier's arm and he flung her off. She fell and lay on the ground beating the earth with her fists and weeping hysterically. The other women still followed hurling shouts and abuse until one of the soldiers swung around and pointed his gun at the woman on the road. He snarled something and Marie gasped.

'What did he say?'

'He said if they didn't shut their mouths he'd come and use their pretty daughters.'

More women had now emerged from their houses and as the soldiers manhandled the struggling crying boy down the road they stood a silent accusing line of witnesses.

The boy's mother had now struggled to her feet and was running after them, screaming.

Again they turned on her levelling their guns. She halted and cringed, her whole body crouched over with despair. The boy still wept as they dragged him along. He didn't fight any more but was limp and lifeless as a rag doll.

Halfway down the street they released him and stood back. A sigh went up from the women. It had all been just a terrible game. His mother took a faltering step towards him. He hesitated a second, glancing briefly and fearfully at his captors. They were smiling. He ran. They raised their rifles and shot him twice in the back. He threw up his arms and fell and a shaft of sunlight impaled him.

Shock drove me to my feet as I prepared to run toward the boy. Marie grabbed me. 'No, Judith.' She clutched my arm. 'Sit. You can do nothing.'

'It's Harry,' I gasped, 'in Victoria Square. He looked like that, Marie.'

'It's not Harry, Judith. Nothing like.'

'Yes,' I sobbed. 'You're wrong, Marie. It's Harry.'

'You can do nothing,' she insisted. 'Nothing.'

So we just sat there, shivering uncontrollably while the women silently brought a wooden hurdle, lifted the boy onto it, and carried his body into one of the houses. We were ashamed to be so frightened for ourselves and confused as to whether it was more precarious to stay or dare leaving. There was a hideous menace in the power we had seen so suddenly unleashed and a cold-blooded brutality beyond our comprehension.

We felt defenceless.

The soldiers were still occupied searching houses but now they were at the far end of the village.

We determined to risk creeping away as unobtrusively as possible, grabbed our belongings and, on legs boneless and unsteady, stumbled back towards our car. We passed the soldiers' truck but avoided looking at the driver. With trembling fingers Marie unlocked our car door and we tumbled in, grateful for the illusion of safety.

Marie drove a little faster than usual jolting the car nerve-rackingly over the potholes.

It felt strange, even grotesque, to return to the normality of our hotel and the benign smiles of the plump proprietor who inquired casually whether we had enjoyed our day. We couldn't tell him that we had had a glimpse of hell.

That night we lay awake for a long time. Eventually I heard Marie's steady breathing but still the vision of the boy, strangely fair for a Spaniard, reminded me of Harry. I sat up and with apologies to sleeping Marie put on the dim electric light. I took a piece of paper and began to draw.

The boy was spread-eagled on the ground, impaled, as I had seen him, in that shaft of sunlight. Circling him was a band of soldiers but it was their boots that I emphasised – those hellish leather boots that strode the earth with inhuman possessiveness. The boots were monstrous but the bodies above them were miniscule and the faces were the faces of slavering wolves. I wrote FASCISM below the drawing and let it speak for itself.

Marie stirred and woke. 'Whatever are you doing, Judith?'

'Something I must.'

She got up, came to my side and looked down at my drawing. It was rough but she saw its Goya-style brutality. 'Judith, you must destroy that. If anyone here found it, *mon Dieu ...*'

I continued to refine it and she sat beside me silent and anxious. I only had pencils and without fine pens had to be satisfied. Although less than perfect it still had the force of my passionate anger – the same anger that had driven me to draw Harry crucified against the palings of Victoria Square.

'It is wonderful, Judith. Wonderful. But you must destroy it.'

For a minute I said nothing, studying my cartoon. I recognised her good sense, knew with almost a physical pain how much she had done for me and for Harry and how much I was risking. 'No, Marie,' I said. 'I'm sending it to the editor of the *Daily Herald*.'

'Are you mad?'

'No,' I said, 'not completely indiscreet. I won't send it to the office but to the editor's home address and I'll fold it and send it as a small letter rather than in a large flat envelope. But I must send it, Marie.'

I hesitated, fearing to sound self-indulgently dramatic. Then I said in a rush, 'To not protest would leave a wound on my soul that might never heal. It would continue to weep, Marie, like the tears of that distraught mother and I would know that the one thing

439

I had power to do I was too afraid to do. I could make rescuing Harry an excuse but ...' I stopped and looked at her helplessly.

She put her hand over mine and gazed at the cartoon. 'Yes, Judith, you are right. We must not make excuses. Send your work but at the same time send your letters to your mother and father and Winnie so that letters to Australia might cover any suspicion about a letter to England.'

I had drawn it on lighter paper and now folded it and slipped it into an envelope. I searched out the home address of the editor, which he had given me along with his phone number. By the time it reached London and he published it we would be gone from Spain with Harry.

The next morning we went out to our nearby cafe for coffee and breakfast. Neither of us felt hungry but it was necessary to behave normally. Whether many people knew about the tragic event in the village, we didn't know. We should at least appear to struggle out like tourists, even if shocked ones.

But the news had reached Sotrondio. A few coffee drinkers glanced at us uneasily and, when they left, avoided looking at us. However a couple approached us: 'We are very sorry, English ladies,' they apologised. 'What terrible things you will think of Spain.'

It was hard to respond appropriately. To say we were appalled and devastated by such barbarity would only increase their unhappiness on our behalf. To pretend it had not affected us would be a lie and present us as heartless. We compromised. As Marie understood their Spanish she acknowledged their distress and thanked them for their concern but she made no comment on the shooting.

We lingered in the cafe, undecided about what to do next. We were afraid to visit another village and yet our drawing excursions gave us the excuse we needed to stay in Sotrondio. Already we had detected a slight surprise that we stayed on. Packing up and leaving immediately was what most people would do after such a fearful experience in a foreign country. If we didn't have to stay, why did we?

So in a quandary we sat on sipping our third cup of coffee. How I longed for an Australian cup of tea. The cafe emptied.

But there was one man left. He read a paper in a far corner and we sensed that he watched us. I looked at Marie uneasily: 'Should we leave?'

From where she sat she could observe him clearly. 'No, I don't think so. He doesn't look threatening.'

We drank the remainder of our coffee, making it last. He folded his paper, put on his hat and stood up, deliberately, it seemed. He made his way between the tables so that he might pass us. He doffed his hat and murmured, in English: 'Good morning, ladies. A lovely day.'

Marie narrowed her eyes slightly and assessed him. I saw a short, spare man with a square face and receding hair. His eyes behind steel-rimmed glasses were tired but sharply intelligent.

'Artists, I believe.' He smiled down at us.

'Yes.' Marie was cautious.

He looked regretful. 'But Spain is not a good place for artists these days.'

Was he going to make the ubiquitous apology for our experience, just like the others? I felt disappointed.

'I believe,' he continued, 'that you are fortunate in having a friend here to help you.'

Marie took another sip of the dregs of her coffee and watched him over the rim of her cup. She was still suspicious and I was nervous. She didn't hurry to reply and at last gave a brittle laugh: 'Not really a friend. An old lover. Garcia was his name I think. It's so long ago. But I've had second thoughts. Maybe it's not good to dig up the past. His wife mightn't welcome my sudden arrival.'

He looked at her with amusement. Clearly, he didn't believe her. But for some strange reason his disbelief seemed to please him.

441

'Maybe you have other friends here … beside Garcia. The young make so many friends and so quickly.'

There was something odd about this conversation that disturbed me. It wasn't the words – they were innocuous enough – it was something I couldn't quite define.

His expression remained bland. 'I'm sure you'll enjoy catching up with … old friends.'

'Up to now it's been a futile search,' Marie sounded resigned.

'Futile, you say? That's frustrating. And sad.' He looked sympathetic. 'I'm sure that need not be the case. Oh, excuse me, ladies, I didn't introduce myself. I'm the local doctor.' He offered his hand and we each shook it. Was I mistaken or did he press my hand a little too firmly? And look too keenly at the wedding ring on my other hand?

He waited expectantly. I took the initiative: 'I'm Judith,' I said, 'and this is my friend Marie. We're Australians.'

Briefly he looked taken aback. Then he said, 'It's a pleasure, ladies. My best wishes for all your endeavours. I hope you find your friend.'

He moved away and out the door.

'Judith,' Marie was breathless with hope, 'he knows something.'

'Yes,' I said and then was silent.

My thoughts in turmoil tumbled over each other. I hardly dared to let myself hope. I had lived so long in doubt and fear about Harry that this abnormal state of suspended life had become my real world, everything else a mere dream. In my worst moments I had seen myself like the ghostly figures of my childhood flitting along the wharf doomed to endless futile searching.

At last I managed to ask, 'Can we trust him? There are eyes everywhere watching us. It could be a trap.'

'Imagination, Judith!' She was brisk. 'There are no eyes, just a lot of people trying to go about their normal business. We're peripheral to their struggles. Come, let's post your letters. The sooner one of them leaves your handbag the better.'

We paid the bill and walked out into the sunshine. We had been lucky with the weather. It would have been hard to justify hanging around pretending to draw if it had rained all day.

'Do you think he'll contact us again? It would be terrible if we had read too much into an innocent conversation.'

'No.' Marie was certain. 'Not innocent, Judith. Not innocent at all.'

When we returned to the hotel there was a message waiting for us. The proprietor said the doctor had called to say he would visit the un-well English woman in the evening.

I started to deny that either of us was sick but Marie kicked me surreptitiously in the ankle. 'Yes, you do look very pale, Judith,' she said quickly.

The overweight proprietor nodded wisely. He had little twinkling eyes embedded in folds of flesh and when he laughed his whole face quivered jovially. 'English ladies,' he pronounced, in perfect English, 'always get sick in Spain. It is the food or the water or both. We're not as clean as the English. The doctor will come at about eight o'clock after his rounds. He does many rounds at night. Often poor people in the villages need him. He's a good man. He goes twice a week and stays there. He rides a mule.'

This was another odd conversation and I wondered what secret assignations might be going on. 'He's not afraid of the bears?' I asked innocently.

For a second he looked blank. 'Bears?' He seemed puzzled. And then, 'Oh, yes, bears. No, the village people come and protect him with lanterns and staves. He's not afraid of bears. Our doctor's a very brave man. He's braver than the soldiers. They're afraid of bears.' He chuckled. 'You look most un-well Mrs Grenville. So pale. And those purple rings under your eyes.' He was overdoing it a little.

'I'll rest,' I said.

He beamed approvingly. 'Yes. You should lie down in your

room and wait for the doctor. I'll send the maid with some coffee for you both.'

For a time we lay on our beds and read. Marie ventured out for some rolls, cheese and fruit for lunch. The proprietor kept us supplied with plenty of coffee and, panting up and down the stairs, knocked on our door a couple of times to inquire about our welfare and my 'sickness'. He suppressed his excitement and I felt sad for him. Was this small act of defiance in helping us his means of retaining self-respect? Did all suppressed and victimised people assert their power and dignity through little tricks, glorying in miniscule victories? He would have liked us to share more of our secret but we remained cautious and he had to be satisfied with being the liaison.

In the afternoon Marie dozed but I lay awake visualising a new cartoon. In my mind's eye I saw a football field and a team of soldiers with heavy leather boots and wolverine faces. I named them Mussolini, Lerroux, Franco and Dolfuss. In the centre with the football in his hand ran Adolph Hitler. He raced ahead of the rest in the act of kicking the football of the world through the goal posts labelled FASCISM. My fingers itched to draw it. I saw it all so clearly, so powerfully. But if it were discovered I would have ruined our chance of rescuing Harry. I would have blown our covers as innocent tourists, perhaps even thrown our own lives away. I had risked sending one cartoon to London. I must not dare to send a second. It could wait. There would be time later.

The doctor knocked on our door at eight o'clock. He was accompanied by the proprietor who, hoping to be included, hovered expectantly. The doctor sent him away with thanks but a firm hand on his shoulder.

We set the one chair in our room for him and perched on our beds. For a few minutes he gazed at us thoughtfully, cleaning his glasses and taking his time. When he began to speak his words were slow and careful as if he were measuring the weight of each of them. I fidgeted, struggling to control my impatience, and knew that he recognised my anxiety.

He spoke more to me than to Marie, although he often glanced in her direction.

'You know,' he said, 'of the terrible events that occurred here early in October?'

I nodded.

'They didn't end then. They are still going on. You saw the boy shot.'

My mouth was dry. I swallowed and nodded again.

He didn't need an answer. His questions were merely rhetorical. 'There were many shot in those first days. Thousands. And the reprisals have gone on for weeks. Even the wounded in hospital were dragged out and murdered. You might say that we have descended into the abyss and still taste the sulphur of hell. If I hadn't been away at that time ... I tell you this, not to shock you further, but to explain to you that there have been a number of wounded or ill men secreted in the hill villages.'

Marie interrupted: 'And that is why you visit on a mule?'

He gave her a slight smile. 'And very uncomfortable they are, too. But sure-footed on mountain tracks that cling to the edge of steep gorges. But, yes, that is why I go.'

'And my husband?' I could no longer contain myself. 'Did you tend to him?'

He gave me all his attention. 'So you are searching for your husband?'

'Yes.'

'I thought it might be so.' And he glanced again at my wedding ring. 'I would like to tell you that the young Englishman I tended was your husband but there were a few foreigners caught up in it all and I can't give you my complete assurance. He was wounded.'

At my stricken look he hastened to add: 'But not seriously. I treated him a couple of times and then at ...' He named a village we had not heard of. 'Then he was moved and I needed to look after the more seriously wounded. Those who need care are moved to different places according to how well or ill they are. But ...' He looked at me with concern. 'I may be mistaken, perhaps he's not your husband. I asked about him and was told he carried a British passport and that's all I know. There was no mention of him being Australian.'

'Is there nothing more you can tell us?' My voice was thick with despair.

'A little,' he said, 'but it would be cruel to raise your hopes too much. He was a fair young man, in his twenties, I'd estimate, and of a slender build. He was barely conscious when I treated him and I had no time to question him. Of course, we all wondered how a perfect stranger came to be embroiled in our political affairs.'

'If it's my Harry, my husband, it's a long story.'

'And a complex one?'

'Yes, a complex one.' I felt a little more composed. The description fitted Harry. Hope was a reality I could cling to.

'One more thing that might help,' he added. 'There is a man, José, who lives in a village at the foot of the mountains. You can reach there via the main road so long as you turn ...'

Now Marie had his attention as he detailed the route we must take into a remote and secluded valley.

At last he put on his hat, preparing to leave. 'Don't be afraid. You'll be safe there. The soldiers only rarely venture into the mountains.'

'Because of the bears?' I said.

This time he smiled with genuine amusement. 'The bears are a bit of help to us. And the wolves. All our friends.'

I gave him my hand. 'Thank you,' I said. 'Whether it is or isn't my husband I will never be able to thank you enough.'

'Mrs Judith Grenville,' he replied, his eyes penetrating, 'or is it Miss Judith Larsen? Your cartoons are thanks enough.'

I gaped at him, my hand still grasped in his. How could he be so discerning?

'My cartoons?'

'Oh, yes. I visit England. I keep in touch with the editor of the *Daily Herald*. We were at boarding school together there. There'll be more cartoons I hope.'

'Yes,' I said, 'but not here.'

'No, not here.' For a moment he looked desolate. 'But we'll see them you know. Cartoons cross all barriers. Drawings speak everybody's language. The world is a smaller place than you realise.'

When he had departed we dissected every comment he had made, examined the nuances of every phrase and expression. On a roller-coaster of hope and doubt, one minute we convinced ourselves we had found Harry, but in the next feared failure. A British passport did not necessarily mean that the young man was English. Australians also carried British passports. The doctor had said that he had treated more than one foreigner, but his physical description matched Harry.

I agonised over whether Harry might be lying ill in some mountain village accessible only by mule. We had heard of the two-storey wooden houses on stilts that crawled up the sides of gorges and clung there above creeping narrow tracks around escarpments. In the mountains there were even labyrinths of caves where people lived or could be hidden.

Eventually, having exhausted ourselves with wild surmises, we stopped.

'Tomorrow,' Marie said, 'we'll find this José and talk with him. Take heart. Each day we get nearer.'

She spread her map of Spain on the bed and studied it. 'Look, Judith, look here. When we leave with Harry we'll not take the road back through Oviedo and along the coast. We'll head for Pamplona and then north over the Pyrenees to a border post. We'll take our chances with the weather.'

'Better the weather than Franco's soldiers,' I said.

'Oh, yes. Far better. A small border post won't be so officious. They won't have heard of Harry or us, nor probably much about the Asturias.'

'And if he shows signs of having been shot?'

'Wounded, Judith, wounded. There are many ways of being wounded. We won't mention shooting. I think he might have been silly enough to run with the bulls in Pamplona at their festival.' Enthusiastically she warmed to her theme. 'And, heavens above, the things wives have to endure from the stupidity of men. We've had to wait around in Spain for months while he recovered from his injuries and was fit enough to travel.'

Suddenly her make-believe struck home and I felt a surge of anger at Harry. 'Certainly the bit about him being impetuous and unthinking of consequences won't be a deception,' I said bitterly.

She grinned. 'Then you can be very convincing and rail at him all the way to the border.'

'No.' My voice was tight and desperate. 'I'll keep it for France. But after we get out of Spain I'll let him have a few home truths. Oh, Marie,' I pleaded, 'do you really believe this Englishman is Harry? And that José knows where he is? I don't think I can endure much more of this.'

She hugged me. 'I have a good feeling. All these things that have suddenly happened in our favour must mean something. Please have faith.'

I had another rotten night, savagely turning this way and that, my body aching with my struggles to sleep, and praying that dawn would come soon. My brief anger at Harry had dissolved. His impetuosity might appear careless and thoughtless to those who did not know him but to me it was part of his sweet eagerness, his excitement at life, his snatching at new experiences. By comparison I was sober – even, as Jock would term it, dour. That Harry loved me was a strange and beautiful wonder for which I was deeply grateful.

At last a few damp rays of sun struggled through the window. All night the sighing of quiet soft rain had accompanied my restless thoughts. Now the rain had stopped but probably only briefly because the sky was a low pallid grey. We made a point of carrying our easels and stools downstairs and then quite a show of our disappointment and indecision. Finally, in loud clear voices so everyone might hear, we announced that today painting would be impossible and we'd just have to be satisfied with a drive. It was a complete bore but the weather …

Maybe it would improve tomorrow. We shrugged.

We had taken a leisurely breakfast at our cafe because we needed to appear innocently unhurried and later, on the pavement, we expressed again our disgust and disappointment to two cafe patrons who sheltered under umbrellas.

Eventually we climbed into the Citroën. The engine was cold and stammered and stuttered and worried Marie for a few moments before it burst into life.

At the petrol station an attendant filled our tank and Marie bought an extra can for any emergency and he put it into the boot for her.

We set off. I leaned back in my seat with a sigh of relief. 'Pretending is so exhausting. I have no flair for it.'

'No, Judith, not at all. Pretending is delightfully stimulating.'

'I think you love playing a part, as much as I hate it.'

She glanced at me whimsically. 'You fear to expose yourself to strangers and hide behind your cartoons, dear Judith.'

'You think I do that, Marie?'

'Most certainly you do. Me, I hide behind whatever persona I choose.'

We crossed the bridge over the river, the water dark and stale without a bright sun.

'Have we a long drive?' I asked, changing the subject.

'Longish. Further than we have ventured yet. I don't know how

449

extensive the foothills are or how far before we enter the high mountains.'

'And the road?' I always asked about the road, which was useless because Marie had no more knowledge than I did and she had to cope with it. But she always answered me patiently because my questions about the road hid my deeper anxieties.

It was indeed a longish drive before we entered the troughs and crests of the foothills. The road twisted and turned as we climbed steadily around the first low mountain, then dipped into a fertile valley with a small stream. We climbed again, another hill, and then down into another valley.

Then there were a series of hills each higher than the last. As the grade steepened the car occasionally growled in complaint and Marie grimaced. 'Come on, old girl,' she muttered. 'Give her a pat, Judith, and tell her she's doing well.'

In the valleys below us I saw grey-stone villages with terracotta-tiled roofs. All looked similar and our directions for finding José and his particular village seemed dauntingly vague.

As we ascended the slopes above and below us were thickly forested with deciduous trees. A thick carpet of dried brown leaves and acorns told me that many were oaks. A squirrel, alerted by our passing, skittered across the leaves and raced up a tree. The road narrowed. Now it seemed a mere ledge interrupting the slope. Marie reduced speed and we crawled over the dirt track keeping clear of the soft edges that fell into the valley too far below us.

She looked worried. 'I can't turn on this road, Judith. We must go on but where to? If it narrows further I don't know ...' We were both apprehensive. She clung to the steering wheel for the road was wet and she didn't need to warn me that the car might slide uncontrollably on the muddy surface. It grew colder. Marie's rug had fallen off her lap. I leaned over and tucked it securely around her. Our breaths fogged up the windscreen and I tried to clear it with a handkerchief so she could see.

'Thanks, Jude,' she muttered, still concentrating on the road.

I watched her white intense face and felt miserably guilty to have involved her in this. She always pretended that it was an exciting adventure but I suspected this was another of her acts, a brave pretence.

Lately, I thought, I detected new lines on her pretty face that had always appeared so youthful. Were the pitiless demands of our journey ageing her? She had born the brunt of it all – the organisation, the exhausting driving, the emotional turmoil of hope and despair. If this journey were a dead end should we give up? Could I continue to impose so many burdens on her? At what point would we be forced to admit defeat?

The track seemed to narrow even further and then, surprisingly, there was a clearing ahead of us and Marie drove onto a small plateau. She relaxed her hands on the wheel and pulled over.

'I think we may have arrived, Judith.' She took some deep shaky breaths and some colour returned to her face.

In front of us was a village of the customary grey stone. Possibly a miners' village although we saw no sign of pits or workings. 'It's very peaceful,' I said, 'and secluded.'

We got out of the car.

'Very secluded and safe,' she said. 'I don't see a convoy of military trucks grinding around that road.'

Women and children had come out. They stared at us in amazement. Two little boys whispered together and pointed at the Citroën. An old man approached us. The skin on his face was leathery and seamed and his hands were gnarled, the joints thickened by arthritis. He walked unhurriedly supporting himself with a rough knotted walking stick.

I smiled tentatively but received no warm response. I didn't feel we were unwelcome, rather that we were being weighed up cautiously. We waited until he spoke to us.

'*Buenas tardes,*' he said.

'*Buenas tardes,*' Marie replied.

I had a sudden impulse to laugh at these careful courtesies. It was a bizarre situation: two strangers at the end of an inaccessible dirt road bidding good afternoon as if we had just dropped in on the neighbours for afternoon tea.

He was puzzled, even suspicious, and rightly so. We must indeed be a peculiar interruption in their lives. Finally he asked, 'Are you lost?'

Marie rapidly translated for me. At her fluent Spanish he relaxed a little.

'No,' she said, 'at least we hope not.'

He continued to look confused.

'We have been sent by the doctor. To speak to someone named José.'

His surprise was brief and then concealed. 'The good doctor?'

She nodded. 'Yes.'

'To find someone named José?'

'Yes.'

Still he gave nothing away. 'And why would you come all this way to speak to José?'

'He may be able to help us.'

He was suspicious again. 'I doubt if José could be of any assistance to two ...' he hesitated, 'Englishwomen.'

But Marie persisted, 'Yes, we believe he can and so does the good doctor. We are looking for someone.' She regarded him thoughtfully. 'Are you José?'

Her question was blunt. How would he react?

He inclined his head.

'My friend here,' she indicated me and still translating for my benefit, 'my friend here has lost her husband.'

A shutter fell over his face. 'Why would I know anything about your friend's husband. Husbands often go missing. Another woman, perhaps.'

But Marie wasn't to be put off. 'No. Not this one,' she said.

I caught the word Grenville.

'Mrs Grenville is looking for her husband.' she repeated.

He shook his head and all my previous disappointments were mere shadows beside the reality of this one.

He spoke again to Marie and I recognised the word *Inglés*.

Marie replied quickly in Spanish and I knew she explained that my husband was Australian and that we were not English.

'Austrian,' he said.

'No. Australian,' she corrected.

'*Australiano*?' The word lingered on his tongue while he thought. Then he smiled at us for the first time. 'Ah, *Australiano*,' he said. 'So far away.'

She nodded.

For some reason our coming from so far away seemed to reassure him and he spoke volubly and quickly.

He repeated the word *Inglés* several times and once waved his hand towards the end of the village.

She turned to me disheartened, apologetic for my disappointment. 'He says there is a young Englishman resting in the barn at the end of the village. He has a British passport. He was wounded in a street battle. The good doctor has healed him and they have brought him down from the mountains because of the winter cold. He asks if we could speak with him.'

I felt exhausted and cruelly indifferent to the plight of some unknown Englishman. He had probably been as foolhardy as Harry. Then I recalled the dead boy crucified in a shaft of sunlight and the insolent indifference of the soldiers who shot him. In confronting such evil and deciding whose side he was on, had Harry really been foolhardy or had he been incredibly brave?

Wearily I supposed that we should meet this young Englishman. Perhaps we could help him in some way – take a letter for him, alert someone as to his whereabouts. I thought it unlikely but maybe he had met Harry in the street battle. Maybe he knew something of Harry's whereabouts. Maybe, maybe. I was sick of the word maybe: its slimy half-promise that always deceived.

My better self agreed to visit him. I could only hope that someone somewhere was similarly showing compassion to Harry.

'Are you happy to go to see him, Judith? You never know.'

'Of course. What else can we do?'

José had listened attentively to our conversation, straining in a vain attempt to comprehend. Now he looked at me sharply. 'Judith?' he inquired.

'Yes. My name is Judith. Judith Grenville. Judith Larsen.' I felt impatient. Marie had told him my name. But perhaps even in this remote spot someone had seen my cartoons. If it endangered me, too bad.

He spoke again, this time directly to me, in halting English. 'You are Judith Card?' There was an urgent insistence in his question.

Marie looked at him blankly. 'Judith Card? No. Judith Gren ...'

He interrupted her, his old face wrinkling in a beaming smile. And in careful rehearsed English he said very slowly, 'Judith, she is such a card.'

The breath rushed from my body and the world catapulted around. I was aware of Marie's face blazing with excitement.

'The barn,' I gasped. 'Marie, it's Harry.'

'I'll show ...' José started to say, but he was too late. I was running, shouting something unintelligible. The women clustered on the road parted to let me through, their faces astonished. I was stumbling on the broken earth track, running, hurtling towards the barn at the end of the village.

Acknowledgements

For this elegant publication of my novel I wish to thank at Wakefield Press Michael Bollen, Julia Beaven, my editor, for her courteous consideration, helpful advice and artistic production skills, Angela Tolley, Margot Lloyd and Michael Deves – and Stacey Zass for her cover design.

My thanks are also due to those who read my manuscript and offered me generous encouragement: Nalini Scarfe, Hilary Endacott, Bill McIntyre, Jeff and Jo Keith. I am especially indebted to Dr Heather Goodall, Professor of History, UTS, and Michaelie Clark who not only read my manuscript but endorsed it with unsolicited recommendations.

I am indebted to Meredith Blundell at the Port Adelaide Library and Moana Colmer and Andrew Peters at Natrail Museum for their research assistance.

To my husband Allan whose unfailing enthusiasm and assistance made *Hunger Town* possible, my deepest gratitude.

Wakefield Press is an independent publishing and
distribution company based in Adelaide, South Australia.
We love good stories and publish beautiful books.
To see our full range of books, please visit our website at
www.wakefieldpress.com.au
where all titles are available for purchase.

Find us!

Twitter: www.twitter.com/wakefieldpress
Facebook: www.facebook.com/wakefield.press
Instagram: instagram.com/wakefieldpress